For
Thomas Joseph Farrelly

'Joe'

CONTENTS

A NOTE ABOUT TIME

Level 1 Science

Traditional Time versus Geokinetic Time *continued*

Traditional (imperial) Time

Unit	Duration
Second	1/86400 of a day
Minute	1/1440 of a day
Hour	1/24 of a day
Week	7 days
Year	52 weeks and 1 day (365 days)*

Geokinetic (metric) Time

Unit	Duration
Microday	1/100000 of a day
Milliday	1/1000 of a day
Deciday	1/10 of a day
Hand	5 days
Year	73 hands (365 days)

Days of the week

Monday, Tuesday, Wednesday, Thursday, Friday, Saturday, Sunday

Days of the hand

Polexday, Secundusday, Maximusday, Annularisday, Minimusday

Time conversion table

Geokinetic Unit		Traditional time equivalent
Deciday	=	2 hours 24 minutes*
Milliday	=	1 minute 26.4 seconds*
Microday	=	0.864 seconds*

* Correct before the beginning of the time change crisis. Since this was calculated, the days and years have become significantly longer.

PROLOGUE
Tana

(Annularisday)

Mícheál Gonagain walked unsteadily from the poker table. He was ashen-faced and thought he might vomit. He had just been hustled, and had lost everything.

When he had blagged the job onboard the *Cadabra* trading vessel, he had promised his young son that he would be back for his birthday. That day had passed-by some time ago, but he was so keen to establish himself as a regular crew member on the dirigible that he had stayed on. The pay was so good that he justified his actions by imagining his return as a wealthy man.

He had taken ground leave from the *Cadabra* and booked a berth on a stage dirigible. He had only come into the bar to pass the evening before heading home, but had been invited to join the game. He had almost doubled his money at one point, but now he didn't even have the fare home. Even if he did, how could he go home after all this time with nothing? He would have to start all over again. It would take years to catch up.

PART 1
A Crew Cast Asunder

CHAPTER 1
Lubumbashi

(New Year's Eve)

It was just before midnight on New Year's Eve and Oisín Gonagain was pleasantly drunk. That is to say, that it was just before midnight if you used Geokinetic Time, which Gonagain did – when it suited him. If you used Traditional Time, which Gonagain *also* did – when it suited him – then midnight was still a few hours away, at around dawn. But, at present, he was in a Geokinetic region, and in the company of two pretty, young ladies that he was hoping to coax back to his cabin... or maybe just one of them – even though he had the captain's quarters, it wasn't a very big cabin.

Across the other side of The Scrimshankers Refuge tavern, his lieutenant, Bearnárd, was surrounded by young ladies who were currently engaged in squeezing his substantial muscles and gasping theatrically. Bearnárd Strongman was Gonagain's half-brother, but apart from the dark hair and pale complexion, there were few similarities. Despite the number of ladies thrusting their cleavage and swinging their petticoats at Bearnárd, Gonagain knew there was as much chance of him waking up in a cell as in the arms of one of the ladies. Things had a habit of getting out of hand when Bearnárd was out on the lash. Gonagain was firmly of the opinion that he was the brains, and Strongman the brawn.

It was just as the countdown of the last ten microdays to midnight began, and Gonagain was trying to decide which of the lovely ladies to kiss first, when the tavern suddenly erupted with a deafening blast and an earthquake-like tremor. Revellers screamed as they were flung to the floor, and tankards and glasses crashed to the ground around them.

The blast sounded very much like a steam-cannon, and that could mean only one thing – they were under attack from Traditionalists. Gonagain, who suddenly felt quite sober, leapt to his feet, put on his bowler hat, and drew his pulsarnite pistol. He nodded to the two wine-soaked young ladies who were still entwined on the floor.

"Ladies, perhaps another time." Then, more loudly, "Bearnárd! Let's get the hell out of here!" He ran for the door.

Outside the tavern was chaos, with people screaming and running in every direction. As well as the steam-cannon, which Gonagain could hear but not see, there would also be Traditionalist foot-soldiers. He could smell the gunpowder from their weapons. Gonagain needed to get back to *The Reliant* and get it airborne before it caught the attention of the Trads. The blast from the cannon had put out most of the gas-lamps, so keeping to the shadows wouldn't be difficult. But the Trads wore varilight goggles which would make the darkness of midnight look more like dusk, so he wasn't going to head down the broad Lubumbashi Main Street. He would zigzag towards the airdock via Lubumbashi's network of alleyways.

Eventually, he reached Doxies Parade. Normally, at this time of night, it would be heaving with doxies, punters, and voyeurs, but now it was deserted. The lights were off and the presentation windows empty. Doubtless there were doxies and their clients taking cover inside. It was a long straight alley that ended not far from the airdock. There were lots of doorways in which to hide, but no turnings. Once he started down the alley he would be committed. He checked behind him, hoping to see Bearnárd following, but Gonagain was lean and quick and there was little chance of his lumbering half-brother keeping up with him. Besides, he had probably taken the direct route.

He was nearly at the end of Doxies when he saw the dim orange glow of two pairs of varilight goggles. Turning to check the alley behind he saw, to his horror, the glow of about half a dozen goggles at the other end. Going back was not an option – he was surrounded. He slipped soundlessly into one of the doorways and tried the door. It was, of course, locked. The doxies always kept their doors locked except to let their clients in and out. It wasn't safe in any part of town to leave your door open but especially not in this district. Looking up he could see that the terraced buildings were all at least three stories high. He couldn't go through; he couldn't go over and he couldn't go around.

"Feck!" he cursed quietly to himself. He was either going to have to bluff his way out or blast his way out. He considered ditching his pulsarnite pocket watch and pistol. Being captured by Trads in possession of anything powered by pulsarnite was not good – not good at all. But being unarmed with a Trad attack underway was even less appealing and besides, these things didn't come cheaply. Scanning the dark doorway for inspiration, he spotted some empty beer bottles on the floor. He checked his pistol was set to wide angle. On narrow beam, it could punch a hole right through a man – on wide angle it could knock a dozen men off their feet like they had been body slammed by a two hundred kilo sumo wrestler. What the effect of wide angle would be in this narrow alley he wasn't entirely sure, but it should cause a suitable level of mayhem. He tucked the pistol into the back of his shirt collar, undid his button flies and picked up a beer bottle. Then, kicking over the remaining bottles, he staggered out of the alley, fumbling with his flies as he went.

At the sound of the clattering bottles, the goggles entered the alleyway "Hey you!" they shouted, "Hands where I can see them!"

"Wassup?" he slurred, "What's the story?"

"Hands where I can see them!" Goggles repeated.

Gonagain dropped the bottle and put his hands on his head. "I jus' needed the jacks – got caught a bit short, you know."

He sensed, rather than saw, the pair drop their guard and lower their weapons. Reaching behind his head, he grabbed the pistol, took aim, and squeezed the trigger in one swift movement.

There was a brief delay, no more than a fraction of a microday, before the pulsarnite pulsed and the pistol fired, but it was enough time for Goggles to get off a shot of his own.

Gonagain dived back into the doorway for cover, but not quite quickly enough. The bullet fizzed through the thick tweed of his jacket sleeve, clipping his upper arm on the way through. He swore and clutched his bicep. His own shot had a more devastating effect. With his pistol set to wide angle in a narrow alley, the sonic pulse his weapon emitted had ricocheted off the buildings, shattering the windows and peppering the two Trad soldiers with fragments of glass as it knocked them off their feet. Still clutching his wounded arm, Gonagain took his chance and, stepping over the stunned and bleeding soldiers, hurried towards the airdock.

It was when he reached the perimeter of the airdock, that Gonagain first saw the Geokinetic

Guards. Quite how they had got there so quickly, he had no idea, he was just glad they had. Armed with their high-powered pulsarnite rifles and wearing night vision goggles, they would keep the Trad soldiers busy for a while. They streamed around and through the dock and continued toward the red-light district of Lubumbashi.

At last he could see *The Reliant* moored right in the middle of the dock. He was nearly home and dry. Gonagain hoped that the rest of the crew were already in the airship or, failing that, not far behind him.

Just as Gonagain thought he was safe, two more Trad soldiers stepped out from the shadows right in front of him. They had obviously been hiding from the Geo Guards, and Gonagain didn't think they would want to attract their attention with gunfire. Anyway, you would have to be mad to fire a gun-powder weapon in an airdock. The heliagen-filled dirigibles were safe enough, but hydrum was highly flammable – especially if you had illegally filled a soft-envelope dirigible like *The Reliant* with it. He decided to keep it casual.

"Howya!" Gonagain greeted them cheerfully, "Had to dock urgently – any port in a storm, you know how it is."

"That looks suspiciously like a pulsarnite pistol to me."

"I lifted it from a Pulser just now, just after the steam-cannon strike."

"Let's see the pocket watch then," said the second soldier, gesturing with his rifle at the chain running between Gonagain's waistcoat buttonhole and pocket.

"Oh, don't worry it's mechanical," he lied.

"Then you won't mind showing us."

"Look, you're not going to fire those in an airdock are you? Some of those airships are highly flammable, you know. And I've heard some eejit has filled a soft-shell with hydrum."

"But we're pointing our guns *away* from them, aren't we? And *at* you," the soldier sneered.

Suddenly, the steam-cannon fired again, and the ground shook beneath them with a violent force. As the soldiers put their hands out to steady themselves, Gonagain seized the moment and dashed between them. The soldiers turned and raised their rifles, but now they were facing *towards* the airdock. They lowered their weapons and gave chase.

Gonagain was running for all he was worth. The loading hatch of *The Reliant* was down and he could see his engineer, Rajaobelina, silhouetted by the loading bay lights, standing on the gangway, loading a revolver. Gonagain ducked to allow her a shot, and she duly fired over his head. The shot flew above the heads of his pursuers as well, but they knew this was going to be one-way gunfire and it was enough to send them diving for cover.

As Gonagain approached the airship, it began to lift off. The gangway was becoming steeper and as he tried to scrabble up the slope, it completely left the ground. Gonagain's legs dangled comically as he tried to drag himself up to the loading bay. Rajaobelina grabbed his bad arm, hauled him up and began to close the gangplank.

"Thanks, Jao!" Gonagain gasped, "Who's piloting?"

"Bunty."

"Bunty! She's had about ten large gins – she's fluthered!"

"That she is."

"And you're letting her fly *The Reliant*?"

"You want me to pilot and her to shoot over your head?"

Gonagain paused, briefly contemplating that scenario. "Where's Beagán?"

"Not here."

"Bearnárd?"

"No."

"Then get this ship down until they get here! And that's an order!"

Jao looked her captain in the eye. With her chocolate-brown skin and greasy overalls, she was barely visible in the dark, but the steady gaze of her piercing blue eyes emanated calmness and strength. She spoke without an accent, but with the deliberateness of someone speaking a second language. "With respect, Captain, we can hold those two off, but if we don't get out of rifle range before more arrive, they'll either have us trapped on the ground or they'll blow us out of the sky. Beagán will have to take his chances. Bearnárd is a big boy; he can look after himself."

Rajaobelina was right of course. He sighed and leant over to the voice-repeater. “Bunty, take her straight up. Five hundred metres and hold our co-ordinates.”

“Righty-oh skipper.”

Rajaobelina popped open a porthole and fired a volley of shots in the general direction of the Trad soldiers. *The Reliant* was ascending fast and, within a milliday, they were out of range. “Right” she said, “Let’s get you to the medical bay!”

******

Rajaobelina was *The Reliant*’s engineer, but she was also the ship’s medic and a healer. Her grand-mother had been a healer and had known, the moment that Rajaobelina was born, that she also had the gift. She gave her all the guidance, encouragement and training she could – healing did not work alone, so Rajaobelina was also taught basic medical skills.

Her mechanical prowess was borne out of necessity. Growing up on the outskirts of Antsirabe she had nothing, and mend and make-do was a way of life. She loved fixing things and had a facility for it. Picking up discarded bits and pieces and making something from them was a way to earn a living. One day, she came across an old broken rotavator and took it apart to see how it worked. She cleaned it, reassembled it, and got it working. She gave it to her grandfather, a subsistence farmer, and it changed his life. After that, people began bringing broken farming equipment to her, and her career as an agricultural mechanic took off.

Then, one day, a neighbour came to her saying that a handsome young dirigible captain was looking for her. At first, she thought it was some sort of practical joke, but eventually she was persuaded to pick up her tools and hitch a ride to the airdock. Sure enough, there was a handsome – if rather dishevelled and worse for wear – dirigible captain eagerly awaiting her arrival. Apparently, he could not find anyone prepared to mend the burnt-out engine of his airship, and had been told that there was a girl who could fix anything. She had never even seen a dirigible engine before. "Yes, I fix it," she said.

She worked day and night on that engine for almost a week. It was a steep learning curve, and there was a lot of trial and error involved. She slept in the hold when she couldn't stay awake any longer and 'The Captain' bought her food and scavenged-for spare parts. In the evening, whilst his navigator and lieutenant went into town, he would stay with her and drink whiskey and make her coffee. He never lost faith in her ability to fix it.

Eventually it was ready, and they took it for a test flight. He was so delighted with the way it flew that he paid her far more than she asked for. Rajaobelina had never seen so much money. It was a happy time for her, but she was sad to see The Captain leave. At least now she had enough money to buy a small hut near the airdock and could begin fixing dirigible engines as well as farm equipment.

Several months passed, and Rajaobelina had all but forgotten the handsome captain and his tatty airship, when she heard the familiar sound of an engine she knew well. She had butterflies in her stomach as she watched *The Reliant* land awkwardly in the dock. Either The Captain was a terrible pilot or the steering was damaged – she privately hoped it was the latter. The repair took only a few hours and the airship was, sadly, on its way again. "Jao, you are a genius" he said as he waved goodbye.

Rajaobelina hated being called "Jao". Or "Belle". Or "Lina". And, definitely, not "Raj". Her name was Rajaobelina and that was what she liked to be called. But somehow, when The Captain called her Jao, she didn't mind at all – she even quite liked it. Perhaps it was because it was said with genuine affection, rather than just out of laziness. Perhaps it was just because he was handsome and she liked him.

The Reliant became a regular visitor to Antsirabe Airdock. The Captain would, apparently, not get his vessel repaired or maintained by anyone else.

On the last occasion that the ship docked at Antsirabe, *The Reliant* was riddled with bullet holes. Not only were both the hull and the envelope in need of repair, so was The Captain. He was covered in bruises and had a gash on his head which needed stitches. She used her healing powers first, then stitched the wound. She stitched and tarred *The Reliant's* envelope too, and patched the hull with scrap brass and reclaimed timber. It was then that The Captain offered her a position on his ship. She could not believe her luck. The next day she sold her hut, and brought her tool bag and a brand-new traveller's trunk, containing all her worldly possessions, to the airship.

In the beginning, she had wondered if she and The Captain might become romantically involved, but it didn't happen. Either she had misread the situation or The Captain just wanted to keep things on a professional level. She didn't mind – she was used to not getting what she wanted and she just moved on. She had the friendship and respect of The Captain, she was seeing the world, and she had a comfy cabin to sleep in at night, and that was enough.

Now though, as she tended the bullet wound on The Captain's upper arm, she felt those early feelings come to the fore. Fully-dressed he looked dapper and lean, some might say skinny, but sitting shirtless in the medical bay she could see he was all muscle with good definition. His chest was almost hairless and had a few scars.

The medical bay was, really, just the tiniest cabin on the ship (with a few bandages, tinctures, and ointments) and the intimacy of the space and the physical contact made her feel like a teenage girl. It was foolish and she needed to concentrate. After cleaning the wound, she sat with her face close to it. She began a low, deep humming which induced a trance-like state. Then, as she stared at the wound, her eyes emitted an invisible light into it, which would make the healing process quicker and more complete – although for some reason her healing was never quite as successful on The Captain as it was on other people. She felt perhaps he didn't believe in it.

After a few moments, she came out of the trance.

"I'll just put a couple of stitches into that,' she said gently. "And give you some laudanum and cannabis – it will ease the pain and make you drowsy."

******

Gonagain wasn't inclined think of Jao romantically. Not that she wasn't attractive. With her flawless skin and pale-blue eyes she was quite beautiful – he had noticed that the first time he set eyes on her. It was more her demeanour. Apart from the silly healing nonsense, she was practical and pragmatic. She never really showed a passion for anything, except for engines and machinery, or anything else that needed fixing. She wasn't the remotest bit 'girly'. He rarely saw her out of her greasy, shapeless overalls; she always had dirt under her nails and her jet-black hair was always messily tied up. On the rare occasion that he saw inside her cabin, he noticed she didn't even have a mirror. He just came to think of her as one of the boys.

The only exception was when she was in her second role, that of ship's medic, and he was her patient. It somehow felt very intimate. It didn't help that the space was so small. She was so caring and careful and gentle. She would certainly make a good mother, but he imagined that she would be a good lover too. He had to fight the urge to kiss her. He was the ship's captain and she was crew, and it was too confined on an airship to get into a messy relationship. He didn't want to spoil anything. Jao was an invaluable member of the crew, although he never really intended having a permanent engineer. It had been a miscommunication that led to Jao coming on board.

He had been on a long journey to Tana to buy up some goods to trade – they made good quality silk in Tana, along with trinkets made of silver, inlaid wood, and zebu horn. The engine had been making a noise for days and burning bloquettes like there was no tomorrow. If they could just make it to Tana, he could have it repaired whilst he went about stocking-up the loading bay.

In the end, they were forced to dock at a godforsaken place called Antsirabe. When the dock engineers looked at *The Reliant*, they just laughed. "That was a worthless pile of junk before it broke down. It's even more worthless now," they had said.

After two days of failing to find anyone to fix the ship, Gonagain was in a bar drowning his sorrows. *The Reliant* had been left to him by his estranged father and, in a way, so had Bunty Goodtime. Come to think of it, Bearnárd had been kind of left to him in his mother's will. And now he was going to be forced to abandon them all. He had been telling the barman his woes when someone overheard him. "Listen," the earwigger said, "it's a bit of a long shot, but I've heard there's a girl on the outskirts who can fix anything."

When Gonagain met the girl with the beautiful eyes and the unpronounceable name he was, to say the least, dubious. She was just a slip of a girl, no more than seventeen. Tall and slender, she would probably have been elegant if she wasn't wearing a dirty tunic and carrying a bag of rusty tools. She seemed confident that she could fix *The Reliant*, but at the same time didn't seem to know very much about dirigibles. Perhaps it was just the language barrier – her native tongue was Gassy. He gave her the benefit of the doubt.

After two or three days, he was beginning to regret his decision. She was a tireless worker, but he wasn't convinced she knew what she was doing at all. The dock engineers watched with great amusement and started making jibes about flying tractors. There were also some wagers going on. Every time Gonagain went by, they made a sly comment behind their hands and laughed. He didn't know what to do. He was trying to save face with the dock engineers by pretending he knew something they didn't, but really, he wanted to call a halt to the whole thing. In the end, he just continued backing the strange girl –

he was stuck in Antsirabe anyway.

Then, one afternoon, when he was dozing, she came to him. "You want fly test?"

When they took *The Reliant* up, he was dumbfounded. He had never heard it sound so good. "That is unbelievable!" he exclaimed. "How much do I owe you?'

"Ten thousand ariary?"

"Ten thousand?"

"Too much?"

"You need to sort out your prices; for so much hard work those gobshites down there would charge ten times that."

"Hundred thousand? No, too much. Fifty thousand."

"Alright, fifty thousand ariary, you have a deal."

After that, he always went to Antsirabe for repairs and maintenance.

Later that year he ran into trouble with the Southern Air Guarda. Apparently, some of his stock was stolen goods. Gonagain knew it – you don't pick up emeralds at that price if they're legitimate. The Air Guarda chased him, shot at him, and eventually boarded *The Reliant*. They were corrupt, and they tried to take his stock for themselves. They beat him up for not handing over all the emeralds. Eventually, Bearnárd broke free, overpowered them and threw them, literally, off the ship. Somewhere there is probably an empty Guarda dirigible still floating around. They headed straight for Antsirabe for repairs, and Jao tended to his wounds as well. She was gentle and tender and, for a moment, Gonagain thought he might fall for her. Afterwards, she fixed up the ship. She was amazing.

"I could do with you full-time on *The Reliant*," he said.

It was a throwaway comment, and Gonagain was taken by surprise the next day to find her at the airship, with her tools and the tiniest trunk he had ever seen. She had taken him at his word and had even sold her hut. He didn't have the heart to tell her he hadn't meant it.

He took her to one of the unused cabins. It was small, dusty and untidy, and smelled a bit musty, but Jao was delighted. She had never slept anywhere so nice.

"It is lovely," she beamed, "I will have to share?"

"No, it's all yours," he cleared a lump in his throat, "I'll leave you to settle in." He left the cabin quickly – his voice had nearly cracked, and his eyes were decidedly watery.

Gonagain was bought out of his reverie by the sound of Jao's voice.

"I'll just put a couple of stitches into that,' she said gently. "And give you some laudanum and cannabis – it will ease the pain and make you drowsy."

CHAPTER 2
Lubumbashi

(New Year's Day)

Gonagain awoke in his cabin. He didn't really remember getting there – the effects of alcohol, cannabis, and laudanum. He wondered if he had got himself to bed, or if Bunty and Jao had put him there. He was still wearing his trousers, which was good, but his flies were undone. Memories of his escape from Doxies Parade came flooding back to him. Had his flies been undone the whole time Jao was treating him? Or worse, had someone had to help him go to the toilet?

"Pull yourself together, man," he mumbled to himself. "You've got bigger problems than that."

In his cabin, he had two cabinets with one door. The door was hinged in such a way that it closed either one cabinet or the other. Looking in the open cabinet, he saw his pulsarnite pocket watch had been hung on its hook and his pulsarnite pistol was on its mount. The calendar read 1.01.1910 – the first day, of the first hand, of the year 1910. The clock read 3.98. As both the clock and the calendar were powered by pulsarnite they needed no maintenance. Even as the world slowed on its axis, and the days and nights grew longer, pulsarnite timepieces automatically adjusted to match.

He unlocked the door and revealed the other cabinet. There was only one page left on the paper calendar and it read "December 33, 1909". He took the calendar off its hook and dropped it into the bin. From his bureau drawer, he dug out a new calendar and hung it on the now vacant hook. He tore off the cover to reveal the first day, "January 1, 1910". Out of curiosity he flicked through the pages looking at the last day of each month until he came to "May 34, 1910". That was an extra day they didn't have last year. He wound both the aero chronometer and his double half-hunter pocket watch. The time, just after midnight, was correct despite it being dawn.

Gonagain had no real allegiance to either time system – but he didn't really understand why the Trads had reverted to Traditional Time. Geokinetic Time made so much more sense. Ten decidays to a day; one hundred millidays to a deciday; and one hundred microdays to a milliday. All the odd units that traditional time used – twenty-four hours to a day, sixty minutes to an hour, and sixty seconds to a minute – seemed unnecessarily complicated. The Trads also refused to adjust the system to match the slowing down of time. Instead they wore those ridiculous varilight goggles to turn daylight to darkness and darkness to daylight whenever their time was out of sync with the day. What made him angry though, was that they had decided to start a war over it – to try to force the 'Pulsers' to revert to Traditional Time too.

He checked his Peacemaker revolver and his supply of ammunition, and closed and locked the door, revealing the Geokinetic Time again – he was, after all, still in a Geokinetic region.

Whichever time system he used, it was still the first day of the year and he still had two crew members stranded, or worse, in Lubumbashi.

Checking his reflection in the mirror, he saw that he was looking pretty rough. He set about smartening himself up – he was very particular about his appearance. After a quick wash, he shaved off his dark stubble with a cut-throat razor and neatened his sideburns with a small pair of scissors. He oiled his hair with some pomade, and took out a fresh, white, collarless shirt. After putting on his waistcoat, he checked his boots – they were shiny enough. He put them on and, putting his pocket watch in his waistcoat, he checked his reflection again. He still looked rough, but he felt more able to face what was left of his crew. Straightening his back, he set off towards the bridge.

******

Keeping a dirigible hovering in the same position takes more skill and much more concentration than flying in any given direction. When Gonagain arrived on the bridge, Bunty Goodtime was still at the helm and *The Reliant* was still in position, 500 metres above the airdock. Her eyes looked like they needed matchsticks to hold them open.

"Bunty, that was great piloting last night. Fair play to you."

"Thanks, Skipper. I used to go out with a pilot when I was younger," she said by way of explanation.

"I still don't know how you did it; you looked like you could barely walk when you left the tavern."

"Adrenaline, Skipper. There's nothing like a soft envelope full of hydrum and a bunch of people firing gunpowder weapons to sober you up." Rubbing her nose, she added, "Of course, the snuff helped."

Gonagain felt guilty. It was unfair putting his crew in such danger by filling the envelope with hydrum. Especially after the incident with the corrupt S.A.G. officers. If the envelope had been filled with hydrum on that day, none of them would be here today.

He had taken on a haulage contract that *The Reliant* couldn't really handle – not with an envelope full of heliagen. Hydrum was easily manufactured and, as a result, cheap. It was also twice as light as heliagen, giving *The Reliant* twice the lift, and allowing him to take double the payload. It was a huge risk, but he felt it was worth it for the contract. He had paid his crew danger money and treated them to a night out in Butare. The problem was, that he had continued to pay them danger money whilst the envelope was filled with hydrum, and now he couldn't afford to refill it with heliagen. Heliagen was a natural gas and there wasn't a limitless supply. That made it very expensive.

"You best get some shut-eye, Bunty. I'll take over now."

"Aye-aye, Skipper. You will wake me if you go looking for Beagán and Bearnárd won't you?"

"I will, Bunty – I promise."

Adjusting the bat-wing aerofoils and putting the propellers into reverse, Gonagain tilted the ship forward to get a better view of Lubumbashi through the glass dome of the bridge. As he did so, he tried to make sense of the previous night. Attacking whilst Geos celebrated the new year was tactically sound – if a little underhand – but why would the Trads attack a market city like Lubumbashi? And how had the Geo Guards responded so quickly? Where had they come from? Something was not quite right about the whole thing.

Lubumbashi was, almost entirely, surrounded by forest. There were half a dozen roads in and out of the city, many of which went through towns and villages in other clearings in the woods. In Lubumbashi itself, it all looked quiet now, but it was impossible to know what was going on elsewhere in the forest. Gonagain decided to let Bunty get some sleep, and give the Trads time to clear out before landing again.

******

As *The Reliant* bumped gently down on the air-dock, Bunty emerged from her cabin with her pulsarnite pistol in its holster over her bodice and her fedora perched on her head. She sniffed and rubbed her nose.

"Are we going to see if we can find the chaps, Skipper?"

"Yes, I think it's time. You ready?"

"Born ready, Skip, born ready."

"Perhaps we should bring the cart, Captain," chimed in Rajaobelina.

"I suppose we might have chance of a bit of looting," said Gonagain.

Bunty and Rajaobelina shared a silent look. Bunty realised that Rajaobelina was thinking more about bringing back their dead or injured crewmates, rather than any booty. It seemed like Gonagain was trying hard not to consider that possibility.

After bringing the cart down the gangplank and locking up the ship, they set off in single file, Bunty in front and Gonagain pulling the cart, with Rajaobelina bringing up the rear. Many of the dirigibles from the previous night had made their escape – a few had been left on the dock.

The main street was both busy and quiet. People

were busily clearing up the debris from the previous night's attack in a dazed silence. They passed an apothecary which had taken the full blast of the steam cannon. The cannon ball that had wrecked it almost filled what was left of the shop – it must have been a full metre in diameter. An apothecary was hardly a key target. It was either badly aimed or just an arbitrary shot. Gonagain made a mental note to have a rummage in there on his way back – they were running low on Vin Mariani.

As they continued through the city, there were two things that were noticeable; the lack of any obvious objective of the attack and, thankfully, the absence of casualties. They decided to head straight to The Scrimshankers Refuge – the last place that Bearnárd had been seen – and work their way outwards.

Upon arriving at The Scrimshankers, Gonagain realised how lucky he and Bearnárd had been. The outhouse, ice house and other out-buildings had been demolished by the steam cannon. Another huge cannon ball was nestling in the wreckage. Sticking out of the ruins of the outhouse was a pair of legs, the first casualty. It was not a pair of legs that any of them recognised. They were just about to enter The Scrimshankers when Rajaobelina froze.

"Listen!"

They all stopped, still as statues and listened. There was a whimpering coming from the wreckage of one of the store sheds. It was the least damaged building of them all – destroyed at the front, but still upright at the back. They began to carefully pull the debris away. After a few minutes, they reached the source of the sound – a small white dog with black and brown ears. Gonagain recognised it as the tavern's ratter, a scruffy little thing which toured The Scrimshanker's tables on an hourly basis looking for scraps and treats. Once the opening was big enough, the dog started to pull itself out. It was in a bad way, using its front legs only and dragging its back legs behind it.

Suddenly the tavern door flew open, and the taverner emerged, pointing a clunky-looking weapon at them. It was some type of hybrid gun that fired actual bullets, but used a tiny grain of pulsarnite to propel them.

"What are you doing?" the taverner growled.

Gonagain raised his hands in the air. "We were here last night," he replied, "We've lost some of our crew; one of them was here."

He lowered the gun "I remember. Big fella, came in with the two of you," he gestured to Bunty and Gonagain. "He ain't here. He helped some of the ladies who were in shock – real gentleman he was – and left."

For the second time today, Gonagain felt a pang of guilt.

It was then the taverner saw the dog. He raised his gun again.

"No!" shouted Rajaobelina, stepping between him and the dog. "I can save him."

"Better putting it out of its misery. Step aside,

lady, I'll end it's suffering."

"She has a gift," said Bunty. "She can make it better."

The taverner lowered his gun again and turned back towards the tavern door "It's all yours then," he muttered.

"What's his name?" asked Gonagain.

"Ain't got a name; just the ratter."

Rajaobelina gently scooped up the whimpering mutt and headed out of the tavern yard, back to the handcart. Bunty and Gonagain followed.

"Captain, the cart! It's gone."

"There it is, Skipper." Bunty gestured to the cart, which had been moved halfway up the road, and had something new on it.

After laying the dog on the cart, nestled in some old sacking, the three examined the small trunk that had been left on the cart. It was perhaps twice the size of Jao's tiny trunk. Gonagain tried the catches. It was locked. He then lifted it a couple of centimetres off the cart. It was heavy. Bearnárd could probably carry it around all day, but Gonagain would have struggled to get it all the way back to *The Reliant* without stopping to rest.

"What are we going do with it?" asked Bunty.

"Well it's on *our* cart," said Gonagain. "It must be ours."

They continued spiralling out from The Scrimshankers, asking everyone they encountered about Beagán and Bearnárd as they went. Eventually, they spoke to a general store owner who was washing down the street outside his store.

"There were a few casualties," he said, nodding to the area he was scrubbing. "Try the undertakers; you might save yourself some time." Then, realising how harsh he sounded, he added, "Or put your mind at rest."

"Where's the undertakers?" Gonagain asked.

"Black Horse Square."

The three of them looked at each other vacantly, then back at the storekeeper.

"At the end of Longest Walk Lane."

Again, the three looked nonplussed.

"Not far from the hospital."

"Which tavern is it near?" asked Bunty, a little impatiently.

"The Vigil and Wake."

"Righty-oh, Skipper, let's go!"

******

When they arrived at Gerhaert Undertakers, there was a row of bodies laid outside on the ground – about a dozen of them. They were all covered, but it was clear that none of them were big enough to be Bearnárd. Gonagain let out a quiet sigh of relief.

"Right," he said, "I'll start at this end, you two start at the other."

The first body that he uncovered, Gonagain thought he recognised the legs from The Scrimshankers outhouse. The next two he didn't know. Then, from the other end, he heard Bunty's voice, more gentle than usual.

"Skip, it's Beagán."

Gonagain looked towards the sky "No! No, no, no, NO!" He slumped to his knees beside Beagán's body and held his hands, which the undertaker had placed, loosely clasped, over his midriff. "You were a good lad, Beagán, this should never have happened to you," he said tearfully.

"I'm so sorry, Skip."

"We should never have left him down here!"

It was Rajaobelina's turn to feel guilty. "I'm sorry, Captain," she blurted, before bursting into tears.

Bunty wrapped her arms around Jao. "Skipper, there was no choice. If we'd waited, we'd all have been blown out of the sky," she said calmly, "or we'd have been picked off one-by-one on the ground."

The undertaker spotted them around Beagán's body and came out. "I'm Herr Gerhaert, I'm sorry for your loss," he said. "You're not local?"

"No. Air traders," replied Bunty.

"So, you won't require my services." It was a statement, more than a question.

"No. We'll take him with us. Where was he found?" Gonagain had recovered some of his composure.

The undertaker checked his notes. "Main Street, towards the river dock end. They didn't shoot many, only those resisting capture."

"They captured some?" asked Gonagain.

"Apparently, yes, quite a few."

"What did they do with them?"

Herr Gerhaert shrugged. "Two airships took off from satellite towns in the early decidays of this morning: a big one in the south east and a smaller one in the north west; my guess would be they were taken in them."

"Which direction did they go?"

"North-west, I think; I didn't watch for very long. I did notice the smaller one was quite badly damaged though. It will probably have to stop for repairs sooner rather than later."

Gonagain had always told Bearnárd, "Rule number one is stay alive." He hadn't thought he needed to lecture Beagán.

The walk back to *The Reliant* was a long one. Minds flitted from sadness about Beagán, to worry about Bearnárd, to concern for the dog, to curiosity about the chest. It was a lot to take in.

******

Back at *The Reliant*, they laid Beagán out on the airdock ground and wheeled the cart, with the dog and the trunk, into the hold. Rajaobelina took the dog to the medical bay. Gonagain didn't hold out much hope for him. It looked as though his back was broken, poor thing. He thought the taverner had the right idea, but he didn't want to appear dismissive of Jao's healing powers.

Whilst Rajaobelina and the dog went to the medical bay, Bunty and Gonagain set about preparing an airman's send-off for Beagán. Beagán was only a boy, still in his teens, but he was fit and strong and smart. He had only been aircraftman on *The Reliant* for about thirty hands, but he had showed promise, and Gonagain had imagined he would be with them for a long time.

They put him into a black, rubber-lined, silk envelope and Gonagain filled a balloon a from a small oxygen cylinder and put it in with him. Bunty stitched the envelope closed. It was a job that Jao or Beagán would normally do, but Bunty was one of those people who could turn her hand to anything if she applied herself, and she made a neat job of it. Meanwhile, Gonagain heated up a pot of tar on a portable stove. Together they painted the tar over Bunty's stitches, to seal the envelope, and they tethered it to three anchor points on the airdock.

Gonagain dragged a large cylinder out from the hold and connected it to a valve on the envelope. He turned a nozzle on the cylinder and the envelope began to fill with hydrum. When the envelope was *almost* fully inflated (the hydrum would expand as the air pressure reduced with altitude) they stopped and sealed the valve. Bunty went into *The Reliant* and came back out with Rajaobelina.

They stood in silence for a moment, each with their own thoughts. Then, taking a rope each, they cut the moorings and the envelope began to rise. It would continue rising until it reached the very edge of the atmosphere. With the reduction in the air pressure, the oxygen balloon would expand and burst. The sudden injection of pure oxygen into pure hydrum would cause an explosive inferno. Beagán and the envelope would be ashes on the wind before they fell back into the troposphere.

The three stood in silence with their arms around each other, Gonagain in the middle, and watched until Beagán was the tiniest dot. It was Bunty who broke the silence.

“Do not mourn, I did not die,
I am with you in the sky,
I am in the wind that squalls,
I am in the rain that falls.
Do not cry, I have not gone,
I am in the blackbird’s song,
I am in the brightest star,
To guide your journeys, near and far.
My dearest friends, please be at ease,
I am drifting on the breeze,
An airman’s soul it does not die,
It travels with you as you fly.”

Gonagain wiped a tear from his eye. “That was a beautiful poem, Bunty, who wrote it?”

“I did, just now.”

“When did you learn to do that?”

“I used to go out with a poet when I was younger.”

CHAPTER 3
Lubumbashi

(New Year's Eve)

The captain liked to have someone minding *The Reliant* constantly, if possible, and ever since the hostilities had stepped up a notch, he preferred *two* people to stay with the ship. Tonight, it had been decided that Rajaobelina and Beagán were to stay behind. It was New Year's Eve and Jao was not much of a drinker, and Beagán was under-aged, the captain had said.

Beagán was furious. He could easily pass for twenty and had been in taverns with the captain loads of times. Captain Gonagain and Lieutenant Strongman were always skipping their turn as dock lookout, and Miss Goodtime was old; she should be tucked up in bed with a good book, instead of out drinking and gambling and flirting with younger airmen. Besides, she never lasted the pace and would probably stagger home before midnight. It had been a mistake to raise these issues with Captain Gonagain though. He was told in no uncertain terms to have respect for his elders and superiors, and put on the dock lookout duty for the next two hands. Ten days of lookout! That wasn't fair! On the upside, Captain Gonagain had said that he could go out if Miss Goodtime returned to the ship early.

He was delighted, then, to see Miss Goodtime weaving unsteadily towards him across the dock.

"Beagán, my boy! Anything to report?"

"No, Miss Goodtime, all quiet."

"Good-oh. It is *raucous* out there, sonny – *raucous*! If you get your skates on, you should still get some action. There are some pretty young things nicely loosened up with grog, just waiting for a handsome young man like yourself to walk into their lives."

Beagán squirmed with embarrassment.

"Righty-oh then, son, off you go. The skipper is in The Scrimshankers, if you're interested."

Beagán straightened his newsboy cap and set off, almost at a trot.

"Oh!" said Bunty "Nearly forgot. Anything to report?"

Beagán rolled his eyes. "No, Miss Goodtime, all quiet," he repeated.

He was in two minds where to go. He liked drinking with Captain Gonagain and the other airmen; it made him feel part of the crew – one of the boys. On the other hand, he would like to go somewhere with a young crowd, and the thought of 'pretty young things loosened up with grog' was very appealing. He decided to go his own way – he wasn't confident about getting served in The Scrimshankers, and he was still angry with Captain Gonagain anyway. He would go to the Bird of Paradise and see what was happening there.

At the Bird of Paradise, he threaded his way to the bar and bought himself a pint of ale. To his delight, the barman didn't ask his age or even give him a second look. He found a seat near the door, subconsciously emulating Captain Gonagain ("Rule number one, Beagán, always take a seat near the door – better for a quick get-away if you need it.")

Beagán looked up to his captain. He was smart, quick-witted, athletic, and handy with his fists as well as with a gun. He was also usually quite successful with the ladies – although not quite as successful as he portrayed himself – and Beagán envied him for that.

Beagán was not as handsome as Captain Gonagain. Back at the orphanage, his nickname was Tayto because, they said, he had a head like a potato. He also had freckles and a very slight ginger tinge to his hair. But other than that, he was not bad looking. He had a strong brow; a strong chin, and he was taller than the captain, and more muscular. He was also braver. It was the one thing he didn't understand about Captain Gonagain. He was good in fight, yet always preferred to talk his way out of trouble, or just make himself scarce. Beagán enjoyed a good brawl, especially when Lieutenant Strongman and Captain Gonagain were on his side. He was always getting into scraps back at the orphanage and it didn't matter how big his opposition was, or how many of them there were – especially when they called him Tayto. He didn't really like living at the orphanage – they were never cruel, but they were rarely kind, and he was always in trouble for fighting or running away.

******

Beagán had run away from the orphanage for the umpteenth time and was loitering around an airdock when he met Captain Gonagain. Every ship that came in, he approached the captain for work. At first, he didn't realise that Gonagain was a captain – he looked too young – and he let him walk right past. It was only after observing him at the dock office and the chandlery that he realised his mistake.

"Need an aircraftman, Captain?" he said, as Gonagain ambled back.

"How much experience have you had?"

"None, but..."

"No, thanks, I don't take beginners."

"I'll work hard and I'm strong."

Gonagain cocked his head and eyed him up. "I'll tell you what," he said, "I've just bought ten large cylinders of hydrum from that chandlery over there. If you can get them from there into the hold in ten millidays, I'll take you on."

Beagán eyed up the distance. "OK, you're on!" He pulled a battered pocket watch with no chain from his trouser pocket and watched the microday hand as it ticked past 70… 80… 90…zero. "Go!" he shouted, and ran towards the chandlery.

Gonagain checked his own pocket watch and smiled to himself. It was smart that the kid had timed himself and not trusted him to do it – he hadn't expected that – but it would have been smarter if he had started from the chandlery and not the ship. He reckoned that he'd get seven or eight to the ship in ten millidays. Gonagain would then only have to get two or three himself – or pay a stevedore to do it.

The young fella struggled to get a grip on the first cylinder, and Gonagain lowered his expectations, but once he had worked out a technique he was up and, quite literally, running. He set off at a cracking pace, but by the time he was on number five, the sweat was pouring off him and he was beginning to slow down. At number seven, his strength was beginning to sap, and he had to stop halfway for a rest. Gonagain expected him to give up after number eight. As he ran back for number nine, the boy checked his watch and it seemed to spur him on – he did number nine without a rest. He had to drag, rather than carry, number ten up the gangway. Then, from the hold, he shouted, "Nine millidays and seventy-two microdays!"

Gonagain checked his own pocket watch. Then

he strolled up the gangway to see that, not only had he got the cylinders into the hold, but stacked them neatly in the rack. Gonagain whistled. “Fair play, son. What’s your name?”

“Beagán Haybailer, Captain.”

“Well, Aircraftman Haybailer, your cabin is first on the right, nearest the hold.”

Beagán grinned the biggest grin. “Yes, Captain. Thank you, Captain.” He grabbed his kit bag and ran inside.

Gonagain hadn’t really wanted an aircraftman, but he had one now. He was just glad he hadn’t agreed to pay him anything.

******

Beagán liked the Bird of Paradise tavern. There was a band with a banjo and a fiddle, and a young crowd. He wished he wasn’t there on his own though. He was just trying to pluck up the courage to ask a pretty girl to dance, when he felt the floor vibrating and a loud rumbling from outside. He decided to go out and see what was going on.

The machine that was rumbling past was like nothing he had seen before. It looked a bit like a steam locomotive, but it was at least three times the size. It didn’t run on tracks, but on huge, metal spoked wheels with solid rubber tyres. At the back of the machine, you could see the engine working nine to the dozen, puffing out plumes of smoke and steam. There was then a system of enormous cogs gearing down and transmitting the power into the slow rumbling movement of the massive vehicle. On the top of the machine was the largest gun barrel he had ever seen – and it was cranking upwards to a firing trajectory. Beagán had slept in smaller spaces than that gun barrel. He didn't even know what this machine was, but he knew it wasn't good. He had best go and warn Captain Gonagain.

He ran as fast as he could, aware that the machine's gun was pointing in his direction. There was an almighty bang, like a clap of thunder, and he came to a stumbling halt as he saw the vast shadow of the giant cannon ball as it soared over his head. Then he saw the cannon ball itself, dropping as it lost velocity, falling right towards The Scrimshankers' Refuge. The ground shook and there was a loud crash, followed by screams. A hot, panicky feeling overcame him. He was glad he hadn't been a bit quicker and hadn't made it to The Scrimshankers, but at the same time, he wished he had been *a lot* quicker and had made it both in and out again with Captain Gonagain. He broke into a run once more.

As he got closer the tavern, he began to feel a bit better – it hadn't been a direct hit. He was within a hundred and fifty metres when he saw, with relief, Captain Gonagain emerge from the tavern and head off to the back alleys of Lubumbashi. Beagán set off in pursuit.

He lost sight of his captain once or twice, but managed to keep on his tail as far as Doxies Parade. As he was approaching Doxies, he spotted about six pairs of varilight goggles glowing orange in the dark. He flattened himself to the side of a building, behind a decorative half-pillar. If he kept going, he would reach the entrance of Doxies at the same time as a bunch of Trads. If they didn't follow the captain, they would probably discover him here. He edged out of sight and then turned and ran back towards Main Street. Perhaps he might find Lieutenant Strongman.

Upon reaching Main Street, he did indeed find the lieutenant, but not as he was expecting. He was one of a group of about two dozen men, being marched up Main Street, hands on heads, in the general direction of the Bird of Paradise. The men were walking in two columns. There was an armed Trad soldier at the front, two more on each flank, and another taking up the rear. There was also an officer – a sergeant, tall and skinny with an arrogant demeanour and a thick moustache, waxed and upturned at the ends – and yet another private, who was carrying a bundle of pulsarnite weapons and watches that had been taken off the captives.

Beagán crept along behind them, his small pocket pulsarnite pistol drawn and set to narrow beam, getting closer with each step. When he was close enough, he grabbed the rear guard around the neck and shoved his pistol under his chin.

"Let these men go, or I'll kill him!" he roared.

The captured men and the Trad soldiers turned as one. Bearnárd Strongman stared wide eyed with disbelief and gently shook his head. If Beagán backed off now with his hostage, he might still get out of this.

"Let them go!" Beagán shouted again, this time with slightly less conviction.

One of the captives broke rank, and lunged for the soldier carrying the confiscated weapons. The sergeant drew his revolver and shot him dead in one swift movement. Then, when he was sure his men had their rifles trained on the captured men, he strode silently and confidently towards Beagán.

Beagán pulled his pistol from under the chin of the rear guard and pointed it at the approaching officer. Bearnárd willed him to pull the trigger, but he hesitated, and the rear guard took his opportunity. He stamped on Beagán's foot, elbowed him in the ribs and wriggled free. Beagán was winded, but tried to straighten up anyway. Then he heard the gunshot and felt the searing pain in his chest. He fell to the ground. He lay looking up at the stars on a cloudless night, and found himself momentarily admiring their beauty. The last thing he heard was a voice. "Okay, men, as you were, carry on!" Then, nothing.

CHAPTER 4

Lubumbashi to Stanleyville

(Secundusday)

The Reliant had been unmoored from the airdock and was ready to leave. The black funeral envelope, and the used oxygen and hydrum cylinders had been replaced. The cargo hold – which had been full of knick-knacks and tat upon arriving in Lubumbashi – was empty, apart from the cart, various other tools of the trade and, of course, the locked trunk. It had been a very successful visit to the Lubumbashi winter festivals up until New Year's Eve.

"Where to, Skipper?" sighed Bunty

"Well, Herr Gerhaert said the Trad airships were heading north-west and one of them was limping. Where's the nearest Trad town with a repair airdock north-west of here?"

Bunty studied her maps. "Stanleyville is west-north-west. There's nothing north-west for nearly a thousand kilometres."

"Set a course for Stanleyville then."

"Righty-oh, Skipper."

Gonagain released the water ballast and emptied some more hydrum from the compressor to the envelope. The ship gently rose and, with port and starboard propellers working in opposite directions, rotated gracefully towards the north-west. Gonagain took the starboard out of reverse and into forward gear, engaged the single bow prop, and the much-reduced crew said a sad and silent farewell to Lubumbashi, as the ship headed west-north-west.

******

It was later that same afternoon, whilst Rajaobelina was keeping Gonagain company on the bridge, that Bunty burst in.

"Okay, which one of you deviants has pilfered my salty liquorice?"

"I haven't touched it," replied Rajaobelina.

"Bunty, if I was going to pinch any of your food – which I wouldn't – it wouldn't be the salty liquorice I'd be taking. Disgusting stuff."

"Well, one of you has."

Gonagain looked at Jao. "The dog?"

"No – the dog hasn't moved from my bunk."

"Bunty, are you sure you didn't eat it already, maybe when you got back from the tavern?" said Gonagain.

"No. I didn't. Just keep away from my scran – it's not funny, it's beastly!" and with that, she stormed out.

Rajaobelina looked at the captain. "Did you?"

"No. You?"

"No!"

"She must have eaten it and forgotten."

"You don't think she's going prematurely senile do you, Captain?"

Gonagain wasn't sure if Jao was serious or not. She wasn't usually one for wise-cracks but he chuckled anyway. "No. She may be nearly old enough to be my mother, but she's sharp as a knife and fit as a fiddle, that one. She'll probably out-last me."

Rajaobelina and Captain Gonagain slipped into a comfortable silence. The bridge, much like the rest of *The Reliant*, was a bit tatty, but very comfortable and, inside at least, almost stylish. The seats were upholstered in a soft natural leather which was worn and scuffed with age. They were bolted to the dimpled metal floor, but swivelled and reclined. On long journeys across open plains or seas, the captain could often be found with the seat fully reclined and his feet up on the instrument panel. He would – to an untrained eye – appear to be fast asleep, but when he was on the bridge the captain slept like a dog, with one eye open and prepared to take whatever course of action was required at a moment's notice. The instrument panels were really rather beautiful. The various dials and levers were gleaming brass, set into, or protruding from, a fascia of polished billabob wood. The curved walls were a web of narrow, blackened, steel beams with rivets that had been worn shiny. These were inset with lightweight panels of billabob wood which stopped the bridge from becoming like an oven in summer, but provided little protection from the cold in winter. A mesh of copper piping traced the web of steel. These pipes ran to and from the engine boiler and were filled with oil that would be heated up when the valves were opened, to stop the crew from freezing to death. The valves and pipes were also used as hooks and rails from which to hang charts, tools, charms, and goodness knows what else. Then there was the panoramic view provided by the glass dome at the front of the bridge. It was not an unbroken view – there was, again, a web of steel hexagons and pentagons creating the domed shape, which were in-filled with thick glass panes. Most of them were fixed, but on the edges of the dome they could be tilted for ventilation. The noise of the bow propeller meant that they were rarely opened.

Rajaobelina sat beside her captain with a hot cup of coffee and, as she watched the forests gradually give way to savannah, she felt a wave of inner peace and contentment wash over her.

******

Gonagain had been taking a nap in his cabin, when he was woken by the sound of raised voices.

There was some sort of altercation between Bunty and Jao up on the bridge. He briefly considered trying to go back to sleep and letting the two sort it out between them, but he had such a small crew now, and he needed everyone to be working together. He sat up with a weary sigh, pulled on his boots, and reluctantly headed up the spiral staircase to the bridge. When he first took ownership of *The Reliant,* he had envisaged himself barking orders to a bunch of hardy airmen – not mediating between two strong-minded women. To be fair though, this was the first time he'd needed to; despite having literally nothing in common, Bunty and Jao liked and respected each other.

When Gonagain entered the bridge, the two were face to face, inches from each other, and shouting. They didn't even notice him come in. He reached over to a switch on the wall marked 'Emergency drill' (Beagán had crossed it out with chalk and written 'Panic stations') and flicked it on. A deafening klaxon sounded briefly before he switched it off again. The two women suddenly stopped shouting and looked at him accusingly.

"Right! What is going on between the two of you?"

The two women started up again from where they left off, except now they were facing him.

"She took my banana-rice-cake…"

"She accused me of taking her banana-rice-cake…"

"…revenge because she thinks I stole her salty

liquorice...”

“...well, *someone* took my salty-liquorice...”

“...they were home-made...”

“...she can make more...”

“...where will I get bananas this far north...”

“...where will I get salty liquorice this far south...”

Gonagain flicked the klaxon on and off again “ENOUGH!” he shouted. “Right. I didn’t take *your* salty liquorice and I didn’t take *your* homemade banana-rice-cake. Jao, did you take Bunty’s salty liquorice?”

“No.”

“Bunty, did you take Jao’s homemade banana-rice-cake?”

“No.”

“Well, I believe both of you.”

“Ockham’s razor, Skipper, Ockham’s razor. There’s only three of us on board, therefore it must be one of us.”

“Okay, Bunty, lets apply Ockham’s razor, shall we? Some snacks have gone missing and we all deny taking them. What does that tell us?”

“That one of us is a dirty fibber.”

“I’m NOT lying, Captain!”

“Quiet, Jao!” Gonagain reprimanded. Jao gave him a defiant look and pouted – beautifully.

“Okay, Bunty, so one of us is lying, or...?”

“... or we’re all telling the truth and someone else took them, but that’s not possible, there’s no one else...”

"But there is someone else, isn't there, Jao?"

"It's not the dog, Captain. I'm feeding it and sedating it until it's better."

"So, is there any possibility that some*one* or some*thing* else is on board?" asked Gonagain.

"No, Captain. The ship was locked or guarded at all times."

"We still don't know what's in that trunk, Skipper."

"You mean the locked trunk that we can't get into?" said Rajaobelina sarcastically.

"Maybe it's locked from the *inside*, Skipper."

"Now you're thinking," said Gonagain. "There's some weird critters in the forests of Lubumbashi – some of them are cute hoors too."

They headed down to the hold with an air of expectation and nervous excitement and stood around the cart with the trunk on it.

"No air holes, Captain."

Gonagain lifted it up. "What about underneath?"

"No."

He shook the trunk vigorously. It was a dead weight and made no sound. He put the trunk down. The disappointment was palpable.

"Weight!" said Rajaobelina suddenly.

Gonagain and Goodtime waited.

"Wait for what?" said Bunty eventually.

"No, not wait – weight! The weight gauge on the bridge! I noticed it earlier when I was checking the instrument panel, but didn't think it all the way through. The weight of *The Reliant*, fully equipped and crewed but with no cargo, is usually about thirty-five tonnes and three hundred and seventy kilos."

"Right. So...?"

"Beagán was roughly eighty kilos and Bearnárd was... I mean *is* about one hundred and twenty kilos. So, the gauge should be at thirty-five tonnes and one hundred and seventy kilos, but it's not, it's about a hundred kilos over."

"Don't forget the trunk and the dog," said Bunty.

"That's what I put it down to," said Rajaobelina. "But the dog is about seven kilos, and you just saw the captain lift the trunk – it's nowhere near a hundred kilos."

"I *am* quite strong!" Gonagain said indignantly.

Rajaobelina and Bunty each raised an eyebrow and looked at the captain.

"So, we have what? Sixty odd kilos unaccounted for?" continued Bunty, ignoring Gonagain's input.

"Roughly, yes"

"Full sweep of the ship, Skipper?"

"Good idea," replied Gonagain. He was delighted to see Jao and Bunty working as a team again, but still a little offended at their dismissal of his physical prowess. "I'll start at the bridge and the mess. Bunty, you check the cabins. Jao, you take the engine room, the loading bay, and the hold. Report back to the bridge when you're done."

******

Gonagain had checked the bridge, the gun turret, the mess and all the corridors, cubby holes, nooks, and crannies – and found nothing. Rajaobelina had also come back to the bridge with nothing to report. Then Bunty spoke over the voice-repeater. "Sixty odd kilos and missing snacks accounted for Skipper. Be with you in two shakes."

Bunty came on to the bridge pushing, what – at first – appeared to be a very handsome young boy in front of her and carrying a kit bag on her shoulder. It took Gonagain a microday to notice that the stowaway had slightly wider hips than waist, and gentle curves that were not pectoral muscles. Despite the beige, wool, high-waisted boy's trousers with braces, paired with a waistcoat that almost matched, the brown tweed jacket, scuffed brown boots and a cream collarless shirt, the young man standing before him, clutching a brown, tweed newsboy cap was actually a young woman.

"We have a stowaway, Skip," said Bunty, stating the blindingly obvious.

The stowaway was no more than a hundred and sixty centimetres tall. She had a smooth olive complexion and short, dark hair, cut like a pixie. She had dark brown eyes; her nose was small and straight, and her mouth was wide with full lips and sharp white teeth.

Gonagain realised that, whilst appraising the stowaway, he had unintentionally softened his stance and demeanour. He straightened his back. "Who are you and what are you doing on my ship?"

he barked, trying to regain his air of authority.

"No comment," she replied sweetly, revealing a slightly diastematic smile.

"Why are you dressed as a boy?"

The stowaway rolled her eyes. "This is the twentieth century you know." She gestured at Bunty and Rajaobelina.

Gonagain looked at his crew.

Bunty was wearing beige jodhpurs, brown knee-length boots, a brown leather waistcoat and a white blouse. Whilst not traditional ladies clothing, they were – unlike the stowaway's outfit – all cut for the female form. The blouse had lace frills at the collar and cuffs, and the waistcoat laced at the back in a corset style and, although Bunty didn't lace it *very* tightly, it accentuated her wasp waist.

Jao was in her usual shapeless overalls, but that was just practicality. It was the only suitable clothing for a dirigible engineer.

"Is that her kit bag?" he asked Bunty.

"Yes, Skip. Shall I turn it out?"

"Yes. Do."

Bunty pulled the drawstring toggle and tipped the contents on the floor.

"Hey, careful with my stuff!" the young woman shouted.

Bunty knelt on the floor, and started moving things from the pile to create a new pile, about thirty centimetres away. As she did so she called out the objects. "One snub-nosed, six-shot revolver – a Model 10; one cylindrical wicker tube – some sort of bottle carrier maybe; a pencil and pad; one leather pouch containing... soap, face cloth, toothbrush and erm... some ladies' things; and a change of under garments." Bunty scooped the underwear up quickly and tucked it under the other objects – it wasn't fair to leave that on display. She picked up the last object – another leather pouch. Inside was a metal box, slightly smaller than a house brick. It was adorned with dials and buttons and had a cylindrical tube sticking out one side. There was a flip-up rectangular frame on another side.

"What's that?" asked Rajaobelina.

"It's a camera," replied Bunty. "A pretty new-fangled one at that. It probably takes thirty-five-millimetre film." She tutted. "Things have come a long way since wet plates."

"How do you *know* this stuff?" asked Gonagain with admiration.

"I used to go out with a photographer when I was younger."

"How does it work?" Rajaobelina was addressing Bunty.

The stowaway piped up, "It's basically a light-proof box that lets in a bit of light at just the right moment. When the light enters the camera, it creates an image by causing a chemical reaction on photo film. Then you have to develop the film in a darkroom, by dipping the film in special chemicals which make the image visible."

"How did you learn all that?" Rajaobelina asked the stowaway. She was impressed despite herself.

"Someone taught me," the stowaway replied. She clearly thought it was a daft question.

"Oh. Well I suppose anyone can do it, if you don't have to work it out for yourself," said Rajaobelina dismissively. She had decided that she didn't like this young woman at all. She had the air and confidence of a woman that was used to getting what she wanted. Rajaobelina had already seen Gonagain soften towards her.

She had known people like this all her life. They were pretty enough, or educated enough, or Machiavellian enough to manipulate people into giving them what they wanted. Or worse they were just wealthy enough to buy whatever they wanted – whether they needed it or not. This woman seemed to be all those things. These people had always dismissed Rajaobelina, brushing her aside as if she were not there. Rajaobelina had always got everything the hard way, through hard work and patience. She was determined not to be brushed aside on *The Reliant*, where she was finally made to feel important.

Bunty meanwhile was turning the kit bag inside out to check she hadn't missed anything. There was a name stitched to the inside. 'A. Trustworthy'.

"Look, Skipper!"

"Well, Miss Trustworthy. What does the 'A' stand for?"

"No comment."

"I see. Then the next question is, what do we do with you?"

"I think we should stick with tradition, Captain." It was the old tradition of throwing stowaways from the ship during flight that Rajaobelina was referring to.

"Well, without a full name and with no idea what you're doing aboard *The Reliant*, I'm afraid I must agree," said Gonagain. He pulled the pocket watch out of the stowaway's waistcoat by the chain. "Mechanical. So, you're a *Trad* stowaway. That decides it then."

The stowaway had lost her air of defiant confidence, and was now looking nervous.

"My name is Aoife Trustworthy, and I'm a photographer," she blurted.

"And why are you on my ship?"

"I needed to get out of Lubumbashi. I don't think I'd be very welcome there after New Year's Eve. I didn't know this was a Pulser ship."

"We're time neutral on *The Reliant* – at least we were until the Trads killed one of my men and captured another. When did you board *The Reliant*?"

"When you were watching your aircraftman take his final flight," she replied meekly.

"And how did you get *into* Lubumbashi?"

"I stowed away."

"A proper little hobo, this one," said Bunty.

"I still say we stick with tradition."

Gonagain realised that Jao had taken a genuine dislike to Aoife Trustworthy and, unlike himself, was not bluffing about the tradition.

"I think for now we'll just put her in Beagán's cabin, Jao."

"In Beagán's cabin? Beagán's body's not even cold!"

"Well, technically, Jao..."

Bunty shot Gonagain a look.

"No. No, quite right," Gonagain corrected himself. "Put her in the medical bay, please, Jao. Bunty, remain here – I need to talk to you."

Gonagain often sought advice and guidance from Bunty Goodtime. She seemed to have accrued several lifetimes worth of experience and she had a vast range of skills and knowledge that she had acquired by carefully observing others, whilst simultaneously pretending to be totally disinterested in everything they did. She always found knowledge was more valuable if no-one knew you had it. She was an ideal, unofficial advisor and confident to Gonagain, but it hadn't always been this way –Gonagain and Goodtime's acquaintance had got off to a rocky start.

Gonagain's estranged father had left *The Reliant* to Gonagain in his will. "To my son, Oisín Gonagain..." the solicitor had read, "I leave my beloved ship, *The Reliant*, on the provision that he also takes care of my darling mistress, Bunty Goodtime."

It was difficult to know who was more resentful: Bunty, for being passed on like some sort of chattel; or Gonagain, for being lumbered with an apparently useless, much older – though not unattractive, woman.

******

Bunty was the daughter of an army major. He had little interest in his daughter and focused his attention on his sons, in order to equip them for a military future. His plans for Bunty consisted solely of sending her to finishing school, and marrying her off to someone of a suitable rank and class. Bunty, on the other hand, had different ideas. She was expelled from every school she was sent to – for misdemeanours ranging from simple insubordination, to supplying and distributing illegal substances. At sixteen she met a handsome young airman and ran off with him to see the world. Unfortunately, it transpired that he did not have permission to bring Bunty aboard, and she was abandoned unceremoniously at Zalagazeg Airdock. She worked briefly at the Zalagazeg Airdock, doing clerical work, before being spotted by a landscape artist who happened to be passing through. He instantly switched from landscapes to life painting, and Bunty became his muse – until she realised that he was a very average artist and a possessive old pervert. She snuck out of his garret in the middle of the night and hitched a ride on the first dirigible out of the airdock, in exchange for working in the galley. And so, began her career as a serial job swapper, blagger and opportunist. She was canny enough to save money for short stays in inns or hostels when she was between jobs, but she was never between jobs for very long. She was endlessly resourceful, and able – though not particularly keen – to work hard when required. She was, initially, naïve, but she was very intelligent, and soon became a shrewd reader of people and a social chameleon. She was as comfortable in a bawdy cabaret hall as she was at a royal garden party. Of course, it did her no harm at all that she was utterly stunning to look at. With her golden-blonde curls and her curvaceous figure, her flawless tanned skin, and bright green eyes, she turned the heads of men wherever she went, and she used that to her advantage.

As she got older, of course, she was unable to press this advantage as much as before. Her figure barely changed, but her hair was not quite as lustrous as it used to be, and her face began to develop a few laugh lines. She avoided wearing spectacles when she could, but it became increasingly necessary. She had been travelling with a very successful air trader when she discovered she was about to be usurped by a younger model. Not wanting to face that indignity, she packed her bags and left without a word. She had spotted that *Le Cabaret des Etoiles* in St-Gille-Croix-de-Vie was auditioning, and went along to try her luck with a song and dance routine.

“That was... interesting,” said the creative director after her audition. “You have a fantastic figure and there’s no denying that you’re pitch-perfect, but your voice has the timbre of... a parakeet... in a garotte. As for your dancing, you have great rhythm but, you are a touch too... enthusiastic and, frankly, a tad... mature.”

Bunty, who was holding a cane to go with her top hat, adjusted her grip in preparation to hit him with it.

"But I *do* like you," he continued, "I like your personality. How would you like a position in front of house?" he asked. "Mingling with the customers – you can get them to buy you drinks, if you like – making sure there's plenty of atmosphere, even when it's a bit empty. If you still want to be on stage, you can fill in when we're short staffed... at the back."

Bunty released her grip on the cane. She had just been offered her dream job. She would be paid to party! She decided to ignore the bit about being at the back.

"Righty-oh. When can I start?"

It was whilst she was working at *Le Cabaret des Etoiles* that she met Mícheál 'Mickey' Gonagain. It was love at first sight – something that she had never believed in. Within the week, she had packed in her dream job and was back travelling the world again, in a tatty, three-propellered airship with a patched-up yellow envelope. And for several years, that was the most blissful period of her life – right up until the morning she woke up beside her lover's cold body and her world shattered around her.

As relieved as she was not to be made homeless, she was not delighted with the idea of travelling with Mickey's son. She hadn't even known of his existence until the reading of the will. Now he was making it clear that she was no longer the First Lady of *The Reliant*, but his subordinate. Cheeky little upstart – playing at being captain when he had only just been gifted a dirigible of his own. Well, she was going to do nothing to help him. She'd just wait until he messed up and then she'd show him what's what.

His first mistake was to try to fly *The Reliant* solo – it was at least a three-crew ship – but she had to give him his due, he coped very well. Piloting, navigating, *and* stoking on his own was no mean feat. He barely slept whilst they were airborne, but when he did, he would stoke up the engine to full power and set a course full steam ahead – to minimise drift – before dozing off. Upon waking, he would immediately assess their location and adjust their course accordingly. Docking an airship solo is nigh-on impossible, yet he managed it. Ingeniously, he would drop the ballast pump pipe to suck up water, whilst simultaneously increasing the heliagen content in the envelope to compensate. Once the ballast tank was full of water, he would send the heliagen back to the compressor and the ship would gently bump down to the ground. With a full ballast tank and reduced envelope, he could safely leave *The Reliant* long enough to secure the mooring ropes. Bunty was impressed – but didn't let it show. She nonchalantly turned the page of her book, as if she hadn't noticed.

However, all this work eventually took its toll, and shortly after a purchasing trip to Tana, he developed a fever. He was delirious and weak, and in no fit state to do anything. Bunty began to regret leaving him to cope alone. She would now have to nurse him back to health *and* fly *The Reliant* solo herself. They were over the Terrasec Desert so, with no water for kilometres, docking wasn't an option even if she could replicate Oisín's clever technique. She set a course for Zika – there was a hospital for tropical diseases there.

Over the next three days, she mopped Oisín's brow and fed him soup. She struggled to keep *The Reliant* on course, as there were so few landmarks on the Terrasec. On one occasion, the engine started to splutter because it had run so low on bloquettes, but she managed to stoke it up before it stopped completely. Eventually, the Dirty Great Mountains appeared on the horizon, at about ten degrees off their direction of travel. Not long after, Oisín Gonagain appeared on the bridge. He still looked rough, but he was up, and he was lucid. Bunty was delighted – she desperately needed some sleep. How Gonagain had managed solo for so many weeks was beyond her comprehension.

"Where the hell *are* we?" he asked.

"About fifty clicks south of Zika."

"What are we doing there?"

"The hospital for tropical diseases – I wasn't sure..."

"*South* of Zika?" exclaimed Gonagain suddenly. "The Dirty Great Mountains!"

"We're coming in north-westerly; I was going to turn to due east once we passed the Wrecker Peaks."

"Oh. Good plan. Fair play to you," said Gonagain. "Erm... how did you get us here?"

"I used to go out with a navigator when I was younger."

Gonagain wasn't quite sure how that explained her own navigational and piloting skills, but at this point he didn't really care.

"Permission to get some shut-eye, Skipper?" It was the first time she had called him Skipper. It was the first time she had called him anything other than 'son', 'boy', or – if she was in a particularly good mood – Oisín. For a moment, Gonagain wondered if he had heard right or if he was still delirious. Then Bunty smiled.

"Permission granted," he smiled back. "You deserve it."

******

"So, what do you think of our Miss Trustworthy?" Gonagain asked Bunty.

"In what capacity? As a suitor for you?" Bunty replied mischievously.

"I'm being *serious*."

"So am I. I saw you go all mushy when you saw her."

"I did *not* go mushy."

"Come on, old boy, don't tell me you don't find her attractive."

"*Look...*" said Gonagain exasperatedly, "Okay, if it makes you happy, yes, she's a very attractive young woman..."

"Don't let Jao hear you say that."

"*Bunty!*" Gonagain was getting annoyed, "Do you think Miss Trustworthy is a problem and, if so, what do you think we should do with her?"

"Well I think 'sticking with tradition' is just a smidgeon archaic. But I think she's a snollygoster. I don't trust her. Not one jot. Nothing about her accent or equipment says 'poverty', yet she travels as a stowaway dressed like a boy. That doesn't add up for a start. Plus, I just have a hunch she's not all she seems."

"So, what do we do with her?"

"Set her down now and let her take her chances. Or, if you're feeling generous, let her work her passage as far as a Trad town."

"Okay. Thanks for your input, Bunty. I'll mull it over"

"Righty-oh, Skip."

Gonagain went to the medical bay to speak to Aoife Trustworthy.

"Right, Miss Trustworthy..."

"You can call me Aoife, Oisín," she interrupted coquettishly.

"And you can call me Captain," he replied, as sternly as he could muster. She was very attractive and, despite her diminutive stature, the medical bay seemed very small for the both of them. "How do you know my name?" he added.

"The airdock office had all the information I needed. You see, Oisín, I always like to check who I'm travelling with.

"I said 'You can call me Captain'," he managed to sound a bit sterner this time.

"Yes, Captain!" she replied.

Gonagain couldn't decide if there was hint of a mocking tone. He decided to ignore it. "We don't carry passengers on *The Reliant*, so as soon as we find a safe landing spot, we're going to set you down."

"Oh, please, Captain, at least take me as far as the nearest Trad region. After what happened in Lubumbashi, I wouldn't feel safe in a Pulser area." Aoife was playing the damsel in distress to perfection.

"Well, as it happens, our next stop is Stanleyville," said Gonagain, "But, as I said, we don't carry passengers. You'll have to pull your weight."

"I'll do *anything* you tell me to, Captain," she was back in coquette mode again.

"Right, the medical bay will serve as your cabin for now. I'll get Bunty to return your things. Report to the bridge in fifteen minutes." Gonagain left the medical bay and returned to the bridge, only vaguely aware that there was a slight skip in his stride – and not entirely sure why.

Aoife breathed a sigh of relief. This whole mess was beginning to turn out quite well. Having missed the Trad airships out of Lubumbashi, she had found herself stranded and, after struggling with the heavy trunk for hours, she had found a handcart to carry it on. All she needed to do was get it into the forest and send for help. Then *that* all went pear-shaped when the owners of the cart suddenly appeared. She had certainly never intended to stowaway on this ship, she only wanted to stay in contact with the trunk. Now they were both going to be delivered to directly to Stanleyville. All that was needed was a plan to get the trunk off with her.

The captain was clearly both soft-hearted and a little bit vain – which should make him easy to manipulate. And, if she had to resort to sleeping with him it would be no hardship, he was clean and fit and *very* handsome. The older woman was difficult to get a handle on, but she had her weaknesses; she liked a drink and she liked her snuff. She could use that in some way. It was the engineer who was going to be the problem. She would be much more difficult to win over. She didn't think sleeping with *her* was going to be an option – which was a shame. As handsome as she found the captain, the engineer was even more her type.

Fifteen minutes later, on the Bridge, the whole crew – including the newest recruit – were assembled. Gonagain announced that Aoife was going to be working as aircraftman as far as Stanleyville. Bunty struggled to subdue a smirk. She knew The Skipper would want to keep the stowaway on board – the randy bugger. She would just have to make sure she didn't get under his skin and have him thinking with the wrong part of his anatomy. Conversely, Rajaobelina was struggling to subdue her rage. She remained passive and stony-faced but, if you looked carefully, you could see her dark skin reddening with rage. She was also clenching her teeth. Even Gonagain could sense an atmosphere developing.

It was then that the little dog came trotting into the room, its claws clattering on the metal floor. It skipped past the crew, straight towards Gonagain, who was the only person seated. It hopped up into his lap and sat staring at the captain. The atmosphere dissipated almost instantly.

"Jao, I don't believe it!" Gonagain said, "You're a miracle worker!"

Then, addressing the dog he said, "Hello, little fella. Have you got a name?"

"It's not a little fella, Captain, it's a little girl," said Jao, "And I haven't named her yet."

"Well, we can't have a crew member with no name," replied Gonagain.

"She reminds me of a dog that lived at *Le Cabaret des Etoiles*, Skip, Boo-boo her name was."

"Then that's what we'll call her."

"Boo-boo?"

"No, Etoile."

"It seems you have an all-female crew, Captain," said Aoife.

"So it does!"

CHAPTER 5
Isalo Mine

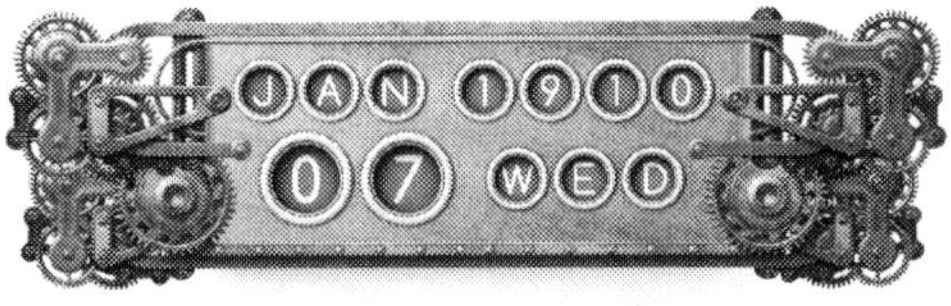

"Rule number one," Gonagain had always said, was, "stay alive."

Well, Beagán had broken rule number one and Bearnárd Strongman was beginning to wish he had too. Since being captured in Lubumbashi, he had been transported via the river dock to goodness-knows-where and put to work in a pulsarnite mine. He had been chained to the hull of the paddle steamer on the journey and was terrified. As hard as he tried, he could not get the iron bolt, that anchored him to the hull, to come out. And even if he could, he would still drown if the ship went down – he couldn't swim a stroke. Of course, he couldn't fly either but, for some reason, that never seemed to worry him when he was in a dirigible. From the paddle steamer, he was transferred to an enclosed trailer, pulled by a traction engine. He had lost all sense of direction and distance.

He was under the command of Staff Sergeant Digby Landowner, who had been promoted from plain old sergeant since capturing Bearnárd and killing Beagán. Bearnárd had been given the job, due to his strength, of carrying crates of pulsarnite *back into* the pulsarnite mine. The crates were stored in a strongroom on the surface, and needed to be carried to the pulsarnite face, deep in the mine – a journey of about four miles. He was to do this, sixteen hours a day. Strongman had tried to take his mind off his weary body by converting miles into kilometres and hours into decidays, but maths wasn't his strong suit and it just made his brain as weary as his body.

The workforce at the mine was made up of captive Pulsers, convicts and, believe it or not, some volunteers. The volunteers only did a few hours at a time and they got a hot shower and a hot meal at the end of their shift. They worked in volunteer-only groups. The captives and the convicts did the full sixteen-hour shift and got a sloppy stew with stale bread at the end of their day.

Strongman was luckier than some. He was able to breath fresh air every time he emerged from the mine with an empty crate. He also got to see daylight now and again, if he remembered to take off his varilight goggles when he emerged from the mine. The small clock that was mounted on the bridge of the goggles had been stopped at midday, meaning he was in permanent 'daylight'. But it was an artificial light, and taking the goggles off and seeing real daylight made Bearnárd feel a bit more alive. Those at the pulsarnite face were not so lucky. Some were exposing and cleaning the unmined pulsarnite. This was hard work in confined spaces and humid conditions, and it was pitch black if you removed your goggles. Worse still, there were people down there with hot torches and tongs who had to heat up the pulsarnite that Strongman bought down until the surface was soft and tacky. They could then fuse it to the pulsarnite face. The heat was murderous.

For the life of him, Strongman could not work out what the purpose of the exercise was. Pulsarnite was a commodity. Businesses went to extraordinary lengths and at great cost to *extract* it from the earth. And here they were putting it back. Each crateful was worth a fortune.

Aside from the conversion of Trad units to Geo units and the purpose of the 'un-mining' operation, there was one other thing occupying Bearnárd Strongman's mind – escape. "How would Oisín get out of here?" he muttered to himself. He ran his mind through Gonagain's long list of 'Rule number ones'. "Rule number one, Bearnárd, always learn from other peoples' mistakes." That was as good a place to start as any.

In the marquee that served as the canteen, Strongman sat opposite a man in a grey boilersuit that the convicts wore. He picked him because he looked like he had been here a long time – the rings around his eyes from wearing goggles were deep. "How long have you been here?" he asked after the convict had eaten most of his gruel.

"Dunno. Any idea what the date is now?"

"Two, two, nineteen-ten... I think," replied

Strongman

The convict scratched his flaky shaven scalp. "What's that on a proper calendar?"

"Oh. Er... seventh of January... I think."

"You do a lot of thinking, don't ya?" the convict smirked, "You don't look the type."

Strongman decided he had picked the wrong man and went back to stirring his watery stew.

"So, it's a new year then?" the convict continued, "Well that means I been here around six months. That's about thirty-six hands to you."

"Have you ever seen anyone escape?"

"Nope. Don't mean it ain't never happened though."

"Have you ever seen anyone *try* to escape?"

"Not many, no," he gestured with his spoon to Staff Sergeant Landowner. "See that long streak with the stupid 'tache? He has a very direct method of discouraging any bad behaviour. You step out of line even once and he'll shoot you dead, no questions asked, no second chances. And he'll make sure everyone sees it happen. So, if you're thinking up a plan to escape, you got to be a hundred percent sure it'll work. Either that or you just don't care anymore."

"Aye, I've seen his methods – first-hand." Strongman subconsciously clenched his fist and his jaw. "Any idea where we are?"

"Blimey, you don't half ask a lot of questions."

"Knowledge is power." That sounded good when Bunty said it. It sounded stupid coming from his own lips. "That's what my navigator always says," he added.

"Navigator, eh? You an airman or a sailor?"

"Airman."

"Well, airman, if you can get a message to your navigator, you can tell him our exact location is the middle of flippin' nowhere." He began using his spoon as a pointer again. "That way, mountains; that way, desert; that way, desert; that way, more flippin' desert."

"I came most of the way by river."

"Yeah, from Boma."

"No, from Lubumbashi."

"Well then, chances are we're not particularly near a point on a river that goes through both Boma and Lubumbashi."

Their conversation was interrupted by a fracas at the counter. One of the new 'recruits' was being simultaneously strip-searched and beaten by the Trad soldiers. Staff Sergeant Landowner strode purposefully across the compound towards the ruckus. There was a momentary calmness as he ascertained what was going on. Then, after slapping the now naked man around the face a couple of times he grabbed him by the hair and shoved him face down into the barrel of stew. He held him there whilst the poor unfortunate struggled for breath. Each time the man seemed about to go limp, the staff sergeant would pull him out and let him get a few gasps of air, only to repeat the process all over again. The rest of the workers were studiously ignoring the whole incident.

Strongman could not sit by any longer and jumped to his feet, only to be grabbed by the wrist by his companion and pulled back down again. "Don't be a flippin' idiot," he whispered, "all the heroes around here are six feet under."

Eventually the staff sergeant's victim was dumped on the floor, naked and coughing up stew. Workers who had been waiting patiently in line stepped over him and slopped stew on to their plates as if nothing had happened.

"What was that all about?" asked Strongman.

"He didn't bring back his spoon. He's either a flippin' moron or he was hoping to make a weapon out of it. He's lucky moustachio boy didn't just shoot him."

The butt of a rifle was banged loudly on the table right in front Strongman making him jump. "Table TEN your time is up! Take your trays *and* spoons to the counter and proceed to your dormitory."

Strongman got up and headed towards the counter, but as he passed table nine, he flicked his spoon off his tray, and it fell to the floor. He knelt to pick it up and had a quick look under the table. There, with the handle wedged in the join of the two planks that made the table-top, was the missing spoon. With a swift movement that Gonagain would have been proud of, Strongman grabbed the spoon and shoved it in his shirt. He stood up clutching his own spoon. "Whoopsie," he said and smiled at the soldier escorting them.

His lunch mate winked at him. “What’s yer name, airman?” he asked under his breath.

“Strongman, Bearnárd Strongman.”

“Charlie Namemaker, pleased to make your acquaintance.”

“One more question, Charlie. How long did you sail from Boma?”

“About a day and a half. Now shut up we’re being watched.”

Despite the arid heat of the day giving way to the chilly air of the night, Bearnárd was not able to sleep that night. Although his body was exhausted, his mind was racing. He was trying to visualise some of Bunty’s maps. He liked looking over her maps and comparing them to what he could see from the bridge or the deck. As far as he could remember, there were two rivers in Lubumbashi: The White Gelada, and The Brown Gelada. The White Gelada was mostly unnavigable, but The Brown Gelada wasn’t, and it did indeed go through Boma. He estimated that paddle steamers and airships travelled at similar speeds, except, of course, that airships could travel more-or-less in a straight line. If Charlie Namemaker had sailed a day and a half from Boma, and he had sailed about two days from Lubumbashi, then he must have been transferred ashore somewhere near Isalo.

Bearnárd Strongman was quite pleased with himself – both for working out where he was and for stealing the spoon. He wasn't sure what he had achieved, but it was a start, and Gonagain was a great believer in starts. Then he thought of his half-brother. He always treated Bearnárd as if he was dumb but, in truth, if he was paying attention, he was usually only a few millidays behind his captain when it came to working things out. Still, he hoped Oisín was trying to track him down. He only wished he could pinpoint his *exact* location and get a message to him.

Suddenly there was a loud bell ringing, and Staff Sergeant Landowner came marching in, shouting, "Stand by your beds!" It was daylight outside, but the circular windows were filled with varilight glass, which was currently in blackout mode. Gas lights were being lit to illuminate proceedings. Convicts and captives got out of their bunks and stood to attention. Bearnárd followed their lead.

Landowner was showing a senior officer, a general, and a man in a white coat, around the dormitory. They were flanked by a dozen privates. It was White Coat who seemed to be in charge. The uniformed men stopped at the first captive in his blue boiler suit, but White Coat just waved them on. It seemed that he was only interested in the convicts. Eventually they reached the poor unfortunate who had been dunked in stew earlier that day. There was a brief conversation and he was hauled away by two soldiers. They continued onwards, past Charlie Namemaker, who breathed a sigh of relief, and picked out four more men. They left the building, the privates putting out the gas lights as they went. For a moment, the men stood by their beds in the total darkness, before realising that they weren't coming back. There was general mumbling in curious tones as they went back to bed. If Bearnárd had been having trouble sleeping before, he would have no chance now.

CHAPTER 6
Lubumbashi to Stanleyville

(Mediusday)

Bunty was at the helm as *The Reliant* cruised steadily on its course to Stanleyville. There had been little to do, other than watch the scenery pass by through the hexagon-panelled dome of the bridge's panoramic screen. The lush forests of Lubumbashi were far behind them and the green savannah had given way to dusty plains. Patches of shale and siltstone, typical of the Stanleyville region, were already beginning to appear. Soon it would be a flat, barren, grey landscape, with only patches of scrub, interrupted by vast slate quarries.

Gonagain was in his cabin and Etoile was, as usual, sitting watching him. At first Gonagain thought that it was quite cute, the way the dog focused so intently on him, but now it was beginning to unnerve him slightly.

He opened his Trad cabinet to wind his time pieces. He decided that he might as well clean and load his Peacemaker revolver too – he'd be in Trad airspace soon. He took some oil, applied it to the cylinder and gave it a spin. With a small brush he cleaned the barrel, squinting through it towards the dog afterwards – to make sure it was clean and true. Then he took six bullets from a box and, one by one, loaded each chamber, spinning it once again to be sure. He cocked the hammer and pointed it towards the dog. "Bang!" he said, just for his own entertainment. Etoile instantly dropped to the floor and rolled on her back with her legs in the air. So convincing was her performance, that Gonagain was momentarily concerned that she'd had a heart attack. Then he saw a gamey eye looking at him from under a hairy eyebrow. Gonagain burst out laughing and, at the sound of his laugh, Etoile jumped to her feet, spun three times, and launched herself at him, licking his face all over. The more Gonagain laughed, the more Etoile licked his face. The more Etoile licked his face, the more Gonagain laughed.

Etoile had not yet endeared herself to the rest of the crew. Rajaobelina was a little upset that, after all the effort nursing her back to health, she didn't seem to like her quite as much as she liked Gonagain. Bunty was also put out that Etoile, Gonagain and Jao seemed to be forming a little clique that she was not part of. Aoife was most concerned – the dog bristled and growled whenever they were in the same room. Apart from the fact that the dog didn't like her, she was worried that the rest of the crew would pick up on her distrust.

Aoife was in her cabin, the medical bay, when Gonagain called for a crew meeting on the bridge over the voice-repeater. She went to the medicine cabinet and cleared some of the bottles to the side so that she could reach a medium-sized, brown, glass bottle at the back. It had had the residue of a dark red liquid in it when she found it, but she had cleaned it out with a bit of old sacking she had found in the hold and deposited the key of the trunk in it. She tipped the bottle into her hand and the key popped out. She tucked it into her underwear and replaced the bottles. She should really keep the key in her underwear the whole time, but it was heavy and the cuts on the key chafed her skin. The bottle looked like it had not been used for some time and there had not been enough of the liquid to fill a teaspoon. She checked her reflection in the cracked mirror and left her cabin. The door had a cabin hook on the inside, for privacy, but there was no locking mechanism on the outside. She plucked a hair from her head and snagged one end of it on a brass rivet on the door and the other end on a similar rivet on the door frame – at least she would know if anyone had been snooping in her cabin – and headed to the bridge.

Rajaobelina had been pottering restlessly in the engine room when the meeting was called. She had dropped everything and ran towards the sleeping quarters. Hiding in a store cupboard opposite the medical bay, she had watched Trustworthy leaving her cabin, and emerged as soon as she was gone. She saw that she had done something to the door, but from the angle she had been watching, she was unable to tell what. A quick scan of the door frame was all it took to discover the hair. As far as Jao was concerned, this was proof that she was hiding something.

She tried to unsnag the hair, but it snapped. She swore to herself in Gassy. She entered the cabin and began to search it methodically, without really knowing what she was looking for. She found a pair of tweezers, went back outside, and removed the broken ends of the hair. In the bin she found a bit of old sacking. There was nothing made from sacking in Trustworthy's kit bag that she could remember. It was damp with dark red liquid and smelt tart – like vinegar. Vin Mariani! She went through the cabinet until she found the right bottle – she knew it was empty, but she hadn't cleaned the bottle and nor would anyone else. This was definitely suspicious. She left the cabin and plucked a hair from her own head to replace the one she had broken. Her hair was blacker than Trustworthy's and not as fine, but she reckoned she could get away with it.

Rajaobelina was last to arrive on the bridge. "Sorry," she said, "I had to make myself decent."

Aoife looked at Rajaobelina and, appraising her tangled black hair and greasy overalls, raised an eyebrow. Etoile looked at Aoife and bared her teeth with a barely audible growl.

"We'll be in Stanleyville very shortly, so all pulsarnite-powered equipment should be hidden away – mechanical watches and gunpowder weapons only. Remember to use Trad units when you're speaking – no kilometres, kilos, or litres and – definitely – no decidays. We'll be needing our varilight goggles too. Aoife, presumably you'll be leaving us as soon as we arrive?"

Rajaobelina mumbled something in Gassy. No one knew what it meant, but they all assumed it wasn't, "Lovely to have met you!"

"Not immediately, if that's okay with you. I may need some time to find some contacts."

"We won't be delaying our departure on your account, Aoife; if you or your belongings are still on board when we're ready to leave, we'll leave regardless."

"Understood."

"Jao, I'd like you to come with me and see if we can find out if any airships have come in for repair, or if anyone has seen more Trad military around than usual. Bunty, you'll be on dock lookout duty."

"Captain, I have some maintenance to do in the engine room" Jao lied "perhaps I could do dock lookout duty and Bunty could go with you?"

"Okay, Jao, if it's really necessary."

Rajaobelina escorted Trustworthy back to her cabin. "So, who are these contacts you need to find in Stanleyville then?"

"I don't actually know anyone in Stanleyville, but there must be some fellow photographers or journalists who could help me." It was almost the truth – she had never been to Stanleyville.

"Well, be sure to let me know if you need any help. Packing for example," Rajaobelina added pointedly.

There was an awkward pause. They were stopped outside the medical bay, each waiting for the other to move. Eventually Aoife couldn't help herself, she glanced at the door, looking to see if the hair was still in place – it was still there, but she was not quite sure everything was exactly right. It was what Jao was waiting for, and she immediately opened the door for her crewmate. "Well, you must have lots to do," she said.

"Yes." Aoife went into the cabin and shut the door.

Rajaobelina's hair had not snapped, it had just dislodged from one of the rivets. She grabbed it between her thumb and forefinger and pulled it free, taking it with her to her own cabin.

Rajaobelina was not sure why she was so bothered by Aoife Trustworthy – in theory, she would be out of her life by the time they left Stanleyville. But she didn't like the way the captain looked at her, for a start. She knew nothing would ever happen between herself and the captain, but she didn't want him falling for someone like *her*. She also felt that at least *some* of the recent strange goings-on were connected to her in some way and, if she was right, she didn't want her getting away with it. Mostly, though, there was just an irrational dislike and distrust of the woman.

CHAPTER 7
Stanleyville

Later that same day *The Reliant* arrived in Stanleyville. The contrast to the verdant region of Lubumbashi was stark. As they flew over the town towards the airdock, the central square, with its giant clock, dominated the view. The clock was not housed in a tower, as you might expect, but in a huge, cubic, metal frame. The top of the cube had an arched, glass roof to protect the clock from the elements, but the clockwork mechanism was visible from virtually every angle. The dull clanging as the teeth of the escapement wheel hit the mechanism was audible even from this height. The enormous balance wheel whirred as it oscillated back and forth at a tremendous speed, disturbing the air around it. The face of the clock was about three times the size of *The Reliant* – including its envelope. The numerals, one to twelve, were in a gothic font and were about twice the size of a person. The huge steel hands showed the time at eight twenty-five. On the other side of the grey slab square was a similar construction, housing a calendar. The mechanism was similar, but instead of hands that moved it was the face – four metal discs, engraved with numbers, months, and days – that rotated. At the top was a black rectangle of steel, within which the outer disk showed '0', the next '7', the third 'January', and the inner disc showed 'Wednesday'. The year was not indicated. Gonagain noticed that the design of the calendar allowed it to go up to thirty-nine days per month – ample for years to come. The whole square was designed to say – "This is a Traditionalist area; Geokinetics are not welcome."

The people going about their business were as grey as the place they inhabited. Clothing was mostly in muted hues, and even the odd splash of colour had been dulled by the smog created by the surrounding industry. Many of the passers-by wore scarves to protect them from the damp, foggy air. It was daylight and most people had their varilights hanging loosely around their necks – they would be needing them again soon as noon had already passed, and sunset would be around midday – but a few were still wearing them, purely out of habit.

The airdock itself was a series of circular docks, each with twelve docking points around the perimeter. In the centre of each was a dock office. Each dock office had a five-sided clock on the roof, allowing them to be seen, not only from north, south, east, and west, but from directly above as well. Gonagain didn't remember ever seeing so many clocks simultaneously.

"Captain, I could use some help in the engine

room for a few millidays… sorry, *minutes*. I know you and Bunty are keen to get going, so perhaps our aircraftman could spare me some time before she goes looking for her contacts?"

Aoife narrowed her eyes and looked at Rajaobelina suspiciously.

"Okay, Jao, but don't keep her long; she wants to get going, and so will we."

"It won't take long, Captain. Aircraftman Trustworthy, follow me please."

Rajaobelina took Aoife down to the compressor and pointed her towards a valve. "I need you to hold this valve closed while I replace the return spring." She placed Aoife's hands in the required position and deftly began to remove a spring. Once it was out, she dug another spring from her overalls pocket and began to put it in position.

"This one's not going to work," Jao said, "I have another in the hold. *Do not* let go of that valve; if all the hydrum goes to the envelope, it will split – and hydrum is extremely volatile when it mixes with air. I'll only be a couple of minutes." With that, she ambled off.

It was dangerous leaving her like that – she had disabled the safety valve for authenticity, so if Trustworthy let go of the valve she would hear the hydrum pass through and see the gauge move. If she left the valve unattended, the envelope really could burst.

Aoife knew that she was being played, and that

Rajaobelina was trying to keep her here. She suspected that nothing would happen if she let go of the valve, but wasn't sure enough to do so. How long should she wait before she could be certain it was a trick? She didn't know if the engineer intended leaving her here indefinitely, or if she just wanted to keep her occupied for a few minutes. She momentarily loosened her grip on the valve, and it immediately began to turn under the pressure from the compressor. There was also a faint acrid smell. The valve *was* active, and it *was* hydrum. Aoife knew very little about the workings of a dirigible, but she knew about the volatility of hydrum and air.

As soon as she was out of view, Rajaobelina switched from an amble to a trot. She headed straight to the medical bay. She deftly removed the new hair that was snagged from door to frame and went straight to the Vin Mariani jar. It rattled as she lifted it. She opened it and tipped it into her hand. A key! It looked remarkably like the key to her own tiny clothes trunk. Still moving at speed, she went to her own cabin, unlocked her trunk, and removed its key. She swapped the two keys and ran back to the medical bay putting her own key in the Vin Mariani bottle. She re-snagged the hair on the door and, moving as quickly as possible, headed back to the engine room. As she reached the engine room, she slowed back to an amble. "This will do it!" she said casually, producing the exact same spring she had just removed.

Aoife was surprised to see Rajaobelina back so quickly with another spring – she had thought that she was going to be left here for ages. As she began to replace the spring, Aoife studied the engineer. She had not been this close to her before and was surprised to see that her skin really was as flawless as it seemed. Her eyes were absolutely stunning – the pale blue of her irises and the bright whites of her eyes were such a contrast to her chocolate-brown skin. Her nose, much like her own, was neither hooked nor ski-tipped, but completely straight. Her lips, if anything, were slightly fuller. Despite the grubby overalls, greasy hands, and the untidy hair, she smelled good – not perfumed, but clean and fresh, like a baby. *My goodness, she's beautiful,* thought Aoife.

"Okay, all done. You can go and do whatever it is you were going to do. Thanks for your help," said Jao chirpily.

"No problem," replied Aoife warily.

Aoife headed straight to her cabin. The hair was still stretched from door to frame. She removed and discarded it. Once inside, she scanned the cabin to see if anything had moved. She hadn't been sure, earlier in the day, whether everything was as she had left it, so she had started memorising the location of objects before she left the cabin. It was all the same. She took the key from the Vin Mariani bottle and put it in her underwear. Perhaps she was being overly suspicious of the engineer and she had indeed only needed a second pair of hands.

Rajaobelina was on dock lookout, sitting in a folding chair at the open loading bay, when Aoife set off for Stanleyville town centre. “Do you need anything in town, Jao?” she asked.

Rajaobelina was surprised at the question and at the tone of Aoife’s voice. It was the first time she had sounded genuine, and she felt a tiny bit ashamed of her deceit. “No, thanks. I’ll be going into town myself, as soon as I’m relieved from duty.”

As soon as Aoife was out of sight, Rajaobelina took the key out of her overalls pocket and went to the hold. The key slotted straight into the lock of the trunk, just as she had suspected. It took a bit of jiggling before it turned. Rajaobelina realised she was subconsciously holding her breath and let out a puff of air. “Let’s see what we have on board then, Miss Trustworthy,” she said to herself. She lifted the lid, to reveal the largest piece of pulsarnite she had ever seen. In fact, it was possibly the biggest piece of pulsarnite *anyone* had ever seen. It was slightly larger, and much heavier, than Etoile. This thing was worth a fortune.

******

Bunty, Gonagain and Etoile checked into the dock office at the hub of their dockyard. There was a junior clerk with docking forms, and he had a docking record for just this one dockyard, for today only. He was a thin young man with a beaky nose, thick glasses, and crooked teeth. As Gonagain filled in the forms, Bunty draped herself over his desk. She had undone the top buttons of her blouse, revealing a very impressive cleavage.

"You must be an awfully clever young man, to have a such a responsible job as this," she said.

"Not really, ma'am" he replied, "it's just filling in paperwork, really." He was desperately trying to stay focused on Bunty's face.

"Please, call me Bunty. So, what happens to this very important paperwork once you've done your duty then, airman?"

"Well, it goes over to the main office at the dock entrance, ma'am... I mean, Bunty."

"And what happens to it there?"

"It just goes into the records file, so we know who's been in and out, ma'am."

"And you must have some fascinating stories of who's been in and out – the rich and famous, pirates, the military..."

"Not really, ma'am... I mean, Bunty, it's mostly just airtraders."

"Not even a few military men?" Bunty began to sit up straight and pretended to lose interest.

"Well, we did have a couple of military dirigibles come in earlier in the week, on dockyard two."

Bunty leant back down again "*Fascinating!* Tell me more," she said in her deepest, huskiest voice.

"Well, I don't know much more, Bunty. Two came in. One of them was shot up pretty bad, but it was a hard-shell and it held okay."

"*Really!* So, what happened to these military dirigibles then?"

"Well, I think the damaged one might still be in the hangar. They transferred a load of stuff to the other one and left."

"Gosh. So where is this hangar then? I'm fascinated with military aircraft. I'd love to see this ship."

"Well, it's just here, Bunty," said the clerk pointing to a site map, "but you won't be allowed in, I'm afraid."

"Oh! Okay. So, what sort of things did they transfer? Prisoners?"

"No, I don't think there were any prisoners – with all the soldiers and weapons from both ships they'd never have taken off with prisoners too. It was mainly crates and trunks."

"What's your name, airman?"

"Eugene. Eugene Waterboy."

"Well, I have to go with my captain now, Eugene, but I'd *love* to hear more of your stories when I get back."

"I'll try and think of some, ma'am… Bunty."

As Gonagain, Bunty and Etoile left the dock office, Gonagain was grinning and shaking his head. Bunty caught his eye. "Still got it! Not bad for an old bird, eh?"

"Oh, you have *definitely* still got it, Bunty," Gonagain laughed, "and what's more, you know how to use it!"

******

If Stanleyville had any military presence at all, it would have an office in, or near, the town hall. That was where Aoife decided to go first. Sure enough, she found a tiny recruitment office, with just one junior officer.

"Good morning, Miss, how can I help you."

Trustworthy pointedly eyed his stripe. "Is there anyone more senior I can speak to?"

"Well, you can speak to me first, and if I think..."

"Trust me, Lieutenant, this is above your pay grade."

"Perhaps you should let me decide, Miss...?"

"Trustworthy. *Commander* Trustworthy."

The lieutenant jumped to his feet and saluted. "Apologies, Commander. I'm the only military personnel in Stanleyville at present; my captain is away on military business. This is just a recruitment office, really."

Aoife sighed with exasperation. "I need to get a message to Victoria."

"We can send a telegraph."

"That will do. Presumably you also have some pigeons?"

"Yes, Commander."

"Then get me one from Victoria."

"Yes, Commander," he left the room.

While he was out of the office, Aoife retrieved a wicker tube from her bag – it was the one that Bunty had mistaken for a bottle carrier. She then began to roll up her left sleeve.

The lieutenant returned with another wicker

tube, containing a pigeon and a sheet of paper. "Sorry, Commander, but I've just checked our records, and the only Commander Trustworthy is listed as missing in action."

"Commander Trustworthy; 001529; missing in action, December 33, 1909; Lubumbashi."

"Yes, that's right," the lieutenant said, checking the paper.

Aoife showed him the small tattoo on the inside of her upper arm, which simply read '001529'. "Well, I'm no longer missing."

"Excellent news, Commander," he said, as he exchanged the empty tube for the one containing the pigeon. Aoife put the pigeon in her bag.

"What do you want the telegram to say?"

She dictated as he wrote neatly in his notebook. "001529. Jan 7. Stanleyville. Have prize. Have company. *The Reliant*. Hydrum."

"I'll send it right away, Commander."

******

Stanleyville Airdock was huge. So much so, that bicycles were used to get around it. Gonagain and Goodtime borrowed a pair of 'ordinary' high-wheeled bicycles – the new 'safety' bicycles with equal sized wheels had apparently not yet caught on in Stanleyville. As they pedalled towards the hangar, Etoile cantered alongside, occasionally jumping up at Gonagain's ankles for fun.

When they reached their destination, they

parked the cycles in a bay alongside some others. The huge doors of the hangar were closed and the human-sized door within them was locked. Bunty gestured to a damaged air vent, high up in the brick wall – the metal grille was bent and hanging off, probably from storm damage.

"How are we going to get up there?" asked Gonagain.

Bunty was looking at one of the brick buttresses and making strange pawing movements in the air with her hands. She paused to look around her, and her eyes alighted on the bicycle she had just been using. She propped it against the buttress and began the pawing movements again.

"Righty-oh. Let's go!" she said to herself.

Using the high-wheeler bicycle as a climbing frame, Bunty made it about halfway up to the damaged vent. At that height, the pointing on the corner of the brick buttress was weather-damaged, providing footholds and handholds. Bunty continued up the corner of the buttress, until she was slightly higher than the vent. She then made the difficult traverse. The footholds were shallower away from the corner and Bunty's soft leather boots slipped a couple of times. Gonagain held his breath below and prepared himself to try to catch her if she fell. Eventually, using the bent vent cover as support, Bunty slid into the opening, feet first.

For a few long moments there was silence, then the sound of Bunty kicking the inner vent cover open. Her head popped out again.

“Don’t tell me,” said Gonagain, “you used to go out with a mountaineer when you were younger.”

“No, but I was once a lookout for a gentleman thief. Just one problem. I didn’t think this all the way through – I can’t get back down on either side.”

“Wait there,” said Gonagain, as if she had a choice. He disappeared around the corner, re-appearing quickly with a mooring rope. It took a few attempts, but Gonagain eventually managed to throw it high enough for Bunty to catch it. She went into the hole with the rope, only to pop her head out again a moment later.

“Nothing to tie it to.” She threw one end back to Gonagain, “Can you tie it around your waist?”

Gonagain had barely finished tying the knot when he was jerked upward with violent force. He felt a couple of vertebrae move. He put both feet against the wall and braced himself as Bunty lowered herself down on the other side. A few moments later, he landed flat on his back with a slap. Bunty had let go of the other end of the rope. The rope piled up on his chest and the end, which had been dipped in wax to stop fraying, hit him in the face. As he lay there, trying to work out which bit of him hurt the most, he heard Bunty’s voice. She was standing beside him, having opened the door from the inside.

“What are you doing down there?” It was a genuine question, but she didn’t wait for an answer. “Come on, quickly, while the coast is clear.”

Inside the hangar was a medium to large dirigible. It was clearly once a beautiful craft – probably based on a Dreamcloud Executive, or something similar, but heavily customised. The envelope was a hard shell, made from some sort of lightweight metal, like mercuriumite. It had a mirror finish and polished brass fittings. The mirror finish was both aesthetic and functional – it would reflect the sky around it, making it difficult to spot. Riveted on the side were brass letters spelling out the name of the craft – *Grande Complication.* The envelope had taken a lot of damage from pulsarnite weapons and the massive dents in it gave it a fairground hall of mirrors effect. The gondola was a mixture of mercuriumite, brass and billabob. The underside was a mottled blue, white and grey – camouflaged from those viewing from below.

Gonagain and Goodtime advanced the time on their varilight goggles by a couple of hours, to enhance the light. It was gloomy in the hangar and it would be more so on the dirigible.

"Etoile, stay!" said Gonagain.

Inside the *Grande Complication*, the use of quality materials continued, but the overall effects were of efficiency and reliability, more than luxury. Although the furniture and fittings were all intact, it had the look of a place that had been recently raided. Empty drawers were left open and cabinet doors revealed no contents inside. It was also not the kind of ship that held prisoners; it was a flying HQ for some sort of operation.

At the centre of the operations room was a large

desk, with clips on its edges. The clips had obviously held down a large sheet of paper which had been torn away, leaving fragments still in the clips. Gonagain examined the fragments. It had clearly been a map, but most of the fragments revealed nothing he could recognise. One piece though, the top right, had some writing on it.

BASHI
NITIONS
TORY
AID

"Bunty, what do you think this says?"

"I don't know. Lubumbashi Munitions Factory Raid?"

"That's a thought," said Gonagain

"Except there's no munitions factory in Lubumbashi, Skip."

"But if there was, it would explain two things. Why the Trads attacked Lubumbashi, and how the Geo Guards got there so quickly."

It was then that Etoile started barking frantically.

******

As soon as she was sure the rest of the crew were well away from the airdock, Rajaobelina had gone to the chandlery to make a couple of purchases. She needed a trunk, similar in size to the one in the hold, and the sort of sandbag that some of the smaller dirigibles used as ballast.

"I need a trunk about this size," she had said, gesturing with her hands, "and a thirty-pound sandbag."

"Certainly, madam," the chandler had replied, "a popular combination today."

Rajaobelina didn't know what he meant by that, but she didn't give it much thought.

She put the new trunk in her cabin, locked, with the massive chunk of pulsarnite inside. The sandbag was locked in the trunk in the hold. Her final task was to swap the keys back. Swapping the keys back again would be easy enough, but she would need to distract Trustworthy again. She was contemplating how to do this when Aoife returned.

Aoife had been doing some thinking of her own. She had two options: one was to try to get the pulsarnite rock off *The Reliant* here in Stanleyville; the other was to use Gonagain and his crew to get both her and the pulsarnite to Victoria. She had decided there was no reason why she couldn't keep *both* options open. She would have double the chance of success. On her way back from the town hall, she had bought some 'farewell' presents. Over the time she had spent with the crew of *The Reliant*, she had genuinely developed some affection for them, but the real purpose of the gifts was to try and keep them occupied.

For Gonagain, she had bought a book, *How to*

Train and Domesticate Your Canine Companion. This would have the advantage of keeping both him *and* the damn dog busy.

Bunty Goodtime was easy; she had bought her a bottle of good quality gin.

It was the engineer that was the problem. Knowing how much she liked to fix things, she had initially scoured the markets looking for some mechanical gadget in need of repair. She needed something that would really pique her interest. The only problem was that her own mechanical knowledge was so limited that she didn't know what was too easy to fix and what was just a pile of junk. Eventually she came up with another idea. Having explored every inch of *The Reliant* whenever the opportunity arose, she was aware that Jao had no mirror, or cosmetics of any kind in her cabin. Perhaps she could convince her to fix *herself* up.

She arrived back at *The Reliant* to find Jao sitting on her folding chair in the doorway of the loading bay, drinking coffee.

"Did you find any contacts?" asked the engineer.

"Yes, he sent a message for me."

"So, have you come back to pack?"

"Not yet, no. I'll see what kind of reply I get."

"There's dozens of Trad airships here... aren't you going to hitch a ride on one of those?"

"It sounds like you're trying to get rid of me."

Rajaobelina shrugged her shoulders noncommittally.

"Well, I got you all a present anyway, just in case

we *do* part company in Stanleyville." She waved her bag in the air.

Rajaobelina eyed it suspiciously.

"I'm just going to put them in my cabin, then you can have yours if you like."

Aoife returned after a few moments and presented Jao with a wooden box.

"What is it?" asked Jao

"A vanity case!"

The box was made of beautiful walnut. Jao lifted the lid. The inside was lined with silk, and contained ornate crystal bottles and silver containers. There was a matching hand mirror and hairbrush decorated with mother of pearl, and a little set of tweezers, scissors, and a nail file. The inside of the lid was also a mirror. Jao had never owned anything so beautiful. It had never even occurred to her to own such a thing. She was quite touched.

"Thank you, Aoife! I don't really know what to do with it all."

"There's a little pamphlet that tells you what everything is and gives you beauty tips. You are very beautiful, you know. You should make more of your looks."

Aoife took the brush, untied Jao's hair, and started to brush it. There were a few tangles, but they were dealt with after a few brushes. Aoife continued to brush and Jao's hair began to fall into rich, glossy tresses. Aoife could not believe what good condition her hair was in, as she had never seen it given any care at all. It was a little coarser than her own, but it was so thick and shiny.

Jao was also surprised at how good it looked. She had never been taught any grooming. Growing up in Antsirabe, such things were considered frivolous. In a way, she was enjoying the attention, but it did feel a bit intimate, and that made her uncomfortable – perhaps *because* she was enjoying it. "I might just take this to my cabin to work out what's what, if that's alright with you?"

"Of course it is!" replied Aoife.

As soon as Rajaobelina was out of sight, Trustworthy made a dash for the chandlery. "I've come to pick up the trunk and sandbag you put aside for me earlier."

She put the sandbag in the trunk and staggered with it back to *The Reliant*. Back in the hold, she fished the key out of her underwear and slipped it into the lock of the pulsarnite trunk – it wouldn't turn. She took the key out, re-inserted it and tried again. *Dammit* she thought *the lock must be stuck*. She hid the new trunk under some sacking, and was about to try one more time when she heard Etoile barking in the distance, followed by the sound of gunfire.

Within seconds, Rajaobelina was running through the hold. "Gonagain's in trouble. Come on!"

Aoife patted her ribs to check that her little snub-nosed revolver was in its holster under her jacket, and followed without hesitation. It was only when she had been running for a few moments that she started to question what she was doing. *The Re-*

liant was now unattended and unlocked – she could just go back, take the trunk and the cart and head to Stanleyville town hall. Yet here she was, running to the rescue of a Pulser she had only met a few days ago. She hadn't managed to check inside the trunk though. What if the pulsarnite was no longer in it? But of course, it was... she had the only key. What if it wasn't even the same trunk? Maybe that's why she couldn't open it. It had to be the same trunk – what were the chances of there being an identical trunk on board? Why was she trying to justify her actions with all these unlikely scenarios? The reality was that she just didn't want to see Gonagain, or Goodtime, getting hurt. There was no reason why she couldn't help them and still get the trunk off *The Reliant*. She kept running.

CHAPTER 8
Stanleyville

Lieutenant Penman hadn't liked the way Commander Trustworthy had treated him. After he had sent the telegraph, he had studied his notebook.

001529. Jan 7. Stanleyville. Have prize. Have company. The Reliant. Hydrum.

The first three parts were obvious. He studied the rest of the message. 'Have prize' was probably the target of some operation secured. 'Have company' must be non-military personnel, perhaps non-traditionalist. '*The Reliant*' meant nothing, but the mention of hydrum must mean it's an airship. He decided to round up some reservists and head down to the airdock.

He sent a runner to all the volunteers who would form the section, and within half-an-hour he had a dozen men at his disposal. They headed down to the airdock. If he could rescue a 'prize' from a Pulser airship, he would surely get a promotion.

Infuriatingly, the airdock was divided into multiple dockyards, and the main office would not know who was docked where until the paperwork came through from the various dock offices. Lieutenant Penman could have split up his section and searched all the docks simultaneously, but he didn't trust them to do it right. He also didn't trust them not to try and take the glory themselves. So instead, they marched around as a unit, from dockyard to dockyard, looking for *The Reliant*. Eventually he spotted a tatty, yellow-enveloped, three-propellered dirigible in dock four. *The Relia* was emblazoned on the envelope – it looked like the *nt* had been blocked out by one of many patches – but it was a softshell and therefore had to be a heliagen dirigible. There was a young, southern-looking woman in greasy overalls sitting outside on a folding chair, drinking coffee.

He led his team to the dock office and told them to wait outside. Inside, he found a young man, who introduced himself as Eugene Waterboy.

"Tell me about that yellow ship outside," demanded the lieutenant.

The young clerk searched through his papers – he seemed a little flustered.

"Ah. Here it is!"

Vessel: The Reliant.

Buoyancy agent: Heliagen.

Business: Airtrade and haulage.

Senior Officer: Captain Oisín Gonagain.

Crew: Five.

Passengers: Zero.

Cargo: None.

"Is that it?" asked Penman, incredulously.

"Yes, that's all that's required," he replied nervously.

"Did they say anything suspicious?"

"No, they... actually the woman, Bunty, was very interested in what kind of vessels came in and out. She had a particular interest in military craft."

"You told her nothing, presumably?"

"Erm, I may just have mentioned the *Grande Complication*... just in passing... and not by name."

"You blithering idiot!" Lieutenant Penman was turning a kind of puce colour. "Was this Bunty a young, southern woman in overalls?"

"No, she was mature... but very attractive," he added as if this explained his mistake in some way.

"Take us to the *Grande Complication,* NOW!"

At the hangar, Lieutenant Penman had hoped to have the element of surprise, as well as superior numbers on his side. Unfortunately, the moment he stepped inside, his presence was announced by a small dog who barked incessantly and ran in zigzags, circles, and various non-geometric paths. The lieutenant took a few shots at it, but its erratic movements made it a difficult target.

Inside the *Grande Complication,* Gonagain and Goodtime had heard the commotion and were going from one porthole to another, trying to get an angle where they could see what was happening. Eventually Gonagain spotted a motley crew that were getting themselves organised.

"About a dozen men, including your boyfriend, Eugene, and a Trad officer," said Gonagain.

"The two-faced, four-eyed, bucktoothed... rantallion! What were they shooting at? Etoile?"

"Yes."

"That's beastly! What's the plan?"

"First priority, we need to stop them boarding the ship. I'll go back and shut the hatch; you keep them occupied from one of the portholes. Have you got much ammo?"

"Yes, lots." She patted her satchel.

"Good. Take it handy now!"

"I will. You be careful too."

Bunty peered out of the porthole. The posse of men were dividing themselves into groups and were about to disperse. Bunty took her opportunity and fired a quick volley of five shots into the posse. One man dropped to the ground like a sack of potatoes and didn't get up. Two more fell, but dragged themselves behind a handcart. The rest ran in every direction, bumping into each other as they went, and fighting over hiding spaces when they found them.

Bunty reloaded her revolver. She had decided to reload every five shots, even though she had six chambers. It was a trick she learnt from an old boyfriend – a Coca thug. *Someone* would be counting shots between reloads and assume she only had a five-chamber cylinder. If she got caught, she would still have a bullet they wouldn't know about. She moved to a porthole about seven or eight down from the one she had fired from as she reloaded. She would have a different angle from there and they would struggle to work out where she was if she kept moving.

Gonagain burst into the loading bay, just in time to see three men stalking through the hatch. They were walking with a kind of crouching stoop, as if it would make them a smaller target, but they were more prepared for Gonagain's sudden appearance than he was for theirs. A single shot rang out and Gonagain dived for cover.

"Feck!" He cursed to himself. He was, he realised, sitting behind a rack of hydrum cylinders. He hoped they were armoured cylinders – or empty. On the wall opposite was a clock with a polished brass case. It offered him a very distorted reflection but, when the amateur soldiers moved, he could just about make them out. They were approaching slowly, one up the near wall, one up the far wall, and one up the middle. He moved his hand in order to find his own reflection and work out his position relative to the three volunteers.

"You might as well surrender now, chum – you're completely surrounded."

The gruff voice sounded about ten metres away. So now Gonagain had an idea of direction *and* distance. He took a deep breath and rolled out into the open and on to his belly. Fanning the hammer with his left hand, he emptied all six chambers, spraying bullets from left to right and back again, and rolled back behind the cylinders. He deftly reloaded and looked up to the clock again. This time there was no movement in the reflection. There was also no sound. Could he really have hit all three of them? He briefly popped his head above the cylinder rack. All three were on the floor. He peeked above the rack again, this time more slowly. None of them were moving. Cautiously, he stepped out and walked to the prone figures. He gave each one a hard kick. Stone dead – all three of them.

"Fair play to you, Oisín, old son, fair play," he congratulated himself. He scanned the hanger for Etoile, but she was nowhere to be seen. He cranked up the loading bay hatch manually and bolted it.

Back in the operations room, Gonagain found Bunty firing a couple of shots from a porthole. She dashed to the other side of the room, which spanned the full width of the gondola, and fired another three shots from the other side. She was barely even looking where she was firing.

"Skipper! Good to see you," she said with casual bravado, "What's the score?"

"Three-nil to me. What about you? Have you actually hit anyone?"

"I have actually, yes. One definitely dead, two definitely injured, and two more I've either hit or they've run out of bullets. They're not firing back any more, anyway. Have you got Etoile?"

"No."

"So now what?"

"Well, you've taken care of at least one... potentially five, and I've taken care of three. So, there *may* be only about four of them left. If we stay holed up here, they'll probably send for backup. Do you fancy making a dash for it? See if we can find Etoile on the way?"

"Sounds like a plan, Skip – not an especially good one, but a plan nonetheless."

They returned to the hatch that Gonagain had just closed. Stepping over the three bodies, Gonagain headed towards the crank that lowered and raised the hatch. With the engines running it could be opened from the bridge or from here, but with the ship dormant it could only be cranked by hand. He was about to begin lowering it when he paused.

"What's on your mind, Skipper?"

"If they see the hatch coming down, they're going to be right outside by the time it's fully open."

"So, we find a way to open it quicker or we find another exit." It was as much a statement to herself as it was to her skipper.

They scanned the loading bay for inspiration. Gonagain's eyes alighted on an axe, mounted beside the fire alarm. He took it in his hands and felt it for heft. Then he eyed the steel cable that ran from the crank to the hatch.

"You won't cut through that in one go, Skip! Wait there." Bunty positioned herself at the nearest porthole. "Okay, Skip, on the count of three. One... two... three!"

Gonagain swung the axe and Goodtime simultaneously fired a shot from the porthole, masking the clang of metal against metal.

"Again!"

"One... two... three!"

Again, Goodtime fired and Gonagain hit the cable with the axe.

"One more will do it."

Bunty reloaded the empty chambers of her revolver and joined Gonagain at the hatch.

"Once we're out, you cover port and I'll take starboard."

"Righty-oh, Skipper, and don't run straight – zigzag."

Gonagain swung the axe one more time, cutting through the last few strands of the cable. The hatch dropped like a stone, hitting the hangar floor with a mighty crash. They ran down the gangplank and did a U-turn at the bottom, Goodtime going right and Gonagain left. Zigzagging as they went, they ran at a fast-faster-slower velocity, as they tried to make themselves difficult to aim at. They fired random shots, Goodtime to the left and Gonagain to the right, in the direction of anything that could be used to hide behind. Bullets fizzed passed them from the return fire. It was lucky the posse hadn't thought to adjust the time on *their* varilights and were operating in a relative gloom.

They were just at the hangar door, when a huge, burly man in docker's overalls and a flat cap stepped out in front of them – a shotgun in his hand. Gonagain fired, but he was out of ammunition and his revolver just made a click that seemed to echo in the hangar, as if to announce the fact to all concerned.

"Gotcha!" said the docker in a gruff voice. Then his eyes widened as he felt the barrel of a gun on the back of his head.

"I don't think so," panted Rajaobelina, as she pressed the barrel harder into his head.

"Do you not?" Said Lieutenant Penman, as he emerged from the shadows, his gun trained on Rajaobelina, "I'm afraid I must disagree."

"Put your weapon down, Lieutenant." This time it was Aoife's voice, as she stepped through the hangar door with her gun aimed at the officer.

Gonagain looked from one person to another; he was beginning to lose track of who was going to shoot who.

Two more armed men emerged from their hiding places, one was Eugene Waterboy and the other looked like a money lender, judging by his clothing. Bunty raised her pistol and pointed it at Waterboy, and he paused uncertainly. Gonagain, feeling somewhat left out, pointed his empty pistol at the money lender.

"Don't worry about those two," said the lieutenant, "he's fired his six shots and she's fired her five."

"Except," said Bunty, "if you look closely, this is a Modéle 1892, which is a six shooter."

There was a protracted silence, as everyone tried to work out the situation. Everybody was pointing their weapon at someone. Everybody had a weapon pointing at them. Everybody knew that

Gonagain's weapon wasn't loaded. One by one, as they worked it out, they started to look towards the money lender. He was the last to catch on, and then seemed somewhat hesitant to shoot the petite young lady who had stepped into the hangar, perhaps because he was now the centre of everyone's attention.

As if to offer encouragement, Lieutenant Penman spoke to Aiofe Trustworthy. "I'm surprised at you. You're a traitor, falling in with this crowd. When news gets back to Victoria, that a commander..."

Aoife shot him dead. At the same time, a white ball of fur and teeth emerged from nowhere and leaped at the money lender, biting at his throat and face. Shots were fired and people fell to the floor, or dived for cover. Gonagain dived behind a crate and reloaded in record time. Emerging from his safe place, he fired a couple of shots.

"Get the hell out of here!" he yelled, "Use the bicycles!"

It was then that he spotted Etoile. She was lying on her back beside the money lender, in a puddle of blood.

"Oh no! Etoile?"

Etoile looked up at him with a gamey eye.

"Etoile, stop acting the maggot and get out of here!"

The little dog jumped up and shot out of the hangar like a startled hare, leaving the money lender to bleed to death from the bullet wound in his stomach.

A shot rang out. It was one of the injured men, who had dragged himself from behind a crate. The shot clipped Gonagain on the arm, just above where he was hit in Doxies Parade. “Feck!” he cursed as he backed out of the hangar, firing back. Not only did it hurt, but it was another jacket and shirt to be repaired.

Outside, he grabbed a high-wheeler and started pedalling after his crew. Jao was firing back over her left shoulder without looking. Gonagain had to veer to her right, where Aoife was running, to avoid being hit. He pulled alongside Aoife Trustworthy.

“Why didn’t you take a bicycle?” he yelled.

“My legs are too short to reach the pedals!” she turned and fired, very accurately, through the hangar doorway.

“Get on the mounting peg!”

Aoife threw her arms around Gonagain’s waist and put her foot on the peg used to mount the high-wheeler. The bicycle wobbled, dangerously close to crashing but, somehow, he kept it upright. He made much slower progress, cycling with two on board, and the others were beginning to disappear into the distance. Etoile was just a dot.

When Gonagain and Trustworthy reached *The Reliant*, the hatch was down, the mooring ropes were cut, and the envelope was full to bursting-point with hydrum. The other high-wheelers were abandoned outside, but Gonagain didn’t stop. He ducked his head as they cycled up the gangplank and through the hatch, stopping only when they crashed into the loading bay wall. There was a huge splash of water outside as the ballast was released, and *The Reliant* rose vertically, like it had been fired from a cannon.

In the hold, Gonagain and Trustworthy were disentangling themselves from both the bicycle and each other.

"Thanks for the lift," said Trustworthy.

"Well, I couldn't just leave you after you came to my rescue, could I," he replied.

"Whatever. It's appreciated."

Aoife stood on tiptoe and planted a kiss on Gonagain's lips. Gonagain's lips parted and their tongues met, entwining, tenderly at first, but then with more urgency.

Gonagain stopped suddenly and pushed her away. "No! Sorry... no. Not this. Not now."

CHAPTER 9

Isalo Mine

Things were changing at the pulsarnite mine. The man in the white coat, it turned out, was a scientist and one of the head honchos. His name was Dr Conceptuloco, and he was not impressed with the way things were being run.

The mine had originally had a pulsarnite-powered railway for hauling the pulsarnite out of the mine. It had been decommissioned when the Traditionalists defeated the Geokinetics in the region, along with all other pulsarnite-powered machinery. Dr Conceptuloco wanted the railway back in use – he planned to power it purely by gravity which, as they were taking pulsarnite *down* into the mine, seemed perfectly feasible. All pulsarnite repatriation operations were suspended until the tracks had been repaired.

Bearnárd had been put to work taking sections of damaged track out of the mine and moving sections of good track from the end of the line to replace them – the line would have to be a bit shorter until they procured some extra track. It was backbreaking work in hot and humid conditions, and keeping hydrated was difficult. Bearnárd had spotted an upside though – there were a lot more tools around and, although they were rigorously checked in and out each day, he occasionally found himself alone with them, and had begun to fashion a weapon from the spoon. He had hammered the scoop section into a crude cylindrical ring. The handle, he had bent back over the scoop and then bent outwards. All he needed to do was sharpen the end of the handle to a point and slip it over his finger to create a lethal knuckle-duster. He had already spotted a grinding wheel to do the sharpening.

He had also spotted that the man who was nearly drowned in stew was back. He had hoped to talk to him, if he could, to see if he could learn anything and, as luck would have it, he found him sitting with Charlie Namemaker in the canteen. Namemaker made the introductions.

"Koko, meet Bearnárd Strongman; Bearnárd, this is Koko Stewdiver."

Bearnárd offered a hand and they shook without any verbal greeting. Koko was a Madaka name, and his frizzy auburn hair and freckly skin was typically Madakan. But the Madaka, like the Gassy, did not use surnames. 'Stewdiver' was obviously a surname that Charlie Namemaker had just given him.

"What was the story with Conceptuloco last night?" asked Bearnárd, without any preamble or small talk.

"I dun't know. They took us; they give us eye

test, I dun't pass eye test; I wus sent back."

"What about the others?"

"Passing eye test."

"And then?"

"I dun't know. Still there, I suppose."

Bearnárd turned to Namemaker, "Any ideas?"

"He's a mad fella, that Conceptuloco. A genius – but mad as a box of frogs. He's probably gonna do some awful experiment on them."

"It wus like huspital, but none of us wus ill."

"I bet they are now," said Namemaker.

There was a momentary silence.

"I wunt my spoon now," Koko said, looking Bearnárd in the eye.

Bearnárd shot Namemaker a look, but he raised his palms and shook his head, "Not me!"

"Komondor, he tuld me you had it," said Koko

"Who's Komondor?"

"Swaruban man – white dreadlocks – he wus taken with me, he saw you take it."

"What did you want with a spoon anyway?"

"Make a weapon."

Bearnárd was silent for a moment. He didn't want to give up the spoon, especially since he was nearly finished fashioning it into a weapon. But Koko had paid dearly for trying to steal it. He had more right to it. He was looking directly into Bearnárd's eyes. He didn't blink or flicker. His expression was unreadable. Bearnárd reached inside his overalls and pulled out his home-made weapon. He slipped it over his finger and mimed a punching action. He slipped it off and palmed it across the table.

"You just need to sharpen the end."

"Whut wus you gunna use for?"

"Escape."

"You have a plan?"

"No."

"Count me in anyway."

Koko slipped the spoon into his overalls just as a guard approached.

"What are you lot talking about? You look very suspicious to me."

"We were just discussing the recipe for your delicious... slop," said Namemaker, "I imagine it's a well-kept culinary secret though."

And with that, the three men got up, handed in their bowls and spoons, and dispersed.

It was later in the night, when the sun was probably rising outside, that Charlie Namemaker spotted a man, sitting on his bunk, with long white dreadlocks.

"Komondor?"

The man turned his head and Namemaker flinched, jumping back a step. "Flippin' 'eck!" he exclaimed.

"Is it bad?" asked Komondor.

"It's... it ain't great."

Embedded in the man's forehead, raw skin stretched uncomfortably around it, was a clock face the size of an old eight pence piece. Where the man's eyes used to be, were two glass discs in brass frames, slightly larger than the clockface and heavily tinted. Again, there was raw skin stretched tightly around them. The glass was of the type used in varilight goggles and the tint was the same hue that the circular varilight windows were showing.

"Does it hurt?"

"Like nothing I've ever felt before. I tried to look in a mirror but it's too dark." The effect of double varilights – both windows and eyes – must have made it pitch black.

"Come with me," said Charlie. He guided him to the window and fished a single match out of his overalls. He struck it against the wall and held it near Komondor's face. His reflection was visible in the black window.

"What have they done to me? I'm a freak," he whispered.

The match burnt down to Charlie's fingers and he dropped it, plunging them into darkness again. He guided Komondor back to his bunk. "I'm sorry mate, really I am. What about the others?"

"I never saw Koko again."

"He's back safe and sound. The others?"

"They were lucky; they either died on the operating table or went blind. They'll never see what I've just seen."

"So, you're the only one?"

"No, my friend, I'm not the only one… just the first one. Now they've done it once, they're going to modify everyone."

CHAPTER 10
Stanleyville to Lubumbashi

(Annularisday)

With Rajaobelina at the helm and Bunty in her usual role as navigator, *The Reliant* had headed south-east out of Stanleyville at a rate of knots, back to Geokinetic territory. It was the one of the fastest getaways Oisín Gonagain had ever witnessed and he found himself marvelling at his crew. They had to be one of the tightest, slickest units in the air. He would need to buy new mooring ropes though, with the current ones having been cut instead of untied. Gonagain and Trustworthy had joined Bunty and Jao on the bridge.

"What's our bearing, navigator?" asked Gonagain

"East-south-east, Skipper."

"Back to Lubumbashi?"

"Yes, Skip."

"Good woman yerself!"

"Captain, my contact in Stanleyville said the larger airship had continued on to Victoria. That's north-east of Stanleyville," interjected Aoife.

"Is that right, *Commander* Trustworthy?" replied Gonagain.

"I'm sorry?" said Aoife

"Just before you started World War V down there, that lieutenant called you 'a commander'.

"I… I think you must have misheard."

"'I'm surprised at you. You're a traitor, falling in with this crowd. When news gets back to Victoria that a commander…' I think those were his exact words," chimed in Rajaobelina, who had an echoic memory.

"A commander's daughter – my father was a commander," lied Trustworthy without missing a beat.

There was a pause, as the rest of the crew digested this new piece of information.

It was Gonagain who broke the silence. "You seemed very keen that he didn't finish that sentence. Why was that?"

"I'm not proud of him, but he's still my father. I don't like him being used against me," Aoife's tone became more indignant as she grew into this new lie.

"Well, regardless, *our* intelligence is that there were no prisoners on that airship. We'll not find Bearnárd by chasing it down. We have a new lead and it's back in Lubumbashi."

Jao changed the subject. "Bunty, can you take over at the helm please, I need to look at the captain's injury." She gave Gonagain a stern look that said there was more than his injury on her mind.

In Aoife Trustworthy's cabin, which was also still the medical bay, Jao tended to Gonagain's arm. First, she gently took the dressing from the previous gunshot wound and examined the skin beneath. There wasn't a mark there. It was as if he had never been shot in Doxies Parade. She smiled to herself when Gonagain caught sight of it in the mirror and his jaw dropped. She cleaned his new wound, used her healing powers on it, and began to dress it.

"Captain, we need to talk about our aircraftman."

"This sounds ominous."

"She has secrets and can't be trusted."

"We *all* have secrets, Jao."

"I think she's dangerous."

"Well... I think you're probably right," conceded Gonagain, "I'm not convinced by her 'commander's daughter' story."

"I'm not convinced she's a Traditionalist," said Jao.

It wasn't the accusation that Gonagain was expecting.

"Where is this coming from, Jao?"

Jao finished dressing the wound before continuing. "I've been suspicious of her from the start," she explained, "so I've been doing a bit of snooping. She takes measures to ensure no-one comes into this cabin without her knowing. That made me think she was hiding something in here." Jao reached for the Vin Mariani bottle and shook it – it was empty. She then took a key from her overalls pocket. "I found *this* key hidden in *that* bottle. The key fits the trunk in the hold. I've had a look inside the trunk. What would a Trad be doing with a thirty-kilo piece of pulsarnite in a trunk?"

"Whoa there! There's a trunk containing a thirty-kilo lump of pulsarnite in the hold?"

"No."

Gonagain looked confused.

"There's a trunk containing a thirty-kilo ballast bag in the hold. The thirty-kilo lump of pulsarnite is in another trunk now, in my cabin. She has the key to my *little* trunk in her underwear, but she thinks it's this key."

Gonagain looked confused.

"So, let me get this straight," he said, "The trunk *we* brought aboard belongs to Trustworthy?"

"Yes."

"And it contained the biggest lump of pulsarnite I've ever heard of?"

"Yes."

"But now it has a bag of sand in it?"

"Yes."

"And you have the key, which you found in *this* cabin."

"Yes."

"But Trustworthy thinks *she* has the key in her underwear?"

"Yes."

"But it's really the key to *your* little trunk?"

"Yes."

"And the pulsarnite rock is now in *another* trunk in your cabin?

"Yes."

"And the key to that trunk is...?"

"In *my* underwear."

Gonagain paused thoughtfully.

"Show me," he said eventually.

Jao stuttered and blushed for a microday before regaining her composure. "Oh, you mean the pulsarnite."

In Jao's cabin, Gonagain stood eyeing the trunk with anticipation. He turned to Jao, and was slightly taken aback to see her undoing her overalls and rummaging in her underwear. The gentleman in him wanted to turn away, but his nature got the better of him and he found himself admiring the view. Jao's overalls were as dirty and greasy as ever, but she looked different. Her hair was not messily tied up – like it usually was – but hanging in silky tresses around her shoulders. Her white cotton underwear was figure hugging and, in contrast to her overalls, immaculately clean. Her chocolate-brown skin was still glowing from the exertion of the escape from Stanleyville. She smelt divine. As Jao fished out the key, Gonagain averted his gaze. He didn't want her to catch him ogling her. She passed him the key and Gonagain could feel the warmth of her body off it.

Gonagain cleared his throat, kneeled, and unlocked the trunk. He realised he was holding his breath, and let out a sigh. He lifted the lid and there it was – a boulder of pulsarnite. It was a pinky-grey colour and shiny, as though it had been varnished. There were smooth sections here and there, but mostly it was rough and grainy. Gently, with reverence, he put his hands on it and felt it pulsing.

Turning back to Jao, he said, "This is worth more than all the cargo we've ever had on *The Reliant* combined. We need a meeting – you, me and Bunty – as soon as Aoife is out of the way."

Squeezing past Jao, he left her cabin and headed back to the bridge. This was massive. Not just the piece of pulsarnite, but the ramifications of having it on board.

Sitting back in the captain's seat on the bridge, Gonagain's mind was racing. First there was the huge lump of pulsarnite. Then there was 'Commander' Trustworthy, the kiss, the possible munitions factory in Lubumbashi, and the whereabouts of his half-brother. Yet his mind kept going back to Jao's figure hugging underwear, the smell of her skin and the warmth of the key.

******

While Aoife was in the galley preparing supper, the rest of the crew were on the bridge. Bunty Goodtime was now fully up to speed with the trunks, the keys and the pulsarnite.

"Well, Skipper, I don't think we should challenge her over it. She's pretty adept at thinking on her feet, and we'll probably get another tall tale from her. It's better for now that we know something that she thinks we don't know."

"So, what do we do next?" asked Jao.

"String her along. If she makes a run for it, she'll be doing so with a trunk full of sand," replied Bunty

"What if she decides to deal with us the way she did with that lieutenant in Stanleyville?" said Gonagain.

"There's three of us and one of her, Skipper; we should be able to handle her."

Etoile barked.

"Okay, four of us!" Bunty rolled her eyes.

"I think we should all be armed ten-five," said Jao.

"Agreed," said Gonagain.

"I don't understand why she didn't take the trunk in Stanleyville and just hitch a ride to Victoria. She had the opportunity, but she helped us get out of there instead," added Jao.

"Our main problem, as I see it, Skip, is that we don't know which side she's on or who she's working for. She shot that lieutenant in cold blood, which would indicate she's not Trad. Yet she seems pretty keen to get to Victoria. I wouldn't like to get caught in a Trad city like Victoria with a thirty-kilo piece of pulsarnite."

"Maybe that's why she let *us* bring it on board. If we didn't know what was in that trunk, we'd lay claim to it. She could deny all knowledge," said Gonagain.

There was a moment of silence that Gonagain took as agreement.

CHAPTER 11
Lubumbashi

(Minimusday)

As *The Reliant* touched down in Lubumbashi Airdock, Gonagain could barely believe that it had only been two hands since New Year's Eve. He had always liked the lush, verdant region around Lubumbashi, but it would forever have melancholic connotations now.

Rajaobelina, Goodtime and Trustworthy each took a mooring rope and tied the airship down. This was managed with some difficulty, as the ropes were now very short. Gonagain manoeuvred the ballast pipe into a water tank and set the pump going.

"Where are we going to start looking for this munitions factory, Captain?" asked Rajaobelina "It's not in any part of Lubumbashi we know."

"The undertaker said one Trad airship took off

from the south-east and another from the north-west," replied Gonagain, "So we'll have to try both."

"Which way first, Skipper?"

"No idea. South-west?"

Trustworthy let out a sigh. "Listen," she said, "I haven't been totally up front with you all."

"Tell us something we don't know," mumbled Jao under her breath.

"The reason I was here in Lubumbashi was to photograph a munitions factory I had heard about," continued Trustworthy. "It was for a newspaper," she added, "I know exactly where it is. It's north-east. I'll take you. It won't get you any closer to finding your lieutenant though."

She took out her revolver, checked the chambers were full, spun the cylinder, and re-holstered it. She marched off in a north-easterly direction. The others stood open-mouthed for a few microdays, looking first at Trustworthy and then at each other.

Trustworthy turned, "Are you coming or what?"

The group marched deep into the Lubumbashi forest, Aoife Trustworthy leading, and Gonagain and Etoile at the rear, keeping a keen ear and eye on the path, such as it was, behind them. The thought crossed Gonagain's mind that Trustworthy might be leading them into a trap. Or that she could just abandon them here. He doubted he could find his own way back to *The Reliant*. He drew his pulsar-nite pistol and set it to a narrower beam before re-holstering it under his tweed jacket. The muggy air and the exertion of traipsing through the forest was making him feel decidedly clammy.

Trustworthy was holding a compass out in front of her, but she barely looked at it.

"How do you know this route so well?" asked Goodtime, who was second in the line.

"I worked here undercover," replied Trustworthy, "We all had individual routes into work, so we didn't make a well-trodden path that would lead unwanted visitors to the factory. This was my daily commute."

"How long did you work here?"

"Shhh. We're getting close now. It's guarded even on Minimusdays."

Minimusday, the last day of the hand, was not a working day but, as they reached a clearing in the forest, there were Geo Guards, just as Trustworthy had predicted. The guards were walking around a large rectangular, grassy knoll. It was about four hectares in size.

"Where's the factory?" asked Gonagain.

"Underground."

So that was why they had never seen it from the air.

"So how do we get in?" asked Goodtime.

"No idea. There are several entrances cut into the ground, but they're all guarded. I was searched *every time* I went in or out. It was impossible getting anything in or out without blowing my cover."

"So, you didn't get your photographs then?" asked Rajaobelina.

"Yes, but not whilst under cover. That's why this

is as close as I'm going. I'm wanted around here now."

"Is that right?" said Gonagain, "That gives me an idea."

"No! Absolutely no!" said Trustworthy, after Gonagain had outlined his plan.

"That's not a request, Aircraftman Trustworthy, it's an order."

"I'm just not doing it."

"Insubordination is grounds for dismissal. I'll leave your stuff on the air dock... *if* I'm feeling more generous by the time I get back to *The Reliant*," Gonagain began walking away, hoping he was going in the right direction. Etoile followed.

"You're bluffing," said Trustworthy

"You said yourself, we won't find Bearnárd by going to the munitions factory. We can look for him just as well, with or without you."

Bunty and Jao began to follow Gonagain.

"You'll never find your way back to the airdock."

"I won't," said Gonagain, "but Etoile will."

"All right, all right. Just don't leave me alone with any of the guards okay?"

They skirted around the clearing along the edge of the forest and emerged at the main entrance to the factory. It was a ramp, about fifty metres wide, that went down into the ground and ended at a huge metal shutter of the same width. They walked directly towards it, Trustworthy at the front, her wrists and thumbs tied together behind her back with her own bootlaces. Rajaobelina gave her a rough shove forward, partly for effect and partly for her own pleasure.

Two guards approached them, their pulsarnite rifles raised. "What do you want? This is military property – you're trespassing."

"Who's in charge of security around here?" Gonagain nudged Trustworthy with the muzzle of his pulsarnite pistol, "I believe there's a bounty on this one. We're here to pick it up."

"Go and get Captain Warehouse," said one guard to the other.

After a few millidays, the guard, a private, emerged with the captain. He was a short, stout man with grey moustache. "You shouldn't be here; this is not a tourist attraction you know."

"We believe there's a bounty on this one. We're here to pick it up," repeated Gonagain.

"Ah! Young '*Aiden*' Trustworthy. How lovely to see you again! You must think we're a bunch of fools. We knew all along you weren't a boy you know – but we were prepared to overlook your deception because of your skills and intelligence. It turns out that wasn't your only deception was it? You were working with the Trads all along."

Trustworthy decided her best bet was to stick to the story she had told the crew of *The Reliant*. "No, I wasn't. I'm an independent journalist who spotted an opportunity," she lied.

"You were spotted in here on New Year's Eve with the Trad soldiers."

“I was outside looking for a loophole in security when the Trads turned up. I just followed them in.”

“A likely story.” The captain turned to Gonagain, “I don’t know where you got your information, but there’s no bounty. Thank you for bringing her here though. These men will escort you from the premises.”

Gonagain, Goodtime and Rajaobelina, who up until now had their weapons trained on Trustworthy, transferred their attention to the three men in front of them.

“No bounty, no prisoner,” said Gonagain. “In fact, we might just take you all to your field marshall and tell them you were in cahoots.”

“Now look here…” began the captain, before spluttering to a halt.

“We could have taken her to headquarters, but we bought her straight to you so you can redeem yourself. Now, I’m sure there is some way you can offer us recompense for our efforts,” said Goodtime.

“Well… let’s discuss this in my office. Follow me.”

The captain and one of the guards escorted them to the captain’s office. The guard stationed himself outside the office as the rest went through.

“If you would leave your weapons with young Private Cooperson…”

Gonagain and Goodtime handed over their pulsarnite pistols, Rajaobelina, who preferred gunpowder weapons, gave up her revolver and Trustworthy’s snub-nose. The captain and private shared a wary look when they saw the gunpowder weapons.

"Those are hers," said Rajaobelina.

"Check them for hidden weapons, Private," barked the captain.

Private Cooperson made them stand with their arms up as he frisked each one in turn. He spent an extra-long time checking Rajaobelina, and his hands lingered longer than was entirely necessary as he felt her thighs, buttocks, and breast pockets. He was almost as thorough when he was frisking Goodtime.

"I say!" Bunty exclaimed. "Are you going to let your subordinate *grope* me like this, Captain? I had you down as a gentleman, not a cad and a scoundrel."

"That's enough, Private," shouted the captain. He turned to Bunty, "I'm sorry, madam, but you can't be too careful."

Whilst Bunty was creating the distraction, Rajaobelina dipped her hand into Trustworthy's trouser pocket and palmed a small pulsarnite stun gun into her own pocket.

The captain sat behind his heavy, wooden desk on a plush, leather, swivel chair. As there was not enough seating for everyone, Gonagain and his crew stood. Jao wandered around the room, studying the contents of the shelves.

"Now. There is no bounty for the return of this traitor, or spy, or whatever she is. However, I am grateful that you bought her back here. What kind of arrangement are you looking for?"

"How about some information?"

"What kind of information?"

"What you do here, what was taken in the raid, what use it is to anyone else, where you suspect it was taken to..." listed Gonagain.

"That's all classified information. Totally out of the question I'm afraid."

"I thought you might say that," said Rajaobelina, who was now behind the desk with the captain. She pulled the stun gun from her overalls and pressed it to his neck. He jerked briefly and then slumped unconscious in his chair. "Shall we go and have a snoop?"

"After you," said Gonagain, gesturing to the door. "Don't forget there's a guard on the door."

Jao waved her stun gun. "I'm sure he won't be a problem," she grinned.

After Goodtime had untied Trustworthy, Gonagain and his crew wound their way through corridors and staircases down to the lowest level – they must have been fifty metres below ground. Pushing open a heavy steel door they emerged on to the massive factory floor. None of them, except Trustworthy, were prepared for what they saw. Machines the size of houses with pulsarnite weapons to match; pulsarnite powered vehicles; handheld pulsarnite weapons; but most amazing of all, a small army of metal, human-shaped soldiers, all standing in rank and file.

"This," said Trustworthy, spreading her arms

out wide, "is what I wanted to stop." She gestured to the largest machine in the room. It looked like a municipal building on caterpillar tracks with a giant's pulsarnite rifle stuck on top. "This, on its own, could destroy a town the size of Victoria. But it won't work without a massive lump of pulsarnite."

Bunty and Gonagain shared a look. Jao, however, wasn't listening. She was standing by one of the automatons. "I would *love* to take that apart and see how it works," she whispered in awe.

"Well, why don't you take one and you can take it apart at your leisure," replied Gonagain.

"I don't think I'd ever work it out."

"Sure you would," said Gonagain, "You're the girl who can fix anything."

"All I know," said Aoife, "is that you'd need one of those crates over there."

"What's in it?" asked Jao.

"No idea. I just know you need whatever is in it, to make one of these things work." And with that, she disappeared around the corner, only to emerge a moment later at the wheel of a pulsarnite-powered cart. It had two seats, a cargo crate and the most massive rubber wheels that could be imagined. She pounded one of the wheels with her fist. "These are a great idea. They fill them with air – they don't weigh as much as solid rubber and make the ride less bumpy. Load what you want and let's get out of here.

At the main entrance, the lone guard was just starting to wonder when his partner was coming back, when the shutters were smashed open and a cart with big rubber wheels came hurtling through. On it was the motley crew of bounty hunters, their dog, their captive and a metal man. The captive was driving, and the older lady and the dog were in the passenger seat. The other two, and the metal man, were being bounced up and down in the cargo crate. The dog barked excitedly as they went past.

The guard raised his pulsarnite rifle but, before he could fire, he was slammed into the shutters by the wide-angled pulse from Buntys's pistol. By the time he had staggered to his feet, the cart had disappeared into the forest. He could just hear the sound of saplings snapping under the thick rubber wheels.

******

Back at *The Reliant*, Gonagain was feeling despondent, fearing that he would never find his brother again. He sat in the captain's seat and looked sorrowfully through the domed window at Lubumbashi airdock.

"We ought to get out of here lickety-split, Skipper – where to?"

"That," sighed Gonagain, "is the trillion-ariary question."

Aoife looked at Gonagain's face and she felt overwhelmed with sadness for him. "Don't give up, Captain. What other leads have you got?"

"None. The airships were a red herring. They

only led us to the munitions factory – and that led us nowhere."

"What else did you learn from searching Lubumbashi? What did you see yourself?"

"A couple of great big cannon balls that destroyed half of the town and a row of corpses at the undertakers."

"Where were the corpses found?"

"Beagán was found on Main Street, at the river-dock end."

"And where were the cannon balls fired from?"

"By the looks of it, from the east end of town."

"Isn't the river dock in the east end?"

Gonagain sat up. "Yes. You're right!"

"Skipper, we really need to leave. Now!"

"Okay, set a course to the east and stay low. I want a good look at that part of town."

Aoife sat on her chair and thought through her actions. Technically, she hadn't given any military secrets away – she had asked the right questions and Gonagain had worked it out for himself. Well, almost.

******

It was after supper, and the crew were drinking in the mess as they discussed the day. Having followed the Brown Gelada north for several miles, they had docked *The Reliant* on the west bank, so they could all get some rest. They had taken in some Gelada water as ballast and moored the ship to some billabob trees. Gonagain was satisfied that they were safe for the night.

The east end of Lubumbashi had been quite revealing. The cobbled stones on Main Street had been crushed in two parallel curving lines – the result of the massive weight of the steam cannon wheels. The track that they left led straight to the Brown Gelada river dock and ended there. The machine must have been boarded on to an enormous steamer and sailed off down the river. They had decided to follow the river north, towards Boma because of the preponderance of Trad towns in that direction – south west led towards Toliara – and that was mostly Geokinetic country.

Gonagain and Aoife seemed confident that they were heading in the right direction. Bunty and Jao were a little more circumspect but, without any evidence to the contrary and not wanting to burst the captain's bubble, they offered no arguments and merely suggested caution.

Bunty had imbibed a few gins (she had started a bit earlier in her cabin, with some of the quality stuff that Aoife had bought her) and was feeling a bit woozy. She had briefly considered sharpening herself up with a bit of her special snuff – but decided that an early night was probably a better option. She excused herself and headed off to her cabin, bouncing off both sides of the corridor as she went.

Jao, who wasn't a big drinker, had had her fill of Madeira some time ago and switched to coffee, but if she drank any more, she would be awake all night.

She was reluctant to leave Gonagain and Trustworthy alone together, especially as they seemed to be getting along rather well, but she wanted to get up early and investigate the automaton they had stolen from the munitions factory. Eventually she decided she couldn't chaperone them ten-five and went off to bed too.

Gonagain opened another bottle of wine, and he and Aiofe settled in for the evening. They pondered their options regarding Bearnárd and talked about parents and siblings and relationships. They discussed the munitions factory and their subsequent flight from it, and the Stanleyville escape. Then there was a moment of silence. Whether it was a comfortable silence or an awkward one, neither could quite decide. Eventually it was Aoife who broke it.

"That moment after we escaped the hangar in Stanleyville. It must have been the adrenaline needing to go somewhere. It was stupid of me. I'm sorry."

"No, *I'm* sorry," replied Gonagain.

"You have nothing to be sorry about."

"No, I mean I'm sorry – I regret my actions. I couldn't work you out – I still can't – but one thing I've realised today is that your intentions are good. Stopping the manufacture and use of those weapons is a commendable objective. You're a good person, whatever your methods. If I had known that then…" Gonagain trailed off.

Aoife stood up walked around the table to Gonagain. She sat astride his lap and put her arms around his neck. There was a momentary hesitation as they looked into each other's eyes, and then they kissed. It was a gentle kiss at first, but it became more eager, more urgent as it went on. It was a moment of passion and pleasure that would have been perfect if they weren't both trying to ignore the low rumbling growl that was emanating from the throat of Etoile. Gonagain pulled away and Aoife was half expecting him to reject her again.

"Etoile, shut the feck up! You're cramping my style." He scooped up the wine bottle and the glasses. "Shall we take this to my cabin?"

CHAPTER 12
Isalo Mine

"I hereby announce the inaugural meeting of the Pulsarnite Mine Escape Committee open," announced Charlie Namemaker grandly. "Present at the meeting – please raise your hand when I call your name: Charlie Namemaker;" he raised his hand to signal that he was Charlie Namemaker, "Bearnárd Strongman; Koko Stewdiver; Komondor... Clockhead; and Dympna Tinkerbelle."

Dympna Tinkerbelle had obviously once been a very beautiful woman. It was also obvious that that was quite some time ago, and that she had lived a tough life since. Her raven hair still had some of its lustre, but her lips had thinned, her face had hardened, and her tall frame was carrying some extra weight. She didn't raise her hand, but uttered a simple, "Howya". Bearnárd could almost hear Gonagain's voice. "I'd rather dance with her than fight with her," he would say.

"The reason for this meeting," Namemaker continued, "is to formulate a plan for escape. There are no bad ideas. All ideas are welcome," and with that, he sat down.

Koko was first to speak. "I haven't got ideas, I just wunt to show this." He pulled the spoon from his pocket. Unlike Bearnárd's idea it hadn't been sharpened to a point, like a nail, but flattened and sharpened on one side *and* at the end like a knife. It was a small weapon, but the only weapon they possessed.

"That's a bit shite!" said Dympna, "But we can use it to trade up."

Koko looked crestfallen. "Whut do you mean?"

"We use the spoon to take a switchblade, we use the switchblade to take a gun, we use the gun to take a cannon, we use a cannon to take a fecking..." at that point she fizzled out, but the others took her drift. Koko brightened.

"What about hostages?" asked Bearnárd. "They can prevent an awful lot of gun fire." This wasn't another of Gonagain's 'rule number ones' but still drawn from past experience on *The Reliant*.

"That Doctor wud be gud hostage," said Koko, "Or Landowner."

"I want Conceptuloco," said Komondor flatly.

"We'll aim as high as we can," said Namemaker, addressing Komondor directly, "but we mustn't let revenge get in the way of escape."

"I'd drink to that," agreed Dympna.

It was at this point that a group of guards appeared. "Bearnárd Strongman. Come with us – Staff Sergeant Landowner wants to see you."

The committee exchanged nervous looks.

"Come on! Staff Sergeant Landowner is *not* a patient man."

Strongman rose cautiously and, flanked by the guards, headed towards the mess.

"Well, that's shite luck. It's probably the last we'll see of him, poor fecker," said Dympna

There was a moment's pause as they each considered the potential fate of Bearnárd Strongman.

"Anyhow," Tinkerbelle continued brightly, "A wise auld bird tells me the track for the end of the railway is coming in soon. There'll be an empty cart heading back to the river. I want to be on it, so."

******

Staff Sergeant Landowner was drinking gin with Dr Conceptuloco in the mess. It was a tatty old marquee on the outside, but inside it was furnished in oak and leather. The ground was covered with expensive-looking Persian rugs, and dark-coloured silks adorned the inside of the canvas, covering the stains and patches that could be seen on the outside. Landowner and Conceptuloco were seated in comfortable wing-back chairs, upholstered in dark green leather with brass pins. There was a third, empty, chair at the circular oak table, but it wasn't offered, and Strongman didn't take it.

"Ah! Mister Strongman," Landowner smiled like a man who needed more practice at it. "You *are* Bearnárd Strongman of *The Reliant*, aren't you?"

"No comment."

"Let's not mess around, Mr Strongman, we know

who you are. It was a rhetorical question. Now, we had a bit of a problem in Stanleyville recently, and lost a lieutenant and most of a volunteer division. It seems it was the handy work of the crew of a dirigible called *The Reliant.*"

Strongman failed to conceal a smirk, but Landowner missed it as he sifted through some papers.

"One Captain Oisín Gonagain in command." He pronounced Oisín incorrectly. "A little bit of digging in some of the more meticulous airdocks and we found the names of the crew. Navigator Bunty Goodtime; Engineer Rajaobelina... no surname for him yet; Aircraftman Aiofe Trustworthy – she's of special interest to us; and Flight Cadet Etoile... no surname for him... or her, yet either."

The lack of recognition from Strongman, especially for some of the names, was clearly bothering Landowner but he pressed on. "Now, further investigation revealed that, up until New Year's Eve, there was also an Aircraftman Beagán Haybailer and a Lieutenant Bearnárd Strongman." He smiled his awkward smile again. Bearnárd remained impassive.

Landowner cleared his throat, "Now, I hate to see a good crew cast asunder, and that's why I'd dearly love to bring the rest of your crew here, to be with you, down the mine. So, to that end, I'd like you to write a letter begging for rescue and giving them your exact location."

"I'm not going to do that, and I think you know it."

"We have examples of your writing, albeit just your name, but I'm sure we can forge something pretty convincing. Slightly child-like, not joined up, with an exaggerated curl on the tail of the 'g'. So, you see, we don't really need you at all," Landowner drew his army issue revolver, checked the cylinder was full, and cocked the hammer.

"Let's not be hasty," interjected Conceptuloco, "he's a fine specimen. He'd be ideal for some of my hybrid human experiments."

Strongman swallowed. Gonagain had never actually said: "Rule number one, don't get turned into a hybrid human", but Bearnárd thought that was probably just an oversight.

"Alright. What do you need me to write?"

Landowner pushed a pencil and paper across the table. "In your own words, I think, would be most authentic."

"But I don't actually *know* my exact location."

"I can give you the information you need."

******

The 'P-Mec' were surprised to see Strongman back so soon.

"What the feck was that all about?" asked Dympna.

"We need to get out of here fast," replied Bearnárd.

"Well, as luck would have it, old chum, Dympna

here has the start of a pretty decent plan," said Namemaker.

"If it helps, I now know exactly where we are," said Strongman, "I also know that there may well be a rescue attempt fairly soon, but it's a trap. I've got to get out and find them before they come here."

CHAPTER 13
The banks of the Brown Gelada

(Pollexday)

It was 2:90 in the morning and Jao was up already, drinking from a large flask of coffee and tinkering with her metal man. He was a bit of a giant, and would even tower over Bearnárd. She had already opened him up and found an arrangement of cogs, springs, cables, and cams that were beyond her comprehension. There were literally millions of moving parts. The largest cogs were the size of a side plate, but the smallest were so minute that even the smallest tweezers from her pocket-watch repair kit might not be delicate enough to work with. The tiniest cogs were mostly in the head section of the automaton, along with some sealed units that she dared not open. She didn't even know where to start.

She had then opened the crate to see if that shed any light on things and, to her astonishment, she had found it full of large reels of paper. On closer examination, she discovered that the paper was punched with millions of pin holes, arranged in grids of eight by eight, but only some of each grid was punched, there were lots of blank spaces as well as holes. There was also an empty reel. She could not imagine what they were for.

She plonked herself on her work stool despondently and sipped her coffee. She didn't think she would ever be able to fathom this. She let her mind wander to the munitions factory and all the other equipment there, and to their escape. Gonagain's voice rang in her head "You're the girl who can fix anything."

Jao took another sip of coffee, stood up, and took a deep breath. "Right," she said aloud, "This thing must need power, and *everything* in that place was powered with pulsarnite. So... where would a piece of pulsarnite go?" She picked up a screwdriver and re-opened the chest section. She decided she would start at the largest cog and, sure enough, when she located it, she could see through the spokes, a metal box. She removed the cog with a socket spanner and opened-up the box with a screwdriver. Inside was a length of fine, mercuriumite wire that spiralled tightly around a cylindrical copper scroll. One end of the wire was welded to the inside of the metal box, the other was fixed to a ratchet that would turn the large cog she had removed. It would probably move it one tooth per pulse. She would need a piece of pulsarnite roughly the size and shape of a sherry schooner – and she knew exactly where she could get one. She would need a drill with a diamond hole cutter bit, a hammer and bolster, and a lot of elbow grease.

******

Oisín and Aoife were lying awake in Oisín's cabin, their limbs entwined, and the sheet loosely draped over them. They were both nursing hangovers, and there was an annoying grinding sound emanating from another part of *The Reliant*, yet they both felt quite content.

Gonagain had broken rule number one – never sleep with one of the crew – but, he rationalised, she was only a temporary member of the crew and besides, the sex was phenomenal. Aoife had a great little body. She was petite but she was well-toned, almost muscular, like an athlete. Her breasts were small and pert, her buttocks were round and firm, and her stomach was like a washboard. She also knew her way around the cabin – when to tease, when to please and, when they made love, she moved her body rhythmically, in perfect synchronicity with his own.

Aoife traced one of the scars on Oisín's chest with her finger. "What did you mean last night, when you said you can't figure me out?"

Gonagain contemplated the question. “I’m not naive – I know there’s no such thing as good guys and bad guys. People are more complex than that, and so are their cultures and beliefs. Sometimes people do bad things for good reasons. Sometimes they do good things for bad reasons.”

“So…?”

“I know you’re keeping a fair few secrets from us. I just couldn’t work out whether you were one of the good guys or one of the bad guys.”

Aiofe punched him playfully in the arm. “And now…?”

“You’re one of the good guys – trying to close down those weapons before they can be used – but I still don’t know what it is that I don’t know about you.”

Aoife lay back and wondered what more she could – or should – tell Gonagain about herself.

“Have you any idea what kind of weapons the other side are developing?” asked Gonagain.

“Something powerful, hopefully.”

Gonagain sat up. “Hopefully? I thought you wanted to stop the mass destruction?”

“I do! But it’s not just about weapons. It’s about the biggest threat to all of our futures – time change.”

Gonagain looked at Trustworthy with disbelief.

“The mining and use of pulsarnite is what’s causing the world to slow on its axis,” Trustworthy elucidated. “If we keep up the pulsarnite mining, the days and years will get longer and longer. The temperatures on such long winter nights and summer days will become unbearable. The world will eventually be uninhabitable."

It was a theory Gonagain had heard before, but completely dismissed. "Do you really believe that?"

"You don't?"

"No."

"Ugh! I never had you down as a time-change denier."

"I'm not denying time change – that would be ridiculous – I just don't think it has anything to do with pulsarnite."

"There's solid scientific evidence. The correlation of time slowing and the use of pulsarnite..."

"None of this is the point!" interrupted Gonagain. "The point is, I thought you were trying to sabotage the war, but you're only sabotaging one side. You're a part of this war!"

"Sometimes you have to do bad things for good reasons."

"Rubbish!"

Aoife jumped to her feet and scooped up her clothes. "I don't believe this," she muttered to herself.

Bunty emerged from her cabin, rubbing her nose and sniffing. She was ravenous and decided to get up early and head to the galley to poach herself some eggs. It was a surprise to hear raised voices – the others must be up already.

As she marched purposefully down the corridor, the captain's cabin door flew open, almost hitting her full in the face. It was slammed shut, revealing Aoife Trustworthy standing naked in the corridor, clutching her clothes in front of her. Her face was flushed with anger as she turned and glared at Bunty.

"Excuse me!" she demanded.

Bunty stepped aside and watched Aoife's firm, white buttocks as they disappeared down the winding corridor towards the medical bay.

"Arse," muttered Bunty. "Today will *not* be fun."

******

Jao was back in the engine room with the metal man, but now she was in possession of a cylindrical piece of pulsarnite, that fitted snugly into the copper scroll. It was a bit crudely cut (ideally it would have been polished smooth) but Jao had neither the tools, nor the patience, so it would have to do as it was. Her arms ached like crazy from winding the drill, but her enthusiasm and impatience was spurring her on.

She closed the metal box that was now housing the pulsarnite wrapped in the copper scroll and the mercuriumite coil. She replaced the screws and then slotted the large cog back on its spindle and bolted it in place. She closed the chest plate and, instantly, the lights in the eye sockets began to glow bright orange. This was followed by a gentle whirring sound as the automaton's scalp opened, on both sides, and two slender arms unfolded. It was like watching a giant ladybird preparing for flight.

The metal man fell silent. Jao stared in wonderment. It reminded her of something. Then she remembered the night out in Butare, before Gonagain had changed the heliagen for hydrum. They had gone to a moving picture show. The rest of the crew had enjoyed the slapstick antics on the screen, but Jao had been more interested in the projector itself. She had watched with fascination as the projectionist had loaded the reels and fed the shiny tape through the machine so it could roll from reel to reel. That's what these two slender arms were for!

She went back to the crate and picked out two reels, the empty one and the one with the big '#1' written on it. "Now," she said aloud, "which way? Left to right, or right to left." It was a fifty-fifty choice. "Left to right, I think."

The empty reel slotted easily on to the spigot on the right arm, as did the full reel on the left. Jao located a slot on the side of the automaton's head and pushed the end of the paper tape into it. The tape began to feed through on its own, and stopped when about thirty centimetres had come out the other side. Jao hooked the tape into a clasp at the centre of the empty reel.

Nothing happened. Maybe it was right to left. Maybe she had broken it. She wound the empty reel by hand until the paper was taut. She didn't want to apply too much pressure in case she tore the paper.

Then, suddenly, the reels sprang to life. Rajaobelina sat in exited anticipation as she watched one reel of paper grow smaller and the other larger. This was going to take a while. She looked in the crate. There were seven more reels. She decided to go and tell the others.

Jao burst on to the bridge. “Guess what! I’ve worked out the automaton!” she announced brightly.

Trustworthy stared straight ahead and didn’t respond. Gonagain smiled weakly.

“Good-oh,” said Bunty, somewhat unenthusiastically.

“Well, don’t get too excited,” replied Jao, feeling a bit deflated.

There was a heavy silence.

“Have I missed something?” asked Jao.

“So, is it actually working or do you just know *how* it works?” asked Bunty, more brightly this time.

“Well, it’s… doing something.”

Trustworthy spun around in her chair. “You’d need a big piece of pulsarnite for that. What are you powering it with?”

“A big piece of pulsarnite taken from the massive lump we’re carrying in a trunk I would imagine,” replied Gonagain on Jao’s behalf.

Trustworthy, who already looked in a bad mood to Jao, suddenly looked furious. “*My* piece of pulsarnite?”

"*Our* piece of pulsarnite. *We* found it on *our* cart, and *we* brought it aboard. You have never once laid claim to that trunk," responded Gonagain.

"What do you want it for? You wouldn't even know what to do with a lump of pulsarnite that big!"

"I'd sell it to the highest bidder. There's a facility in Lubumbashi that would pay good money for it, for starters. Anyway, Jao knows what to do with it. She's already taken a piece off for her metal man."

Trustworthy leaped to her feet.

"Where are you going?" snapped Gonagain.

"To the trunk in the hold. I'm going to check."

"There's just a sandbag in it now, but you won't be able to see it; you don't have the right key."

Trustworthy sat back down. That's why she couldn't open it. It wasn't a stuck lock at all. And everyone knew except her. The day was going from bad to worse.

"So, where's *your* piece of pulsarnite now?" demanded Trustworthy

"Jao has it, obviously," replied Gonagain.

Another heavy silence filled the bridge.

"Well... erm... I'll be with my metal friend if anyone needs me," said Jao.

"Need any help dear?" asked Bunty hopefully.

"I need you here on the bridge, Bunty, if we're going to rescue Bearnárd from these bastards," said Gonagain.

Bunty raised her eyebrows and grimaced at Jao. "Oh good," she muttered as she returned to her maps, compasses, and anemometers.

******

It was almost on the stroke of the sixth deciday that the last paper reel had finished winding through the automaton's head and, like the previous ones, had automatically rewound back to its original reel. Jao removed both reels and placed them carefully back in the crate. The thin arms folded back of their own volition and the metal scalp returned to seal the domed head.

There was a moment's pause before the eyes changed from orange to green, and the automaton's head turned to face Rajaobelina. It was looking at her.

"What are you, and what do you do?" Jao mused aloud.

"I. am. Mechanical. Life-form. Emulator. version. two. point. two," it replied in a tinny voice. It spoke with a staccato cadence. Each word sounded like the start of a new sentence. "I. do. anything. I. am. instructed. to. do. and. more. I. can. also. learn. new. things." It continued. "Who. are. you?"

Jao was taken by surprise. She wasn't expecting a reply. She wasn't sure what she was expecting. "Er… I'm Rajaobelina, the engineer."

"Hello. Raj. jao. bel. in. a. the. engineer."

"My name is Rajaobelina. The engineer is my job. Just call me Rajaobelina."

"Hello. Raj. jao. bel. in. a."

"On second thoughts, just call me Jao."

"Hello. Jao."

"What do I call you?"

"I. am. Mechanical. Life-form. Emulator. version. two. point. two."

"Hmmn. That's a bit of a mouthful. Don't you have a shorter name I can call you?"

"You. can. call. me. M. L. E. 2. 2."

Jao laughed. "Emily Tutu?"

"Yes. M. L. E. 2. 2."

Rajaobelina studied the automaton. Because of its massive height she had been referring to it as a 'him', but its body shape was, in fact, quite androgynous. *Another* female crew member; that'll please Gonagain, she thought. "Okay then, Emily Tutu. I suppose the first thing is to introduce you to the crew. Follow me."

Emily Tutu moved with more fluidity than she spoke, however, when she stopped moving, it was a sudden and complete stop, as if she had broken down. It then took you by surprise when she started again.

Up at the bridge, Jao introduced her new crew member. "Everyone, this is Emily Tutu; Emily Tutu, this is the crew."

"Why have you called it Emily? It doesn't look like an Emily," said Gonagain.

"I didn't call her Emily, that's her name. Go ahead and introduce yourself Emily."

"I. am. Mechanical. Life-form. Emulator. version. two. point. two. but. you. can. call. me. M. L. E. 2. 2."

"This is Bunty Goodtime; she's our navigator."

"Hello. Bunty. Goodtime."

"Hello, Emily," replied Bunty

"This is Oisín Gonagain; he's the captain."

"Hello. Oisín. Gonagain."

"No, you call him 'Captain'," said Jao.

Emily Tutu turned to Jao, her head slightly cocked to one side. "But. his. name. is. Oisín. Gonagain. Captain. is. his. job."

"That's correct," said Jao, "but captains are addressed as 'Captain', not by their name."

"That. is. inconsistent. and. confusing."

"Yes, I suppose it is," said Gonagain, "but you'll get used to it."

"This is Aoife Trustworthy; our aircraftman."

"Hello. Aoife. Trustworthy."

Aoife just scowled back.

Emily somehow managed to create an expression of confusion on her metal face. "Should. I. address. you. as. Aircraftman?"

"I'd prefer if you didn't address me at all," said Trustworthy sulkily.

"Moving swiftly on," continued Jao, "this is Etoile."

Etoile looked up at the metal person that loomed seemingly miles above her. She lay down meekly with her head on her paws and wagged her tail as if she were sweeping the metal floor.

"She. is. very. small. What. does. she. do?"

"Officially, she's our flight cadet but, really, she's a mascot, a friendly face, and a kind of counselling service."

Suddenly, Emily moved towards the domed front of the bridge, and stared into the distance. "Urgent. message. for. Captain. Gonagain. Go. to. your. nearest. skydock. Over."

Gonagain turned to Jao, "What's the story with that then?"

Jao shrugged.

Bunty picked up a pair of binoculars and followed Emily's gaze. She eventually spotted a dirigible that was so far away it was only a dot, even with binoculars. When she focused in on it, she could see a tiny pinprick of light flashing. "Morse code, Skipper!" She grabbed a pencil and wrote as she deciphered, letter by letter. When she had finished, she looked down at her notepad and read aloud, "Urgent message for Captain Gonagain. Go to your nearest skydock. Over."

Gonagain peered out of the dome; he still could see nothing. He turned to the automaton. "Good work, Midshipman Tutu, welcome aboard. Bunty, set a course for our nearest skydock."

******

Later that evening, Rajaobelina paid a visit to Bunty's cabin. All the cabins, with the notable exception of the captain's quarters, were more-or-less the same – although they became progressively smaller with increased proximity to the stern.

The bunk consisted of a single metal bar, which spanned the length of the cabin, and some metal eyes on the walls. A rope was then woven and linked like chain mail to form a 'sprung base'. There was a vice handle that could be turned and locked into position to adjust the tension in the rope. A thin, but well-stuffed, horsehair mattress sat on top of the rope, and a thinner, feather-stuffed mattress was an additional layer that Jao didn't have. Bunty's bunk was topped with mulberry-silk sheets and a velvet, quilted bedspread, stuffed with eider duck down.

The space beneath the bunk was used for storage. An array of trunks, cases and hat boxes slotted in neatly, like a three-dimensional jigsaw.

Opposite the bunk, a shallow locker provided hanging space and a shelf, spanning the space between the locker and the cabin wall, served as a desk. An up-ended trunk fitted neatly under the shelf and doubled as a stool.

The whole cabin was adorned with nick-nacks collected from around the world, and a plethora of photographs and daguerreotypes – many of them featuring Bunty herself. Pride of place was a photo of Bunty with Mícheál Gonagain in front of *The Reliant.*

Bunty poured herself a large gin and a schooner of madeira for Jao. Jao sipped at her drink. It was kind of Bunty to keep some madeira in her cabin, specifically for Jao's occasional visits, but she would have preferred a coffee.

"I'm really annoyed that the captain told Trustworthy about the sandbag in her trunk," said Jao, "She might have left with it and been none the wiser."

"It was stupid and petty of him," sighed Bunty, "He just said it to let her know that he knew. What do you know about that other trunk with the sandbag in it?"

"What other trunk?"

"There's another trunk, identical to the one you put the pulsarnite in. It's in the hold, with a sandbag in it."

Jao's echoic memory kicked in. "Certainly, madam," the chandler had said, "a popular combination today."

"That sneaky cow was going to swap the pulsarnite for the sandbag!" Jao exclaimed.

"You mean just like you did?"

"That's different!"

"Well, now that she knows you have the pulsarnite locked in *your* trunk, she'll probably try to swap the trunks over. Why don't we put the pulsarnite back in the *original* trunk? She doesn't have the keys for either. She'll end up swapping one trunk with a sandbag for another," suggested Bunty.

"Now that *is* sneaky," smiled Jao

"I'll take that as a compliment."

"I might see if I can find the keys to *her* new trunk. If she can't open any of them, she'll really be confused!" The two women giggled with delight.

"What's going on with the captain and Trustworthy anyway?" asked Jao with a hint of glee. "They're really at each other's throats today."

"I don't know. Whatever it is, it happened in the captain's quarters last night."

Jao sat bolt upright. "That dirty... sneaky... eugh. I hate her! How do you know about that?"

"I saw her coming out of his cabin in her birthday suit this morning."

"This morning? And you're only telling me now?" Jao downed her madeira and slammed the schooner down. "You can't rely on anyone on this rotten ship." She stormed out of the cabin, slamming the door behind her.

Bunty sat open-mouthed for a moment. "Well, that went well," she muttered to herself eventually.

A few moments later, Bunty heard a shuffling noise outside her cabin. It was probably Jao, back to apologise. She yanked open the door, to find Etoile pacing back and forth. Etoile looked up at her soulfully and trotted in. She hopped up on to Bunty's bunk.

"At last, someone sane," said Bunty, "Fancy a drink, old girl?"

CHAPTER 14
Skydock 101

2.03.1910 (Secundusday) /
January 13, 1910 (Tuesday)

Skydock 101 was one of the more recently built skydocks. The envelope was a huge donut, which looked like it had been made by stitching the envelopes of a hundred enormous dirigibles together – which was, more or less, how it *was* constructed. The perimeter of the circular gondola was spiked with a similar number of docking bays. These consisted of radial, billabob beams, which cantilevered from the gondola deck. The gap between them diminished as you got closer to the gondola, which made them suitable for dirigibles of varying sizes, however, docking a large dirigible meant you could only get to the gondola deck by balancing on the beams. Many a drunken airman had met his end trying to get back to his craft, and new laws were being introduced to include safety nets below. Security locking bars, also made from billabob, were supplied to stop your airship from floating away. Once you were away from the perimeter, it was easy to forget you were kilometres above the ground.

Skydocks were not a new idea – they started building them a long time ago. Originally, they had been floating post offices and chandleries, where you could pick up messages and supplies without having to go down to the ground, but each new one was built bigger and better than the last, with cafés, inns, trading posts, hostels and more. These days, they were more like floating towns. Initially, they hadn't proved as popular as people had expected – dirigible crews wanted proper ground leave, not just swapping one floating domicile for a bigger one – but since the time war began, they had increased in popularity. They were overtly time-neutral, with everything being open ten-five (or twentyfour-seven, if you preferred) and every establishment displayed times and dates in both formats, side by side.

Messages were passed from one skydock to another via Morse code. The more diligent captains, like the captain of the airship Emily Tutu had spotted, would also repeat Morse messages they had picked up, in the hopes they would eventually find their intended recipient.

If you wanted messages sent more privately, each skydock post office had a pantelegraph machine. These were enormous pendulums, taller than a man, that swung back and forth metronomically. The pendulum drove a small pen-like instrument, which replicated its movement in miniature. All pantelegraphs were synchronised using a flashing light. Each time the pendulum reached the end of its arc, a white light flashed. The sending and receiving pantelegraph needed to have their white flashing lights synchronised. A green light went on and off sporadically. This indicated whether the pendulum was above inked or blank paper. As the sending machine swung back and forth over the message, the receiving machine put the pen down when the green light showed and replicated the message, line by line. You could even send pictures, or sign documents remotely with it. It was an ingenious invention, but it was also very slow.

Gonagain was in the pantelegraph room, in the post office of Skydock 101. "The original is in Skydock 42," said the operator, "that's not too far from here. If you're going in that direction it might be quicker to pick it up from there."

"I'm not sure where I'm headed at the moment," replied Gonagain. "Does this skydock have a library?"

The operator was surprised by the question. Dirigible captains did not have a reputation for being avid readers. "Yes, in the dockhall, near the centre of the dock."

"Get me the message and I'll come back for it."

******

Bunty, Jao and Etoile were sitting in the warm sun outside a cafe on the periphery of the skydock, not far from where *The Reliant* was moored. Jao hadn't slept a wink and had gone to Bunty first thing in the morning to apologise for her outburst. Bunty accepted her apology readily and gave her a big hug.

Jao had then burst into tears. They agreed to go out for a proper chinwag as soon as they docked.

Bunty was stirring three sugar cubes into her coffee, wishing it was ice cubes in gin. Jao was absent-mindedly stroking Etoile, who was sitting up at the table beside her. She sipped at her coffee, which she took black, without sugar.

"I know nothing will ever happen between the captain and I," she said. "If it was going to happen, it would have by now."

"Oh, my dear girl, I knew you were very fond of the skipper, but I never realised you were carrying such a torch for him," replied Bunty.

Jao shrugged her shoulders noncommittally. "I just don't like the idea of him with *her*."

"You don't think she's good enough for him?"

Jao stared thoughtfully into her coffee. "I just don't trust her," she said eventually.

"Well, I don't think it went terribly well, judging by the way they were yesterday. I really don't think you have much to worry about there."

"But he still slept with her. He always implied that relationships on board were out of bounds. Yet he slept with *her*. How could he?"

"Yes, it's beastly. He's been a real bounder. But you know the skipper, he's a good man really. Sometimes he just lets his libido get the better of him, especially when he's been at the wine."

"I just don't want to think of the two of them together."

"Then don't, dear heart. What's done is done. He

can't take it back now. Forget it and forgive it, otherwise it will drive you potty," advised Bunty.

"I suppose I will," conceded Jao, "Eventually. But I'm not ready to forgive just yet."

******

Gonagain felt slightly out of place in a library; he hadn't been in one since his mother used to take him and Bearnárd as children. Even then, they had never really done much reading; they preferred to play hide and seek amongst the bookshelves.

As a young child, Oisín had been a bit of a mammy's boy. He had never really known his father – Mícheál Gonagain had gone off on business when he was a toddler and never came back. So, it had just been him and his mother, and they were very close.

One day, completely out of the blue, a stern old woman had arrived with a tall, stocky child, around the same age as Oisín. Apparently, the boy's mother had recently died of whooping cough and they were trying to find his father. If they didn't find any next of kin, the boy would be sent to the workhouse. The boy and his mother had reverted to her maiden name, Strongman, after discovering that his father was a bigamist. His father's name was Mícheál Gonagain.

It was the first that Eibhilin Gonagain had heard of her estranged husband's bigamy, but she didn't even flinch. She was such a kind-hearted, generous woman that she took in the young boy, Bearnárd, and looked after him as if he were her own, even though she could barely afford to keep herself and Oisín clothed and fed.

Young Oisín was furious. He mocked and teased the boy for being an orphan and for being a bit slow on the uptake. It was only after Bearnárd had called Eibhilin 'mummy' for the first time, that Gonagain pushed Bearnárd too far and he lashed out. He punched Oisín, square on the chin, and knocked him out cold. After that, the loathing had turned to grudging respect and reluctant tolerance.

Although Bearnárd was several hands older, Oisín took on the role of big brother. He helped Bearnárd with his learning and protected him with his superior street smarts. Bearnárd, in return, taught Oisín to box and protected him with his superior strength. Before long, the two became a united duo and an irresistible force.

******

"Can I help you?" asked the librarian, spotting that Gonagain looked a bit lost.

"I'm looking for some scientific research, something that's easy to understand."

"In what field."

"Time change, specifically in relation to pulsarnite."

"From which perspective? Traditionalist or Geokinetic?"

"Er... I was hoping for something balanced –

neutral."

"How refreshing, good for you! Most people only want to read something for bias confirmation. But I'm afraid nothing like that has ever been written, at least to my knowledge. I'll get you one from each perspective and you can make up your own mind. That'll be the best."

******

While she was washing up after breakfast, in the galley, Aoife Trustworthy had been assessing her situation. She was further away from Victoria than ever, and heading in the wrong direction. Her position on the ship was now untenable. Gonagain hated her and so did his damn dog. Rajaobelina had hated her from the beginning and Aoife didn't think that sleeping with the captain was going to ameliorate *that* situation. Goodtime clearly didn't trust her, but at least she was polite and civil.

The lump of pulsarnite was now smaller than before and, worse, a part of it was being used to power one of the pulsarnite army. One of the key objectives she had been instructed to prevent had happened right under her nose, albeit in a very minor way, whilst she was supposedly in possession of the pulsarnite rock. That was going to go down like an osmium dirigible back at headquarters. She would already be in enough trouble over the Stanleyville debacle. She had been with the crew of *The Reliant* for far too long now. If she didn't turn up soon with the pulsarnite rock... well, she shuddered to think.

Trustworthy made a snap decision. She was parting ways with *The Reliant* and her crew immediately. A skydock was an ideal place to hitch, or stowaway, or whatever. She had no idea where the rest of the crew had gone, or when they would return, so she needed to act fast.

She opened the porthole in her cabin and groped around for the string she had attached to the hinge. She reeled it in, pulling up the cylindrical basket with the pigeon. The poor creature had been in the tube for days now, with only a walk around her cabin, pecking for crumbs each night before Trustworthy went to bed. Trustworthy quickly scrawled a note.

001529. Jan 13. Skydock 101. Have prize. Parting company. Destination Victoria.

She attached the note to the pigeon's leg and released it through the porthole. Plucking a roll of bandage from the first aid kit, she let it unwind to the centre, where she had hidden the key to her *new* trunk. The end landed loosely on the floor, without the expected 'clunk' of the key hitting the ground. Her new hiding place had been discovered. "Damn it!" she cursed. "Damn it, damn it, damn it." Why hadn't she checked for the key before releasing the damn pigeon? She took a deep breath. "Right," she said aloud, "The pigeon is gone, there's nothing I can do about that."

She quickly packed her kit bag, making extra

sure she had the camera. At least she still had the Lubumbashi Munitions Factory photos.

Finally, she did a tour of the ship, looking for any crates or trunks that could possibly house the pulsarnite. Rajaobelina's cabin revealed only a tiny locked trunk, which was too small for the pulsarnite rock, but the engine room had a larger locked trunk, identical to the one she had bought at the Lubumbashi chandlery. It was sitting beside the automaton. The automaton itself was completely motionless, but the eyes were glowing amber. Aoife stood on the crate and waved her hand in front of its face. It didn't react.

The hold had two trunks in it. Her original black one that still sat on Gonagain's hand cart, and the other burgundy trunk from Lubumbashi chandlery. All the trunks were locked. "Bugger," she cursed under her breath. She sat down on the trunk to think.

They knew that she knew that Rajaobelina had the pulsarnite. So, the obvious thing for them to do would be to swap the pulsarnite back again. But then, they might try to double bluff. They had now taken the key for *her* Lubumbashi trunk so, obviously, they knew about that one too. They would also know that she would know that they knew about *her* Lubumbashi trunk, because of the missing key. Her mind was beginning to boggle.

She went up to the gondola deck and stood on one of the two massive wooden bars that were bolted across *The Reliant's* gondola to stop it from floating away from the skydock. She paused and briefly considered stealing *The Reliant*. She would definitely have the pulsarnite then – but she realised she could never fly it solo. She caught the eye of a stevedore. “Hey!” she shouted, “Do you know of any ships bound for Victoria? Or any other Trad town?”

“No, but I can ask at the office.”

“Thank you. Can you find out if any of them will take a passenger? I’ll pay you for your efforts.”

“No problem.”

Aoife went back to the engine room and lugged the heavy trunk up to the hold. She put it on the handcart and then added the third trunk. By the time she went back to the gondola deck, the stevedore was back.

“It’s your lucky day,” he shouted, “There’s a cargo vessel leaving for Victoria any minute now and they have a spare cabin. It’s *The Oscillator*, and it’s in dock twenty.”

Aoife traversed the wooden docking bar and jumped down on to the skydock, landing elegantly. She took out a thousand ariary note and palmed it to the stevedore as if she was shaking hands. “There’s three trunks on a handcart in the hold. Bring them to *The Oscillator* and I’ll meet you there with another thousand ariary.”

******

Gonagain was back in the pantelegraph room

again. He had skimmed through a lot of scientific research at the library and most of it went way over his head. Eventually, the librarian had found two textbooks that he was able to understand. The Traditionalist book had some pretty compelling theories that linked time change to pulsarnite. What really caught his eye was the graph comparing the growth of pulsarnite use, with the speed of time change. There was also a damning explanation of why pulsarnite timepieces stayed in sync with the earth, no matter how quickly or slowly time change occurred.

The Geokinetic book, in contrast, had not offered any detailed theories for time change, other than, as an unexplained, natural phenomena. It had attempted to dispel the arguments put forward by Traditionalists, but it was largely unconvincing.

It looked like he owed Aiofe an apology. There was only one thing Gonagain hated more than being wrong, and that was having to admit being wrong.

"Captain Gonagain? The pantelegraph has finished transcribing your message."

The pantelegraph operator passed Gonagain a slightly damp piece of paper. Gonagain instantly recognised Bearnárd's handwriting.

Dear Captain Gonagain, I am being held at a pulsarnite mine near Isalo. The co-ordinates are 051w 457s. Please rescue me. Lieutenant Strongman.

"Thanks," said Gonagain, handing the operator an arbitrary amount of cash as he rushed out of the door. "Keep the change."

As luck would have it Gonagain bumped, almost literally, into Bunty, Jao and Etoile as he was marching towards the skydock periphery. They were in the retail zone, and Jao was carrying several bags.

"The message was from Bearnárd; I know where he is," blurted Gonagain. "Come on! Let's get back to *The Reliant*."

Back at dock fifty-one, *The Reliant* was empty. "Where's Aoife?" asked Gonagain.

"No idea, Skip. She was here when we left… I think."

"Well, we need to find her and get moving. You two split up and see if you can find her on the skydock. I'll double-check the ship and stay here in case she comes back. Meet back here in fifteen millidays."

Fifteen millidays later, Gonagain and Goodtime were back on the bridge. "Her cabin is empty; she's gone," said Gonagain. "She's taken the trunk of pulsarnite with her."

"I don't think so," said Goodtime. "I switched the pulsarnite trunk with an identical one in the hold. She's got a trunk full of sand."

"Another trunk?" replied Gonagain. "Show me."

Down in the hold, Bunty rummaged through the sacking bags in the corner. "Blast! She's taken that trunk too." They both turned to the hand cart. That trunk was gone too. There was a noise coming from the deck. Gonagain and Bunty sprinted up the spiral staircase, hoping to see Trustworthy with the trunks. Instead they found Rajaobelina.

"She's gone," said Jao, "Hitched a ride to Victoria on *The Oscillator*, according to the stevedore I spoke to."

"She's taken the pulsarnite too," said Bunty.

"I doubt it," Jao smiled, "I moved it."

"You moved it? So did I – but it doesn't matter anyway; she took all the trunks."

"That's alright. She's now the proud owner of two sandbags and a broken compressor motor. The pulsarnite is in my bunk, under a pile of blankets and between the sheets, where *no one* will find it." Jao looked pointedly at Gonagain as she imparted the last piece of information. "Shall we go and get Bearnárd then?"

CHAPTER 15
Isalo Mine

Dympna Tinkerbelle's plan was far more detailed than Charlie Namemaker had given her credit for. She had been watching the daily routines of all the guards and eavesdropping on the officers as she went about her cleaning duties. The delivery of steel railway tracks and wooden sleepers was due the very next day, at around eight in the evening, and it was imperative that Bearnárd Strongman was in the vicinity. With his size and strength, he would inevitably be seconded to unloading duties. Dympna would be positioned on the roof of the outhouse, next to the canteen, so she could watch the unloading process and send the signals. The others were to go about their business until they heard the first signal.

Bearnárd lay in his bunk and stared into the darkness. The plan seemed very risky to him – there was so much that could go wrong. He thought about his half-brother and wondered what he would say. Gonagain was usually quite meticulous, and liked a plan that had everything buttoned down. Having said that, if the situation was desperate, or the rewards were great, or both, he would take whatever risks he deemed necessary.

Bearnárd felt that the very real possibility of being turned into a hybrid human, whilst the crew of *The Reliant* flew straight into a trap that could lead them to the same fate, constituted a desperate situation. *Not* being turned into a hybrid human was a great reward. Overall, he felt he was doing the right thing.

Charlie Namemaker was less certain. He had been here a long time, waiting for an escape opportunity to arise. He had felt certain he would recognise that opportunity when it showed itself and he really wasn't sure this was it. The plan itself was... adequate, but the make-up of the P-Mec bothered him. Strongman was as sound as anyone here; he didn't really know Tinkerbelle that well, but she had her head screwed on and he trusted her well enough. It was the other two that played on his mind. It wasn't that he didn't trust them, it was more that they both seemed a bit... flaky. He was worried they might not stick to the plan if it wasn't exactly going like clockwork, and it almost certainly wouldn't go like clockwork – someone would react in way they weren't expecting, or something would happen that wasn't part of the plan. They would have to improvise, but without abandoning the basics of the plan. He rolled over in his bunk. If he didn't get some sleep it might be *him* that mucks up.

Dympna Tinkerbelle was also staring at the ceiling. “This plan is utter shite,” she whispered aloud to herself. What on earth was she thinking? They were all going to get killed. She would have to call the whole thing off, first thing in the morning. She couldn’t do that – what would the rest of the Pulsarnite Mine Escape Committee say? They’d never trust her again. Why was she more concerned about what the others would say than she was about being shot? “Better to die with pride, than live in shame, Dympna darling,” she whispered to herself as she turned on to her side.

Komondor Clockhead didn’t even know why he was trying to escape. He could never present himself to his wife and children looking the way he did now. Even if they accepted him, he would be too ashamed. Where would he go? How would he survive? He’d probably end up in some circus freak show. But he wanted this small victory – to escape. And if he died trying? So what? He might take a few of them with him.

Koko Stewdiver slept soundly.

CHAPTER 16
Isalo Mine

It was after eight o'clock in the evening, and Bearnárd Strongman was in the latrines near the canteen. He had been there too long already, and the delivery of the railway track had still not arrived. The plan was that he would be walking past, on his way back to the mine, when the delivery arrived, but if he stayed in the dunny much longer one of the guards would surely come looking for him. Bearnárd actually did need to use the toilet – his nerves were getting the better of him – but he couldn't do it knowing that Dympna Tinkerbelle was perched on the roof above him. All his earlier doubts were coming back to him.

Suddenly there was a loud bang on the roof – it was what he had been waiting for, but it still made him jump. The thump on the roof was Dympna's signal that the traction engine bringing the railway parts had appeared on the horizon at last. Strongman pulled up his trousers (he had taken them down for authenticity), and headed back towards the mine via the entrance gate. He was unsure whether he needed to walk faster or slower than usual to be at the entrance at the right time. He ended up with an odd gait that betrayed his sense of urgency without actually adding any speed.

Dympna was beginning to regret not cleaning the latrines (which was one of her duties) before climbing up onto the roof. The smell up there was awful, but there was nothing that she could do about it now. She was lying flat on the roof and watching the proceedings at the site entrance. The traction engine hauling the enormous cart had pulled into the compound and traced a huge semi-circular arc to face the exit. The entrance guards had checked the drivers' papers and opened the massive doors on the back of the cart, and they were now in the cart, checking the inventory, whilst some other guards rounded up a group of captives for unloading duty.

"Come on, Bearnárd, where the feck are ya?" Dympna muttered to herself.

By the time Bearnárd emerged at the compound gate, an unloading posse of about a dozen men had already been formed and there were five guards supervising. Bearnárd lingered in the area, stopping to tie his bootlace, but no-one paid him any heed.

"You're too late, ya big feckin' eejit!" cursed Dympna under her breath.

Bearnárd stood up and walked confidently to the growing pile of railway tracks. He began organising them into a tidier layout until two of the unloading posse arrived with another length of track.

As soon as they dropped the track, Bearnárd started giving out to them. He pushed them around and even gave one of them a clatter across the back of the head. He then left him to finish tidying the unloaded materials and marched purposefully back to the cart with the other worker to continue the unloading. The whole charade was witnessed by several of the unloading posse and at least two of the guards, but Bearnárd had acted with such authority that everyone assumed that one of the guards had designated him as foreman.

"Good man yerself, Bearnárd, and fair feckin play to ya!" Dympna Tinkerbelle punched her palm. She flattened herself on the roof and continued to observe as Bearnárd and the rest of the posse unpacked the cart.

After a while, Bearnárd and his work mate put yet another piece of track down and, as he straightened up, he looked directly toward the latrines. He mopped his brow, tugged his earlobe, and wiped his nose on the back of his hand. That was the signal that the cart was nearly empty. Dympna scrambled down from the roof of the outhouse, with surprising agility for a larger lady, and crept over to the canteen gong. She gave it two sharp raps with the rubber mallet. Five rings meant breakfast, three was supper, and one was 'attention everyone', but two meant nothing. She scurried back to the outhouse and scrabbled back up to the roof again. Within a few seconds, a guard appeared. He stood at the gong, looking around vacantly. Dympna flattened herself against the outhouse roof so she couldn't be seen, but the birdbrained guard didn't even look up. He looked confused and obviously wasn't sure if someone had struck the gong or if it had just blown in the wind – or if he had imagined it.

Down in the mine, they could just about hear the gong. Charlie Namemaker looked towards Komondor Clockhead, gave a barely perceptible nod, and turned to the pulsarnite mine wall. He crouched down.

"Flippin' 'eck! Look at that! What is it?" One of the guards, followed by Komondor, came marching across to see what Charlie was looking at. As the guard crouched beside Namemaker, Komondor Clockhead grabbed his varilights and snatched them from his face, yanking his head back in the process. Namemaker elbowed him in the Adam's apple and he fell backwards to the floor, clutching his throat and struggling to breath.

"Oi!" a voice behind them shouted. It was the other guard.

Namemaker and Clockhead turned, just in time to see the other guard raise his rifle and squeeze the trigger, but before he had pulled it far enough, a fist wearing a lethal-pointed knuckleduster was punched into his throat and he fell to the ground with blood spurting from his carotid artery.

"That wus too quick and easy for that bustard," said Koko Stewdiver as he looked down at the dying guard. It was one of the guards who had beaten him for not bringing back a spoon – the same spoon that had eventually killed him. "Come on, let's get out of here."

Birdbrain, at the dinner gong, had disappeared and Dympna Tinkerbelle had turned her attention to the mine entrance. Before very long, she saw Namemaker, Clockhead and Stewdiver emerge. They had been joined by half a dozen or so mine workers. Namemaker, Clockhead and two of the other mine workers were now toting rifles taken from the mine guards. The rest carried hammers and wrenches. Stewdiver was heavily splattered in blood and grinning from ear to ear. He had clearly done the lion's share of the work in overpowering the guards, maintaining their stealth by using his improvised weapon. Namemaker was struggling to maintain control over his new squadron.

Dympna scrambled down from her vantage point once again and tiptoed to the gong. She gave it two sharp raps – to let Bearnárd know the others had reached the surface – and scurried back to her hiding place. Whilst Birdbrain returned, to wander purposelessly around the gong once more, Dympna watched the Namemaker squad approach the compound entrance with as much stealth as could be mustered by an excited bunch of men, with revenge in their hearts and rebellion on their minds. Scanning across to the compound entrance, she watched as Bearnárd Strongman emerged from the cart. He was carrying a length of railway track on his own. "He's as strong as a mule that lad," Dympna mumbled to herself in admiration.

The guards at the compound gate were equally impressed by Bearnárd's show of strength, and stood awe struck as he walked towards them with the length of railway track on his shoulder. But their look of amazement and admiration turned to one of horror, as Bearnárd launched the length of track at them with a roar. The sheer weight of it knocked both guards over like a pair of skittles, and there was an audible snapping of bones as it landed on them. One of the guards was lucky; the track landed on his neck and killed him instantly. The other was less fortunate. His ribcage shattered and a lung punctured. He lay coughing up blood and groaning in agony. The remaining three guards were caught by surprise and it took them a moment to realise that it wasn't a horrific accident of some kind. It wasn't until Komondor opened fire that they knew for certain that this was a riot.

Komondor wasn't particularly proficient with the weapon, but compensated for his poor aim by spraying bullets in all directions. He took out all three guards, and two of the unloading crew were collateral damage. Bearnárd lay flat on his belly among the unloaded materials with his hands over his ears.

Dympna scrambled down from her vantage point once more. It was high time she got herself to the compound entrance. She was built for neither speed nor stamina, and all the climbing up and down had already taken it out of her.

By the time she arrived at the compound entrance, red-faced and panting like an overheating dog, Komondor was driving the traction engine through the gate. The rest of the P-Mec were in the cart, along with several other escapees. Namemaker had his rifle poked through a gap in the cart doors and was picking off anyone who appeared to be trying to stop them – he was considerably more skilled with a rifle than Komondor Clockhead. He spotted Dympna struggling to catch them as the traction engine overcame its initial inertia and began picking up speed. He reached a hand out to her. "Come on girl, you can do it!"

Dympna was clutching her belly with one hand; she had a stitch and was slowing down. The gap between her and the cart was widening. Charlie Namemaker looked over his shoulder. "Bearn, she ain't gonna make it!" he said.

Suddenly, the doors of the cart burst open and Bearnárd leapt out. He ran towards Dympna and hauled her on to his shoulder in a fireman's lift. He spun neatly round and chased after the cart. Namemaker was now hanging right out, his legs held tightly by Stewdiver and another man. Bearnárd had nearly caught up with them, but he had underestimated Dympna's weight and was already flagging. Just as he thought they were both going to be left behind, the burden that was Dympna Tinkerbelle began to lighten as she was dragged, by the legs, into the cart like a sack of potatoes. With his load lightened, Bearnárd gave one last spurt of effort and was hauled aboard by Dympna and Charlie.

Dympna threw her arms around Bearnárd and kissed him on the neck. She pulled away with tears in her eyes. “You, you’re a...” she was lost for words. She punched him playfully and hugged him again.

The traction engine had built up a decent head of steam and was chugging along at a fair speed. Komondor was navigating the dunes in the desert with great expertise – he had grown up in a desert environment and knew exactly what to do. You should never attack a sand dune head on – that’s a guaranteed way of grounding your vehicle on the crest, especially if your vehicle has a long wheelbase. Equally, if you summit the dune at too shallow an angle, you are liable to tip your vehicle over and roll it down the other side. Finding the optimum angle for each dune is more an art than a science. The traction engine wasn’t built for desert use, but the huge rollers that functioned as wheels spread the weight of the vehicle very well. The adaptation of spikes in the rollers gave an adequate grip in the soft sand. The huge cart had been fitted with the new air-filled tyres, but they had been filled with heliagen instead. This would have resulted in a loss of traction if the wheels were driven, but as the cart was being drawn, it stayed nicely on top of the soft sand and was very unlikely to get mired.

It was a good while later, as Komondor tacked for the umpteenth time, that Charlie Namemaker opened the doors a crack and peeked out of the back of the cart towards the mine compound.

"Bugger! Looks like we've got company."

A handful of steamcars were in pursuit. They were small, open-top vehicles which could carry two people – a driver and a gunner. Like the traction engine, they expelled plumes of black smoke – giving away their presence, even when they were behind a dune. Unlike the traction engine, they were quite manoeuvrable and had decent acceleration.

"We need to get a message to Clockhead to drive this flippin' thing straight!" shouted Charlie.

"He knows whut he's doing!" replied Koko Stewdiver curtly. "This is how you stay upright and moving in a desert."

Namemaker cursed, poked his rifle through the gap and trained it on one of the vehicles, waiting for it to come into range but, as Komondor continued tacking, it disappeared from view. "This is flippin' impossible. With us weaving all over the place, and them disappearing behind dunes and popping up on top again..."

"Close the doors," said Bearnárd. "Next time we tack, we'll open them up and hit them with all barrels." He gestured to two of the other escapees. "On my word, you two open the doors, then flatten yourself to the side of the cart. The rest of you get on the floor."

Bearnárd, Charlie, Koko and Dympna each took one of the four rifles and lay on their bellies at the back of the cart. Within a few moments, they had crested the summit of a dune and Komondor tacked left.

"Open up!" shouted Bearnárd. The doors flew open. Only three of the vehicles were visible but, from the plumes of smoke, it was obvious they had all gained a lot of ground.

Bullets flew from the gatling guns mounted on the steamcars, but they didn't have an angle. Mostly they lodged into the ceiling of the heavy oak cart or ricocheted off the cast iron framework. The P-Mec returned fire.

Namemaker fired a single shot, hitting one of the gunners right between the eyes.

Bearnárd missed with his first shot, but hit a driver in the neck with his second.

Dympna aimed at a plume of smoke that hadn't yet summited its dune. She fired into the peak of dune, hoping that the bullets would penetrate all the way through. The driver swerved as he crested, and the vehicle ploughed into the soft sand at the top.

Koko fired wildly, emptying his rifle of ammunition, and hitting nothing. Charlie nudged him to one side and took aim. They were close enough to see that the gunner was none other than Dr Conceptuloco himself. As the cart reached the valley between two dunes, the angle was becoming more acute. Namemaker rushed his shot and missed. He cursed. "All right, close the flippin' doors."

"We'll do the same again next time we tack," said Bearnárd.

A few moments later, they crested a dune and Komondor tacked left. The huge doors of the cart were kicked open and the P-Mec got ready to fire again. There were still some plumes of smoke billowing up where they left them, but no steamcars in pursuit.

"The bustards have given up!" exclaimed Koko. He grinned his manic grin and hugged Charlie Namemaker.

Dympna was a bit more circumspect. She turned to Bearnárd. "Hey big fella, would ya give us a leg up?" She gestured to the roof. Bearnárd linked his fingers and cupped his hands for Dympna to step into. He lifted her, with a roar of effort, as she hauled herself up until her arms and head were at roof level. She glanced around and then let herself drop back down. "Two of the feckers have gone around the outside."

Up front in the traction engine, Komondor had already spotted the two steamcars. He was quite exposed in the cab and he tried his best to keep his head down. He rummaged around hopefully underneath his seat and found what he was looking for, a large long-barrelled revolver. One quick glance over each shoulder told him what he needed to know. There was a steamcar either side of him, but it was the one on his right he was interested in. The gunner on that particular vehicle was the man who had mutilated him – removed his eyes and replaced them with the varilight discs that now sat uncomfortably in the stretched skin of his face. He had also embedded a clock in his forehead. Komondor now had an advantage. Dr Conceptuloco did not want him dead – Komondor was his guinea-pig and he wanted to observe him. For his part, Komondor very much wanted Dr Conceptuloco to suffer, but would also be happy enough to see him dead. It was tricky to drive and shoot at the same time, but Komondor took a pot shot. The air-filled tyre on the front of the steamcar exploded, and car, driver and gunner tumbled over and over, down the side of the dune.

The car came to rest upside-down at the bottom of the massive dune. The driver was trapped beneath, his neck bent awkwardly against the ground. Dr Conceptuloco was thrown clear about halfway down, but continued his descent, rolling and sliding on the soft sand until he was in the path of the huge traction engine. He rummaged under his coat for his pistol but couldn't locate it, so instead tried to climb the dune he had just tumbled down. He scrambled up using hands and feet, but every few yards he caused an avalanche of sand that sent him cascading halfway down again.

Komondor swung the steering wheel to the right and drove toward Dr Conceptuloco. The heavy rollers compressed the sand and the spikes dug in deep. Komondor dropped a gear and slowed slightly, and the traction engine began to haul itself steadily up the steep slope. Dr Conceptuloco looked over his shoulder, an expression of panic creeping onto his face. He tried to traverse the slope, but that caused him to slip further, and a small readjustment of the wheel meant Komondor was on his tail again.

Back inside the cart, the rest of the escapees

were incapacitated. They had managed to shut the doors just in time, but the steepness of the dune – and the fact that Komondor was driving straight up it without tacking – had left them all in a crumpled heap at the back. They had each tried to find something to hang on to, but one-by-one they had slid to the back, crashing into the pile of people whose fingertip grip had already let them down.

"Whut is he doing up there?" exclaimed Koko. "He's going to ground us on a dune!"

There was a piercing scream, followed shortly by a gunshot from outside the cart. Bearnárd, Charlie and Dympna looked at each other questioningly – Charlie shrugged. The traction engine continued its steep climb for a few moments longer, before the feeling of motion ceased. The engine continued chugging.

Finally, the bolts on the cart doors could take the weight of multiple human beings no longer. The long, black, cast iron nails creaked as they pried themselves free of the heavy oak. The doors flew open, and the group of escapees were dumped unceremoniously on to the soft dune in a pile of tangled limbs.

As Bearnárd sat up, he was faced with a horrific sight. At first, he almost laughed – it reminded him of a scene from the moving picture show he had seen in Butare. In the show, the villain had been run over by a traction engine and his legs completely flattened. In reality, of course, the actor had been waist deep in a hole, with a pair of well-pressed trousers laid out in front of him like flattened legs. Bearnárd wasn't quite sure how the actor had suddenly jumped up again – Oisín had said it was probably done with mirrors, but Bunty explained it was done by stopping and starting the movie camera. One thing was certain though, Dr Conceptuloco wasn't going to be jumping up again any time soon. Even if the soft sand had negated some of the crushing, the sharp spikes welded to the roller had ripped his flesh to shreds.

Koko, who was small and light and used to a desert environment, scuttled on his elbows and knees, like a sand lizard, to the grounded traction engine. He climbed up to the cab. The clock in Komondor's forehead was shattered and a slow trickle of blood ran down the side of his nose. Even without any eyes, it was clear he was dead.

"Ah, Komondor! You poor bugger." He kissed his first two fingers, but then didn't know what to do with them. He couldn't close Komondor's eyes, or press them against his forehead. In the end, he put them on his lips – even though he would normally only do that with a woman or a child. He had really liked Komondor. He looked back to Charlie and shook his head before sliding back down the dune.

"What d'you reckon?" asked Charlie, "Can we dig it out?"

"I dun't think a hundred men could dig it out."

Charlie turned to Bearnárd and Dympna. "Now what?"

Dympna looked at the upturned steamcar that

Conceptuloco had fallen from. "We could try and right that and get it going."

"That'd be fine for two of us," said Bearnárd.

"Why dun't we just walk?"

"You're flippin' joking, I hope!"

Koko grinned and gestured to the dune. "This is the last one. It's flat from the bottom of this dune to Isalo. You can see the river port from the top." He pulled a battered pair of brass opera glasses from his overalls. "Have a look."

Charlie hauled himself up the dune, using the grounded traction engine for support. He looked out for a while and then looked back. "It's still a flippin' long way – but it's do-able."

******

The ground was flat, but it was a mixture of sand, gravel, and boulders, that sapped your energy as you walked. It was also, as Charlie put it, 'a flippin' long way.' On top of that, it was hot and there was no shelter save the occasional acacia tree. Dympna was still grumbling about the steamcar.

"It wus upside down!" Koko was taking the grumbling personally. "The pellettes would have spilled out and so would the water."

He took his opera glasses out and looked around. They hadn't been walking for very long, but even he had to admit that Isalo didn't seem to be getting any closer. He scanned the sky hopefully, looking first in front and then behind. "Look an airship! We could make an SOS in the sand."

"It might be one of theirs," Bearnárd took the opera glasses to get a better look. The magnification wasn't great, and the image was a little fuzzy, but there were two notable things about the dirigible. It had a yellow envelope, and Bearnárd was pretty sure that there were only three engines. "I don't believe it! I'm going to have to go back."

CHAPTER 17
Skydock 101 to Isalo

(Mediusday)

The Reliant had left Skydock 101 and set a course full steam ahead for the *Isalo* dessert. With Aoife missing, and the rescue attempt for Bearnárd imminent, the atmosphere on board was tense.

"Skip? I don't want to malign him, but you don't think Bearnárd's message could be a trap, do you?"

"Of course it's a trap." Gonagain threw the pantelegraph message to Bunty. "*Dear Captain Gonagain? Lieutenant Strongman?* Bearnárd would never write like that. It's a warning that something is up."

"So why are we going there?"

"One, he's in serious trouble – he would never have sent the message at all if he wasn't. Two, it's only a trap if you don't know it's a trap – we can guess what we're getting into. And three, he's my brother and, more importantly, he's one of the crew

– rule number one: no one gets abandoned."

"Fair enough, Skip, just checking. What's the plan?"

"Be careful and get him out." replied Gonagain impatiently.

"Not too much detail then – playing it by ear. Jolly good."

Jao had been quizzing Emily Tutu about what had happened when she was left in sleep mode. Emily had gone into a passive state as she ran a search through her sleep mode memory. Then, without warning, her left eye shone bright white and a rectangle of light was projected on the wall. Just like at the moving picture show in Butare, a jerky monochrome moving image appeared. It was Aiofe waving a hand directly in front of her and then taking the trunk – nothing useful that they didn't already know.

"We're going to land in a Trad region soon, Jao. We'll need to hide all the pulsarnite-powered stuff, and that includes Emily."

"Hide a two-metre-tall automaton? On a pokey airship gondola? And how exactly do you expect me to do that Captain?"

"I don't know, Jao, just... just do it, okay?"

"Come on, Emily, let's see if we can find a place you can hide."

"But. I. can. help. to. rescue. Bearnárd. Strong-man."

"I think the captain wants to pretend we are Traditionalists. We can't do that with a two-metre, pulsarnite-powered Emily Tutu standing beside us."

"I. understand."

Jao took Emily Tutu down to the engine room. It was full of bits of machinery, both working and otherwise. Jao was hoping that Emily would look less conspicuous down there. She cleared a space in the corner and got the automaton to stand there whilst she piled pumps, cylinders, compressor motors and goodness knows what else around her.

"This is no use. You're just too big!"

"I. can. make. myself. smaller," Emily gracefully sat herself down with one knee bent and the other leg outstretched, and then became totally inert.

Jao laughed. "Emily, that doesn't make you small, you're just sitting dow..."

Suddenly, the outstretched leg of the automaton bent to ninety degrees at the knee... backwards. The foot of the other leg rotated one hundred and eighty degrees as an arm wrapped itself around the shin. The torso leant forwards and the head bowed until it was facing the pelvis. The remaining arm bent itself backwards and up towards the neck. Emily would now have fitted neatly into a cubic box.

A voice emerged from the centre of the pile of metal. "Does. this. help?"

"*That* is very neat indeed. Yes, Emily, it does help, it helps a lot!" Jao propped a few bits of old machinery around and on top of the pile of metal limbs and finished it off with a few oily rags. It just looked like a pile of old junk. “Emily Tutu, standby mode.”

The green glow emanating from the middle of the pile of old junk changed to bright amber and then dimmed until it was barely visible.

Rajaobelina was just about to leave the engine room when Gonagain’s voice came over the repeater. “Jao, are you in the engine room?”

Jao walked over to the machine and pressed the speak button. “Yes. Why?”

“I want you to soak some old rags in oil and throw them into the furnace with the bloquettes.”

“That won’t do the engine much good, Captain. Why do you want me to do that?”

“I want the engine to pump out some black smoke – make it look like we’re having mechanical problems. Will it do any long-term damage?”

“No, I suppose not. We could be pumping out black smoke for days though – maybe even weeks. If I have to dismantle the engine and clean it out, I won’t be happy – and I’m not climbing into the furnace to scrub that down either.”

Gonagain was already feeling a bit guilty for snapping at Jao about hiding Emily. He sighed, “If either need doing, I’ll do it – you’ll just have to tell me what to do.”

“You can be putting that in writing whilst I dig out some oily rags.”

Jao went to her tool station and dug out some rags. She also pulled out a large tin that was half full of dirty oil from the last engine service. She lay out a square piece of tarp on the floor and began dunking the rags in oil and laying them on top. When she had enough to fill a small hat-box, she bundled up the tarp and threw the whole bundle into the furnace. With a sigh, Jao headed up to the gondola deck to see what the effect was.

Up on the deck, Jao found Bunty unfurling two white flags and mounting one on each side of the gondola. Jao raised a questioning eyebrow.

"Skipper's orders," Bunty responded.

A few moments later, the grey smoke from the chimney began to burn black and thick. This time it was Bunty who looked questioningly at Jao.

"Captain's orders."

The two women were just heading back below deck – Bunty was already halfway down the alternate tread stairs – when they heard the starboard prop slowing to a halt, followed by the creak of the port aileron lifting to stop them going around in circles.

When they arrived back the captain was on his hands and knees with Etoile.

"Is there a problem with the starboard propeller, Captain?"

"Nope. I've just put it in neutral," he replied, without looking up.

"Is there a good reason for that, Skipper?"

"Yes – all part of the plan."

"Perhaps you'd care to elucidate, Skip – Jao and I are somewhat in the dark here."

Gonagain looked up. "Yes. Sorry. I'm still sort of

formulating it – it's not quite clear in my own head yet – but here it is. We fly over the mine with one 'broken' prop and black smoke billowing from the chimney. This will give us a reason to land nearby – to make repairs – plus they'll think we're not able to make a quick getaway. We'll have the white flags out, just to make sure they don't shoot at us."

Shooting at a ship carrying white flags was against the Victoria Convention, and even pirates adhered to it most of the time.

"Okay, Skipper, so we have a reason to land and can do it safely – then what?"

"We make it clear we're Trads – revolvers, mechanical watches and varilight goggles – and ask for help. We generally play nicely with them and distract them whilst Etoile goes and find Bearnárd.

"Sorry, Captain – you say Etoile is going looking for Bearnárd? How does *that* work?"

"It's a trick we've been working on from *How to Train and Domesticate Your Canine Companion*. She's got it sorted – she can find either of you two, or Aiofe, with one hundred percent success rate."

"But she's never even met Bearnárd, Skip; how is she expected to find him?"

"That's a worry, but according to *How to Train and Domesticate Your Canine Companion*, she doesn't need to have met him – it's all done by scent. I've been using one of your hankies, one of Jao's hairbands and a pair of... a garment belonging to Aiofe."

"Okay, Skip, so let's say Etoile finds Bearnárd whilst we're keeping the guards busy. What happens then?"

"Well, that's why I'm trying to strap Beagán's little Smith and Wesson to her tummy – so Bearnárd can free *himself*. The trouble is, it's a hammerless safety, and it's so smooth I can't find a way to secure it properly."

"Captain, I don't want to put a damper on your plan, but if this is a trap – as we suspect – won't they be expecting us? They'll just arrest us on sight."

Gonagain fished his double, half-hunter mechanical out of his waistcoat pocket and opened it up. "It's nearly eleven thirty in the evening Traditional time. All the senior officers will be tucked up in bed. The junior officers and the rank and file won't have been briefed about us – trust me, I know how these people work."

"Okay then, Captain, give me Beagán's pistol and I'll take Etoile down to the engine room and get her ready."

Down in the engine room, Jao cut a rectangle of netting from a bag of bloquettes. She melted some sealing wax and dripped it on to the cut ends to stop them from fraying. Next, she took some heavy-duty envelope repair thread and weaved it around the perimeter of the rectangle, pulled it and knotted the ends. The netting was now slightly dished. Then, she used two more lengths of thread and wove them through each end. She tied one of the threads around Etoile's neck and one around her waist. Finally, she popped the Smith & Wesson hammerless into the new netting pouch.

Momentarily, she thought of Beagán. He hated that revolver. "It's a ladies' gun," he used to complain. "I can't wait 'til I can afford a proper pistol." Then he'd become wistful, "I want a Webley Mark Four."

Jao smiled at the memory. "Okay, Etoile, you're ready for action."

******

Private Lamplighter was busy thinking about his lady friend back home when he first heard the engine noise and so it didn't really register. It was only when it became much louder that he stood up to look around. It was nearly twelve o'clock and he couldn't see anything overhead. He waved his gaslight around him, to check nobody was watching him, before removing his varilights. It was ridiculous that he had to wear his varilights for night shift when he was on lookout and the sun hadn't yet set. Why make it dark when you're supposed to be on lookout? He hadn't dared question it though – wearing varilights when the time was out of sync with daylight was law, even if you *were* a soldier on lookout duty. With the goggles off, he saw a tatty yellow airship, flying low and coming in their direction. He raised his rifle and looked through the sight. One of the props had failed and the engine was burning badly. It was flying white flags. He popped his varilights back on and called to his partner.

"Incoming dirigible with engine problems, flying white flags."

The other guard looked up as the airship was almost directly overhead. "How do you know it's got engine problems?"

"I... I can tell by the sound," he lied.

"So, what do white flags sound like then?"

"Erm... well it stands to reason, doesn't it? If you had engine problems, you'd land if you saw a facility like this. And you'd land with flags of truce at any military facility – just to be sure."

His partner eyed him suspiciously, "Assuming they *are* coming here, we'd best go and meet them at the gate."

******

The Reliant bumped down about a hundred yards from the mine compound. Gonagain sent as much hydrum as possible down to the compressor – as there was no water available for ballast – and released the mooring ropes from their pods.

"Bunty, Jao, before you jump out and secure the ropes, we're all pulsarnite free – yes?"

"Yes, Skip."

"I am."

"Is Emily Tutu hidden?"

"As much as possible, Captain."

"And the pulsarnite rock? Is it still in your bunk?"

"No, Captain, I have to sleep in my bunk."

"So where is it then?"

"I've hidden it in the compressor chamber."

"How'd you get it in there?"

"Emptied all the hydrum into the envelope whilst we were in flight, closed the valve, unbolted the flange seal, popped the pulsarnite in, re-bolted the flange seal, re-vacuumed the chamber and re-opened the valve."

"Oh. Okay. Well done!" Gonagain was stunned. "Right. We stick together at all times, we play nicely with the Trads, we keep our eyes and ears open and we trust no-one."

Gonagain picked up a brown, newsboy cap that belonged to Bearnárd and then picked up Etoile with the same hand. He adjusted the cap to make sure it completely covered the hammerless revolver strapped to Etoile's tummy.

"Okay, let's go."

"Er... Skipper. Maybe take off your bowler – you look a bit odd with two hats."

Gonagain removed his bowler and hung it on the instrument panel. He smiled at his crew and put on his varilight goggles, before leading them down to the loading bay and out the hatch.

Two guards were waiting at the compound gate, lit by their lanterns. Gonagain approached slowly but confidently, whilst Bunty and Jao pegged the ropes.

"Howya? I've got a few mechanical problems. I was wondering if I could get some help?"

"Hands where I can see them, stranger," Private

Lamplighter growled, pointing his rifle at Gonagain.

Gonagain raised his right hand, whilst slowly lowering Etoile to the ground. He slid the cap from under her belly and passed it in front of her nose. "Go find!" he whispered as the little dog sniffed the cap. Etoile scuttled off as Gonagain put the cap on his head and raised the other hand.

"That dog has no loyalty – the first inkling of trouble and she's off."

Lamplighter's colleague approached Gonagain and frisked him. He pulled Gonagain's Peacemaker revolver from its holster, "I'll hang on to that." He then pulled out his double half-hunter, pocket watch by the chain and examined it. He flipped open the front cover and saw the Roman numerals which went all the way up to twelve. He turned the watch over and flipped open the back cover. Inside were the beautiful workings of a mechanical watch – the mainspring, the hairspring, the balance wheel, and escapement, and twenty-one tiny rubies. He snapped it shut and tucked it back into Gonagain's waistcoat pocket.

"Okay, mate, you can put your hands down. I'm going to have to frisk the ladies too, I'm afraid."

He went through the same process, trying to be as brisk and perfunctory as possible. He withdrew with a Saint-Etienne Modéle 1892 and a Colt M1877. He turned to Lamplighter.

"Okay, they're Trads and they're unarmed now."

"What kind of help do you need?" asked Lamplighter.

"If you have a nine-inch, ninety-tooth cog and a one-and-a-half-inch, fifteen-tooth cog going spare, we can fix the propeller drive and be on our way in an hour or two," replied Jao, fitting as many Traditional units of measurement into a sentence as possible. "Failing that, if you have a work bench with a clamp and a diamond file, I can re-tool our damaged ones. And a big tub of engine grease, if you have one."

"You wait out here with Private Lamplighter. I'll see what I can find," replied the guard. Then he turned to Private Lamplighter, "Don't let them back into their dirigible until it's been searched."

The group were still waiting in awkward silence when the steamcars arrived. Lamplighter was impatiently waiting for some help to arrive – he didn't like being left to guard this group on his own. Gonagain was wondering if Etoile would be able to find Bearnárd and, if so, how long it would take. Rajaobelina was hoping there were no good engineers around – they'd soon realise there was nothing wrong with the prop drive if there were. For her part, Bunty was mainly concerned about the loss of their weapons. She felt naked without a pistol and she was rather attached to her Saint-Etienne Modéle 1892.

But the silence was broken, and the thoughts dissipated, when the steamcars hove into view. Two of the vehicles were fully crewed with both driver and gunner. They were driving parallel to each other and the gunners were occupied with holding one end each of a makeshift stretcher, which was made with a pair of tree branches and two jackets. The man lying on the stretcher looked in a very bad way indeed. The two gunner-less steamcars were taking up vanguard and rear-guard positions, so the four vehicles were in a diamond formation. There was an air of panic about the group. The calmest was the driver of the vanguard vehicle. He was a tall, skinny sergeant with a waxed moustache. He eyed *The Reliant* with great interest as he drove past it, and then headed straight for Gonagain and his crew.

"Captain Gonagain, as I live and breathe," he announced, as he stepped off the steamcar and drew his pistol.

"How do you know my name? I don't believe we've met?" replied Gonagain.

"I was given a description. A pavonine captain, of a flying yellow junk heap, who can only get women to crew for him." He looked from Gonagain, to *The Reliant,* to Bunty and Jao. "Check. Check. And check. Spookily accurate."

"For your information, I can get whoever I like to crew *The Reliant*. However, I choose to have only the best. My engineer," he gestured to Jao, "is second to none. There is nothing she can't fix or build. I'd pit her against any of your engineers. My navigator is also first class and there is so much more to her than navigating. She has more skills and knowledge than anyone I have ever met. They are my crew by merit, the fact that they happen to be female is totally irrelevant. They could be captains in their own right."

Landowner shook his head and smiled. "Female captains? Whatever next? So, we have Miss Bunty Goodtime and Miss Rajaobelina...?" his pause was met with silence, so he continued, "And what of Miss Aiofe Trustworthy? Where is she?"

"We parted company – just recently."

"That is a shame. She has something that we want, you see."

"She took all her belongings with her."

"And where was she headed?"

"Victoria, I believe."

"She has a brass neck showing her face in Victoria after fraternising with your motley crew and that debacle at Stanleyville Airdock. We lost some good men there. Still, if she has what we're after, she may yet escape the noose – an achievement that is probably beyond your reach, Captain. And there was another crew member, if I remember rightly – a Miss Etoile...?" He paused briefly again but, realising his mistake, pushed on. "Where is she?"

"We also parted company... even more recently."

"Tsk. You do seem to have problems with your crew, Captain. Okay, Private, take the captain and his crew to the cooler. I'll deal with them later. And have someone search that floating junk heap."

The cooler was a bunker with thick brick walls and no windows, except for the small, barred square in each of the steel cell doors. They looked out into the corridor they came in through. Rajaobelina was locked into the first cell, opposite the main entrance. Gonagain was next, with Bunty Goodtime in the third cell. They could hear some moaning coming from some of the cells further down the corridor.

Gonagain put his face to the bars, "I'm sorry crew, I've let you all down. That was a reckless plan."

"It's not over yet, Skipper; there are still two crew members at large."

"Two?"

"Well, Etoile is still running around somewhere with a pistol strapped to her belly, and Emily Tutu is still hidden in *The Reliant.* Any chance you could get her to come and rescue us, Jao?"

"Not from here."

There was an uncomfortable silence for a few moments, until Jao broke it.

"That was a lovely speech you gave to that sergeant. You said some really nice things about Bunty and me."

"Well, it's all true. Every word of it."

"What impressed me most, Skip, was that he insulted you, *The Reliant and* us – but it was *us* you chose to defend."

"*The Reliant* and I are nothing without a good crew, and you're the best crew I could wish for. Besides, I couldn't really defend *The Reliant,* it *is* a floating junk heap – it wouldn't even be in the air if it wasn't for Jao. And I couldn't defend myself either – he called me 'pavonine'. I don't even know what pavonine means."

There was a pause, before Gonagain asked, "*Am* I pavonine, Bunty?"

"Well… you *are* quite particular about your appearance, and you *do* enjoy the attention of the ladies, but I think calling you pavonine is harsh, Skipper."

Gonagain absorbed this bit of information. If taking pride in your appearance and enjoying the company of young ladies made you pavonine, then being called pavonine wasn't really much of an insult, in his opinion.

CHAPTER 18
Isalo

When Bearnárd announced he was going back to the mine, he was met with a chorus of objections. He had escaped, so his colleagues could do the same… they'd taken their time getting to him, why was he rushing back… and various other reasons.

"If they didn't escape, I'd never forgive myself. And if they do escape, I want to be on that airship with them."

Bearnárd didn't have the nerve to ask anyone to go with him. He looked around at the other escapees, hoping someone would volunteer. They stared back at him vacantly. Surprisingly, it was Koko who first realised what he was waiting for.

"Uh, no. Surry. I'm nut going back. No way!"

Bearnárd looked hopefully at the others.

"Flippin' 'eck, Bearnárd. If it was anyone other than you, I'd tell 'em to stuff it. Go on then."

"Well, I feckin' owe you for getting me on the cart, so I suppose I'm in."

There was another volunteer – a Swaruban man who had ditched the traditional dreadlocks and wore his white hair in corn rows.

"I'm hoping to get back in one of those steam-cars – so it'll have to be just two of us." Bearnárd looked at the Swaruban – he was lean and fit looking and used to the desert environment – but he barely knew him. "Charlie. You and me?"

Dympna gave a sigh of relief. "Listen big man, good luck. I'm headed to the Gold Coast. Come by someday and I'll buy you a beer. Charlie love, look after yerself. Don't get into any more trouble than you need to." Dympna gave them both a hug and turned to Koko, "Koko, ya eejit. Is this river port any closer or what?"

******

By the time Charlie and Bearnárd got back to the traction engine, the steamcar driver who was trapped under his upturned vehicle had managed to free himself and was struggling in vain to right it.

"Need a hand there, mate?" Charlie shouted from behind him.

The driver spun around and began to reach for his pistol.

Bearnárd raised his rifle. "We're not going to hurt you fella, so just hand that over, nice and gently."

The driver grasped his revolver between thumb and forefinger and handed it over.

Bearnárd put it in his belt and slung the rifle

over his shoulder. He stepped up to the steamcar and got a good grip. "On the count of three –one... two... three." The three men got the machine upright again, although it was Bearnárd who did the lion's share of the work.

"There should be a bucket somewhere on this thing," said Charlie, looking at the traction engine. "I'll get water from the boiler and refill the boiler on the steamcar. You two try and find as many pellettes in the sand as you can, and feed them back into the fuel hopper."

Charlie climbed up to the cab to find the bucket. A pair of confused looking carrion starlings were perched on Komondor's head and were pecking futilely at the glass disks where his eyes should have been.

"Shoo!" Charlie waved a hand at them and they flew to a safe distance before turning to watch. As he returned with the first bucket of water, Charlie spotted the bloodstained sand where Dr Conceptuloco had been. "Hey! What happened to Conceptuloco? Was there a whole flock of carrion starlings or something?"

"The others came and took him back."

"And left you?"

"His need was greater than mine, and besides, I had to stay with the steamcar, in case any scavengers came by."

"He's not dead?"

"No."

It wasn't long before the steamcar was up and

running again.

"Now, what?" asked the driver.

"Now, we take your steamcar. We need to go back to the mine."

"But… but if they get the steamcar back they won't come back for me!"

"Well, mate, I suggest you fill your canteen from the traction engine and start flippin' walking."

"But I'll never make it back! If I don't freeze in the night, I'll be cooked by the sun tomorrow."

"Don't go back. If you go that way, you can make it to Isalo Port. If you catch up with the others, tell them Bearnárd said they're not to shoot you."

Bearnárd climbed into the driver's seat and Charlie took the gunner's position. They headed off, literally, into the sunset.

Bearnárd slowed right down as they approached *The Reliant,* trying to keep the engine noise as low as possible.

"You fly around in that thing?" asked Charlie. "You're a braver man than I thought."

Bearnárd ignored him. "Keep a look out. I'm going on board."

Namemaker parked the steamcar behind the dirigible, to keep it out of sight, dismounted and snuck to the bow of the gondola and poked his head around. The compound entrance was completely deserted.

Bearnárd made a swift, silent tour of *The Reliant*; he checked the bridge, the cabins, and the engine room. All the crew's pulsarnite cabinets were closed and locked – their Trad cabinets were all empty. He retrieved his own revolver from his cabinet and was surprised to find Beagán's little hammerless was missing. He remembered Landowner referring to crew members he didn't know. Maybe Beagán had been replaced already. The engine room was a mess – that wasn't like Jao at all. There was a massive pile of junk in one corner. Bearnárd hoped Jao hadn't been replaced too. Then he heard Charlie calling in a stage whisper.

"Bearn! Incoming troops, starboard side!"

He hurried out of the loading bay at stern and around the port side where Charlie and the steamcar were.

"Nothing of any note inside. How much ammunition have you got left?"

Charlie clicked the safety into place and pulled back the bolt on his rifle, careful not to lose an unspent cartridge. "Just one in the chamber."

Bearnárd opened the floorplate of his own rifle and caught the cartridges that fell from the magazine. He then pulled back the bolt, releasing the one in the chamber. "There's three more." He discarded the empty rifle in favour of his own, familiar revolver.

"I know you don't want to hear this, mate," whispered Charlie, "but we should start with worst-case scenarios. You check the morgue and I'll go to the cooler. There's a void under the reception shack; I'll meet you back there."

"I don't want to do the morgue. I don't think I can face that."

"You have to. If they're there, I won't know – I don't know what they look like."

As the search team entered the loading bay of *The Reliant*, Charlie and Bearnárd scuttled into the compound and split up.

Charlie Namemaker headed towards the cooler. The cooler was used for short-term punishment and, also, as death row. He slipped quietly in through the main door and peeked into the first cell. A young, southern woman was sitting in the corner, eyes closed as if meditating. She was scruffy and wearing greasy engineer's overalls, but she was also quite beautiful. It was possible she was *The Reliant*'s engineer, he supposed, but Bearnárd had never mentioned a female engineer.

He moved on to the next cell, where a slim, dapper young man was pacing back and forth. He sensed Charlie looking in and turned sharply. He had Strongman's complexion and colouring.

Namemaker smiled, "Captain Gonagain, I presume."

Gonagain looked at him in surprise. "Am I some sort of celebrity around here? I've never been to Isalo before, and yet everyone seems to know who I am."

Charlie extended an arm awkwardly through the bars, "Charlie Namemaker is the name. I'm with Bearnárd; we've come to get you out of here."

Gonagain shook his hand. "Did Etoile come and

find you?"

"Who's Etoile?"

"The little dog with the gun."

"A dog with a gun? Are you talking in flippin' riddles or something? We'd just escaped when we saw your... airship... at the mine – so we came back to get you."

"So, where's Bearnárd?"

"Searching the morgue."

A lady's voice came from the next cell along, "Well, he doesn't have much faith in us, does he?"

Charlie moved along, to see who owned the voice, and came across a beautiful-looking lady who was a similar age to himself. She was wearing beige jodhpurs and a brown leather waistcoat, cinched in at the waist. She had an amazing figure and long golden curls. Charlie thought he was probably in love. "Who are you?"

"Bunty Goodtime, navigator."

"Crikey – Bearnárd never told me his crew mates looked like a beauty pageant."

"Well, that's very charming of you to say, Charlie, but, rather than standing around making chit-chat, is there any chance you could actually get us out of here?"

"Ah... well, our plan only really got as far as finding you. Getting you out is going to be much trickier. I'm not sure how to go about getting the keys to this place."

Another female voice from the first cell called out, "Charlie?"

Charlie went back to the first cell and found himself face to face with the most striking blue eyes he had ever seen. “Flippin’ ‘eck,” he muttered in astonishment.

Jao ignored his comment. “Listen, this is going to sound odd – both to you and to Bearnárd – but it’s important you follow this exactly. Go and find Bearnárd and tell him to go to the engine room of *The Reliant*. When he gets there, he needs to say, ‘Emily Tutu, awake.’ He then needs to introduce himself.”

“You’re right – that does sound odd. Engine room; Emily Tutu awake; introduce himself. Got it.” Charlie turned to leave.

“Charlie!” Rajaobelina shouted.

Charlie paused and looked back.

“Thank you.”

Bearnárd and Charlie stood in the engine room of *The Reliant*. The search team had been and gone. They hadn’t really disturbed very much – they probably didn’t even know what they were looking for.

“If I didn’t know you better, Charlie, I’d think you were making fun of me.”

“It’s what your engineer said – word for word.”

Bearnárd took a deep breath, for no apparent reason, and announced theatrically, “Emily Tutu, awake!”

Charlie couldn’t help but giggle.

From within the pile of junk in the corner,

Charlie spotted a throbbing amber glow. He nudged Bearnárd and nodded towards it. The glow grew brighter and then turned green. Suddenly, the pile of junk began to move. A few old bits of machinery that Jao had been working on – plus a few she had *intended* to fix – fell to the floor. A couple of old rags followed suit. The clean metal machinery which was now exposed appeared to be moving on its own. Gradually, the shape of a metal man began to emerge.

Bearnárd and Charlie stood open-mouthed. Charlie backed off a step, cautiously, "What the flippin' 'eck is *that*?"

The automaton turned to face Charlie Namemaker. "I. am. Mechanical. Life-form. Emulator. version. two. point. two. Who. are. you?"

Bearnárd, remembering Jao's instructions, interjected, "I'm Bearnárd Strongman, lieutenant of *The Reliant*. This is my friend, Charlie."

"I. am. Mechanical. Life-form. Emulator. version. two. point. two. but. you. can. call. me. M. L. E. 2. 2. Your. presence. indicates. that. Captain. Gonagain. had. a. successful. mission."

"No, not exactly. He needs your help."

"Good. I. was. feeling. superfluous. to. requirements. Let's. go."

Charlie looked at Bearnárd and smirked, "You heard her – let's go!" Then, muttering to himself, "Emily Tutu – M L E 2 2. I like that – that's funny."

By the time the two escapees and the automaton returned to the compound, the sense of chaos from the escape, the return of the injured Dr Conceptuloco, and the arrest of the airtraders, had abated and the entrance gate was guarded once more. “Stop where you are and put the guns down!” shouted Private Lamplighter in a shaky voice.

Bearnárd and Charlie raised their guns and the three continued walking. Lamplighter took a shot at Emily Tutu – she was both the most intimidating and the biggest target. The shot ricocheted off her mercuriumite chest plate, leaving barely a scuff, and the three continued walking. Bearnárd cocked his revolver and straightened his arm. Charlie checked he had one in the breech and took aim. The two compound guards turned and ran.

Bearnárd strolled into the cooler, and looked into the first cell. “Hello, Jao.”

“Bearnárd!”

He moved on to the next cell. “Hello, Osh. What are you doing in there then?”

“I’d have thought that was obvious – I’m rescuing you!”

“Well, get on with it then!” replied Bearnárd, folding his arms.

“Bernie, as entertaining as this banter is, do you think you could stop being a clever bollix and get us out of here.”

“Okay, what’s the plan!”

“Did you bring Emily Tutu with you?”

“She’s outside.”

“Emily Tutu, will you open these doors please?”

shouted Jao. "Start with Bunty's cell."

Emily Tutu strode purposefully into the cooler and stopped at Bunty's door. She took a firm hold of the bars in the door and began to pull. She didn't yank the door, and it was hard to see how much effort – if any – she was putting into it, but cracks began to appear in the brickwork. Suddenly, accompanied by the crash of falling brickwork, the top of the door – complete with doorframe and the odd bit of mortar – was free, leaving a narrow gap to step through.

Bunty emerged through the cloud of brick dust. "Thanks, Emily old girl!" she said casually as she brushed her clothing clean.

Emily repeated the process with Captain Gonagain's door with the same result. Oisín Gonagain and Bearnárd Strongman embraced in a long bear hug.

Gonagain held on as he fought back his tears. "I thought I'd lost you Bernie. I thought I'd lost you," he whispered.

"Rule number one – stay alive," replied Bearnárd.

They both began to laugh. Then Bearnárd became solemn. "Osh. Beagán – he didn't make it."

"I know. We gave him an airman's send off in Lubumbashi."

Bearnárd nodded, "That's something, at least."

Meanwhile, Emily Tutu had set about freeing Rajaobelina. This time she succeeded in removing the door entirely.

"Right," said Jao, "let's get out of here!"

It was precisely this moment when Staff Sergeant Landowner marched in – his revolver cocked and aimed at Gonagain. "Ah, the crew of *The Reliant*. Together again at last – most of you, anyway. How nice that you will all be hanged side-by-side."

Landowner's head was suddenly jerked backwards and a chunky hand, wearing Koko's improvised, bladed knuckle-duster appeared at his throat. The top of Charlie Namemaker's head was just visible over his shoulder. "You know," said Charlie, "that just ain't gonna happen."

Landowner dropped his revolver.

"Do it, Charlie!" said Bearnárd.

"I think we might be needing a hostage, mate – a human shield. Those compound guards have rounded up some support."

"We're not all going to be able to hide behind that skinny yoke." Gonagain gestured to Landowner as he spoke. He looked around for inspiration and his eyes alighted on the door to Jao's cell. "Emily Tutu, can you shield us with that door?"

The automaton strode towards the door, grasped it by the barred window with one hand and by the food hatch with the other, and hoisted it, horizontally, so that it covered the area from her knees to her belly.

The others hunched behind it experimentally. Their legs were exposed, but otherwise they were well-covered.

"Right," said Jao, "*now* let's get out of here!"

"Charlie, would you lead the way?"

Charlie stepped out into the night with Staff Sergeant Landowner in front of him. He moved the blade from the soldier's throat to his eye. "All of you put your weapons down or I start removing bits of him starting with an eye."

"Do as he says, please, men." There was a definite wobble in Landowner's voice. The sound of safety catches and guns being thrown to the floor echoed around them.

Emily Tutu stepped out sideways behind Name-maker. She turned to face the soldiers and repositioned the cell door across her as before. The others scurried through and took shelter behind the door. Gonagain was toting Charlie's rifle, Bunty had Landowner's revolver and Bearnárd was carrying his own pistol. Only Rajaobelina was unarmed.

Crab-like they made their way around the perimeter of the grounds, making sure that nobody snuck behind them. Bunty was keeping an eye on the area outside of the compound. Soldiers followed at a distance. They had surely retrieved their weapons, but none dared show them. Eventually they reached the compound gate and began to back towards *The Reliant*. As they drew level with the yellow dirigible, Gonagain called Charlie towards him.

"Right, Landowner, I'm going to let you into a little secret. My airship is filled with hydrum. If they start shooting at us, we all go up in a ball of flames. So, you tell them whatever you need to, so we can get out of here in one piece."

Landowner nodded nervously.

“Well, go on then!” Gonagain said impatiently.

Landowner cleared his throat. “Listen men! These people are dangerous, desperate and heavily-armed. Do *not* to try to rescue me. I don’t want to put you all at any unnecessary risk. I’m going to go with them. I believe I will be able to convince them to turn themselves in. Failing that, I will bring them to justice myself. So, keep your weapons down and, most importantly, do not shoot at them. I have this under control.”

Charlie Namemaker shook his head in disbelief. Landowner had managed to make his cowardice look like an act of bravery. “What a flippin’ turnip,” he muttered.

One-by-one, they edged their way into *The Reliant*. Emily Tutu was last. She dropped the huge steel door and cranked up the hatch after her.

Gonagain was already at the helm. “Jao, get her fully stoked, quick as you can. Bunty, set a course to the nearest hill, mountain, valley… wherever we can get out of sight the quickest. Emily, get up into the gun turret – make sure they all do as he told them. If anyone even raises a weapon, shoot them. Don’t let them get a shot in first. Lieutenant, get that envelope full and get us off the ground.

“Yes, Cap’n!” replied Bearnárd, then added, “Charlie, search Landowner and tie him up – there’s rope in the hold. Don’t let him out of your sight.”

Charlie looked at Bearnárd open-mouthed. “Yes, Sir!” he replied, with more than a hint of sarcasm in his tone.

"Bunty, what's our bearing?"

"Absolute bearing is one hundred and seventy-five degrees, Skipper. I'm just getting a reading from the anemometer... set a course for one hundred and eighty-nine degrees."

Jao's voice came over the repeater, "We're fully stoked, Captain, engines ready to roll, but won't reach full power for another three millidays."

"Lieutenant, why are we still on the ground?"

"Envelope pressure was very low, Cap'n – we had no ballast or moorings."

"How much longer?"

"We're virtually at sea level but unladen, about seventy-five kilotarps should do it."

"So? How much longer?" snapped Gonagain.

"Seventy-three... seventy-four... seventy-five... seventy-six... seventy-seven... we're off the ground, Cap'n."

Gonagain slammed the port prop into reverse and the starboard into forward.

"Cap'n, there's a steamcar parked right alongside – portside. You're going to need at least one metre relative altitude before you manoeuvre."

Gonagain put the propellers back into neutral and checked his altimeter before realising he hadn't checked their altitude before lift-off. He looked out of the window instead. "Feck it, that'll do," he muttered to himself before re-engaging the props. *The Reliant* spun gracefully to a bearing of around one hundred and eighty degrees and the propellers roared as Gonagain put all three to full speed ahead. He could adjust their course more precisely once they were safe and travelling. He craned his neck to watch the compound guards until they were out of view, then leaned to the voice-repeater.

"Emily, any sign of action down there?"

"They. are. not. taking. up. arms. Captain."

Within a couple of millidays they were out of firing range.

"Good work, crew!" said Gonagain, as he relaxed in his chair. "Fair play all round."

******

Etoile had searched all over for the scent her master had given her. She had gone the long way around, as she didn't like the men her master had been talking to. She had found the scent everywhere, but hadn't found the owner of the scent. It was strongest where the people slept, but most recent in the rooms with broken doors. In the end, she had found it mixed with her master's scent, and followed it back the floating home.

But when she got there, the home was already floating again. She had run around to the big window at the front, but, as she did so, it had turned around and faced the other way. Etoile had found herself under her home as it went higher and higher. She ran along underneath, barking as loudly as she could, but the floating home was making so much noise she could barely hear her own bark.

Eventually her home began to disappear into the distance, and she gave up chasing and sat down. She had never had a nice master before, and she had never belonged anywhere. Now her nice master had abandoned her. She wandered back to where her home had been last and sniffed around, in the vain hope her master – or any of the others – were still there. After a while, she gave up and found a scraggy shrub to sleep under. Not only had she been abandoned, but she was thirsty and cold, and the thing strapped to her belly meant she could not get comfortable. She was thoroughly miserable.

PART 2
Into the Lions' Den

CHAPTER 19
Isalo to Amur

(Annularisday)

Gonagain sat bolt upright in his pilot's chair. He felt a hot flush come over him, followed by a cold sweat. "Etoile! We've forgotten Etoile!"

"Who's Etoile?" chorused Bearnárd and Charlie.

"Etoile! The dog with the gun. Do try to keep up chaps," replied Bunty.

"I've just escaped from that place twice; I'm not going back again for some flippin' mutt."

Gonagain jumped up and marched over to Charlie Namemaker and squared up to him. They were almost the same height, but Charlie was much stockier. "*I'm* captain of this airship, and *I* say where we go and where we don't go. Anyone want to tell Namemaker what rule number one is?"

There was a pause whilst the crew tried to work out which *specific* rule number one was most appropriate for this occasion. Gonagain didn't wait. "Rule number one is 'No man gets left behind'."

Charlie opened his mouth to speak, but then paused, glancing at Bearnárd. "Aye-aye, Chief."

Gonagain retained eye contact with Charlie. "Bunty, find us somewhere to hide, and maintain co-ordinates above. Lieutenant, take the helm. I'm going to get the kite."

Down in the hold, Gonagain located the kit bag marked 'night kite'. He emptied it into a pile of bamboo canes, brass fittings, and a black silk sheet. He began to assemble the kite – passing the canes through sleeves in the silk, then bending and joining them with the brass fittings. Before long, he had a huge crescent-shaped kite which filled the hold entirely.

Rajaobelina appeared at the door. "Do you want me to fly it? I'm much lighter than you."

"Thanks for the offer, Jao, but I wouldn't put you at such a risk. Besides, I have to show Namemaker that *all* crew members are important and that I wouldn't ask anyone to do anything I wouldn't do myself."

"You don't have to prove anything to anyone, Captain."

"I need to lead by example; it's the only way I know."

"I bought you your pulsarnite pistol, a pair of my overalls and one of Bunty's scarves."

"Thanks, Jao. Will you get all the ropes you can find and tie them together? I'll send up a flare."

"Of course," Jao turned to leave and then turned back, "Captain. Be careful. Please."

Their eyes met and there was a moment of connection more intimate than between captain and crew. Gonagain smiled, "I will Jao. I promise."

Gonagain set his varilight goggles to midday; he wanted maximum light for landing. He wore his pulsarnite pistol holster *under* his jacket and put on a sherpa bag *over* it. He wore the bag on his front, rather than his back – the kite was going to be on his back. He dropped a flare gun and a bunch of flares into it. Over the top of everything, he wore Jao's overalls. Jao was tall for a woman and wore her overalls baggy. He was decidedly average height for a man and very trim. As a result, the overalls fitted him quite well. Finally, he tied Bunty's scarf over his bowler hat, knotted under his chin. Fixed firmly in place, it served as a crash helmet. It was as he was crawling under the kite, that Charlie Namemaker appeared at the door.

"Jao said you needed help."

Gonagain didn't need any help, but understood what Jao had done.

"Help me get into this kite and out of the hatch without damaging it will you," Gonagain said.

Charlie helped to strap him in and then held the kite steady.

"Get Lieutenant Strongman to open the hatch."

Charlie leaned over to the voice-repeater. "Open the hatch Bearn… Lieutenant."

"Will do."

As the hatch opened, Gonagain side-stepped towards it until, one wing out and one wing in, he stood on the edge of the gangway. He crouched down. “Hands away!” he said and, as Charlie stepped back, Gonagain toppled sideways into the abyss. The trailing wingtip cleared the top of the hatch by mere millimetres.

Charlie ran to the edge of the gangway, just in time to see Gonagain plummeting into the darkness and out of sight. “Flippin’ ‘eck! I thought he was brave to fly around in *this* pile of junk.”

******

Gonagain was falling like a stone. He twisted his body around until he was facing the ground and the rushing air caught the kite. Suddenly he was gliding on the thermals like a raptor. He spotted a level area of scrub near – but not too near – the mine compound and, pulling a string with his right hand, steered the kite towards it. He passed over it a couple of times before attempting the landing. Landing wasn’t anywhere near as dangerous as leaping from the airship, but the last thing he needed was to damage any of the bamboo poles. Eventually, pulling and releasing the strings on both sides, he eased down and landed as if he had just jumped off a small step.

After weighing down the kite with some stones, Gonagain set a tiny flare. It was too small to be visible from the compound, and was a slow-burner that would keep going for at least thirty millidays. He made sure it was far enough from the kite not to set light to it.

"Right," he muttered to himself. "Where would Etoile have gone?"

******

Etoile was shivering under her sparse little shrub. The desert was virtually silent, but every now and again she would hear a noise and look up. It was one these occasions, when she was looking up, that she sniffed the air. *Master!*

She emerged cautiously from her hideaway. It was pitch black now and she couldn't see more than a few metres in front of her. She sniffed the air again and followed her nose. Then she heard a voice. It was just a whisper, but she knew that voice. "Etoile? Etoile? Here, girl." Etoile barked loudly and ran towards the voice. "Shhhhh, Etoile. Quiet now." Etoile barked loudly again. Then, coming out of the gloom, she saw him – Master. She ran to him and jumped up – hitting him squarely in the groin.

"Ouch! Shhh, Etoile. Shhh."

She licked him on the face and neck and jumped around him whimpering with joy and excitement. Her master had come back for her!

The sound of Etoile barking, in the normally silent desert, caught the attention of the compound guards. Within seconds, the bright white searchlights were on and sweeping over the sand dunes and the scrub. Etoile barked again. "Shhh, Etoile, you'll get us in trouble." A low hum began, which quickly increased in pitch to a headache-inducing whine. The security siren.

"Now look what you've done!"

Gonagain lifted Etoile and put her in the sherpa bag, taking the flares and gun out to make room. He buttoned up the overalls to secure her, so only her head was visible. They were both glad of each other's body warmth.

Gonagain set off at a trot to find the kite, but soon found himself re-tracing his steps. He had forgotten to take stock of his landing position and had no idea where the kite was. The sound of shouting voices was just audible, and dozens of lanterns bobbed up and down in the distance.

"Where the feck is the kite?!" he whispered angrily to himself. His heart was racing. "Right. Take a deep breath, keep calm, don't panic."

Zigzagging across the scrub as methodically as he could, he searched for the black kite while the voices got louder and louder. He reached the point where the scrub gave way to dunes. He had gone too far and would have to retrace his steps once more, and walk *towards* the searching guards. Their varilight goggles had changed from a dull purple glow to a warm orange as their artificial dawn grew brighter. Gonagain was aware that his own goggles were set to midday and would be a bright yellow. He tugged the brim of his bowler hat down and kept his eyes to the ground.

Eventually Gonagain stumbled across his kite, literally, and breathed a sigh of relief. The dull ember of the faulty flare glowed nearby. He strapped himself back into the kite and, crouching down, tried to use the black silk kite as camouflage. He could hear the voices of the search party loudly now, and the searchlights were sweeping ever closer. At least Etoile had quietened down and was contenting herself with licking his neck and chin.

With his varilights set to midday, he could see *The Reliant* drifting towards him; the dim lights of the bridge were quite bright when viewed through the goggles. He hoped the search party's dawn setting was less clear.

When the airship was within about a hundred metres, Gonagain lit another, brighter, flare. Instantly, the voices behind him became more animated; the guards would be right on top of him in no time. He watched as *The Reliant* adjusted its course and increased its speed, he could actually see his crew – they were all on the bridge looking for him – Emily Tutu was pointing straight at him. The dirigible passed straight over his head and Gonagain spotted the rope they were trailing behind them – it narrowly missed the tip of his wing as it came past, and he had to turn and chase it, fighting against the resistance his wings created. He grabbed at the rope and it ran through his hand, burning his palm as it went, but he held on regardless. Eventually he found a knot with a loop that Jao had thoughtfully tied; he slipped it around his wrist and it pulled tight, yanking him off the ground and nearly dislocating his shoulder in the process. He was airborne again and gaining height. He covered his bright goggles with his free arm until he was high above the ground. As he passed over the heads of the guards, he could see that they were still intent on reaching the flare and they didn't even look up. He found that Jao had also passed a short metal bar through a knot in the rope – giving him somewhere to put his feet and taking the strain from his arm. Etoile had not stopped frantically licking his neck throughout.

"You're okay, girl," reassured Gonagain, "No-one gets left behind."

Emily Tutu hauled in the captain and his dog – hand over hand – until they were within a few metres, before tying off the rope. They would have to land before they could safely board the ship.

******

Rajaobelina handed her captain his fourth cup of hot tea. He was sitting in the mess, wrapped in every blanket aboard the ship – about a dozen of them. He had started shivering now, which was a good sign. He had been towed behind *The Reliant* for over half a deciday before they found somewhere safe to land, and both he and the dog were freezing. She had struggled to get him to take off his cold clothes, but eventually convinced him that he would warm up quicker if he was naked under the blankets. Etoile was in there with him – she would not be separated from her master for *any* reason.

Jao felt a huge rush of love for her captain, and thoughts of Aoife Trustworthy were forgotten. It wasn't a passionate, yearning love, but the love of a special friend. He had risked his life to save his dog. It was a matter of principle to look after his crew – human or otherwise. It was his underlying self-doubt that meant he was constantly proving himself to others – and himself. It was his natural empathy that meant he couldn't leave Etoile behind. And now he was sitting naked, shivering, and vulnerable and swaddled in blankets, drinking hot tea, and looking adorable.

"I don't know why I'm still shivering. I actually feel quite hot now," he said meekly.

"Your body is confused. As soon as you stop shivering, you can go to bed and get some rest. You'll be fine in the morning."

"Where are we heading?"

"Amur."

"What's in Amur?"

"Charlie says it's a big market town – a Geo region, but with a black-market in Traditional paraphernalia. We've lost half of our weapons and we're short on supplies – it sounds like a good place to stock-up."

"We need to start trading again too – we've not

bought or sold anything since New Year's Eve."

Jao smiled. "We'll get back to that soon enough," she paused. "What are we going to do with that big lump of pulsarnite?"

"I don't know, Jao. I'll have to think on that," he replied pensively.

CHAPTER 20
Amur

(Minimusday)

None of the crew of *The Reliant* had ever been to Amur before, and Gonagain was keen to find the market. He had fully recovered from his kite flight and so had Etoile – although she hadn't left his side since.

"I'd come with you and show you around," said Charlie, "only I can't go out like this." He gestured at his convict's overalls.

"What do you think, Jao? Would it be worth trying on some of Beagán's clothes?" asked Gonagain cautiously.

"Well… yours are too slim, and Bearnárd's are too long…" she eyed up Charlie. "He *might* just squeeze into some of Beagán's."

Five minutes later and Charlie emerged from

Beagán's cabin, pulling the gusset of Beagán's breeches from between his buttocks as he went. "They're a bit snug, but they'll do for now," he grinned. "I don't suppose I could borrow some cash to buy something that fits properly?"

Everyone looked to Gonagain.

"I'll tell you what, we have a vacancy for an aircraftman. You could earn a few ariary if you like – and I'll give you an advance"

"I dunno," replied Charlie, "It's a kind offer – and I'm grateful – but… aircraftman, at my age, and with my experience?"

"You have flying experience?" queried Gonagain.

"Well… I'll put my hands up and say I don't think I've ever piloted a Sparrow 3 before – not one as old as this, that's for sure – but I have flown a Dream Cloud Club Class, a Guppy Whale, a Hawk Irascible, and just about everything in between."

Bearnárd whistled his admiration.

"Seriously?" asked Gonagain.

"Deadly."

"In what capacity and what rank?"

"I was a err… supplier, and I was the skipper."

"It looks like you're over-qualified and out of my price range then."

"Look… I'm not in a great bargaining position here," he gestured to his ill-fitting clothing and pulled the gusset from between his buttocks again. "An aircraftman's salary will do for now, if you could just do something about the job title. It's flippin' embarrassing at my time of life."

"How about 'Pilot Officer'?" suggested Gonagain.

"That'll do. What did you pay your previous aircraftman?"

"Bed, board and beer-money."

Charlie looked Gonagain askance.

"He had no experience!" Gonagain exclaimed defensively, "or negotiating skills."

Charlie grinned, despite himself.

"How about ten thousand ariary a week?" suggested Gonagain.

"Fifteen thousand."

"Twelve."

"Thirteen."

"Done."

"I flippin' have been," muttered Charlie.

******

Amur Market was everything Charlie had promised and more. Gonagain was stunned that he had never discovered it before. It was a long, broad, cobbled boulevard with a glass roof that covered it in its entirety and made it a perfect venue in all weather. The roof was supported by ornate steel, gothic arches, which rose grandly from the half-pillars which decorated the adjacent buildings. It reminded Gonagain of a cathedral, or a grand, city railway station. It was vast and, unlike many markets which were a hotchpotch affair, organised into departments. Consumables were at one end and non-consumables at the other. They were then subdivided into, for example, clothes and shoes, tools, and materials. Above it all was a sign which read 'Amur Super Market'.

Charlie caught a glimpse of Gonagain's and Bearnárd's expressions of awe.

"We're lucky – it's Minimusday. The 'Pinkyday' market is always the best."

Gonagain loved being at a market – it was a microcosm of society. Everybody had a social standing, and everyone knew their place. You could tell who was who, just by looking at them. In fact, you could tell just by their hats.

Standing by an elaborate cast-iron stove, outside an exclusive lodge, were the top-hats. These were the gentry, the landlords. They owned the land the market was on, the land that the produce was from, or the factories the goods were manufactured in. They were sipping port and keeping a watchful eye.

Then there were the black bowler-hats – the money lenders. *Everyone* hated the money lenders, but nobody would dare say so. They were a necessary evil.

Next in the social standing were the brown bowler-hats. These were self-made men, airtraders, importers, exporters, shopkeepers, and manufacturers. The newsboy caps were their right-hand men – shop assistants, security, and deputies.

The flat caps were porters and stevedores – usually employed by the market, but some enterprising young men were freelancing.

At the bottom of the pile were the hatless – beggars, scroungers, and thieves mostly. Some were there in the hopes of earning a few ariary. No one respectable would *ever* be seen at a market without a hat.

"Right," said Charlie, "I'm going to get myself some new threads. I won't be long, and then I'll introduce you to the right people – you have a look around."

"I'm going back to *The Reliant* to keep Jao company, Skipper. We'll come back when someone returns to watch over Landowner and the ship."

Gonagain was surprised, but pleased. He had expected Bunty to be straight into the market, rooting around for bargains, but she and Jao had become much closer recently, and had taken to going out together during the daytime. "Okay, Bunty. Bernie, it's just you and me, and Etoile. Let's see if we can find a stall selling firearms."

"Don't rush into buying anything, Chief," said Charlie, "I know who's who around here – I can get you a good deal."

When Gonagain and Bearnárd met up with Charlie again, he was sporting a dapper three-piece suit, a penny-collar shirt, and a knitted tie. He looked almost respectable.

"Charlie! Are you going to a wedding?" Bearnárd

jibed.

"Bog-off Bearn, you turnip – you're just jealous 'cause I've got a bit of style."

"We found a trader with pulsarnite pistols, but Osh needs a replacement for his Peacekeeper."

Charlie gestured for them to follow him. "I know just the man for both of you."

They weaved their way through the market until they reached a huge stall selling reams of fabric. The stall holder had his back to them but, with his shaved head and stocky build, he looked not unlike Charlie Namemaker.

"Morning, Commodore!" shouted Charlie cheerfully.

The stall holder spun around; he was sporting the most splendid handlebar moustache. "As I live and breathe!" he exclaimed, "Charlie Namemaker! I 'eard you was brown-bread."

"Rumours of my death have been greatly exaggerated. The S.A.G. finally caught up with me. They reported me dead and sold me off to Trad extremists," he explained, "But it takes more than death to keep Charlie Namemaker down."

"Well, I never! What are you up to now?"

"P.O. on a trading vessel."

"What are you flying?"

"It's a, erm... Sparrow 3."

The stall holder let out a belly laugh. "Pilot officer on a Sparrow 3? You've gone down in the world, haven't you?"

"It's temporary." He gestured to Gonagain and

Bearnárd. "This is Captain Gonagain and Lieutenant Strongman. And *this* is Harry 'The Commodore' Twoships."

The three men shook hands cautiously.

Charlie lowered his voice. "The captain, is in need of a gunpowder handgun, and Bearnárd needs a pulsarnite pistol. Have you got anything?"

"Step right this way, gentlemen." Harry Twoships' stall was made up of almost a dozen handcarts arranged roughly in a rectangle – he took them to a cart in the far corner. "I believe I have exactly the fabric you're looking for right here," he announced loudly.

Twoships moved several reams of fabric aside, and located a trapdoor in the cart. Using his fingernails, he lifted the door to reveal a hidden compartment. "Feast your mincers on that lot. Something for everyone. Whatever takes your fancy."

There was an array of firearms, displayed neatly. Gonagain immediately spotted a Peacemaker. He lifted it carefully and opened the chamber, bringing it up to eye-level to check the barrel. Twoships put his hand on Gonagain's and pushed it down.

"Keep it below the height of the screen, if you don't mind," he said, gesturing toward the piles of fabric surrounding the secret stash.

"Oh. Right. Sorry. How much for the Peacemaker?"

"Normally twelve hundred ariary, but as you're a friend of Charlie's, fourteen hundred," he joked and nudged Charlie theatrically. "I can let you have it for a grand."

"Flippin' 'eck, Commodore! These people are my friends!" protested Charlie. "Seven hundred."

"Nine hundred."

"Eight."

"You'll bankrupt me, Charlie Namemaker! Go on then, eight hundred."

Charlie looked at Gonagain. Gonagain shrugged. Charlie gave a barely perceptible nod.

"Eight hundred it is then," said Gonagain, tucking the Peacemaker into his belt and fishing in his jacket pocket for his money pouch.

Twoships re-covered his secret stash and cleared a new space, revealing another compartment.

"Now, Lieutenant, what's your preference for a pulsarnite piece? I've got Daison, Bæliss or Çinclair."

"Bæliss. Çinclair are cheap tat and Daisons are overpriced."

Twoships nodded, "Very wise." He picked out a weapon. "The Bæliss Deka. Ten whole grams of pulsarnite in these – very powerful. Some people find them a bit bulky, but a man of your stature and frame…"

Bearnárd felt it for heft and grinned, "How much?"

"Fourteen hundred – the pulsarnite alone is worth eight hundred."

Bearnárd turned to Charlie. "Do your stuff Charlie."

******

The three men made their way back to *The Reliant* – Etoile followed Gonagain so closely she kept clipping his heels.

"So," said Bearnárd, "is Harry Twoships really a commodore?"

"Nah. It's just his nickname."

"Why do they call him that?" asked Gonagain.

"On account of him having more than one ship," replied Charlie, as if it was a stupid question.

"Of course. Harry Twoships. He has two ships."

"Actually, he's got four. Done very well for himself has Harry Twoships."

When they arrived back at *The Reliant*, Bunty was sitting in Jao's folding chair, soaking up the warmth of the weak winter sun.

"Anything to report, Bunty?"

Bunty opened one eye. "No, Skip – all quiet." She closed her eye again.

Inside, Gonagain and Strongman found Jao in the mess making breakfast for Digby Landowner, whilst Emily Tutu stood guard.

"What's *he* doing in here?" demanded Bearnárd accusingly.

"He needed to use the latrine and he was hungry," Jao replied defensively.

"You know it was him that killed Beagán? Shot him in cold blood. Beagán had already been overpowered."

Rajaobelina turned to Landowner, waiting for him to deny it, but he returned her gaze with a sheepish look. She hurled a bowl of hot porridge at him.

"No, Bearnárd, I did *not* know that," she said as she left the mess.

Landowner hurriedly scraped scalding porridge from the inside of his collar, bleeding from a gash on the bridge of his nose where the bowl had hit him.

"I didn't know that either, Bernie," said Gonagain.

"So, what are we going to do with him then, Osh? A bullet in the head would seem appropriate, but a bit too easy."

"We're not going to kill him, Bernie, that would make us as bad as him."

Bearnárd looked at Gonagain with an expression of shocked disappointment. "You're kidding? It's not like we've never killed anyone before."

"It's always been self-defence though – or at least a fair fight. Killing him now would be an execution. We're better than that."

Bearnárd sighed an acknowledgement and turned to leave.

"Where are you going?" asked Gonagain.

"I can't sit and play nice with *him*, Osh."

"No-one said you had to play nice, Bernie, I just said you can't *kill* him. Why don't I leave the two of you to work it out?"

Bearnárd brightened. "I could live with that."

"Emily, stand guard outside. I'll be on the bridge

if anyone needs me."

Twenty millidays later, Bearnárd joined Gonagain on the bridge. He had a nasty bruise coming up on his left cheek and a slow trickle of blood coming from his left nostril, which he was dabbing with a handkerchief.

"Feeling better, Lieutenant?"

"Yes, Cap'n. Much better, thank you."

"And how is our guest?"

"He'll live – I expect."

******

Whilst Jao and Bunty were perusing his selection of revolvers, Harry Twoships pulled Charlie Namemaker to one side.

"So honestly – what are you doing as a pilot officer on a Sparrow 3? Are you working an angle?"

"The lieutenant helped me escape from the Trad fundamentalists and the captain flew us out of there. I sort of owe them."

"You don't really believe that, do you." It was a statement rather than a question. "You make your own destiny. You always say that yourself. Why don't you come and work for me? I'll make you a captain."

"I owe him hard cash as well, Commodore."

"I'll lend you the money to pay him back."

Charlie had serious reservations about working under Captain Gonagain – he hadn't liked the way he had been spoken to a couple of times to start with.

He also didn't know where he stood with Gonagain *or* Strongman – one minute it was all 'Osh' and 'Bernie', the next it was 'Lieutenant' and 'Captain'. But he had seen the way that Harry Twoships operated, and he hadn't gotten rich through altruism. Being indentured to The Commodore was not appealing at all.

"That's a kind offer, Commodore, but I think there's an angle here, if I can find it. Besides," he nodded towards Bunty, who had just found a Modéle 1892, "I haven't had the chance to turn on the old Namemaker charm with the navigator."

"You sly old dog," Twoships winked. "Well, the offer is there."

When Bunty, Jao and Namemaker returned to *The Reliant*, it was deserted except for Emily Tutu, who was standing stiffly beside the loading bay gangway, keeping guard.

"Hello, Emily old girl, has the skipper got you on lookout?"

"Yes. he. and. the. lieutenant. have. taken. the. captive. to. the. Amur. Geokinetic. Guards. headquarters."

"Good. I'm glad he's not on board anymore," said Jao.

"Here. is. the. captain. now."

Bunty and Jao turned, to see Gonagain and Strongman strolling toward them. There was a lightness to their gait that gave off an air of breezy good-humour. Bearnárd was sporting a dark bruise on his cheek.

"What happened to your face, Bearnárd?" Jao asked with concern.

Bearnárd touched the bruise, winced slightly, and then laughed. "It's nothing, Jao. You should see the other fella." The brothers chuckled as if at some in-joke. "We just turned Landowner in to the Geo Guards. They gave us a reward – a thousand ariary each – drinks are on us tonight."

"We'd probably have got more if he was in better condition." They laughed again, childishly. They were clearly enjoying being back together again. "Where's Charlie? I want to find out where the craic is in Amur."

******

The Malomir Club and Casino was vibrant and *very* upmarket. There was a good atmosphere, but it wasn't the craic that Gonagain had in mind. His good humour of earlier in the day had dissipated anyway. He was at the bar, ordering another round, when Bunty joined him.

"What's on your mind, Skipper? You look like you have the weight of the world on your shoulders."

"I've been thinking about something that gobshite Landowner said about Aoife. 'If she has what we're after, she may yet escape the noose.' She doesn't have what they're after, does she? It's in *The Reliant's* compressor chamber."

"Ah. I see. We really aren't responsible for her, Skip. We just got caught up in her business. She was never honest with us."

"I know, I know. But... I just feel..." he didn't finish the sentence.

"Are you in love with her, Skip?"

"No! No, nothing like that. I do like her, though. And we parted on bad terms. And she was right about a lot of stuff. The thought of her facing the noose really doesn't sit right."

"You want to save her, don't you?"

"Yes."

"Listen, Skip. Why don't we talk about this in the morning? This is supposed to be a celebration! We have Bearnárd back, we have a new pilot officer, and you got two thousand ariary for turning in Landowner. Both you and Charlie look like you lost a diamond and found a garnet."

"What's wrong with Charlie?"

"I don't know, Skip. Why don't you go and talk to him? Make him feel welcome."

Charlie was nursing a large whiskey and half-heartedly joining in with Bearnárd and Jao, who were both in a jovial mood. He had played the charming gentleman all day with Bunty, but she and Jao had been so busy shopping and chatting that she had barely even acknowledged him. He had ended up carrying a trunk and a bag of clothes back to *The Reliant* whilst they walked on ahead, gossiping in hushed tones. The captain and Bearnárd were thick as thieves as well. Why wouldn't they be?

They were blood after all. Charlie was a spare part, socially and functionally. He needed to get his life back on track and he didn't think the opportunity would arise whilst he was working on *The Reliant*. He was pondering it all when Gonagain got his, and everyone else's, attention by tapping his glass with a knife.

"Everybody... everybody please. I'd like to start by thanking Jao and Bunty for everything they have done over the last few hands to help me find and rescue Bernie."

Bearnárd snorted loudly.

"Well... finding him anyway. It's great to have him back. I'd also like us to take a moment to remember Beagán. He was a good lad and we will all miss him. But we have a new crew member now and, as this is supposed to be a celebration. I'd like to propose a toast, to welcome Charlie Namemaker on board. To Charlie!"

"TO CHARLIE!"

Charlie brightened a bit as they all raised their glasses and Gonagain slipped into the seat beside him.

"Welcome to the crew, Charlie. How are you finding it?"

"It's good, Chief, it's good..."

"But?"

"I'm not sure where I stand. One minute you and Bearnárd are all friendly like... and the next, it's all official – Captain this, and Lieutenant that."

"You know what it's like captaining a ship, Charlie. It's not the time or place for democracy. You need a chain of command. When we're on *The Reliant*, especially on the bridge, we keep it all official. And I'm captain. Off-duty, we're all equal."

"So, I can call you Oisín when we're off duty, can I?" Charlie asked sceptically.

"Yes."

"And you'll call me Officer Namemaker whilst we're on board?"

"If you want me to."

"You don't do that with the ladies." Charlie nodded towards Bunty and Jao.

"They always call me Skipper or Captain!"

"But you never call them Officer."

"No, you're right. I should probably address that," Gonagain replied pensively. There was a brief pause before he changed the subject. "I heard you tell Twoships that the S.A.G. finally caught up with you – why were they after you?"

"Oh, err… I was a wanted man for a while."

"Obviously. What were you wanted for?"

Charlie hesitated, then sighed, "Piracy, hi-jacking and dirigible theft."

Gonagain glared at Bearnárd accusingly.

"I never thought to ask, Osh. We had other things on our minds. He doesn't look like a pirate."

"What do you think pirates look like? Wooden legs, hook hands and eye patches?"

"To be fair," interjected Charlie, "most pirates *do* look a bit like that."

"Shut up, Charlie! Bearnárd, you bought a hi-jacking, dirigible-thieving pirate on board *The Reliant.*"

"I'm sorry, Osh – but you never asked either!"

Gonagain opened his mouth to respond, but Bearnárd was right – he'd taken Charlie on without due diligence. There was an uncomfortable silence for a few moments, which Charlie eventually broke.

"So… Oisín, shall we find somewhere livelier?"

The Pioneer tavern was much more suitable for a celebratory night out. There was music and dancing and a much livelier clientele. Gonagain had been up dancing with Jao.

Jao was wearing a green velvet dress and her hair was loosely, but elegantly, tied up. She was also wearing make-up. Her eyes had a smoky, sultry look about them, and her lips were red and shiny. She looked stunning and, when Gonagain wasn't dancing with her, other men were virtually queueing up to ask her to dance.

As Gonagain came back to his seat (Jao had only made it halfway back before being whisked back to the dancefloor), Bunty caught his eye. She was gritting her teeth and staring pleadingly at him. Charlie was beside her, topping up her glass with champagne. Gonagain read the situation.

"Would you like to dance, Bunty?"

"I suppose it would be a sackable offence to turn the captain down," she replied, as she leaped eagerly to her feet.

On the dancefloor, Bunty let out a sigh of relief.

"Thank you, Skipper, I've been trying to get away from Charlie for ages."

"I think he's a bit smitten. I take it you're not interested?"

"Flaky scalps and barrel-bodies are not really my cup of tea. Besides he's old enough to be my… my older brother. You know I like them younger."

"Oh, poor Bunty!" Gonagain replied mockingly. "You can't blame him for trying. He's a red-blooded man who's been stuck in an all-male dorm, and you're a very attractive woman."

"That would have been flattering if you hadn't mentioned the all-male dorm."

She had expected Gonagain to laugh, but his attention had been distracted as Jao spun past in the arms of a Geo Guard.

"Talking of very attractive women, Jao looks beautiful this evening, doesn't she?"

"Yes," replied Gonagain, his eyes still fixed on Jao. "Now you come to mention it, I suppose she does."

Bunty and Gonagain returned to the table, shortly followed by Jao. She looked worried.

"Captain – we have a problem. The man I was just dancing with – it was Private Cooperson."

Gonagain wracked his brain, trying to remember where he had heard the name before.

"I thought he was familiar, but it wasn't until he said his name that it came to me. And it gets worse, his captain is here too."

Suddenly it dawned on him and Gonagain's eyes

widened, "From the Lubumbashi munitions factory?"

"That's him."

"Did he recognise you?"

"Not yet – but he kept saying he knew me from somewhere."

"Okay, crew, we need to get out of here."

Bearnárd and Charlie looked confused.

"What's the problem, Osh?"

"The men we stole Emily Tutu from, after Jao immobilised them with her stun gun, are in this tavern. We need to leave before they recognise us. We may need you or Charlie to create a diversion."

"I think we may be too late, Skipper, they're coming over."

Charlie Namemaker jumped to his feet and picked up his tankard of ale. He stepped back towards the dancefloor until one of the dancing couples gently bumped against him and then he dropped the tankard. He spun around and grabbed the gentleman by the collar. "Oi! You just spilt my drink." He punched him in the face, sending him crashing into a table of young bachelors. Suddenly there was mayhem. The bachelors had assumed the man was drunk and started to attack him. Charlie, suddenly switching sides, dived in to rescue him, and tankards and glasses began to fly. Within a few moments, half the tavern was involved.

"Okay, let's get out of here!"

"Osh, I should stay and help Charlie."

"He'll be arrested. We'll need you to go and bail

him out in the morning. You're the only other person the Geos aren't after."

Bearnárd hesitated.

"Come on, Bernie!"

The group skirted around the melee, mingling with as many people as possible. Through the tangle of bodies, Gonagain could see the Geo captain. He was looking toward the table they had just vacated, but was apparently unable to see it, or get to it, because of the fracas in front of him. As they left the tavern, Gonagain turned to see how Charlie was doing. He was fairing pretty well against a disgruntled dancer, a table full of bachelors and the intervening Geo Guards. He looked like he was even enjoying it.

CHAPTER 21
Amur to Victoria

(Pollexday)

The next morning, Bearnárd returned from the Amur Geokinetic guardhouse, a few thousand ariary lighter but with Charlie alongside him. Charlie was given a standing ovation by the rest of the crew. He was sporting a bruise on his left cheek that matched Bearnárd's and made it look like they had joined some sort of cult.

"Well done, Charlie, that was mighty. Above and beyond the call of duty."

Charlie smiled modestly, "I saw what you did for the mutt, Chief. I knew you wouldn't leave me there. And a couple of bumps and bruises never did anyone any harm."

"Well, as a reward for your valour, the money I advanced you for your suit is yours. There's no need to pay me back." Gonagain turned to the rest of the crew, "Right. Shall we get out of here before anyone else gets captured, arrested or detained in any way?"

"Chief? About the piracy thing. I promise I won't try and steal *The Reliant* from you."

"That's good to hear, Charlie."

"There ain't much of a market for Sparrow 3s anyway."

As soon as they were safely away from Amur, Gonagain called the entire crew to the bridge. He was in official business mode.

"We've set a course for Victoria," he announced, "and I want to explain why we're going there. Whilst you were in Isalo, Lieutenant, we briefly had an aircraftman who was also a Traditionalist spy. She left the ship to go to Victoria, believing she had some pulsarnite she had stolen from the Geos – but that pulsarnite is still on-board."

Charlie's eyebrows raised involuntarily.

"When the Trads discover she doesn't have it, they'll probably hang her. I intend to use the pulsarnite to buy her life. They may not be amenable to this; in which case I will try to rescue her another way. Now I realise that some of you have never met her, and others may not particularly like her, but she *was* crew and I can't leave her to her fate. If any of you are unhappy with this mission, I can leave you on a skydock and pick you up afterwards. Obviously, I'd be grateful for your support, but there will be no hard feelings and no loss of wages if you choose to stay behind."

There was a moment of murmuring.

"I'm in, Cap'n"

"Me too, Chief."

Bunty looked apologetically toward Jao. "You can count on me, Skipper."

All eyes turned toward Jao, who was standing beside Emily Tutu.

"I. will. go. where. Jao. goes."

"Well... I suppose it's best if we all stick together. Will there be anything else, Captain?" Jao replied tersely.

"Would you retrieve the pulsarnite from the compressor?"

"I bought a trunk to put it in."

"Thank you, Jao. Thank you, everyone."

Charlie's interest had been well and truly piqued. He had watched Bunty and Jao buy that trunk and he had carried it back to *The Reliant*. There had been smaller trunks on sale, but they had been passed over. The very idea that there was enough pulsarnite on board to fill it made the hairs on the back of his neck stand on end. He wondered what grade it was. Sand? Gravel? Maybe something bigger? A couple of money pouches of gravel-grade pulsarnite would really set him up.

******

The journey to Victoria was a long one, and Charlie Namemaker was bored. He had been sitting on the bridge with not much to do, except think about pulsarnite. He had thought about asking to pilot *The Reliant* – he was supposed to be a pilot officer after all – but they were high over flat, featureless savannah, and there was so little to do that Gonagain was piloting with his feet up and his eyes half closed.

Bunty was reading a book called *Time Change and Pulsarnite: Is There Really a Connection?* which she had borrowed from Gonagain. She periodically glanced at her anemometer, but the headwind was not blowing them off-course, merely slowing them down.

Bearnárd was on his hands and knees playing with the mutt and a length of rope with a knot at each end. The mutt occasionally went back to the captain, who smiled at her indulgently, and then launched herself back into the game.

"Permission to take a break and stretch my legs, Chief?"

"Permission granted, Officer."

Charlie wandered down toward the engine room. As he approached, he could hear Jao muttering in disgruntled tones. At first, he thought she was talking to the automaton but, as he drew closer, it was apparent that she was grumbling to herself. He paused to try to make out what she was saying, but soon realised she wasn't speaking any language he recognised. He sauntered into the doorway and leant against the door jamb.

"Need any help, Officer… Blueeyes?"

Jao looked up and glared at him aggressively. He changed his casual stance to a more upright one.

"No?" he asked, referring to 'Officer Blueeyes' rather than his offer of help.

"No," confirmed Jao. "If you want to be formal, it's Officer Rajaobelina."

"I did wonder if Jao was short for anything," he mused. "Need any help, Officer Rajaobelina?"

"No, thank you. I can do this on my own."

Charlie eyed the compressor chamber, which was split into two pieces. From the angle he was looking, he couldn't see if there was any pulsarnite inside. He noticed the trunk was already in the room.

"You don't seem happy about this mission?"

"I didn't much care for Aircraftman Trustworthy."

There was an uncomfortable silence, as Charlie tried to think of an excuse to stay in the engine room. The engineer was a spiky character and he didn't want to irritate her.

"So, you've pumped all the heliagen into the bag then? That explains why we're so flippin' high." He edged closer, trying to get a better look.

Rajaobelina casually moved a large toolbox, blocking Namemaker from getting any closer in the process. "It's hydrum, and yes, I have."

"Hydrum? In a soft-shell? I thought the Chief was bluffing when he threatened Landowner! And you're alright with that?"

Jao shrugged, "The captain looks after us in

other ways."

"You're all barking on this ship!" Charlie was thinking about Gonagain plummeting sideways out of the hold with a bamboo kite strapped to his back.

"Was there anything else, Officer Namemaker?"

"No. No, I s'pose not." He slunk away, leaving Rajaobelina to resume her work – whilst grumbling to herself in Gassy.

Namemaker went up to the gun turret and sat himself in the gunner's seat. The gun was a Bæliss, dual-pulsarnite, alternate rapid-fire rifle – definitely not standard on a Sparrow 3. It was detachable, and Charlie suspected they had a gatling gun somewhere that would fit in its place. From the turret, you could see three hundred and sixty degrees without mirrors – something that was not possible from the bridge – but you couldn't see the ground below. You could also see the port and starboard props. They didn't look standard either. Now that he thought about it, the lumpy looking envelope wasn't the original either. It was one of the ugliest-looking dirigibles he had ever been on, but it was a more impressive vessel than he had first thought. He spun the chair around. Beyond the ship he could see nothing but sky and cloud and, way off in the distance, another dirigible, which appeared to be following a similar course.

******

Jao didn't know why she didn't trust Charlie Namemaker. Sometimes she just *knew* whether someone was going to have a positive or negative impact on her life – it was as though she could actually *see* it, like an aura – but that wasn't the case with Namemaker. She could not figure out what it was that made her so wary. He hadn't even committed the usual crime, that always got her hackles up, of calling her Jao.

When she was young, she was so poor that she had, literally, nothing but the clothes on her back and her name. And, even then, she had just the one name. The worst thing you could do was diminish it.

Then, of course, she met Gonagain and that all changed. It made her *happy* to hear Gonagain call her Jao. He had introduced her to the rest of the crew as Jao, and it was too awkward to say that only 'The Captain' could call her that. And so, on *The Reliant* at least, she became Jao. As time went on, she got used to it and, because she had so many more material possessions, a fulfilled life and the respect of her fellow crewmates – it was no longer a problem. But if a relative stranger called her Jao – that was too familiar and disrespectful, and it was a guaranteed way to get into her bad books.

Charlie had been nothing *but* respectful. He hadn't done a thing to earn her mistrust. Somehow though, she felt the equilibrium of *The Reliant* was upset with him around. And, as far as Jao was concerned, there was something about him that was just not quite right.

******

Half a deciday later, Charlie reappeared on the bridge.

“You were a long time, Officer Namemaker. Where were you?” asked Gonagain casually.

“Just familiarising myself with the ship, Chief. I was up in the gun turret. I think we’re being tailed.”

Gonagain was suddenly more alert. “By who?”

“They’re too far away to tell, Chief – even through the gun sight.”

Gonagain relaxed, “They’re probably just going to Victoria, same as us.”

“What’s the wind speed, Officer Goodtime?” asked Charlie.

Bunty checked the anemometer, “Twenty-eight knots – headwind.”

“That must be slowing us down.”

“Hugely. What’s your point, old chap?”

“I’ll bet the wind ain’t half as strong at a lower altitude.”

“No – but we’re stuck up here until Jao re-assembles the compressor.”

“So, unless they’ve got their compressor in bits as well, what reason would *they* have to be at the same flippin’ altitude as us?”

Gonagain looked questioningly at Bunty and Bearnárd, who both shrugged. He leaned over to the voice-repeater. “Jao… Officer Rajaobelina, is Emily Tutu there with you?”

"Yes, Captain."

"Send her up to the gun turret, please. I want a report on a dirigible following the same course at a similar altitude."

"Yes, Captain."

The crew waited in anxious silence. Gonagain was looking from one rear-view mirror to another – he could see nothing. Everyone else stared expectantly at the voice-repeater. They jumped when Emily's voice broke the silence.

"Captain. Gonagain. The. vessel. is. a. Hawk. Interceptor. with. Southern. Air. Guard. livery. It. is. travelling. on. a. course. of. twenty. two. degrees. at. an. altitude. of. approximately. six. thousand. four. hundred. metres. and. a. velocity. of. approximately. thirty. eight. knots."

"Skipper, that's an identical course, four hundred metres lower, and two knots faster."

"And perfect if you want to be in my blind spot."

"Chief, I can't get caught by the flippin' S.A.G. again."

"It might not be you they're after, Charlie; we've had our own run-in with the S.A.G."

"So, you're a person of interest to the Geos, the Trads, *and* the S.A.G.? Flippin' 'eck, you're worse than me! We need to re-negotiate my wages."

"Not *now*, Officer Namemaker!"

"... an' flippin' hydrum an' all," muttered Charlie under his breath.

Gonagain leant toward the voice-repeater. "Jao... Officer Rajaobelina, how long before the compressor is back in one piece?"

"I've just checked the seal, Captain; it's functional as of now."

"Stoke the engine and report to the bridge."

The whole crew was gathered on the bridge.

"Okay, crew, take your positions and strap yourselves in – I'm going for a manoeuvre. Emily Tutu, you may have to just hang on to something."

Emily Tutu just planted her feet further apart. "I. am. ready. Captain."

Gonagain put all three propellers into 'safety' – they stopped spinning and locked into position. "Lieutenant, put the compressor on full power and reduce the envelope to sixty kilotarps – when we hit five hundred meters reverse the compressor until we stabilise."

Bearnárd looked at Gonagain questioningly but got no reaction. "Aye-aye, Cap'n." He pulled a lever fully toward him and *The Reliant* began to lose altitude, slowly at first, but soon they were plummeting like a stone.

Etoile, whom everyone had momentarily forgotten, had been happily licking herself, until she found herself weightless and hovering in mid-air. She whimpered and began a futile running motion.

"Four thousand metres, Skipper... three thousand... two thousand; nine hundred; eight hundred; seven; six; five hundred!"

Bearnárd slammed the lever forward again.

"Four, three, two; one-fifty... one hundred... fifty

metres... forty-five metres..."

Etoile landed heavily on the metal deck, whimpered again, and ran under Gonagain's legs with her tail between her legs.

"Forty-one metres and stable, Skipper."

Gonagain took the props out of safety and rattled through the gears rapidly. Within microdays, they were up to sixty knots.

"Flippin' 'eck! What kind of compressor is that?"

"I harvested it from a wrecked Dreamcloud Express," replied Jao proudly.

"That ain't a Sparrow engine either, is it?"

"Engine and props are from a Hotspur Goose."

Emily Tutu had somehow remained stolidly rooted to the deck. "That. was. fun!" she said impassively.

The whole crew turned to look at Emily Tutu in astonishment.

Gonagain's manoeuvre had achieved two things: it had put some distance between them and the S.A.G. dirigible; and, it had proved Charlie right. The S.A.G. had now abandoned their stealthy stalking, and were in all-out pursuit.

"Chief, we ain't gonna outrun them! As souped-up as this craft is, that's a Hawk Interceptor chasing us."

Gonagain adjusted the mirrors and looked behind. The S.A.G. dirigible was visibly closer than the last time he looked. "I know, I know, but what else can I do? The terrain is flat as pancake – there's nowhere to hide."

Charlie went over to Bunty's station and looked at the map over her shoulder. He tapped on a shaded area. "What kind of forest is that?"

"The map doesn't specify but, in this region, I'd imagine it's acquoia forest."

Charlie tapped another shaded area, totally encircled by the first. "And that's a lake, right?"

"It is. What's on your mind?"

Charlie turned to Gonagain. "Permission to take the helm, Chief?"

"Permission denied. This is not the time to learn to fly *The Reliant*."

"With respect, Chief, I've handled much more complicated craft than this – straight off the bat. I've seen what this ship can do – thanks to your earlier demonstration – and as a pirate, pursuit and evasion has been my schtick since I was a boy."

"What's your plan?"

"To hide in the forest until they're looking the wrong way, and then double back with a tail wind."

"Hide a dirigible in a forest? Have you gone feckin' mad?"

"I've done it before."

"Really?"

"Well… similar. It was a canyon, but the principle's the same."

Gonagain was silent. He had nothing better to suggest, but the plan seemed insane, and he didn't like surrendering control in this sort of situation.

"Skipper, acquoias have massive, high canopies

and bare trunks below. There's a lot of space between each tree."

"Enough for *The Reliant*?"

"I don't know, Skip. It does seem a *bit* risky."

"Trust me, Chief – I'm a flippin' good pilot."

Gonagain stood up. "The helm is yours, Pilot Officer Namemaker. Please be careful with my ship."

Charlie settled himself into the captain's seat and rubbed his hands together. "Officer Goodtime, what's the course to that forest? We want to enter where the river is."

"Seventy degrees absolute," she checked the anemometer, "Allow seventy-nine for drift."

He adjusted the aerofoils but kept the props at full speed. Within a few millidays they were tracking the course of a river, which was little more than a stream, and heading toward the forest.

Charlie pulled a lever toward him and damped down the engine. Then dropped down the gears. The propellers reduced to a gentle twirl and Charlie checked his mirrors to see how far behind the S.A.G. were. "That'll do," he muttered to himself.

"Lieutenant Strongman, take us down to five metres."

"Aye-aye, Cap… aye-aye, Officer Namemaker."

Charlie put both port and starboard to neutral, leaving only the bow prop running. They were now tracking the river at walking speed. Charlie scanned the forest left and right. "There!" he exclaimed.

The rest of the crew looked 'there', but had no

idea what they were looking at.

Charlie carried on at walking pace for another forty metres and then put the bow prop into neutral. Putting port into reverse and starboard into forward, he spun *The Reliant* on a pinhead, ninety degrees to the left. The gap between the trees was wider here, but still little more than the width of the dirigible. Using just the bow prop again, he edged the ship forward.

Jao realised she was holding her breath and let out a breathy sigh. The rest of the crew followed suit, and there was a brief murmur of mirth from everyone except Gonagain (who had resumed holding his breath), Charlie (who was concentrating too hard for levity), and Etoile (who had resumed licking herself and didn't understand humour).

Charlie repeated his manoeuvre, turning left or right as the opportunities presented themselves. At one point, they hit a dead end and he had to perform a full one hundred and eighty and retrace his steps for a while.

"Of course, this thing would be a lot easier to hide if it wasn't the colour of a flippin' canary. They won't spot us from above, anyway."

Gonagain moved closer to the domed window of the bridge and looked up. The canopy was completely closed-in above.

"I think this is it, Chief! I think this is where we need to be."

They were still under the canopy of the trees, but immediately ahead was a navigable path to the lake in the middle of the forest.

"Will your ballast hose stretch as far as the lake, Chief?"

"Just about."

Charlie released the hatch and the ballast hose.

"Emily Tutu?" Gonagain spoke, without turning from the bridge window.

"Yes. Captain."

"Take the ballast hose to the edge of the lake, please."

"Yes. Captain."

The whole crew stood and watched as Emily Tutu emerged from under *The Reliant* carrying the end of the large bore ballast hose. She trudged, knee-deep through the mud, until she reached the water's edge. Emily dropped the end of the hose into the lake and turned to give a double thumbs-up. It was unnerving, the way the automaton occasionally, and unexpectedly, adopted human mannerisms.

"Lieutenant, fill the ballast tank to bursting, but keep us off the ground. Where's the anchor release?"

"We don't carry an anchor," admitted Gonagain. "The extra weight reduces our payload."

"Why doesn't that flippin' surprise me? I'm going to need your automaton to act as an anchor when the time comes."

Right on cue, Emily Tutu arrived back on the bridge, caked in mud up to her knees.

"Emily, tie one of the mooring ropes around your waist and await further instructions. What next, Officer Namemaker?" asked Gonagain.

"Is the ballast tank full yet, Lieutenant?"

"Yes, and I've topped up the envelope – so we have an altitude of one metre."

Charlie killed the engine. "Well, Chief – now we wait."

The Reliant remained stationary, a metre off the ground, hidden under the canopy of the acquoia trees, whilst the S.A.G. Hawk Interceptor criss-crossed overhead. The S.A.G. had followed them into the forest as far as possible but, being a bigger craft, they were forced to rise above the canopy. Now they were working on the principle that *The Reliant* would have to come out sooner or later, and they were waiting overhead and scouring the forest from above.

From the bridge of *The Reliant,* the crew could hear the S.A.G. dirigible, but could not see it – and so they waited. And waited. They waited for nearly a deciday – until, eventually, it emerged in the clear sky above the lake. And it was moving away from them.

"This is it!" Charlie said suddenly. "Aircraftman Tutu, I need you to tow us out to the lake and keep us anchored for as long as you can."

Without a word, the automaton left the bridge. She emerged from beneath them moments later, trudging back through the mud. *The Reliant* began to move through the forest – shrubs scraping the belly of the gondola as they went. Emily Tutu lumbered on into the lake, sinking deeper into the mud with each step, until *The Reliant* was clear of the canopy.

"Okay, Lieutenant, fill the bag up as quick as you can," instructed Charlie.

Bearnárd put the compressor at full power into reverse, filling the envelope. The ship began to rise, tugging at Emily Tutu, who was anchored deep in the mud.

"Okay," said Bearnárd, "the envelope is full."

"Release the ballast."

Bearnárd released the ballast. It splashed down with a roar, battering Emily Tutu, who was yanked unceremoniously from the mud. They shot up like a bullet, with Emily dangling below. *The Reliant* swooshed, almost silently, past the rear of the S.A.G. craft, so closely that they could see the rivets in its hard-shell envelope. They carried on up above the clouds, eventually levelling out at about six-and-a-half thousand metres. The wind caught them, and they started to drift back in the direction Amur.

Gonagain looked at Jao, "We should put the sails up."

"You carry sails, but no flippin' anchor?" Charlie shook his head.

Up on the gondola deck, Gonagain and Jao erected the sail masts. The masts projected from a central post to either side of the deck at an angle of about forty degrees. They each attached a boom to the same post, slightly further down. A carefully pleated sail was attached to each mast, and ropes fed through loops on the boom. Jao and Gonagain stood well back with the taut ropes in their hands.

"On the count of three," said Gonagain. "One... two... three!"

They each gave their ropes a good hard yank and the sails unfurled, catching the wind immediately. The ship lurched forward. Gonagain and Jao fought the ropes but they were both dragged, skidding towards the central post. They crashed into each other and the sails were momentarily flaccid.

"Pull!"

They pulled the ropes, hand over hand, until the sails billowed again. Gonagain secured his rope to the cleat on his side but, with the strength of the wind, Jao was struggling to hold and secure the rope simultaneously. Gonagain grabbed the rope and pulled, giving Jao enough slack to tie it off. The ship lurched forward again, and the two collapsed breathlessly to the floor, laughing, as *The Reliant* moved silently away from the forest and the S.A.G.

Jao turned to Gonagain and their eyes locked. They were inches from each other. Their laughter subsided. They moved closer, each of them unsure of the other, until their noses were almost touching. Then, without warning, Gonagain became distracted and looked beyond Jao. Jao turned to follow his gaze.

A metal hand was reaching over the balustrade, strands of pondweed trailing from the wrist. The hand was closely followed by the rest of Emily Tutu. She was coated in mud from the thighs down and draped in pondweed, including a rather fetching pondweed toupée. She clattered to the deck before quickly standing up erect, as if on parade.

“I. am. going. to. get. cleaned. up. and. oil. my. joints.” she announced haughtily, before marching past and disappearing below deck.

Gonagain and Jao dissolved into hysterical, childish laughter. Jao laughed until her sides ached. Gonagain was literally crying with laughter. He eventually gathered himself. “I suppose we should go below deck and find out where we’re going.”

CHAPTER 22
Cabinda

(Pollexday)

The Reliant sailed where the wind took them, until Bunty identified the town of Cabinda as a suitable place to lay low.

Cabinda was a drab little place, with no obvious sign of industry or economy. The people were drab, uninteresting, and uninterested in the yellow dirigible that had landed at what passed for an airdock. Bunty and Jao had been on a short reconnaissance of the town and found very little of note. There were two bars – the unimaginatively named The Tavern and the equally uninspiring New Tavern Inn. Both were squat brick buildings with shallow pitched roofs. The Tavern was marginally less uninviting.

"It's the perfect place to stay lost, Skipper. I can't think of any good reason to come here."

"We won't stay long – just long enough for the

S.A.G. to realise that they've lost us and give up."

Gonagain was aware that the S.A.G. were probably more interested in Charlie than anyone else on *The Reliant*, but Charlie was crew now, his safety was as important as anyone else's. He was also the 'man-of-the-moment', with his quick thinking in the Pioneer Tavern, and his piloting skills in the forest. But Gonagain was keen to get to Victoria none-the-less. "We'll get moving first thing tomorrow."

"We might as well get some scran and grog, Skip. Can I entice anyone to The Tavern?"

The entire crew descended on The Tavern, instantly doubling the number of patrons (who were only briefly curious about Emily Tutu).

The vegetable broth was possibly the blandest thing they had ever tasted, but the bread and cheese was acceptable, and the ale was surprisingly good. The atmosphere, though, was sterile; the crew's mood was muted, and Etoile was restless.

"I might take the pooch for a walk, Oisín."

Gonagain was surprised, as Charlie had never shown any affinity with Etoile but, as the weather was quite inclement, he was happy to let him take her out.

Outside, the wind that had bought *The Reliant* to Cabinda had turned blustery and was accompanied by a heavy mizzle. Charlie Namemaker turned his jacket collar up. "Okay, dog, do a quick wee so we can get back to the jalopy; there's something I need to check out."

Back at *The Reliant*, Namemaker put Etoile into the pile of sack cloth and old clothes that served as her bed. "You stay there and keep quiet."

He headed straight to the engine room and found what he was looking for – the chest he had carried back from Amur market. After trying the lid, he lifted the chest a few centimetres off the ground. It was heavy. If that was all pulsarnite, then this was a very valuable chest indeed. He shook it to see what sound it made – it made no sound at all. Probably not gravel grade then. But even sand grade was valuable to watchmakers, and he could probably take a few money-pouches full without anyone noticing.

Charlie scanned the engine room, looking for a key. It was probably the tidiest engine room he had ever seen. There were scores of drawers, ranging from ones the size of the chest to those not much bigger than a matchbox. He opened a few of them. They were full of tools and spare parts, meticulously organised, cleaned, and greased. He could search all night and not find a key hidden in here. He checked the lock on the trunk. If he had any lock-picking tools it wouldn't be a problem.

Jao's cabin was as meticulously tidy as her engine room. There was nothing out of place and not a key to be seen. Charlie opened a tiny travel trunk and a locker but doubted he was going to find anything here either. He was just about to open an expensive-looking vanity case when he heard Etoile barking. Charlie poked his head out of the cabin, "Oi! I told you to be quiet, you stupid flippin' mutt."

Charlie stepped back into Jao's cabin, but Etoile resumed barking. "Flippin' 'eck!" He marched angrily towards the hold, where Etoile's bed was, and stormed through the door.

"Hello, Charlie old boy, what are you doing here? I thought you were walking Etoile."

"Bunty! Yeah, I, erm... She didn't want to go. Probably the weather. I just bought her back here and was about to come back to the tavern. What are *you* doing back so soon?"

"There was no craic in that tavern, at all. We left a message behind the bar for you," replied Gonagain. "Why did you want Etoile to keep quiet?"

"No reason, Chief. She was yapping a lot. The sound of a dog yapping gets on my nerves – that's all."

Gonagain eyed him suspiciously. "Well... we're all turning in early. I want to make an early start tomorrow, so I suggest you do the same."

Several hours later, Gonagain was woken in his cabin by the squall outside. He could feel the wind buffeting the envelope and hear the rain pelting down. There was a flash of lightning and a roll of thunder. It was unlikely they would be going anywhere anytime soon.

CHAPTER 23
Victoria

Aoife Trustworthy didn't know whether it was the agony from her fingers that woke her, or the need to urinate. Her cell was in darkness, but that didn't mean anything. The only window was high up the wall. It was heavily barred and faced out into a gloomy alleyway, and Aoife occasionally saw a pair of feet pass by, but it barely let in any light at all. It did, however, let in the cold. The walls were brick and heavily scarred with the names of previous occupants, and a count of the days they had spent in the cell. Aoife had already started a day-count of her own. She had also read all the other names and she thought she recognised one that she had brought in herself. There was no door to the cell, just a sturdy, iron-barred gate – the bars were *just* close enough together to prevent her from putting her head between them. The cell had a dirt floor and Aiofe had begun digging with a spoon, before realising that the cell was semi-subterranean. She had tested the ground under the gate but found a solid stone threshold less than an inch below the dirt.

The bed she was lying on had a tubular metal frame and flat metal slats for the reed mat, which served as a mattress, to sit on. The metal slats were too narrow and too far apart to be properly functional. The blanket was so thin that it was little more than a sheet. The only other thing in the cell was a metal bucket in the corner.

Aoife lay huddled on the uncomfortable bed until her bladder was ready to burst. Reluctantly, she swung her legs down and sat up. She waited for her eyes to become accustomed to the gloom and she was able to locate the bucket. She paused to listen for any approaching guards, before dropping her prisoner's boiler suit to her knees and squatting over the bucket. It was freezing in Victoria in January and she was naked under the boiler suit. She could see her own breath and the steam from the bucket. She shivered. At least the cold numbed the pain in her fingers.

Aoife still could not believe that she had been stupid enough to turn up in Victoria without breaking into the trunks first. She was usually so careful and thorough in her thoughts before she made her next move. Why had she just assumed that if she had all three trunks, one of them would contain the pulsarnite? When the third trunk had been forced open to reveal a piece of machinery, she had stood there opening and closing her mouth like a goldfish. The blood had drained to her feet and it was a struggle not to faint. She had been in this cell ever since.

As she pulled her boiler suit back on and huddled on the reed mat on her cot, she wondered whether they were going to torture her again today. The forcing of needles under her fingernails was mostly vengeful punishment, but also an attempt to get information on *The Reliant* and its crew, and the whereabouts of the pulsarnite rock. She had told them precious little – partly out of some misplaced loyalty to Gonagain. There was also the fact that she didn't have all the answers to their questions but, most importantly, she also knew that once she had told them everything, her next stop would be the gallows.

She began to ponder her life and her decisions. There were things that she regretted doing, and even more that she regretted *not* doing.

She had never reconciled with her father after joining the Traditionalist paramilitary. It had been a strained relationship all her life.

She didn't remember her mother – she had been knocked down by a horse when Aoife was just a child. She was a strong-minded woman from an influential family. She had been politically motivated and quite a visionary, and was also independently wealthy. Aoife could not imagine what she had seen in her father.

Her father was a frivolous man who was drawn to strong women. Like Aoife, they never really respected him. He was an artist by trade, but a mediocre one and a bit of a pervert. Aoife had felt sure his art was just an excuse to ogle naked ladies.

To be fair, his earlier works were all landscapes, so perhaps the art did come first. Aoife was embarrassed by his hedonistic lifestyle and his lack of convictions or morals. It was only when she got involved in the Traditionalist movement that she discovered he was a sincere and heartfelt pacifist. The angrier he became about Aoife's acquaintances and her actions, the more she grew to respect him. And so, she got more and more involved, partially so she could respect her father a little more.

By the time the Traditionalist paramilitary had become a proper army, young Aoife was already a high-ranking officer and she became more focused on her career. There were older colleagues, who became father figures, and other colleagues, who became friends or lovers. Her father was all but forgotten. She even changed her name – initially to her mother's maiden name but then, on the advice of another officer, to Trustworthy.

She had never been great at relationships – she was selfish; her own career came first; and she fell in and out of love too easily. Her life was littered with missed chances.

At school, she had fallen in love with Hinrika Helgusdottir. They were best friends for years but, as they became adolescents, it evolved into much more. When rumours of their relationship spread, Aoife had disowned Hinrika, pretending to be disgusted at the idea that she was in love with her. She had never forgiven herself for that.

Even recently, on *The Reliant*, there were opportunities that she had let slip by. Gonagain was a real catch for somebody. He was gregarious and fun, he had his own moral code, he was handsome, and he was good in bed. But she had messed it up.

And then there was Jao. Rajaobelina. She was beautiful and intelligent, and *genuinely* trustworthy. She probably would not have been interested in Aoife, but Aoife had never told her how she felt. Maybe there could have been a chance.

Aoife decided that if she got out of here alive, she would change her ways. She would still be true to her beliefs, but she would not let them get in the way of relationships.

Her train of thought was interrupted when a guard came with food. Every meal was stale bread and a salty broth, and she had already lost track of whether her one meal a day was for breakfast, lunch, or dinner. The guard shoved the metal tray under the bars and left without a word, slamming the metal door behind him. Aoife greedily guzzled the bread and broth, before turning the metal bed on its end and climbing it like a ladder. With the handle end of the spoon, she began scraping at the mortar around the barred window.

CHAPTER 24
Amur

(Secundusday)

Digby Landowner was beside himself with anger. In the last couple of days, he had been taken hostage by a motley crew of vagabonds, had his personal effects taken away, been scalded by hot porridge, beaten up by a thug from the mine, and handed over to the enemy. His cell could have done with a good clean, the springs in his mattress were on their last legs and the man in the adjacent cell snored. He had to ask to use the latrine and the food was mostly offal, potato, and root vegetables – except for the breakfast, which was *always* plain porridge. No – angry didn't even begin to describe it – he was apoplectic with rage.

The worst thing was that he had been denied any opportunity to negotiate with a senior officer. He had used threats and offers of rewards, to try to ameliorate the situation but, alas, the Landowner name didn't seem to carry any weight in these parts. If those buffoons on that tatty yellow dirigible hadn't taken his hand-crafted, diamond-jewelled pocket watch, he could have bribed a guard with that. It looked very much like he would have to sit-out the war in this dump.

The main door opened and a scruffy looking private wheeled in a trolley of food. He slid the dish through the hatch and moved on to the next cell.

Landover lifted the dish and sniffed it. Liver, boiled potatoes and carrots in a thin gravy. At least there was no turnip. He took it over to his little table and tasted it. "Goodness me. How did it come to this?" he sighed. "Have they never heard of seasoning?"

Landowner heard a tapping and turned to see his scruffy waiter knocking a tin cup against the bars of his cell door. "Oi! Come over by yur!" he said in a stage whisper.

"Are you addressing me?"

"You got anyone else in there?"

"What do you want?"

"Over by yur!" he whispered impatiently.

Landowner dabbed his moustache with his hand, wishing he had a napkin. The man was only a private and he didn't feel inclined to take orders from him. Nevertheless, he pulled out his chair and walked slowly and deliberately toward the man. "*What*, do you want?"

"One of the other guards says you reckon you're

a Landowner."

"That's right. I am."

"One of the Limnio Landowners?"

"Yes!" Digby was interested now.

"What relation are you to old Monty Landowner then?"

"Montgomery was my great grand uncle."

"Really? So, you'll have one then."

"One what?"

"A Landowner special pocket watch."

"Yes! I don't have it right now – it was taken when I was bought in."

"Yeah, right." The scruffy private went back to his trolley and began to wheel it away.

"I *am* a Landowner! I'm Digby Landowner. I can reward you if you get me out of here."

The guard paused. "Digby. Okay. I'll be back."

CHAPTER 25
Cabinda

(Secundusday)

Bearnárd and Bunty were already in the mess when Gonagain emerged from his cabin.

“Doesn’t look like we’ll be going anywhere today, Osh!” Bearnárd nodded to the raging storm through a porthole. As if to drive home the point, the wind buffeted the ship, enough for Bunty spill some coffee.

“Oh buggerisation!” she exclaimed as she dabbed her waistcoat with a hanky.

Gonagain grunted and felt the coffee pot for heat and weight before pouring a cup.

Bunty looked him up and down. He still had a couple of days’ worth of stubble, he was monosyllabic, and his waistcoat was unbuttoned – he was in one of his moods. She turned to Bearnárd and raised an eyebrow. Bearnárd shrugged. He recognised the signs too but, other than the weather, was not aware of the cause.

"Any news?"

"Well, Osh, you probably noticed we're not on our own anymore – there's another ten dirigibles here now."

"And?"

"No-one to cause us any concern; stage-ships and traders mostly. All here because of the storm. Stanleyville, Victoria, Amur and one from Tana."

"That covers a wide area."

"We could be land-bound for a while, Skipper."

"Ugh!" Gonagain turned and slunk back toward his cabin with his coffee in his hand.

"Morning, Chief!"

"Hmn."

Charlie sidestepped Gonagain and stepped into the mess. "What's up with the gaffer?"

Bearnárd and Bunty shrugged. "Where are you off to, old boy?"

Charlie was draining the dregs from the coffee pot. "Eh?"

"What's with the oil skins?" Bearnárd elucidated, gesturing to the cape and sou'wester Charlie had borrowed from Beagán's locker.

"Oh… I thought I might take the dog for a walk."

"You're getting very attached to Etoile all of a sudden."

"Nah. Not really. Truth is, I get bored easy. It's a dull old place this and I get a bit stir-crazy when I'm tied down. The mutt just gives me an excuse to get out."

******

Gonagain stood at his cabin porthole and watched Charlie Namemaker disappear into the rain, with Etoile fighting him every step of the way. He thought about following him, but Etoile was already looking like a drowned rat and he didn't fancy it. He drained his coffee cup and left his cabin on tiptoes. Why he was tiptoeing around his own vessel, he wasn't quite sure, but he was going to rummage through someone else's things and it just felt appropriate.

In Beagán's cabin, Gonagain was disappointed to find very little belonging to Charlie – he had forgotten that he had arrived with nothing. In the locker, some of Beagán's clothes were folded on the floor – to make hanging space for the few clothes that Charlie had bought. He rifled through the pockets, methodically, to be sure he didn't miss anything. Then he went through Beagán's clothes in a similar manner, but with a little more reverence. Finally, he took out the pile of clothes at the bottom of the locker and, even as he lifted the neat bundle, he could feel the weight of something hidden amongst the clothes.

Gonagain carefully lifted the folded items of clothes, one by one, until he came across the source of the extra weight – Beagán's old, ticking-fabric satchel, containing Digby Landowner's personal effects. Gonagain had forgotten all about them. He emptied the bag carefully onto the floor.

The heavy item was a Model 1900 Parabellum pistol. There was also a pocket watch. Gonagain took it to the porthole, where it was brighter, so that he could examine it. Like his own timepiece, it was a double half-hunter, but that was where the comparison ended. It was a beautifully crafted object, made from solid silver. It had ornate engravings on the case and the seventeen jewels were diamonds instead of rubies. Gonagain trousered the watch. He would substitute it with an old, broken watch that Rajaobelina had been promising to fix.

He rummaged through the remaining items – a 'dog-tag' with Landowner's name, identification number and rank crudely embossed on it, a crumpled wad of notes in two currencies – ariary and pula – and an official looking envelope. Gonagain pulled a card from the envelope and studied the ornate script.

To Staff-Sergeant Digby Landowner and guest. You are cordially invited to the annual, grand ball of the Traditionalist Revolution Army at:

The Great Hall
Hotel de Ville
Victoria

On:
Saturday 24th of January, 1910.

There was a hand-written note at the bottom.

I have heard great things about you, Staff-Sergeant Landowner. We, all at HQ, are looking forward very much to putting a face to the name and the reputation.

Yours sincerely

Field Marshall Silverspoon

Gonagain's mind began to race. He'd heard about the Hotel de Ville in Victoria – it was an enormous, multi-functional building. It had the grand hall and beautiful gardens, but it also had barracks and cells. The cells would be where they would keep Aoife – if they hadn't executed her already. And now he was holding an invitation to enter the building. Okay, so it was addressed Digby Landowner, but they had no idea what he looked like – the letter said so. And Landowner wouldn't be turning up, as he was in the hands of the Geokinetics. Gonagain tucked the letter into his waistcoat pocket and put the empty envelope back in the satchel with everything else – making a mental note to come back with his old pocket watch. He paused. He should probably take the ID as well... and the pistol. "Just take the fecking lot of it, Oisín," he muttered to himself. "None of it belongs to Charlie anyway."

Once he was sure everything else was left as he found it, he left the room – consciously stopping himself from tiptoeing. His mood had lifted slightly. He hadn't found out what Namemaker was up to, but he had potentially found a solution to a much bigger problem.

******

Charlie Namemaker had trudged all over Cabinda and been to every shop, market, and bazaar that he could find, which, in truth, was not very many. He wondered how all the dull, miserable people of Cabinda lived here at all. He was on the verge of giving up when he had stumbled upon a dilapidated shop selling second-hand tools and assorted used rubbish. Amazingly, he had found everything he needed there.

As he sloshed through the teaming rain, he began to hum tunelessly to himself. Under his cape, he carried a small, wet dog (who had refused to leave the shop and go back into the storm) in one arm. In the other, he held a sack containing eight pairs of wire-framed glasses, two pairs of needle-nosed pliers, a very small hack saw and a file.

When *The Reliant* came into view, he put Etoile down. He didn't want to be seen carrying the mutt and, anyway, his arm was aching. Etoile spotted the tatty, yellow dirigible and began pulling at her lead to get home. He found Jao and Bunty in the mess drinking coffee.

"You couldn't dry the dog off for me, could you? I'm soaked under this cape and I need to get *myself* dry."

"You were a long-time, old chap. Where were you?"

"Just exploring. The dog didn't want to come

back – she missed out on a walk last night, so I suppose she was full of energy."

"That's unusual," said Jao, "Etoile doesn't normally like the rain."

Back in his cabin, Namemaker threw off his cape and sou'wester. They had, in fact, kept him remarkably dry. He tipped the sack of tools and glasses on to his little desk and set to work, employing skills he had learnt from a man named Jeremiah Lovehats. As he began sawing the arms off the glasses, he thought about Lovehats and smiled to himself.

Jeramiah Lovehats didn't love hats at all. As far as Charlie knew, he owned just one battered, brown newsboy cap. He was born Jeremiah Gotstuff, after his father Joshua Gotstuff, who had made his living as a money-launderer and a fence. But young Jeremiah didn't want to go into the family business and set off into the world to find his own niche. He worked as a hired thug for a while but, eventually, discovered both a talent and a passion for safecracking and lockpicking. He learnt his trade remarkably quickly. He was often faster than his tutors, and he began to market himself as 'the man who can crack any safe'. Unfortunately, his hubris got the better of him and he pitted himself against a safe that was way beyond his level. He spun and twisted the multiple dials, listening for the clicks, but could not get the safe open. Reluctantly, he resorted to blowing the door off but, having never had to use explosives before, made a complete mess of it and blew his own finger off in the process.

Jeremiah was desperate to put this gaffe behind him. He studied every known lock and safe, and started to build his reputation again. He had a friend who made him a very effective prosthetic finger from wood and leather – it even had a capital 'E' inked on the knuckle, to complete his existing tattoos. That was when he came to work for Charlie.

Jeremiah helped them break into the Dreamcloud factory and steal a brand new Dreamcloud Club Class. As they flew to meet their buyer, they had one hell of a celebration. Jeremiah passed out from too much grog, and one of the lads sanded the 'E' off his prosthesis and carved a deep 'S' in its place. It was about four weeks before Jeremiah noticed that his knuckle tattoos now read 'LOVE' and 'HATS'. He was furious, and discarded the prosthetic, but the crew had already embraced his new moniker and, as Jeremiah Lovehats gained a reputation as the best safecracker in the business, he was forced to adopt the name.

Charlie chuckled to himself as he used the pliers to bend the ends of the arms of the glasses into the right position. He filed off the last few burrs and stood back to admire his work. He now had a functional, if rather ugly, sixteen-piece lockpicking set, that should get him, pretty much, into any lock he wanted – assuming his skills weren't too rusty. He should certainly be able to open the trunk full of pulsarnite.

******

"Bunty, have you got a moment? In your cabin."

Bunty clutched her hands to her heart and fluttered her eyelashes theatrically. "Oh Oisín! I didn't know you cared!"

Gonagain gave her a faux, stern look from under his eyebrows.

"Course you can, Skip. Tell me what's on your mind."

In Bunty's cabin, he explained his plan – working it through in his own head at the same time.

"What if there's someone there who knows Landowner? You'll be rumbled as soon as they see you."

"I hadn't thought of that. I'll ask Bernie if he thinks anyone else from Isalo might be invited."

"He had a life before Isalo, Skipper. One of his previous senior officers might be there."

"People of that rank don't take notice of *anyone* until they get to a certain level. You could serve under their command for years and they'd forget you the day you leave. I know it's a gamble, but I think I can get away with it."

"You should at least *try* to impersonate him," Bunty eyed his stubble. "You've got nearly a week to cultivate *that* into a stupid-looking 'tache. You should get a pair of Cuban heeled boots too – he's taller than you. But the big problem is getting hold of a Traditionalist uniform – Charlie might know where we can find one."

"I'd rather keep Charlie out of it, if we can. I don't quite trust him – that's why I wanted to chat in the privacy of your cabin."

Bunty pouted. "You know how to hurt a girl's feelings."

Gonagain laughed and nodded to the invite. "I think I can make it up to you. I want you to be my plus one."

"Oh goodness me, no! If you want to avoid attracting attention, the last thing you need is someone who looks like your aunty – albeit your glamorous aunty – as your date. No. You'll have to ask Jao."

"But you know how to behave at these functions. I'll draw attention to myself by messing up the etiquette. And with Jao... well, it'll be the blind leading the blind."

Bunty stood up. "Get that chin shaved and leave your top lip. Talk to Jao and see if she'll be your date. Then both report to me for etiquette lessons." She opened the door of her cabin and gestured for Gonagain to leave. "Oh... and think of a plan for getting a uniform."

CHAPTER 26
Amur

(Mediusday)

"Psst… psst! Come over by yur."

Digby Landowner emerged from a semi-slumber and peered into the darkness. It was that scruffy guard again. Digby wished he would address him less informally – he was both a lower rank *and* a lower class.

"What do you want?"

"I want you to keep the noise down and come over by yur. I'm not supposed to be here – off duty I am."

Landowner reluctantly got out of his bed and walked to the cell door. He was only wearing his union suit long-johns and wasn't happy about this chap seeing him in his underwear.

"Right. I've been doing some digging, see? Down at the library. All the society pages of every rag for the last seven years." He pulled a crumpled piece of newspaper from his pocket and unfurled it. It was a photograph from a wedding. He read from the caption below. "From left, Artemis Lightbringer, Apollo Lightbringer, Digby Landowner... that's you, is it?"

Landowner, who was surprised to discover that the man could read, snatched the piece of paper. It was a photograph from his cousin Hestia's wedding. "Yes! Yes, that's me. That proves I am who I say I am."

"Right. So, next time I'm on duty, I'll spring you and you'll make me rich, will you?"

"Absolutely. I'll send you some money as soon as I'm home in Limnio."

"No, no. No need for that. I'll be travelling with you, won't I?"

"Won't we be a tad conspicuous?"

The scruffy guard looked confused. "Why's that now?"

"For what earthly reason would someone like *me* have a travelling companion like *you*?"

"Well, we'll have to make you a bit more like me then, won't we?" He stuck a badly scarred and pock-marked hand through the bars. "Dafydd Porcwrangler."

Landowner sighed and reluctantly shook his hand. "Digby Landowner." He wiped his hand on his union suit.

Dafydd Porcwrangler raised his eyes to the heavens. "I *know*," he said impatiently. "I'll see you tomorrow."

CHAPTER 27
Cabinda

(Mediusday)

Jao and Gonagain were sitting at the table in the mess when Charlie walked in. Bunty was standing opposite and Bearnárd was grinning at the end of the table.

"No, Skip, you're holding the fork upside down!"

"How are you supposed to eat peas with the fork that way up?"

Charlie paused at the door. "What's going on here then?"

Bearnárd's grin grew wider. "Etiquette lessons."

"What for?"

Bearnárd opened his mouth to speak, but Gonagain interrupted. "We want to be able to pass ourselves in polite company. There's no money in trading with the rabble."

"Listen, there's plenty of rabble with a ton of

money, if you know where to find them – look at Harry Twoships!" Charlie peered through the porthole. "That weather's finally easing up. We might be able to get out of here soon."

"Let's hope so."

"Well," said Charlie, "I'll leave you to it. I'll come back for me porridge later."

Charlie ambled out of the mess but, as soon as he was out of view, broke into a fast mince. He pulled his home-made lockpicking kit out of his breast pocket as he went, and headed straight towards the engine room. He marched into the engine room and his heart missed a beat when he saw Emily Tutu standing in front of him. Her eyes were throbbing amber lights. Charlie put a hand to his heart and exhaled. "Flippin' 'eck. I forgot about you." He waved a hand in front of her face. Nothing.

He got to his knees in front of the crate, selected two of his tools, and began to work the lock. His lockpicking skills were clearly rusty, and it took ages to get any joy at all. After changing implements a couple of times, and nearly snapping one in the lock, the barrel eventually turned and clicked. He got up from his aching knees.

"Right. Let's see what we got." Charlie flung the lid open unceremoniously and stepped back. He stood silent and motionless, save for his jaw, which was moving up and down involuntarily, for several moments.

"Flippin'…" he rubbed his hand over his flaky scalp. "I don't flippin'… This can't be real." He knelt reverently by the trunk, oblivious now to his aching knees. He gently caressed the huge stone, feeling the smooth and the jagged surfaces in turn. He could feel it pulsing. Tingles went through his fingers and up his arms in waves. It had a beautiful, pink tinge (the pinker the stone, the better the quality) marbled with blue, and it shone as if it had been polished and buffed. It looked almost like soft, pink, oiled flesh with blue veins and capillaries – but it felt hard and dry and cold.

After a few more moments of stunned reverence, Charlie's brain began to cogitate. As wonderful as this rock of pulsarnite was, it messed up his plan somewhat. He had intended to take a couple of handfuls – maybe substitute it with some inert gravel or sand – and carry on as normal until an opportunity presented itself. But how could he take just *some* of it, if it was one enormous lump? He studied it again. Somebody had taken just some of it – there was a hole in the narrowest part, which made the stone look like a pendant from a giant's necklace. He had initially thought that it was natural, but on closer inspection it was, most definitely, man-made. But cutting through the stone would take ages and make a terrible racket. No. He would have to take all of it or none of it. Charlie closed the trunk and tidied up his lockpicks. He should have felt thrilled by such a discovery, but in truth he felt confused and conflicted.

Back in his cabin, Charlie Namemaker ruminated on the situation. This was too good an opportunity to pass up – he'd have to do years of piracy to see the kind of wealth that the trunk offered. But the crew of *The Reliant* had been good to him. He didn't mind diddling them a little bit, but he didn't want to shaft them completely. And Gonagain wanted to use it to trade in return for that woman's life – she must really mean something to him. 'You make your own destiny' – that was what Harry Twoships had said. And it was what he had always said himself, before he ended up down that mine.

"What's wrong with you, Charlie boy? You going soft in yer old age?" he said aloud.

If only he had something of value he could leave in recompense, he wouldn't feel so bad. But he had arrived on *The Reliant* with nothing. Everything he had was curtesy of Gonagain... except...!

Charlie went to the foot of his locker and rummaged amongst the folded clothes at the bottom. A diamond-jewelled watch of that quality was worth a pittance in comparison to the pulsarnite, but it was at least a token of good faith... and it was probably worth more than this tatty old dirigible. Charlie reached the floor of the locker without finding the satchel. He began working his way up the pile again. Nothing. Someone had been into his cabin and stolen the stuff he had stolen from Landowner. The cheeky little... Well, that does it! All's fair – and all that.

******

"Okay, chaps, you are introduced to someone of a superior rank to Gonagain… I mean, Landowner. What do you do?

"I curtsey."

"I salute."

"No, Skip, you bow. Well done, Jao. You make inadvertent eye contact with someone of a superior rank to Landowner. What do you do then?"

"I curtsey."

"I… salute?"

"That's right, Skipper, well done. Jao, a full curtsey is over the top in that situation, just a bow of the head will do. What if it's someone of the *same* rank?"

"Bunty, I think that's enough for today – my brain is banjaxed. Besides, look out there," he nodded to the porthole. "It's clear enough to move on. Some of the other ships are already leaving."

"Right you are, Skip, 'til tomorrow then. Read your notes."

Gonagain and Jao gave each other a weary look and sighed. Gonagain leaned over to the voice-repeater. "All crew report to the bridge in five millidays."

******

Five millidays later and everyone was on the bridge, except Charlie. Gonagain went to the voice-repeater. "Pilot Officer Namemaker, report to the bridge immediately."

The crew waited, either for a reply on the voice-repeater or the appearance of Charlie Namemaker. Neither happened.

"Flight Officer Goodtime, go and see if you can find him, will you?"

"Yes, Skipper."

A few moments later, Bunty's voice came over the repeater. "I'm in his cabin, Skipper; there's no trace of him."

"Well, have a look in the mess or the gun turret."

"No, Skip, you don't understand. There's literally no trace of him. It's like he was never here."

Gonagain paused. "Search the mess and the gun turret anyway. Second Lieutenant Rajaobelina, go and look for him in the engine room. See if anything is missing whilst you're there."

Bearnárd watched nervously as Gonagain paced the width of the bridge.

Bunty was first to return. "Skip, I think he's gone."

Gonagain nodded wordlessly. Jao returned next, with Emily Tutu in tow. "Captain, I checked the trunk. This was the only thing in it." She handed over a note for the captain to read.

Dear Captain Gonagain,

Sorry Chief, but opportunities like this don't land in your lap every day. It was too good to pass up – I couldn't resist it. I promise I'll make it up to you some day. I was going to leave you Landowner's pocket watch as a token of my intent, but I reckon you've already taken it – so I couldn't. Really am sorry, I hope there are no hard feel-

ings. Good luck with rescuing your bird in Victoria.
Charlie.

"No hard feelings? No feckin' hard feelings?" Gonagain turned on Emily Tutu. "You were in the engine room the whole time – why didn't you stop him."

"I. was. in. sleep. mode. Captain. I. was. unaware. until. I. checked. my. sleep. memory. just. now."

Gonagain turned to Jao. "Why was she left in sleep mode? She should have been on guard at all times."

"Emily doesn't work like that Captain. She needs sleep just like the rest of us, otherwise her motors will seize or the pulsarnite will expire."

Bearnárd knew what was coming next – even before Gonagain spun on his heels.

"You! This is your fault! You brought him aboard – a feckin' pirate no less"

"He helped rescue you in Isalo, what was I supposed to do? Leave him there? You didn't have to make him crew, Cap'n."

"Well, I assumed if he was anything other than a grand lad – say, a pirate for instance – you would have told me."

"I didn't know he was a pirate. I needed help to escape and he fitted the bill. Was I supposed to check that I was only escaping with upright citizens? Because I'd probably still be there with windows for eyeballs if I did."

"Well, no-one would have had to rescue anyone

from Isalo, if you hadn't got yourself captured in Lubumbashi."

"What about rule number one? Or should I have resisted capture like Beagán did?"

"If you'd kept up with me, instead of being 'Mr Chivalry' in the Scrimshankers, you wouldn't have needed to do anything. And Beagán would still be alive!"

After the raised voices, the silence was deafening. Everyone knew Gonagain had gone too far – including Gonagain himself – but he wasn't going to back down.

Bearnárd stood up slowly and walked to the door, before turning and speaking quietly. "It's not surprising he done a runner, and your bit of frock in Victoria too, having a gobshite like you as a captain. I'm surprised you have any crew at all."

Gonagain looked to Bunty and Jao, but he knew he wasn't going to get any support from them right now – they were both staring intently at the floor. When he looked back to the door, Bearnárd was gone. Through the bridge's domed glass window, he could see that most of the other dirigibles had left too. Namemaker could have been on any of them. One thing was certain – he wasn't still in Cabinda.

"Right. Flight Officer Goodtime, set a course for Lindi. Second Lieutenant Rajaobelina, get the engine stoked up."

"Yes, Captain."

"Yes, Skipper. And Skipper?"

"Yes?"

"You can drop the Flight Officer and Second Lieutenant nonsense. That was for Charlie's benefit I believe – and he's gone now."

"Yes. Of course."

******

After nearly three decidays of piloting *The Reliant* in virtual silence, Gonagain left the bridge, leaving Jao at the helm. He stood outside Bearnárd's cabin for a moment before knocking quietly. There was no response.

"Can I come in?"

"No."

Gonagain slowly opened the door anyway and poked his head around, before stepping in. Bearnárd was lying on his bunk, staring at the ceiling, with Etoile sprawled across his chest. He was gently stroking behind her ears.

"What do you want?" asked Bearnárd without taking his eyes off the ceiling. Etoile gave Gonagain an accusing side-eye glance, but he wasn't sure if she was siding with Bernie or just annoyed at having her ear-rub disturbed.

"I… I just wanted to apologise."

"For what?"

"For what I said – on the bridge earlier."

"You said a lot of things on the bridge earlier, brother; you might need to clarify which one you're apologising for."

"All of them."

Bearnárd finally made eye contact. "You're going to have to be more specific than that."

"I'm sorry for eating the head off you in general. I'm sorry for blaming you for Namemaker coming aboard. But, mostly, I'm sorry for implying that Beagán's death was in any way your fault."

"Implying?"

"I'm sorry for *accusing* you of being responsible for Beagán's death."

"It's all well and good apologising here, in private, but you accused me in front of the whole crew."

"Come back to the bridge and I'll apologise in public."

Up on the bridge, Gonagain cleared his throat loudly enough that Bunty and Jao spun around in their seats. He cleared his throat again. "I want to apologise to my brother, Bernie, for *everything* I said earlier today. Specifically, I want to apologise for blaming him for bringing Namemaker aboard. It was my decision and my decision alone to keep him on as crew. But mostly, I want to say sorry for accusing him of being in any way responsible for Beagán's death. The only person responsible for that is Digby Landowner – and hopefully he's rotting in jail now."

"Hear hear!"

"Finally, I want to apologise for being a gobshite, a hoor's melt and a rat's knackers." He looked at Bearnárd. "Bernie, is there anything else I need to apologise for, whilst I'm on a roll?"

“Yes. That poxy moustache – you look a right gombeen.”

Oisín and Bernie gave each other a big bear hug. Bunty was cheering, Jao was laughing and wiping a tear from her eye. Etoile had picked up on the mood and was jumping up and down around the two brothers, and Emily felt slightly strange in a way which she didn't really understand but quite liked.

CHAPTER 28
Amur

(Annularisday)

Dafydd Porcwrangler was serving Digby Landowner sweetbreads with turnip and mashed potato.

"What are you messing around with this slop for? I thought we were getting out of here," hissed Landowner.

"Shhh. I'll be there now, in a minute."

Porcwrangler continued serving dinner to the prisoners, whilst Landowner pushed the food around the plate impatiently. The scruffy guard passed by the cell a few times, and disappeared for several millidays, until eventually coming back with two well-stuffed, canvas, sherpa bags. He unlocked Landowner's cell and stepped in. "Put this on and stuff your uniform in the bag," he said, throwing a bag at Landowner.

Landowner tipped the bag out and raked

through the clothes. They were clearly second-hand peasant's clothes. "Where did you get this lot – the workhouse?"

"The city morgue."

"Ugh! They stink."

"I won't lie to you, they're absolutely buzzing." Porcwrangler tipped his own bag of clothes on to the floor and began to get out of his guard's uniform.

"It's alright for you," whined Landowner, "you've got your own clothes."

"These are from the morgue too."

Landowner stared in disbelief. "Why? Surely you've got clothes other than your uniform."

"And what do I say if we get caught? 'After he escaped and took me hostage, we popped back to my gaff so I could get changed?'" Porcwrangler looked Digby Landowner up and down. "Come here!" he grabbed him by the twirly point of his moustache, produced a pair of scissors from somewhere and snipped off the end in one swift movement. As he reached for the other end, Landowner pushed him away.

"What in the name of...? What did you do that for?"

"That's a posh moustache. Those are peasant's clothes. Looks wrong doesn't it." He went for the other end of Landowner's moustache and was pushed away again. "I already done one end so you'll 'ave to 'ave the other end matching, won't you?"

Landowner stuck out a hand, "Pass me the scissors."

"You must be joking, mun. I'm not going to give you a weapon. Now, be a good boy and let Uncle Dafydd even-up your moustache." He grabbed the moustache and snipped it before Landowner could protest.

Carrying their respective uniforms in their bags, Porcwrangler led Landowner through the warren of corridors that made up the municipal buildings of Amur. They ducked into doorways several times to avoid being seen. At one point, when there was nowhere to hide, Porcwrangler spun around and pushed Landowner up against the wall. "It's no use, mun, he's on death row, isn't he? All you can do is say hwyl fawr and carry on."

"Oh, I see," replied Landowner, playing along "well, that's a bally shame, is all I can say."

The two guards passed them by with a vaguely curious glance, then disappeared around the corner.

Porcwrangler shook his head. "From now on you're a mute. Got it?"

They eventually emerged in an alleyway from a side entrance. Porcwrangler breathed a sigh of relief. That was the tricky bit. Once outside, they were just two normal men – provided Landowner kept his gob shut. The next guard didn't start his shift for two-and-a-half decidays – they should be kilometres away by then.

After a long walk, they arrived at a wall with a bunch of crates stacked against it. Porcwrangler climbed the crates and gestured for Landowner to follow. They scrambled down the other side of the wall and headed towards some bins.

"What is this place?"

"The city morgue." He opened a huge bin full of clothes. "Throw your uniform into the bin but keep the bag."

They both put their uniforms in the bin.

"Right, let's get out of here."

"We came all the way here and climbed over a wall just to put our uniforms in a bin? We passed hundreds of places we could have disposed of them."

"After you escaped, taking me as hostage, you bought me here to steal some clothes and dump our uniforms. Duw a'n helpo! Try to keep up, mun! Come on, we're going to the station."

At the station, Porcwrangler bought two tickets to Lindi.

Landowner had rarely travelled by train. For short journeys, he would travel on horseback or by stagecoach – point to point. For longer trips, the comfort of a dirigible was preferable. "Why are we going to Lindi?"

Porcwrangler sighed. "From Lindi, we can go cross-country to Massa. From Massa, we can get a train to Limnio. At Limnio, you can pay me off, can't you?"

"That sounds complicated. Why don't we just get a dirigible straight to Limnio?"

"Because people who look like us don't travel by dirigible."

"So why then, did you choose to dress like this

and make things more complicated?" Landowner asked pompously. He had been out-thought by this scruffy low-life at every turn up until now, and was delighted to be able to find a flaw in his plan.

"Because, important people – people like you – never take a blind bit of notice of people who look like us. *Ever*. You look right through us as if we're not even there. And, as you're on the lam, that's exactly what you want them to do."

Landowner almost visibly deflated. Porcwrangler was, of course, absolutely right. As the train pulled into the station – a huge, gleaming monster of brass and steel, huffing and screeching as it fought against its own momentum – Landowner puffed his chest up again "Well, I think you're entirely wrong there. I think you'll find..." he began, knowing full well that his non-point would be lost in the cacophony of the locomotive. When the train finally came to a halt, Landowner spotted a pleasant-looking carriage and headed towards it, only to be stopped by a tug on his sleeve.

"That's first-class! We're over by there. Twmffat."

"You might as well kick your daps off – it's a long journey." Porcwrangler had said. But the seats were hard wooden benches, his travelling companions were smelly, and the carriage rattled and creaked and bounced along and, after a deciday in a third-class carriage, the novelty of train travel had well and truly worn off for Digby Landowner.

It didn't seem to bother his travelling companion, which annoyed Landowner even more.

Dafydd Porcwrangler had folded his scarf and put it up against the dirty carriage window. He rested his head on it, pulled his cap over his eyes, kicked off his shoes and had, apparently, gone straight to sleep.

Landowner eyed him with a mixture of envy, admiration, and contempt. The carriage bounced over a set of points and Porcwrangler's jacket fell open. Protruding from his jacket pocket was the top of his leather money pouch. Even more enticingly, he wore a holster with an ugly, stubby-looking pistol in it. He glanced around the carriage – there was no one facing in their direction. Cautiously, he waved a hand in front of Porcwrangler's face. No reaction.

The pistol looked very snug in the holster, so he decided to go for the money pouch first. He glanced around once more, then reached across the dozing guard. Grasping the top of the pouch between thumb and forefinger, he gave a gentle tug. Porcwrangler's eyes snapped open and, with cat-like reflexes, his hand shot out and grabbed Landowner by the wrist.

"Steal my money, would you?" his nostrils flared, and his eyes widened. He held his gaze for a few moments, before releasing his grip. "It'll be morning when we reach Lindi. I suggest you get some sleep – we have a long day ahead of us." Within a few microdays, he was dozing again.

Landowner glanced around again. A few heads had turned in his direction and he was getting disapproving looks. Chastened, he pulled his own cap over his eyes and feigned nonchalance. He was fuming and felt humiliated. This Porcwrangler man was really getting on his nerves now.

CHAPTER 29
Cabinda to Lindi

(Minimusday)

"So, what exactly is the plan then, Osh?"

Gonagain sighed, "I dunno, Bernie, if I'm honest."

They were in the mess drinking whiskey.

"I can tell you what the plan was *going* to be. I was going to go to this grand ball in Victoria, pretending to be Landowner. I would schmooze the right people, then casually mention that I still have the massive lump of pulsarnite, and was waiting for contact from Aoife. Then pretend that there must have been some massive mix up in communication that meant Aoife still thought she had the pulsarnite. Then I'd send for you, with the pulsarnite, and exchange it for Aoife."

"But now we don't have the pulsarnite."

"Exactly."

"I *am* sorry, Osh, really I am."

Gonagain poured another two fingers of whiskey each. "It wasn't your fault, Bernie. It's just one of those things. If I hadn't made such a bags of things with Aoife..."

"So, where does Lindi come into it then?"

"Well, it's almost on the way to Victoria, and I have a hunch that I can get a Trad uniform made there."

"What gives you that idea?"

"Those fancy suits of Namemaker's and some of the fabrics on Twoships' stall. They were labelled 'Made in Lindi'. And absolutely nothing about those two was legitimate."

"So, you're still planning to go to the ball?"

"I can't rescue Aoife without getting into the building, and that's an easy way in. I may just have to wing it from there."

"Not much of a plan, Osh."

"It's a shite plan, Bernie. And it's reckless. But I can't hang around; I may be too late already"

Bernie poured them both another whiskey and raised his glass. "To shite plans and recklessness."

******

"You don't have to go through with it, old girl. The skipper will understand."

Jao, who was perched on the upturned trunk that also served as a stool in Bunty's cabin, twiddled her glass between her fingers. "I know. But it means a lot to him. You know what he's like about keeping his crew safe and together. And even if *I* didn't like her, *he* obviously does. He'll do everything he can to keep me safe too. I just wish there was a proper plan."

Bunty poured herself another gin and offered the madeira bottle to Jao. To Bunty's surprise, she took it and poured another large glassful.

"Do you think he's in love with her, Bunty?"

"I don't know. If he *is,* he's not admitting it – even to himself. Once you've slept with someone there's always a connection that you didn't have before – but it isn't necessarily love." She sipped her gin. "Does it make a difference if he is?"

Jao stared into her glass of madeira as if she was looking for the answer in there. "No," she sighed, "I suppose not."

CHAPTER 30
Victoria

Aoife had cleared the mortar from around the window and swept it into a pile under her cot, but the bars were anchored deep into the brickwork. Wearily, she stood her cot on its end and began to climb the frame. She only reached the second slat before jumping down again. Her fingers and toes were agony. She was weak. Her spirit was broken. She sat on the dirt floor and hugged her knees and began to cry. Tears streamed down her face leaving clean streaks in the dirt that mottled her smooth, olive skin. After several minutes of sobbing like a child, she had exhausted all the emotion she had left within her. The ragged blanket was at her feet and the cot frame was upright. Her other plan came back into her head. She pulled the blanket towards her and tore it into strips. It was so thin and frayed that it came apart easily. She began to plait it into a rope.

When the guard came to take Aiofe for her daily 'interview', he knew straight away that something was up. There was usually noise coming from the gaol cell but today there was silence. He had been amazed that she seemed to keep herself occupied in the tiny cell but had never been quick enough to see what she was up to. As he rounded the corner, he should have been able to see the end of the cot, but it wasn't there. He reached the cell bars and peered into the gloom. The cot was standing on its end, supported by the bar they used to shackle prisoners' wrists. Dangling from the ankle bar at the bottom of the bed was a noose, made from plaited strips of blanket. The noose itself was empty. The prisoner sat huddled on the floor, hugging her knees, her face buried behind them. She looked up when she heard the guard approach, her dirty face streaked with tears. "Please don't hurt me anymore. I'll tell you everything I know." Her voice was trembling and cracking. She burst into tears again. The guard smiled, "Well, come on then! Get up and you can go spill the beans on your pals."

In the 'interview' room, her interrogator was already waiting. He was a slim, baby-faced man with a gentle lilting voice. He had his briefcase of tools open and was carefully organising them.

"She says she wants to sing," the guard said as he pushed Aoife into the room, "If you don't hurt her anymore." He slammed the door shut and walked away, whistling.

The interrogator looked genuinely disappointed as he closed his briefcase. "I'll leave it here… just in case."

Over an hour later, the guard came to get Aoife. The interrogator gave him a curt nod. Without a word, he led her back towards her cell, but carried on past it and up the stone staircase to the floor above. Aoife was led to a different cell. The brick walls were whitewashed, the window was at head height, the cot had a horsehair mattress, a sheet, and a thicker, cleaner blanket. The guard gestured for her to go through the steel door with its barred window. It was positive luxury compared to the previous cell.

"A nurse will come by and look at your fingers and toes." He locked the door behind him and paused before turning to leave. "You could have made it much easier, you know."

Aoife sat down on the bed. It was soft and comfortable, but it gave her no comfort. She had just told them everything she knew about *The Reliant*, its captain and his crew. She hated herself for it. She should have used the noose, but had not been able to bring herself to do it. Now she had betrayed Gonagain, Jao and Bunty – and the dog and the automaton. And for what? A few more days of incarceration before they hanged her anyway? She lay back on the bed and cried herself to sleep.

CHAPTER 31
Lindi

Emily Tutu piloted *The Reliant* into the dock at Lindi. She was seated in the captain's seat and beside her, in the co-pilot seat where Bearnárd normally sat, Etoile watched intently through the glass dome. They were the oddest-looking dirigible crew you could imagine. Emily was having one of those strange feelings that she had come to recognise as 'emotions'. She decided this was the one they called 'contentment'. It felt good.

She turned to Etoile. "You. should. go. and. wake. the. captain."

Etoile hopped down from the seat and skittered across the metal floor, her claws clattering as she went. She disappeared through the door.

If Emily Tutu was capable of it, she would have had a huge grin across her face.

Oisín Gonagain and Bearnárd Strongman looked every bit the part as they left *The Reliant* and headed into Lindi – two dapper gents, off to their tailor.

Bearnárd whistled, "Well, you certainly called

this one right, Osh. Look at this place!"

Virtually every shop in Lindi was based around the rag trade – tailors, fabric retailers, sewing machine repair shops, dyeworks, bespoke weavers...

"Where do we start, Bernie?"

"One end of the street and work our way down, I suppose."

Their request for a Traditionalist uniform was met with a variety of responses. Generally, they were treated with suspicion. One of the tailors demanded that they leave his premises immediately. As they worked their way down the street, the shops became less salubrious.

They marched confidently into the next shop and Gonagain spoke with without his usual brogue. "I wonder if you can help me. I'm in a spot of bother and desperately need a replacement for my dress uniform."

The tailor eyed Gonagain and Strongman warily. "Dog tags?"

Gonagain tugged at the chain around his neck and pulled Landowner's ID tags from under his shirt.

"Try Aldo Infila Ago. Don't tell him I sent you."

"Where..."

"First left, a hundred yards down. Go now."

Bearnárd looked at Gonagain with raised eyebrows. They were outside a tatty doorway with a flaking, painted sign that read 'Infila Ago's'.

Gonagain shrugged. "It's what yer man said.

Come on." He led Bearnárd down the dingy staircase.

It was surprisingly well lit and opulent in the cellar that served as Aldo Infila Ago's shop. A small, neat man with slicked-down hair and a tidy-pointed moustache approached them. He was impeccably dressed, in a sharply tailored waistcoat, and trousers. This was matched with a striped, collared shirt, a paisley cravat, and shiny Cuban heeled shoes.

"Good morning, gentlemen, Aldo Infila Ago at your service, how can I ah help you?" he spoke with a strong accent.

"I'm in a spot of bother and desperately need a replacement for my dress uniform."

"I'm afraid you have ah come to the wrong shop. Thank you, gentlemen," he gestured towards the door.

Gonagain was about to turn and leave when Bearnárd spoke. "Harry Twoships said this was the place to come."

The tailor, who up until now had focused entirely on Gonagain, turned to Bearnárd. "How do you know ah Signor Twoships?"

"Charlie Namemaker introduced me to him."

"Signor Namemaker? He ah passed many months ago. Gentleman, please." Again, he gestured to the door.

Bearnárd hesitated before blurting out his next sentence. "Well, he seemed well enough when we both escaped from the Trads in Isalo a couple of weeks ago."

"I don't think ah Signore Namemaker would be ah captured by Traditionalists"

"He was captured by the S.A.G. They sold him to the Trads as a slave."

"The S.A.G. *were* after him," Infila Ago mused. "So, Charlie's alive and well?" Aldo's accent slipped. He jerked his head backwards. "Come through to the back, lads. I reckon I've got enough Phoenician red twill to accommodate a fella of your build. When d'you need it?"

"Er... as soon as possible." Gonagain was still slightly bewildered by Aldo's sudden change of accent and attitude.

"I can do it in four hours, but it'll cost you. Arms out!" He whipped the measuring tape from around his neck and began to take Gonagain's measurements.

Outside the shabby doorway, Gonagain raised an eyebrow at Bearnárd. "Well played, Bernie. Well played." He reached for the brim of his brown bowler hat and tugged at the varilight goggles that sat on the brim. "Well, we've got four hours in Lindi. What do want to do?"

"I don't know about you, Osh, but I could eat a horse. Shall we get some breakfast?"

"I saw a café outside the railway station."

Gonagain and Bearnárd walked to the station, varilights on, in comfortable silence. Gonagain was mulling over the possibilities at the grand ball.

Bearnárd was just enjoying the sights and sounds of a new town. He spotted a very smart hansom cab, fully enclosed, with well-to-do passengers, being pulled by a shining black stallion. Shortly after, they passed two street dwellers having a scrap. "It's a funny old town this, Osh," he mused.

******

Bunty and Jao were sitting in the café just outside the railway station. Jao had finished her porridge and was nursing a second cup of coffee. Bunty was mopping the egg yolk and bacon fat off her plate with her bread.

"Fancy a bit of girly shopping?"

Jao adjusted her cup in her saucer. "I've barely worn what I bought in Skydock 101."

"Jao, you're not poor anymore. You don't have to wait until your clothes disintegrate before you buy another outfit."

"It just seems very… extravagant. Wasteful."

"Not if you buy quality and timeless style. They'll last you a lifetime." Bunty caught the eye of the waiter. "We'll have the bill, when you're ready, young man." She watched the waiter's buttocks as he went back to the till.

Jao was putting on her varilights. Despite it being breakfast time, it was already getting dark. "Oh look, there's the captain and Bearnárd. Any luck with the uniform, Captain?"

"Yes. We've got four hours to kill before I can

pick it up though."

"Well, that settles it, old girl; let's go and shop."

The waiter arrived with the bill and made a beeline for Bunty.

Bunty gestured to Gonagain and Bearnárd. "These two kind gentlemen have offered to settle our bill. Thanks awfully for the lovely service." She winked at Gonagain. "Give him a good tip!"

CHAPTER 32
Lindi to Limnio

Digby Landowner had fidgeted in his seat for hours before finally drifting off to sleep, so he was quite irritated to be woken by Porcwrangler kicking the soles of his shoes less than an hour later.

"Come on, mun, we're here."

The powerful locomotive was huffing and heaving and generally fighting the momentum it had built up. Landowner put on his varilights and peered through the smut-coated window. Platform signs with 'Lindi' painted on them trundled past, until the train finally ground to a halt with a protracted hiss.

They alighted at a pleasant, little, rural station, which Porcwrangler marched through purposefully. Outside, he approached the row of horse-drawn carriages and carts – and began negotiating.

Landowner gazed around him wearily. Two women at the café caught his attention. They were facing out toward the street, so Landowner couldn't quite see their faces, but he felt sure he recognised them. He edged further into the station approach to try and get a better angle.

"Have a care!" A hansom cab rattled past on the cobbles, the hub of the enormous, wooden wheel nearly catching him on the hip. Landowner skipped hastily back toward the station and glared at the cab. It was true, what Porcwrangler had said: no one paid you any attention when you looked like this. The cab was a luxury model, completely enclosed for the passengers, width-hinged doors at legs and a fold down glass screen at the top. Even the cab driver, who sat high at the back, had a folding fabric canopy to keep the rain off. It was painted in a glossy black with gold trim.

"Come on, mun, there's no time to ling di long. We have a ride to Massa."

Landowner took one last look at the ladies in the café before turning to follow Porcwrangler. He felt certain he knew who they were. They had not gone more than a dozen steps, when he spotted the two men coming towards him. He might not have noticed them with their varilights on – the smaller one had also grown a stubbly moustache – but the presence of their female crewmates in the café had made him more aware.

"Give me your gun!" Landowner blurted to his companion.

"I'm not being funny, but…"

Landowner lunged at Porcwrangler, trying to grab his gun. The shabby guard was caught by surprise, but he grabbed him by the wrist and began to twist his hand. With his free hand, Landowner gripped his adversary's throat. "I'll give it back, you idiot. I'm not going to use it on you." Porcwrangler spun around, further twisting the man's wrist, and elbowed him in the ribs.

His throat now released, Porcwrangler turned to his assailant and attempted to deliver a headbutt to the bridge of his nose, but the lanky sergeant straightened to his usual upright stance and the headbutt caught him on the mouth instead. Both men peeled away clutching their faces.

Porcwrangler was bleeding from a cut on his forehead and Landowner, who had lost a tooth, was bleeding from the mouth. They glared at each other, trying to catch their breath. Porcwrangler grinned. "Well, that was a right old clatsio, wasn't it?"

Something about Porcwrangler's demeanour and vocabulary made Landowner smile despite himself. It was as he was smiling his awkward smile, that the scruffy guard punched him hard in the thigh. He crumpled to Porcwrangler's height. Porcwrangler wished he'd thought of that before the headbutt.

Grabbing Landowner by the lapels, he pulled him towards his own face. "What it is, is I'm in charge yur, and if you ever pull a stunt like that again, I'll put bullet through your kneecap." Still holding him by a lapel, he marched the limping sergeant to a cart loaded with coal and bundled him on, climbing on himself afterwards. "Okay, Drive, Massa, quick as you can."

The coal cart trundled off as Landowner

watched the crew of *The Reliant* in the café. He swallowed a mouthful of blood. "What would you come to Lindi for?" he mused aloud.

"Clothes. Cheap copies of expensive clothes," replied Porcwrangler.

Digby Landowner nodded. It was a rhetorical question, but he was gratified by the confirmation anyway.

******

The whole crew, or at least the human element, had descended upon Infila Ago's. Gonagain emerged, self-consciously, from the changing room in his new, Traditionalist, dress uniform. The crimson twill, double-breasted tunic was slightly longer than a bolero jacket. The curved hem was cut high over the hips but dipped lower at the front and back. It buttoned at the front with two rows of ten shiny brass buttons. Black epaulettes and a black mandarin collar finished with gold braid and the regiment crest completed the look. The trousers were simple and black with a wide crimson side-taping.

Bunty wolf whistled. "I say! You might have trouble hanging onto him at the ball, Jao old girl!"

Gonagain blushed slightly. Jao, for reasons she didn't quite understand, blushed even more. She didn't think it had much to do with Bunty, and she was glad that her dark skin didn't show quite how flushed she was.

Bearnárd watched the reaction of the ladies. "We're going to have to stay another four hours, Osh, I need to get one of these too," he joked.

Aldo Infila Ago fussed around Gonagain, straightening hems, and brushing off imaginary threads. "Right, from any normal angle, this is an authentic Trad uniform, but do *not* let anyone see the inside of the tunic. The bias is made from canvas because I didn't have enough twill. I've dyed it Phoenician red, but it's not colour-fast, so don't get it wet either."

He handed Gonagain a cap. "I'm a tailor, not a milliner, but this will pass as an authentic Trad cap, as long as it stays on your head or under your arm. Don't take it off and on unless you absolutely need to, and don't let anyone else handle it – it's not nearly rigid enough. Don't leave it upside-down on a table either. To start with, that's not how officers are trained to look after their uniform and, more importantly, the lining isn't accurate – it's too shiny."

Gonagain carefully placed the cap on his head and adjusted it in the mirror.

"Oh!" sighed Bunty, "I *do* like a man in uniform."

Aldo looked Gonagain up and down – and frowned when his gaze alighted on his brown brogues. "You're going to need new shoes. I can't help you with that, but you want black, five-hole oxfords with a dress uniform. Not derbies – and definitely not brogues."

Gonagain took a mental note, wishing he knew

the difference between oxfords and derbies.

******

It had been an uncomfortable ride, along bumpy dirt tracks, sitting on a bag of coal. Landowner's mouth had stopped bleeding, but his dead leg was still very sore. He had blood down his front and coal smuts on his back. His scruffy clothes still smelled of whoever was wearing them when they died. He had a missing tooth, a lopsided moustache, and a limp. He was feeling very sorry for himself indeed.

The coalman had stopped for a call of nature and Digby relished the relative comfort of quiescence. He wriggled himself between two sacks to try and get a less disagreeable ride. A distant humming caught his attention and he searched the sky for its source. A dirigible with – if he was not mistaken – three propellers. It was in silhouette against the dawn sky and, with the colour distortion of his cheap varilights, he probably wouldn't be able to gauge its hue anyway. He was certain that it was yellow though. Working from the position of the dawn sun, he estimated that it was travelling due east.

He nudged Porcwrangler and nodded skywards. "Does that look like it's heading to Victoria to you?"

Porcwrangler's cheeks rose as he squinted under his varilights. "That direction, isn't it?"

Before long, they had reached the railway station at Massa. Porcwrangler hopped down from the coal cart. “Thanks, Drive!” he waved cheerily to the coalman. Landowner hobbled after him.

The station at Massa was, in fact, just a signal telling the driver to stop. A handful of people stood alongside the track, waiting patiently.

Landowner was barely aware of them. He had been deep in thought since spotting the three-prop dirigible and had made a mental assessment. The tatty airship going to Victoria, the moustache that its captain was growing, the visit to Lindi where they made copies of clothes, and the invitation that had been taken along with his Landowner pocket watch and other possessions. The captain of *The Reliant* was going to the ball, as Staff Sergeant Digby Landowner.

It was late afternoon when the train from Massa pulled into Limnio station. The train driver halted the huge, steam locomotive and waited a few cursory seconds before reaching for the brake release, but he was stopped by something he had never heard before – a carriage door opening and closing at Limnio station. The station had been built entirely for the benefit of the Limnio Landowners – an incredibly wealthy family who owned the vineyards that dominated the landscape as far as the eye could see. But the Landowners never used the railway and thus he made this stop, every journey, for no apparent reason. He poked his head out and peered down the unmanned platform. Two scruffy men had alighted – and were wearily plodding down the platform to the path that led to Limnio Manor. The taller one had a slight limp. They were either drunk, lost or looking for work... or a combination. A few curious passengers were leaning out of the window to get a better look. The driver shrugged and released the brake, and the enormous locomotive creaked and chuffed as it overcame the inertia, to continue its journey.

Landowner led Porcwrangler up the compacted gravel road that zigzagged out of the railway cutting, to the gates of Limnio Manor. As the imposing house came into view, Porcwrangler paused to take it all in.

A red brick wall with white capstones, about eight feet high, surrounded the grounds of Limnio Manor. An ornate, wrought-iron, double gate, flanked by enormous brick pillars framed the grand house.

A gravel drive lined with plaster sculptures and planters dissected the lush lawn, and led to the large disembarkation area in front of the grand building.

The red-brick house itself, was entirely symmetrical. A large double door, with a gabled roof supported by white pillars, sat squarely in the middle. A set of white, stone steps that narrowed as they rose, invited you to the door. There were four large, sash windows on either side of the door. Another row of smaller, sash windows on the floors immediately below and above. The black, slate, mansard roof had a fourth row of tiny dormer windows.

"I won't lie to you, that is lush!"

Landowner smiled to himself. For the first time since he met this irritating oik, he felt his natural superiority was being recognised.

The locked gate of the walled garden looked like the pearly gates themselves as far as Dafydd Porcwrangler was concerned. They gleamed like new, and iron swirls framed the Landowner crest beautifully. Digby Landowner clanged the heavy bronze bell that hung on the gate pillar, and the two men watched as a gentleman clad in black and white walked elegantly and sedately down the drive. He stopped halfway and peered at them. "Go away! There's nothing here for you," he shouted and turned on his heels.

"Wait! Wait! Silvertray? Is that you? It's *me*! Sir Digby."

The man turned back and peered at them again. He took a few steps closer and squinted at them once more.

"Silvertray, it's *me* – Sir Digby. I'm in disguise."

The servant marched forward, "I'm terribly sorry, sir, I didn't recognise you." He unlocked the gate, eyeing Porcwrangler suspiciously as he did so.

"That's quite alright, Silvertray. Get father, will you."

As they walked up the gravel drive with Silvertray, Porcwrangler considered his options. Walking into a house with a family member at gunpoint didn't seem the most diplomatic way to start negotiations. On the other hand, he was outnumbered now, and Landowner was on home turf. He felt vulnerable. He took his homemade pistol from his jacket and tucked it into the back of his breeches.

Inside the great house, Landowner and Porcwrangler stood in the grand entrance hall waiting for Silvertray to fetch Landowner senior. The oak floor gleamed and generations of Landowners stared pompously from gilt frames on the oak-panelled walls. The room was dominated by an imposing double staircase and an elaborate chandelier that hung from a ceiling adorned with a large plaster ceiling rose and cornices. There were multiple doors on both sides of the symmetrical room.

A tall man with extravagant grey facial hair emerged through one of the doorways. He was wearing a burgundy silk smoking jacket and clutching a pipe. "Digby! Look at the state of you. What's the meaning of coming to Limnio looking like that? And who is *he*?"

"Hello, father. It's a long story. Suffice to say I've had a trying time. I've been kidnapped and imprisoned, and my companion here helped me to escape. Two bars of bullion from the safe should be enough to repay him and he'll be on his way."

Archibald Landowner harrumphed. "I see. Very well, I'll fetch them." He marched out of the room, mumbling as he went.

There was a protracted silence as Porcwrangler and Landowner waited for Archibald Landowner to return. He eventually emerged from a different door, momentarily catching Porcwrangler off guard. He tossed a double-barrelled shotgun to

Digby, who caught it cleanly.

"Two bars of bullion, loaded. You know where to take him?"

"Yes, father, thank you." He raised the shotgun and pointed it straight at Porcwrangler.

Porcwrangler reached to the back of his breeches, but his homemade pistol was not there. He scanned the floor hopefully,

"No sir, you haven't dropped it." It was Silvertray, standing behind him, who spoke. He was holding Dafydd's pistol between his forefinger and thumb, as if he was afraid of catching something from it. "I took the liberty – for safety's sake."

"Right, you arrogant, irritating, little pleb. Hands on your head and turn around," Digby Landowner hissed.

Porcwrangler did as he was instructed without a word.

"Did you really think I would pay you just for opening a cell door?" He poked him in the back with the shot gun. "Walk."

The scruffy guard was shoved and poked into the grounds of the grand house, down an overgrown path, until they reached a pig sty.

"Quite appropriate wouldn't you say, Porcwrangler? I expect you know why I bought you here."

Porcwrangler turned slowly, to face his foe. "Because pigs eat everything and anything."

"That's right, pig man. In a few days, you'll be nothing but pig faeces."

The sergeant raised the shotgun to Porcwrangler's face. In an apparent act of desperation, his captive lunged, and made a grab for the gun. Landowners fingers twitched reflexively, and he emptied both barrels into the chest of the scruffy guard. The force of the shot sent him flying across the sty. He crashed into the wall, before falling forward into the mud and faeces where he lay motionless with his head in the trough.

Staff Sergeant Digby Landowner turned and walk back to his house. If it wasn't for his limp, there would have been a spring in his step. The natural order was being restored. Next stop – Victoria.

CHAPTER 33
Skydock 21

1.05.1910 (Polexday) /
January 23, 1910 (Friday)

Harry Twoships should have been delighted with himself. He had just brokered a deal that had made him a huge amount of money. He had the cheque in his pocket and had already sent a pantelegraph of it to his accountant. But the fact that Charlie Namemaker had made fifty times that amount from the deal, muted his good mood somewhat. It was only a few days since Twoships had offered him a job on one of his airships, and now Namemaker was buying himself a dirigible that was better than any that Twoships owned. He slouched back into the dirigible dealership, where the salesman was in full flow.

"The Darwin Colugo is a whole new concept. As you can see, the envelope is not the usual lozenge shape. It's only a metre deep but almost fifty metres wide – we call it a 'delta wing'. If for any reason the envelope is breached and suffers a total loss of heliagen, the vessel would simply glide to ground. With the six engines at full power – did I mention that it's the only six-engined vessel on the market? – you can glide for up to fifty kilometres. It's the nearest thing to heavier-than-air flight so far."

"Probably ever," conceded Namemaker.

"Oh no, sir! Heavier-than-air flight is the raison d'etre of Darwin Incorporated. We believe we are only a few years from making it a reality."

Charlie snorted, "So, it's a heliagen craft then?"

"Well, as it is technically a hard-shell vessel, you could legally fill it with hydrum – but I wouldn't recommend it. The envelope is pure mercuriumite so we managed to get it down to less than a millimetre thick. Did I mention that the 'delta wing' makes it the fastest dirigible on the market?"

Harry Twoships shuffled impatiently. "Sorry to interrupt, mate, but I was just checking the board in the pantelegraph room – your name is on it."

"Can't be. Everyone thinks I'm dead."

"Not everyone, apparently. I told him to start printing it out."

"Where's the original?"

"Lindi."

By the time Charlie reached the pantelegraph room, the message was waiting for him. It was from Aldo Infila Ago.

Wotcha Charlie! I had two geezers in here claiming you wasn't dead no more. They said you escaped from some mine shaft. They bought a fake Trad uniform and left for Victoria. Any of this make sense? Aldo.

Charlie re-read it, twice. "Flippin' 'eck!" he exclaimed aloud. "The idiots are going straight into the lions' den to rescue his bit of petticoat."

The pantelegraph operator stared at him, nonplussed.

“I need to send a message.” He grabbed a pencil and some paper, and wrote in a surprisingly elegant hand.

Whatever you may have heard, I’m not dead. I need information on an acquaintance, Captain Oisín Gonagain of The Reliant, and his crew. Keep me informed of his movements and there’s a few ariary in it for you. Charlie Namemaker.

He handed it to the operator.

“Is it a return message?”

“Multiple recipients. Give me another sheet and I’ll write a list.”

As he strode purposefully back to the dirigible dealership, he contemplated his motives. Why did he care what happened to Oisín and Bearnárd? It wasn’t like him at all. He never usually gave a mark a second thought, even after a long hustle. Maybe he was going soft in his old age, but those two brothers had really got under his skin.

CHAPTER 34
Victoria

The Reliant bumped gently down at Victoria West Airdock. It was almost as large as the airdock in Stanleyville, with just as many clocks. Unlike the grey block in Stanleyville, it was white and curved and elegant, with clean lines and geometric symmetry, and the warm sun cast interesting shadows across the edifice. The words 'Victoria West Airdock' were emblazoned on the building in a modern font, which was all circular curves and pointed angles. It was one of three similar airdocks in the town.

Gonagain exhaled loudly. He hadn't realised that he had been holding his breath. He had been half expecting a military welcoming committee.

"Right. I'm going to the dock office to sign-in. Stay here and keep your eyes peeled for anything out of the ordinary and be ready to take off. Emily Tutu, you're going to have to make yourself scarce, I'm afraid. We're in the Traditionalist heartland – they won't take kindly to your sort."

"I. understand."

The inside of the dock office complemented the external structure. There was a lot of mirror-finished metal and glass, in the same modern style but with more curves and geometric shapes. It was a style that Gonagain had not seen before. The clerk was a female Trad soldier and ultra-efficient. She presented him with a pen and a form with barely a break from her filing. He filled in the form as vaguely as he could – with plenty of omissions, but as few actual lies as possible – and handed it back the clerk.

She studied it carefully. "Thank you, Captain Gonagain, that all seems in order." She turned to the next customer.

Gonagain headed back to *The Reliant*. That had all gone smoothly, but he felt unnerved. Something just didn't feel right.

"All good, Skipper?"

"On the surface, at least."

"What's the plan?"

"I need to find a cobbler and buy myself some 'Oxfords' – whatever they are. We should all do a reconnaissance. Get your bearings. Keep together, in groups or pairs. Who's coming to the cobblers?"

"Tempting though that offer is, I'll pass if that's alright with you, Skip," Bunty replied sarcastically.

"Stick with Bernie then. Jao, you can accompany me."

"Okay, Captain."

"Don't go out in your overalls sweetie, you'll stick-out like a sore thumb. This is *Victoria*, you know?"

Jao glanced at Gonagain, who was clearly itching to get going. "I'll be ten minutes!"

Fifteen minutes later, Jao re-emerged in an ivory and pink, ankle-length, floral dress. She wore a layered petticoat underneath, which made her slim, boyish hips more feminine and gave the skirt a gentle, bell shape. The bodice was tight and made her wasp-like waist look tiny. It had a sweetheart neckline and was cut and wired to accentuate her small breasts, enough to create some cleavage. The tight sleeves showed off her long elegant arms.

She had applied some pink lipstick, which contrasted with her smooth chocolate skin beautifully, and the addition of some eyeliner and mascara framed her striking, cerulean eyes.

Her hair hung in silky tresses around her shoulders and, perched on her head, was an ivory-coloured, wide-brimmed bonnet, tied with a pale pink, silk scarf. An ivory choker with a large kunzite stone completed the look.

Bearnárd wolf-whistled.

Jao blushed.

Gonagain, who had been shuffling from one foot to the other impatiently, stood open-mouthed. "Jao, you look... well, you look... you..." he stammered.

"I think what the skipper is trying to say, is that you're absolutely beautiful, Jao."

"Yes... beautiful."

She blushed some more.

Gonagain proffered his elbow. “Shall we take-in the town, Madam?”

Jao slipped her arm in his. “That would be lovely.”

As Gonagain and Jao left the mess, without saying goodbye, Bunty Goodtime winked at Bearnárd. “Nice work if you can get it.”

Bearnárd stood and proffered his elbow. “Shall we take-in the town, Madam?” he asked mockingly.

Bunty fluttered her eyelashes and clutched her hands to her heart. “That would be lovely!”

They burst out laughing.

“Come on, Etoile, let’s hit the town. See you later, Emily,” Bearnárd called out as he left.

“Keep. vigilant. Bearnárd. and. Bunty.”

“We will, Emily old girl, you too.

Victoria was a town that proudly displayed its wealth. The buildings were maintained immaculately. Many were centuries old, with styles from Gothic and Baroque, to the more contemporary houses with their sash windows and cast window ornamentations. But it was the newly-built, ultra-modern buildings that caught the eye. Like the air-dock, they were smooth and sleek, with flat roofs and geometric protrusions. They were bright white with black or grey windows and very minimal ornamentation. When it came to style, Victoria was the place to come if you wanted to see the future.

Jao was observing the style of the clothes. The

more mature ladies were elegantly dressed in a similar fashion to herself – but many of the younger women were attired in a very different mode. Their dresses were quite shapeless and straight, with virtually no waistline at all – their belts were around their hips and the skirts stopped just below the knee. There were lots of tassels and beads to be seen. Hats were largely brimless – some shaped like a bell, some more like swim hat. She even spotted women wearing turbans. Jao didn't like the way it looked. Even though her slender figure would suit the style perfectly, she decided she liked her own clothes better.

As they strolled nearer to the town centre, they became increasingly aware of the strong military presence. By the time they reached the Hotel de Ville in Twelve Bells Square, roughly one in four men were in uniform and as many as one in ten women.

"Feck! Look at all them Trad soldiers. I hope I'm not biting off more than I can chew."

Jao bit her lip nervously and didn't reply.

"We'll do a lap of the Hotel de Ville and then see if we can find a cobbler."

Bearnárd shuffled uneasily from one foot to the other outside the Victoria library. Dogs were not allowed inside, so he and Etoile were forced to wait on the street whilst Bunty did her research inside. He was astounded by the number of people in military uniform walking by. They really were in the

Traditionalist heartland.

Inside, Bunty was chatting with the librarian. "I've just arrived in town and I'm fascinated by the mixture of architecture. The Hotel de Ville is particularly impressive – baroque architecture I believe?"

"That's right – you obviously know your subject. It's one of the finest examples in the world."

"Do you have anything about its construction? Or are there any tours of the building?"

"It's not open to the public, I'm afraid – since those awful Pulsers started ruining the world, the Traditionalist Army has been forced to take it over as HQ. We do have a lovely book about it in our reference section though. Let me show you."

CHAPTER 35
Lubumbashi

(Annularisday)

Deep underground, in the forests of Lubumbashi, a massive steam engine began to rumble. There probably wasn't enough pulsarnite in the world to power the huge machine, so old technology was a necessary evil. Above ground, the unnatural looking rectangular grassy knoll split in two, as one section hinged downwards, forming a grassy ramp, and the other began to rise upward, exposing the munitions factory to the air. Captain Warehouse looked on with tainted pride as the First Century of M.L.E.s marched up the ramp. This should have been a defining moment in his military career, but he was acutely aware that the century was, in fact, only ninety-nine. He glared at the empty space in the tenth row.

The automatons were followed by the Sonic

Missile Launcher (or *The Smile*, as it had been dubbed). A massive machine – the size of house – on enormous caterpillar tracks, with a pulsarnite canon mounted on top. The Captain of *The Smile* saluted as he passed, whilst the pilot's face was a mask of concentration. Captain Warehouse saluted back. Here, too, he was unable to take full pride. The Geokinetic army had been obliged to buy back their *own* pulsarnite rock – at enormous cost – from an unknown agent, who had acquired it after it was stolen in the New Year's Eve raid. There had been no choice – *The Smile*'s 'energy capture unit' had been built around that specific rock, in order to be able to use it in its entirety. Unfortunately, when the rock was returned, it wasn't entire – a cylindrical piece had been cut out of it. It hadn't gone unnoticed that the missing piece was the exact shape and size to fit the missing M.L.E.

The century of automatons parted, allowing *The Smile* to take the lead. It crashed through the forest destroying everything in its path, followed now by the First Century. A cohort of regulars in pulsarnite-powered personnel carriers (triple-PCs) took up the rear as they began the long journey north, to Victoria.

CHAPTER 36
Limnio

Young Dafydd Porcwrangler didn't really remember his parents. He had a very vague sense of his mother but couldn't picture her face. They had both been taken by cholera when he was small. It was left to his reluctant bampi – his *father's* father – to raise him. Bampi was an old-fashioned man and had little time for children. He didn't believe in showing affection either. One of Dafydd's earliest memories was going to his bampi for a cwtch after his parents' funeral, and being told it wasn't manly to cry or cwtch with other men.

Dafydd worked on his bampi's farm from day one. He had no siblings, no friends, and no toys. He talked to the pigs and found ways to entertain himself. When he could, he would run off to the village school and listen outside – sometimes daring to look through the window at the chalkboard. He found old newspapers and taught himself to read. It was a slow process. At first, he just looked for the words he knew and read them aloud. Gradually he learned how letters put together made words. He would read the words aloud, often without knowing their meaning. Later he would ask his bampi what the words meant, or just listen out for people saying them.

He also liked to make things. He made a pulley system to help him move reluctant pigs and heavy sacks of feed. He also created a hopper system, so he only needed to lift the food sacks once and then release the feed gradually through the hopper.

Despite working on the little pig farm, Dafydd never ate pork. "Pork's not for the likes of you and me," Bampi would say.

Bampi's pride and joy was his shotgun. He used it to hunt rabbit, hare, squirrel, or pigeon and that kept them both fed. Bampi showed Dafydd how to clean and maintain the shotgun and it became his favourite job. He yearned to have a gun of his own and set his mind to making one. He collected old pieces of lead piping and branches of oak and other odds and ends. When he found an old spring, he decided he had the materials he needed. He collected Bampi's used shotgun cartridges and refilled them, stealing a tiny bit of gunpowder from as many new cartridges as possible.

The first time he fired his new weapon, it exploded in his hand. He screamed as the gunpowder burned his hand and it was peppered with shrapnel. He ran to the water butt and immersed his hand, struggling to stifle his sobs. He spent the next hour picking fragments of metal from his hand before bandaging it.

"What happened to your hand, boy?" Bampi asked.

"Pig bit it."

Dafydd wasn't deterred, and he continued his quest to build a gun. He had little success and, despite efforts to protect his hand, suffered more – albeit less severe – injuries. Indeed, the development of his hand protectors made more progress than the gun. It was while he was sporting a wrap of bandages, under a gentleman's lost glove, with a layer of wire wool in between, that he realised he should switch his focus.

Several years passed before he decided he was ready to market his new product. He had switched from hand protection to body protection and invented what he called a 'bullet resistant vest'. A double-layered, leather garment with mercuriumite wire weaved through it. By this time, the hostilities between the Pulsers and the Traditionalists had begun in earnest, and Dafydd realised that there was little point in marketing his vest to the Trads – they were being shot at with pulsarnite weapons. He would have to join the Geokinetics. One morning, he packed his bampi's kit bag and left without a word. He hitched his way to the nearest Geo town and signed up with the Geo Guards. He kept his invention secret. He had decided to wait until he met someone of a high enough rank.

******

Dafydd wasn't sure whether it was the sound of a dirigible overhead, or the large, Old Spot pig nudging his head out of the trough, that bought him back to consciousness. For a moment, he thought he was on bampi's farm. The back of his head hurt. He touched it and winced. He studied his hand, which was covered in congealing blood. His chest hurt too. He remembered the shotgun pointing at his head and the desperate lunge to point it downwards. Then it all came back to him – Landowner, the journey, Landowner's father and Silvertray. He sat up with a groan and undid his tunic. His vest was destroyed but it had done its job. His chest was bruised and bleeding, but the wounds were shallow cuts made by the mercuriumite wire.

Using both the trough and a recumbent pig for support, Porcwrangler struggled to his feet and headed towards the big house. Around the back, the door to the kitchen was open. He ambled in as if he belonged there. The first person he encountered was a scullery maid.

"Who are...?"

Porcwrangler put a finger to his lips and she stopped mid-sentence. He ushered her into the larder and, with a silent warning to keep quiet, shut the door and bolted it. No fight and no pride – that was what was wrong with the working class – he thought to himself.

The cook was labouring over a pot of stew on the stove, oblivious to his presence. Porcwrangler snuck up behind her, picking up a carving knife on his way. He reached around and put a hand over her mouth showing her the knife as he did so.

"I'll be honest with you, I don't *want* to hurt you, 'cause you're only staff see? But I will if I have to." The cook nodded her comprehension and he bundled her in with the scullery maid. "I'll be back now, in a minute."

On his way past, he dunked the ladle into the stew and took a sip. "Needs more salt." Then he spotted a box of red apples. "Where on earth do you get fresh apples at this time of year?" he bit into one. "Mmph! That is lush."

Upstairs, just off the hall, Porcwrangler found the armoury. His old, shonky pistol was in a drawer but he passed over it for a Peacemaker revolver. He dropped the apple core and the carving knife in its place. He opened the cylinder and found all six chambers empty. An old tune from his childhood popped into his head and he began to hum as he loaded the revolver, pocketing the spare ammunition. He didn't know the words to the song, but it was one the workmen used to sing in the taverns on a Friday night after payday. It was something about revolution and overthrowing the oppressors, he was sure.

Still humming under his breath, Dafydd Porcwrangler sauntered casually but quietly around the ground floor of the grand house, keeping an eye out for valuables as he went. Passing an open doorway, he felt a sudden warmth envelope him – followed by the sound of a crackling fire. He tiptoed inside.

There, at the far end of the library, was the old man. He was lounging in a large wing-back armchair and Porcwrangler could only see his legs and feet, which he was warming being at the fire. He cocked the hammer of the peacemaker and, moving as stealthily as he could, approached the prone figure. The old man suddenly jolted upright in his seat and craned his neck around the chair, staring with a with a look of disbelief at the filthy peasant in his library.

Porcwrangler realised it was the large ornate mirror above the fireplace that had given him away. "Hello, Archie. Surprise!" he grinned.

A movement in the large mirror caught his eye and he spun around. "Oh look! It's my old butty, Silvertray."

The sound of scraping furniture alerted him to movement behind him, he spun back again to find Archibald Landowner several feet closer. He pointed the revolver at him, and he stopped in his tracks, but Porcwrangler could see Silvertray making another move in the large mirror.

"Bugger this!" He vaulted a writing bureau, using the chair as a springboard, spun around once more, and backed up towards the window. He now had the two men at ten o'clock and two o'clock, rather than twelve and six.

"That's more like it. Now, Silvertray, despite your behaviour earlier, I don't really want to hurt you. You're only staff, see? But Archie here is another matter, isn't it? You want to start preparing your last words Archie."

The butler took two long, graceful strides and stood between Porcwrangler and Archibald Landowner. “You’ll have to go through me first.”

“Don’t be twp Silvertray, you don’t owe him anything. Not your life that’s for sure. Stand aside now.”

“I mean it. If you’re going to kill Lord Landowner, you’ll have to kill me first.”

Porcwrangler sighed, shrugged, raised his pistol, and shot the butler between the eyes. Silvertray had just enough time to register his surprise before slumping to the floor. Archibald Landowner spluttered for a moment, before contenting himself with opening and closing his mouth silently, like a goldfish. He was spattered with Silvertray’s blood.

The sound of the gunshot brought people from around the house rushing to the library.

“Welcome, welcome. Come on in and join the party!” Porcwrangler waved each person in with his revolver until the flow of arrivals petered out. “Now, are we all yur?” His question was greeted with silence.

When he was younger, Porcwrangler had occasionally minded pigs for a local gentleman. He was familiar with the livery of house staff and could easily ascertain who was who. He made a deliberate show of cocking the revolver before addressing the housekeeper. “Mr Silvertray made the mistake of trying to be a hero. I do hope no one else makes the same mistake. Is there anyone in the house who is not in this room?”

"The cook and the scullery maid are missing, and none of the ground staff are here. I couldn't rightly say where all the family are."

"Where is Digby?" Porcwrangler was addressing the whole group.

"He left in *The Swift*. Less than an hour ago." It was the chauffeur who spoke.

"*The Swift*?"

"It's a Tornado Micro, a single-seater dirigible."

Porcwrangler remembered the sound of a dirigible overhead when he came around. He checked his battered pocket watch – he had been conscious less than an hour. "Are there any other dirigibles?"

"There's a Dreamcloud Club Class and a Dream Cloud Express."

"And you can fly either of them?"

"Not on my own." The Chauffeur hesitated before adding, "But with two crew I can pilot the Express."

"How many to pilot the Club Class?"

"Four."

Porcwrangler paced up and down for a few moments. The Club Class would make the right impression. People stop and take notice when you arrive in a Dreamcloud Club Class. But a crew of four would be a lot to handle if they decided to mutiny. He kept the revolver trained on the assembled group and he continued to hum as he deliberated his next move. To the family and staff, he looked as mad as a box of frogs.

"Right. Family over by yur." He gestured with

the barrel of the revolver. "Staff over by yur."

The group split, mostly, as he expected. He approached a young man in the staff group. "What's your job then?"

"Footman."

Porcwrangler eyed him up and down. He was far too elegantly dressed to be staff. "That's not footman livery."

"It's my day off."

"What brand of boot polish do you use?"

"Err... Um."

Porcwrangler shot him in the head and he slumped to the ground. The maids screamed and one of the ladies fainted. A wet patch appeared on the crotch of one of the gentlemen.

"I don't like being lied to and I don't like being crossed. But most of all I don't like to be taken for a twpsyn." He turned to the family. "An idiot," he explained.

"You crossed me earlier didn't you Archie? When you went for the ingots."

Archibald Landowner harrumphed.

"Kneel down and repeat after me – I relinquish my command of the house and you, Dafydd Porcwrangler, are in control."

"I shall do no such thing."

Porcwrangler cocked the peacemaker and pointed it at his head. "I'll give you one last chance."

Archibald Landowner opened and closed his mouth silently again. He glanced, briefly, at his family and staff before straightening his back and closing his eyes. "Never!"

The gunfire echoed around the library. Blood spattered the wall and Archibald Landowner fell heavily to the floor. There were more screams and whimpering.

"Who's next in command?"

There was a moment's nervous silence before the chauffeur spoke up again. "Sir Digby."

"Who's next in command out of the people in this room?" Porcwrangler replied impatiently.

"Sir Humphrey."

"And which one is Sir Humphrey."

"He is." The chauffeur pointed to the corpse who had tried to pass himself as a footman.

Porcwrangler sighed. His impatience was starting to get the better of him. He spoke slowly and deliberately, as if addressing a wilfully obtuse child. "Who is next in command, who is in this room, and is not dead?"

The chauffeur fidgeted nervously.

"I am." The baby-faced gentleman with the wet crotch had raised his hand. "I'm Sir Ivo. I'm next in command."

"Kneel down and repeat…"

Sir Ivo fell to his knees. "I relinquish command of the house and you, Dafydd Porcwrangler, are in control," he blurted.

"And no-one – staff or family – is to disobey me."

"And no-one – staff or family – is to disobey you."

Porcwrangler pulled a ball of twine from his

pocket. "Now, make the rest of your family comfortable and tie their hands and feet." He turned to the staff. "Valet, run me a bath and get me something decent to wear. Footman, gather some valuables and load them on to the Dream Cloud Club Class – nothing shonky mind – don't take me for an idiot. Housekeeper, the cook, and the scullery maid are in the larder. You can let them out now... and tell the cook that the stew needs more salt. Chauffeur, prepare the Club Class for travel – you can be captain but you'll have three crew and no more. The valet can be navigator, Ivo here will be footman and aircraftman and I'll be the third."

"Err... I don't know anything about navigation," the valet whimpered.

"You'll learn. Quickly – if you don't want to be shot."

"Where are we going?"

"We're going to Geo HQ in Butare... via Porcwrangler Farm. I need to pick up some spare vests."

The staff stood looking at him.

Dafydd clapped his hands. "Well, go on then!"

They all scuttled off.

"Tidy."

CHAPTER 37
Victoria

The crew of *The Reliant* were sitting around the table in the mess. A large enamel coffee pot sat steaming in the middle and, on the stove at the side of the room, a copper kettle was heating up for a refill.

"Okay, so what did we discover yesterday? Bunty?"

"I went to the library, Skipper, and I found a book on the architecture of the Hotel de Ville. I couldn't bring the book back unfortunately, but I drew some rough sketches." She pulled some crumpled paper from her pocket and smoothed it out on the table. "There's about twenty steps up to the main entrance, which means you actually enter on the first floor – there are *two* floors below. The stairs in the Grand Hall only go up. The same is true of *all* the staircases in the public areas. You need to find the staff staircases to get to the ground floor and the basement. There are four of these, one in each corner – more-or-less – of the building. It's a bit of a maze but the building is south facing, and all the corridors run north to south, or east to west."

"So, if we all have compasses, we shouldn't get *too* lost," interjected Bearnárd.

"The basement was built entirely for storage – wine vaults, ice rooms, larders, etc. These are the most likely places to be converted to cells. The ground floor was the staff living quarters, another possibility. There are only two other entrances, one via the kitchens and one from the coach yard. The kitchens will be fully staffed – we won't go unnoticed there – but there'll be lots of comings and goings from the coach yard." Bunty tapped firmly on one corner of her hastily-drawn plan. "That's where you should let me and Bernie in."

"Good work! Jao and I had a scout around the building. The basement level is only half below ground. There are windows at ankle height, but they look like they have security bars, so not a way in or out. Ideal for converting to prison cells though. The coach yard doesn't have a gate, so you can get right up to the house, but there is a sentry guard there. Anything suspicious at the airdock, Emily?"

"I. believe. *The. Reliant.* is. under. surveillance. Captain."

"They haven't spotted you?"

"I. have. been. discreet."

"Good. Keep your head down. We don't need you being discovered."

"Is. there. nothing. I. can. do. to. assist. Captain?"

"I'm afraid not, Emily, you're just too conspicuous."

"I. understand." Emily Tutu sounded disappointed.

The meeting ran on for several pots of coffee, until everyone knew exactly what they were doing, including contingencies for unexpected eventualities. Finally, Gonagain called the meeting to a close.

"We'll meet up here at 6pm. Everyone get some rest."

******

Jao was wearing the pink floral dress that she had worn the previous day when Gonagain arrived at the mess in his fake uniform. He paused at the door. She looked absolutely beautiful. Gonagain felt something stir inside him.

Bunty brushed passed him as she marched straight in. "Looking good, Skip. Looking *very* good. Jao, shouldn't you be getting ready?"

Rajaobelina looked crestfallen. "I *am* ready."

"Oh goodness me, no! No, no, no. That won't do at all. It's a grand ball, not a garden party. Come on," she grabbed her by the hand, "Come with me, I'll sort you out."

By the time Bunty returned to the mess, Gonagain and Bearnárd were taking some Dutch courage – in the form of a schooner of whiskey – whilst Emily sat at the end of the long table with Etoile.

Gonagain glanced at his Landowner, diamond-jewelled pocket watch. It was nearly 6pm.

There was a smug grin on Bunty's face, as if she was enjoying a joke that nobody else was part of. "She's on her way."

But the two men were already staring past the navigator with their mouths open. Jao was standing in the doorway, and if Gonagain had thought she looked beautiful before, he was going to struggle for superlatives now.

She was wearing Bunty's black silk top hat with her hair tied up underneath it. Her eyes were made-up with smoky black eyeshadow, mascara, and eyeliner. Her high cheekbones were accentuated with a dark blusher and her lips were glistening with a glossy purple lipstick.

Around her slim neck was a gold choker, decorated with purple jade which matched the elegant, drop earrings. Her dress had a black, velvet, corset bodice, cinched tightly around her wasp waist and a skirt in purple silk. Black velvet ribbons held the skirt off the ground in swags. Her black boots were suede, with hooks and laces up to her ankles. She was clutching a small black leather bag in one hand and her varilights in the other.

"Do I look okay?" she asked tentatively.

"Jao, you look amazing." Bearnárd was clearly stunned by the transformation. "All these years and I never saw you look so good."

"Captain?"

"I'm... I'm just lost for words. There are no

words! You look… stunning!" Gonagain felt a surge of desire welling up inside. He shouldn't be subjecting Jao to such danger to rescue Aoife. He wasn't sure why he was rescuing Aoife anyway. Was it love, or lust, or honour, or principle?

"There's just one thing sweetie," Bunty took the varilights from Jao's hand and strapped them around her top hat, so they sat on the brim. "That's how they're being worn these days."

"Okay, Captain. I'm ready. Shall we go?"

Gonagain pulled his pocket watch from his tunic and checked the time. "I suppose we'd better." He turned to Bunty and Bearnárd. "Take it handy now!"

Bunty and Bearnárd gave them a ten-minute head start. They used the time to double check their pistols and ammunition.

"You ready, Bunty?"

"Ready as I'll ever be."

"Okay, let's get going. Emily, lock up after we've gone and keep your head down."

"I. understand. Lieutenant."

Bunty and Bearnárd had only been gone a few minutes when Emily Tutu became aware of the approaching Trad soldiers. Her instinct was to grab a weapon and see them off, but she was under strict orders to avoid being discovered. She waited until they began to force the loading bay hatch.

"Etoile. I. must. hide. now. You. should. do. the. same."

Emily Tutu took herself down to the engine room. She arranged some mechanical detritus around her and folded herself into her neat cubic form. Etoile slunk under Gonagain's bunk and hunkered down, shivering nervously. Eventually the Trad soldiers gained access.

The corporal spoke in a whisper. "Okay men. Objective one is to establish if there is anyone else occupying the vessel. Our spy has informed us of the captain, navigator and engineer who have left the ship. There is also another man who has left the ship, who we believe to be their lieutenant. Our source also claims that there is a dog and – believe it or not – a man made of metal. We have no evidence of this, as yet."

Some of the men snorted at the mention of a metal man.

"Objective two is to locate the pulsarnite rock. Final word: remember this is a soft envelope dirigible full of hydrum, so no gunfire unless it's unavoidable. We'll meet back here in five minutes. Okay, let's go." The men split into pre-arranged pairs and began to scour *The Reliant*.

In Gonagain's cabin, two privates began rooting through his possessions. They opened the bureau and rifled through his papers, and dragged clothes out of his locker. It was just as one of the Trad soldiers was trying, unsuccessfully, to open his pulsarnite cabinet, that the other decided to check under the bunk. It was dark underneath and, before his eyes began to adjust, he heard a low growling. He just had time to make out a set of small, sharp teeth with large canines before they clamped over his face. The soldier screamed and tried to pull away, but the dog remained attached as he wriggled and writhed from under the bunk, howling in agony.

"Shoot it! Shoot it!" His scream was muffled and distorted with Etoile's jaw clamped around his face.

His partner pulled his standard issue pistol from its holster, but then remembered the hydrum. He was also afraid he'd hit his buddy. He tried pulling the mutt away instead.

"Aarrgh! Stop – don't pull!"

He grabbed his pistol by the barrel and swung it at the small dog. He only caught the back of its furry head with a glancing blow, but it was enough to make it yelp and finally release its grip. His colleague threw the dog across the cabin and it yelped again, before disappearing through the cabin door, which was still ajar.

The soldier's face was bleeding profusely from the bite wound. His partner grabbed the face towel from the hook by the mirror. "Here, stem the flow with this and go back to the loading bay. I'll check the other cabins on my own."

Back in the loading bay, the corporal was waiting. "Crikey! What happened to you?"

"I found the flipping dog."

"That scrappy little mutt did all *that*?"

"Did you see it? Did you *kill* it?"

"It ran through here like a streak of lightening."

"Where is it now? The little…"

The corporal nodded his head toward the open, loading-bay hatch. "Disappeared into the night."

The other members of the search party returned – each pair with nothing to report. No pulsarnite rock and no metal man.

"Private Tunemaker, run ahead to HQ and let them know that all of *The Reliant*'s crew is accounted for, apart from a small dog. They can start making arrests straight away."

******

Jao and Gonagain strolled elegantly through the town, arm in arm. They attracted several admiring glances from ladies and gentlemen alike. Every now and again, they would stop at one of the chic shops and admire the wares in the window. They paused outside a milliner's and looked through the window. Gonagain took a sneaky glance in the direction they had come from. Jao had previously spotted a man trying *too* hard to look nonchalant.

"Yep. You're right. He is most definitely following us. Well spotted, Jao." Gonagain spoke through gritted teeth. "Let's go to Ticklebelly Alley."

Ticklebelly Alley was a very narrow street surrounded by stores and small businesses, that Bearnárd had spotted earlier that day and earmarked as a good place to get lost. There were a myriad of alleyways and paths that diverged from it. Jao and Gonagain continued to stroll casually through the town, as visitors would, and their tail continued to follow them. On the corner of Tickle-belly, they paused and peered through the window of a shop displaying a range of musical instruments, before turning the corner and strolling into the alley.

The young man in the tasselled scarf and news-boy cap broke into a trot – he didn't want them to get too far ahead in that maze of alleys – but by the time he reached the music shop, they were nowhere to be seen.

"Oh *rats*!" he exclaimed as he trotted up the alley, looking left and right into each turning and doorway. He stopped when he was about a quarter of the way up Ticklebelly Alley. They must have turned off before here – he would have seen them otherwise. He retraced his steps and began to explore each turning again, running further up each one in panicked desperation. He was in deep trouble.

About half-way up Ticklebelly, in the entrance of Shamble Lane, Jao was bent over with her hands on her knees and Gonagain was leaning with one hand on the wall. Both were panting, trying to catch their breath.

"That was... a fair auld... sprint, Jao."

"It's alright... for you... I'm... in a dress... and heels!" She straightened up, clutching her side.

"Come on... we'll get our breath back... as we walk."

Bearnárd and Bunty had been observing from

about a hundred yards back.

"They've spotted him! They're heading for Ticklebelly Alley."

"We'll done, Skip." Bunty breathed a sigh of relief, unaware that she had been holding her breath.

"We'd better try and lose our *own* stalker."

Bunty was about to spin around, but stopped herself just in time. "Have we *got* one?"

"I haven't seen one, but it stands to reason."

"Well, we can't use Ticklebelly; there's no point losing our own follower and picking up the Skipper's one."

"We'll go to the brewery."

They took a left and began to head out of town. As they walked, the streets became less and less crowded and, by the time they reached the brewery, there was only one other person on the street, following at quite some distance.

The brewery yard was full of crates of bottles and flagons and barrels of all sizes. Bunty went and stood among the kilderkins and barrels; Bearnárd hunkered down between the stacks of pins and firkins. Moments later, their pursuer stopped at the yard gate, unsure of what to do next. Bearnárd gave Bunty the thumbs up, and she let out a blood curdling shriek.

"HELP! HELP ME! No. No. Let go of me."

The man at the gate came running in.

"Stop! Let me go!" Bunty was grinning from ear to ear, thoroughly enjoying the opportunity to use her theatrical skills.

Their stalker followed the sound until he came face to face with Bunty among the barrels. He stared at her, confused at first, then the realisation that he had been tricked showed on his face.

"Oh, hello, young man," Bunty smiled.

Bearnárd bought a full pin of ale crashing down on his head. He fell to the ground and lay there motionless.

"Quick, drag him in a bit further before anyone else comes. Then we'd better hot-foot it to the Hotel de Ville."

CHAPTER 38
Victoria

As they climbed the stone steps to the entrance of the Hotel de Ville, Gonagain and Jao looked every bit the glamorous, well-to-do couple, attending a prestigious grand ball but, inside, they were both a bundle of nerves. After showing the invitation to security, they entered the main hall. It was the most magnificent room that Gonagain had ever seen. The hall ceiling was four floors high with an atrium roof. The huge staircase was wide enough to walk ten abreast and it swooped and curved dramatically from one floor to the next. The banisters and balustrades were ornately carved, and each newel-post was capped with a its own unique grotesque. White plaster cornices, corbels and architraves adorned every opening and corner, decorated with lions and chimeras. A column of crystals which hung from the ceiling exploded into a pendulous chandelier at each floor.

A young man approached Gonagain. "Good evening, Captain, do you have a room reserved or are you here for the Grand Ball only?"

"Just the for the ball."

"May I?" he gestured for Gonagain to show his invitation.

"Staff Sergeant Landowner, welcome." He passed the invitation back and gestured again – this time towards Gonagain's pistol. "I'm afraid all weapons must be checked in."

It was the first time Gonagain had noticed the weapons check-in. "Is that wise? What if there was a Pulser attack?"

"There are plenty of on-duty soldiers who are armed, Captain, but those attending the ball and consuming alcohol must check-in their weapons." The young concierge smiled apologetically. "I don't make the rules."

Gonagain reluctantly checked-in his pistol while Jao waited in the hall. "That wasn't part of the plan," he muttered under his breath when he re-joined her.

At the door of the ballroom, the invitation was checked for a third time – by the Master of Ceremonies. "Welcome, Staff Sergeant Landowner. And your guest is?"

"Lady Peggy Blueeyes."

"Staff Sergeant Digby Landowner and Lady Peggy Blueeyes," the MC announced loudly. A few heads turned, but generally people carried on with their conversations and drinks.

Gonagain and Jao walked into the beautiful ballroom uncertainly.

"I still can't believe I'm *Peggy Blueeyes!*" Jao

said through gritted teeth. "*Peggy!*"

"What's wrong with Peggy? I had an aunt Peggy when I was little – she was lovely."

A waiter in black tie and white gloves offered them a glass of champagne – which they took, just to have something to hold. They milled around, saluting, and nodding as Bunty had taught them. Gonagain spotted a junior officer looking awkward and uncomfortable and decided to engage in small talk.

Jao excused herself. "I must go and powder my nose."

Having made a point of asking for directions to the ladies' powder room, Jao walked right past it and disappeared into a warren of corridors. She plucked a tiny compass from her cleavage and did her best to travel only south or east. Eventually she came across a servants' staircase – one that went down as well as up. She headed down one floor and found herself amongst the staff, and near to the coachyard.

A sentry guard stopped her at the coachyard. "What are you doin' down 'ere? This area ain't for guests."

"I'm looking for my good-for-nothing staff. They *still* haven't bought my trunk to my room." Jao tried to act as haughtily as possible, but it didn't come naturally – she hated being rude. She marched past the young sentry guard out into the yard, where Bearnárd was waiting with a trunk that he had robbed from one of the coaches – he had tipped its contents into the passenger compartment.

"What are you doing lingering around here? Why haven't you bought my trunk up?"

Bearnárd struggled to suppress a smirk. "Yes, m'lady, just waiting for Goodtime."

Bunty was just out of sight enjoying a flirt and a cigarette with a footman – the one who was supposed to be minding the trunk that Bearnárd had taken. She dashed around the corner. "Sorry, m'lady." Together, she and Bearnárd picked up the trunk to follow Jao inside and up to the first floor.

"You can't just come in – you've got to go through security." It was the young sentry guard again.

"Don't be ridiculous! I'm already in and they're my staff." Jao was getting into character.

"They've still got to do security," the guard protested meekly.

"Well. I think Field Marshal Silverspoon would be very interested to hear that one of his guests of honour was being denied access to their belongings!"

The guard hesitated. "Well, I suppose you *are* already inside." He backed off.

As soon as they were out of sight, Jao dropped the act. "Right, I've got to get back to the captain. You know what you're doing?"

"Stash this somewhere – we might need it to

get Aiofe out – find the southwest staircase, go down two flights to try and find her. As soon as we're out and clear, we fire a shot through the window."

"Good luck."

When Jao got back to the ballroom, Gonagain was speaking to a Major. He introduced them. "Major, this is Lady Blueeyes; Peggy this is Major Beancounter."

Jao gave a barely perceptible curtsey.

"I was asking your young man here about the kidnapping from Isalo. I didn't know he had escaped."

Jao looked nervously at Gonagain – not wanting to contradict anything he may have said.

"Oh, I, erm… didn't tell Peggy about the kidnapping. She doesn't like to hear about the danger of my job."

"I am sorry, young lady – I didn't mean to upset you," the major flustered. "Well, there's a bit of a surprise later – especially for you Landowner – but I do hope you won't be too shocked, my dear."

"I'll do my best to cope."

Gonagain knew Jao well enough to recognise the sarcasm in her voice, but the major was unaware. There was an awkward moment of silence.

"Well, I'll leave you young folk to enjoy the evening," the major said as he backed away.

"What was all that about?"

"Fecked if I know, but I don't like the sound of

it. The last thing we need is any surprises. Are Bunty and Bearnárd in?"

"Heading to the lower floors as we speak."

The orchestra, who had been playing inconspicuously on the stage, came to an abrupt halt. A portly man in a striking uniform emblazoned with ribbons and medals, and with spectacular facial hair, stood behind a lectern, which had seemed to appear from nowhere. He rang a bell and the room fell silent.

"Lords, ladies and gentlemen. It has been a testing time for Traditionalists recently. We have made some gains, but also some losses. I'm sure most of you will have heard about the riot that broke out at the Isalo mine just recently, which has bought the pulsarnite repatriation programme to a temporary halt. There were, sadly, many casualties. It was initially thought that our head of technology and innovation was among them, however, I'm pleased to inform you that this was not the case. And so, with no further ado, I give you... Dr Wilberforce Conceptuloco."

"Conceptuloco? Didn't Bernie mention that name?"

"He did. I think we need to get out of... oh my goodness!"

There were gasps of shock and horror around the ballroom – at least one of the ladies fainted. The man who had trundled onto the stage was wearing a dinner jacket over a white shirt and bowtie, but below the waist he was entirely mechanical. Small puffs of smoke and steam emanated from a flue in the metal pedestal in the place where his legs should be. Either side of the pedestal there was a caterpillar track that ran around three wheels, creating an equilateral triangle with rounded corners. Most horrific, though, were the two large discs where his eyes should have been, and a traditional watch embedded in his forehead.

Gonagain became aware of a figure behind him and turned around. It was the major from earlier.

"It's remarkable, isn't it!" He turned to Jao. "I do hope you're not too shocked, my dear."

"Actually, that is pretty shocking."

"What's most astounding, is that he performed much of the surgery himself, or at least oversaw it."

An anxious hush settled on the room as Dr Conceptuloco began to speak.

"Lords, ladies and gentlemen. Many of you will have heard about the problems that occurred in Isalo recently. As you can see, contrary to what you may have heard, I *did* survive. Some others were not so lucky..."

"Captain, we *really* ought to get out of here," Jao hissed.

"I know, I know, but we can't draw attention to ourselves now. As soon as yer man with the wheels shuts up, we'll go."

Conceptuloco was still speaking. "... little did I know, that I myself would require surgery..."

"What's the plan, Captain?"

"I'm still working on one."

"... however, with this new hybrid-human technology, we can recycle our wounded and maimed, and get them straight back into battle. I believe that this will tip the balance and make victory over the Pulsers, ours."

As the ballroom erupted into applause, Major Beancounter made his presence felt again. "Come on, let's go and say hello to the doctor."

"Oh! I'm sure he has more important people to speak to."

"Nonsense! He'll be delighted to discover that you escaped in one piece."

As they approached, Conceptuloco was descending from the stage – the triangular caterpillars had tilted forwards to keep him upright and were gripping the nose of the steps; when he reached the dancefloor, they flipped over and he continued seamlessly.

"Dr Conceptuloco! Dr Conceptuloco! Look! I have a surprise for you." Major Beancounter gestured towards Gonagain.

Conceptuloco smiled politely. "And who is this gentleman?"

"Don't you recognise him? It's Staff Sergeant Landowner."

"Major, I have no idea who this man is, but he most certainly isn't Landowner."

"Well," said Gonagain in a clipped accent, "we've both changed since we last met. You more than me, it must be said."

"Major, this man is an imposter. Have him arrested immediately."

Gonagain gestured to Conceptuloco's varilight 'eyes' and embedded watch. "Are you quite sure all this surgery hasn't had any side effects? I really haven't changed *that* much."

Major Beancounter was confused; he didn't know who to believe or what to do.

Conceptuloco snatched the cap from under Gonagain's arm. It flopped, limply, in his hand. "Look! This isn't even a real uniform."

Beancounter harrumphed and flushed a shade of puce. "Guards! Arrest this man!"

Gonagain turned to run, but armed soldiers were approaching from every angle and there were literally hundreds of Traditionalists between him and the grand double doors. He turned to Jao and she shook her head imperceptibly. The general hubbub in the room had subsided and the room was in silence. Everyone glared at Gonagain.

The silence was broken when the double doors burst open with such a force that the brass handles embedded themselves in the adjacent wall. A huge, imposing figure stood framed in the doorway. A sou'wester was pulled down over the eyes and a black scarf tied around the face, like a highway man. The massive stranger was draped in a yellow cape, which matched the sou'wester. A pair of brown breeches, which barely reached past the knees, poked out from beneath. The lower legs and feet were wrapped in rags, making a pair of makeshift boots. Suddenly, the attention was no longer on Gonagain.

Two enormous Pfeifer-Zeliska revolvers emerged from the cape, as Emily Tutu threw it open. At least half of the weapons which had been checked-in at the door clung to her shiny, magnetised torso. She was a terrifying sight.

Emily paused, long enough for the assembled bigwigs to take in her awesomeness, before raising the massive weapons and wreaking havoc. She aimed her shots to miss. She did not want to kill or maim, just create mayhem. Chandeliers crashed to the floor, paintings leapt from the walls and guests defenestrated themselves as candelabras exploded and tablecloths caught fire.

"Run!" shouted Gonagain.

Jao and Gonagain ran, ducking and diving as they went, to avoid the chaos. Emily discarded the empty revolvers and plucked a pair of old Mariette, twelve-barrelled, pepperbox pistols from her torso and continued the onslaught but, as Gonagain drew near, she suddenly stopped.

"Drop your weapons or the girl dies!"

Gonagain spun around. Dr Conceptuloco trundled towards them. He had Jao in a headlock, her feet not touching the ground, and a snub-nosed revolver to her temple.

Emily Tutu de-magnetised, and the weapons clattered to the floor.

******

Digby Landowner had run all the way from the airdock to the Hotel de Ville. He ran up the white stone steps to the door, clutching his side – his heart was racing and he had a stitch. He stopped in the grand entrance hall. It was strewn with unconscious bodies. There was a weapons check-in area but, again, the staff were unconscious. The floor was littered with discarded pistols and ammunition.

Landowner heard a groan – one of the weapons-check security guards was regaining consciousness. He leapt over the counter and knelt over him. "What happened here?"

The guard panicked momentarily, wriggling backwards away from Landowner, before realising he wasn't in danger. "Huge man… yellow cape… weird eyes… so strong."

"One man did all this?"

The guard nodded, before going into a foetal position at the sound of gunfire and screaming. It was coming from upstairs. Landowner spun back into the entrance hall and headed up the stairs, but as he reached the source of the mayhem, the gunfire stopped. He approached the large double doors cautiously.

There in the doorway, surrounded by handguns, was the huge man in the yellow cape. Two shiny metal hands were held out to his side, fingers outstretched. Landowner recognised the hands instantly – it was the metal man from *The Reliant*. Behind the automaton, he spotted the captain, Gonagain. He was in Traditionalist uniform with a stubbly moustache shaved into points.

But it was the sight beyond those two that made Landowner's jaw drop. A creature that looked half-human, half-machine, was holding a young lady by the neck, with a gun to her head. It took a moment for him to recognise her.

The half-human turned its attention to him and spoke in a voice he recognised as Dr Conceptuloco's. "Landowner! What on earth happened to you?" He gestured with the snub-nosed revolver at Digby's wonky moustache and missing tooth.

Landowner looked Conceptuloco up and down and snorted. "What happened to *me*?"

Conceptuloco ignored the comment. "This man has been masquerading as you. Would you care to enlighten me?"

"This is Captain Gonagain of *The Reliant.* He's the man who kidnapped me. He's also the man who helped our agent, Trustworthy, to steal the pulsarnite rock and sell it for her own profit. This monstrosity is his midshipman, and the girl is his engineer."

"Well, we already have Trustworthy, so that's the end of their shenanigans."

"Not quite, sir, there's still the lieutenant and the navigator."

Conceptuloco pivoted on the spot, his right caterpillar track in reverse and the left in forward. "Guards! Seal the building. No-one comes in or out. And check on the prisoner, Trustworthy."

******

Aoife Trustworthy was aware of people moving outside her cell, but remained lying on her cot, staring at the wall, until she heard their voices calling in a stage whisper.

"Aiofe! Aiofe! Is that you?"

She turned and got to her feet. Two faces were peering through the barred window in her cell door – one of whom she recognised. "Bunty? What are you doing here?"

"We've come to spring you out of here."

"Really? Why? What about Gonagain and Jao – are they here?"

"Of course. It was Jao that got us in here. She's up at the Grand Ball with the skipper. You look thin, are you..."

"Who has the keys?" Bearnárd interjected impatiently. He pulled at the door, but there was no give at all.

"I don't know. I've only just been moved up from the dungeon."

Suddenly the sound of gunfire and screaming came from within the building.

Bunty and Bearnárd looked at each other. "That doesn't sound good."

"Don't leave me!" Aiofe's voice sounded genuinely pitiful.

"We're going to try and find a key. We'll be back."

Back in the corridor, Bunty and Bearnárd

stopped to debate their next move. “I think we should abort, old boy.”

“What if it’s nothing to do with us? Osh’ll be furious if we give the signal and he comes out to find us empty handed.”

“Rule number one – if in doubt, run. You can always come back when it’s safe.”

Bearnárd hesitated, not knowing what to do. “I think we should stick with the plan. We’d never get back in again.”

Bunty shrugged. “Roshambo?”

Bearnárd nodded and put his hand behind his back. “One, two, three!” He drew his hand quickly, flat, and horizontal. Bunty drew hers simultaneously, two fingers apart, pointing at Bearnárd.

“Scissors cut paper. Come on, let’s get back to the coach yard.”

By the time they had navigated their way back to coach yard, security had been significantly bolstered.

“Sorry love, no one gets in or out. Orders from the top.” One of the many soldiers that had been put on guard duty handed Bunty and Bearnárd a sheet of paper and a pencil. “Write your name, position and reason for being here, and then go and wait over there.”

Bunty and Bearnárd looked at each other and then at the dozen or so armed, Traditionalist soldiers. They were going to have to bluff it. They gave false names and put their positions down as ‘official aids to Staff Sergeant Digby Landowner’ and handed it back to the soldier. The soldier glanced at it and did a double take, before showing it to his colleague. Bunty and Bearnárd knew they were in trouble.

CHAPTER 39
Victoria

Digby Landowner pressed his face against the bars of the cell door. "Well, well. Artemis Lightbringer! How the mighty have fallen."

Aiofe Trustworthy looked up from her cell cot with surprise – no one had called her by her real name for years. "Ugh! Come to gloat, have you?"

"Yes! Yes, I have. For all these years I've heard about how well cousin Artemis was doing in the military; how she was rising up the ranks. And now, here you are on death row. I must say, you look awful. On a brighter note – did you hear? I'm to be made up to sergeant major." He grinned smugly.

"Go away, Digby."

"That's not very nice." He feigned hurt. "After all these years, I thought you'd be pleased to see me. No, I couldn't possibly miss this moment. I only wish father was here."

Aoife turned over to face the wall. "Why don't you send him a telegram? If he hurries, he might get here in time for my execution."

Landowners expression soured. "Father was

murdered. And Humph."

"Well, that's no great loss to the world."

"He was ten times the man *your* pathetic father is! Is he still doing those awful daubings of naked ladies?"

Aoife sat up and glared at Landowner. "If you hadn't noticed, my name is Trustworthy. Not Lightbringer, and not Landowner. I have nothing to do with that man or *any* family. Unlike some people, I didn't need to use family connections to get somewhere in life."

Landowner looked theatrically around the cell. "That's worked out well for you, hasn't it?" He glanced at his pocket watch. "Well, I'll say 'au revoir'... actually I'd better make that 'goodbye' – just in case I don't see you at the gallows."

He strolled away, whistling a jaunty tune.

Bunty was sitting on the chair next to the desk in her cell. Since they were arrested at the Grand Ball – nearly two hands ago – she had done a lot of thinking about her life: what she had done; what she had failed to do.

When all was said and done, she decided, she had lived life well. She had seen more places than she could ever have imagined. She had collected experiences like some people collected... stamps. She had made love with several men – and regretted very few of them. She had loved – real, genuine, love – and lost. Life had been one hell of an adventure, not least when she was aboard *The Reliant*.

She was the oldest of all the crew and, therefore, had the least to grumble about, being on death row. But she was still loving life and had fully intended to grow old disgracefully. She wasn't finished yet. She felt cheated, angry, and helpless.

Bearnárd just felt angry. None of the events of the past six hands had been his fault. They hadn't been anyone's fault. Osh had only been trying to rescue him, and so had Beagán. Osh was always trying to do the right thing (except when he was doing questionable trade deals). He had been lucky to have a brother like Osh.

But, Bearnárd had always imagined settling down some day with a nice girl, building a nice house, getting married, having children and grandchildren. They just needed to clinch that big deal and make their fortune. He couldn't believe that it was all over already. What had been the point?

Emily Tutu hadn't been 'alive' for very long. Emotions weren't pre-programmed and, although she had been learning fast, she just didn't have the emotional experience to deal with the situation. What she did know was that she could escape whenever she wanted. The flimsy cell door was no barrier, nor were the guards outside. But if she escaped, every logical scenario she could calculate, ended with the instant death of at least *one* of the crew – probably more. No, she would have to bide her time and wait for a suitable moment, should one arise.

Jao sat cross-legged on the floor of her cell and meditated. She always meditated (if she could) when she was in a stressful situation. There was only one problem – she didn't feel stressed. Not one bit. And she had no idea why. It wasn't that she had made peace with the world, because she hadn't. She had too many things she would leave unfinished. It wasn't because she believed in an afterlife – despite her up-bringing, she didn't believe in that at all.

Whenever she stopped meditating, she found herself subconsciously making plans for the future. Maybe she was in denial – but it didn't feel like that.

Unexpectedly, she kept finding herself thinking about Aoife Trustworthy. Unlike their own representative, Aoife's counsel had at least made an attempt to defend her – albeit a futile one. The trial, such as it was, had been quite illuminating, and Jao realised that she had been excessively intolerant and opinionated where Aoife was concerned.

Yes, she was gamine, and well-educated, and from a wealthy background. And yes, she used all these attributes to manipulate people. *But*, it transpired, she was a spy. Secrecy and deception and manipulation were the tools of her trade, as much as spanners, screwdrivers and grease were the tools of *Jao's* trade. She was just doing her job. She hadn't used her family connections to enhance her career either – she had even gone as far as changing her name. She had got to where she was on pure merit.

But mostly, it was what the prosecution had

said about Aoife that kept returning to Jao. Aoife had, apparently, endured horrendous amounts of pain at the hands of a torturer, trying to protect the crew of *The Reliant*. Jao had looked across at Aoife at this point of the trial, and seen for herself the pain etched on her pallid face, the scabs on her fingers and thumbs, and the dramatic loss of weight.

Then there were those moments back in Stanleyville, when she had seemed genuinely warm and kind and friendly. When she had brushed Jao's hair with a gentleness that no-one else had ever shown her. And when she had run with Jao to rescue the captain and Bunty. Jao pledged to herself that she would seek reconciliation and friendship with Aoife as soon as this was over.

Gonagain lay on his cot, staring at the ceiling. He had messed everything up. Instead of keeping his crew safe, he had led them to their deaths. He was a disaster as a captain. His mind kept going back to something Bunty had said when they first met.

"Owning an airship and being a captain are not the same thing. One takes money – or in your case luck – the other takes intelligence, guile, charisma, and mental strength. Don't assume because your father had it, that you have too."

She had been right. He was a silly little boy, playing at being captain. Playing with people's lives. He should have let Aoife go and looked after his own crew.

His mind wandered off to his other big regret in

life – the death of his mother. Or, more specifically, the fact that *he* wasn't there when she died.

******

When Oisín and Bearnárd were in their early teens, they had decided – against their mothers wishes – to pay their own way, and not be a burden to her. They had gone to the factories and the mines and the street vendors looking for work, without success. But at Butare Airdock, you could work as a self-employed stevedore – paid per job. Bearnárd was perfectly suited to the work – he was big and strong and could hump the sacks and crates around all day. Gonagain was much stronger than he looked, but was usually passed over for the bigger men.

One day, whilst he was twiddling his thumbs and Bearnárd was shifting sacks of grain, he overheard two captains discussing their difficulty in retaining crew. One of them had, apparently, just lost his aircraftman to another airship. Gonagain immediately leapt to his feet, straightened his clothes, shined his shoes on the legs of his breeches, and approached the two captains. He pretended he hadn't heard the conversation and focused on the one not looking for staff.

"Morning, Captain! I'm a jobbing aircraftman; do you need any help on your vessel?

"No, son, but he does."

"Excellent." He turned to the other captain.

"When do you need me to start? I'm available right away."

"Whoa, hold on, son. How old are you? You can't have much experience."

Gonagain ignored the question about his age. "I've a load of experience." He proceeded to reel off the name of every dirigible he could remember.

"Alright, son – I'll give you a chance."

"What about my brother? Have you got a position for him? He's very strong." He gestured to Bearnárd, who was lugging a sack of grain on each shoulder.

"Him? He must weigh as much as half my cargo. I think he's more suited to dock work, son."

Gonagain took the job on board the *Grande Depart* and left Bearnárd and his mother, Eibhilin, in Butare. The captain of the *Grande Depart* paid well and he saved as much money as he could. He had been working for about forty hands when he received his first ever telegram. It was exciting – for a moment – until he read it.

Mam's not well. Get home as soon as you can. Bernie.

Gonagain went to the captain to ask for leave to go to his mother in Butare.

"Course you can, son. But it'll cost you to get back to Butare, we're less than a day away from Tana, we'll do a bit of trading there and then we'll be heading back to Butare via Port Harcourt. It'll take you... two days longer and won't cost you a single ariary. You'll actually be *earning* money."

By the time Gonagain was home, the pneumonia had already taken his mother. If it wasn't for Bearnárd, her stepson, she would have died alone. Gonagain never forgave himself – he was no better than his feckless father. He had vowed at his mother's grave that he would never leave anyone he cared about again.

CHAPTER 40
Butare

(Annularisday)

Dafydd Porcwrangler was marched into the admiral's office at gunpoint. Admiral Rufousrage was standing at the window looking at the Dreamcloud Club Class that Porcwrangler had arrived in, and the crew of three who were being held at gunpoint beside it.

"This is the man in charge, Admiral," the captain announced. "He says his name is Porcwrangler and he's here to see you or Professor Woollencraft."

The admiral spun around and glared at Porcwrangler. Porcwrangler smiled back at him benevolently.

"What is the meaning of landing your private craft here in a military base? You're lucky we didn't shoot you out of the sky." Rufousrage barked.

"I suppose I am, but it's very important that I see

you." Porcwrangler paused briefly. "Why didn't you shoot me out of the sky?"

Rufousrage nodded to the window. "A craft like that, you might have been someone important. We didn't want to shoot someone of import down."

Porcwrangler smiled to himself – the Club Class was a good choice. "I won't lie to you, Admiral, I *am* someone important. I'm the man who's going to help you win the war, see?"

"I don't believe I've ever met a Porcwrangler before, certainly not one who flies a Club Class." Rufousrage was skeptical.

"Well, we're not all born at the station we belong, Admiral, are we?" He gestured to the chair in front of him. "May I?"

The admiral nodded and sat on his own leather chair. "I think you ought to get to the point of why you're here."

"What it is, is I have an invention that would help you win the war, and I'm here to sell it to you."

"So you say. What *is* it?" Rufousrage was getting impatient.

"It's a bullet-resistant vest."

"And are you wearing one of these vests now?"

Porcwrangler opened his jacket and puffed out his chest. "I am."

Rufousrage opened his desk drawer, pulled out his revolver, cocked the hammer, and shot Porcwrangler in the chest, all in one swift movement. The force of the shot sent him, chair and all, crashing to the ground.

"Ugh! Ow!" Porcwrangler managed to get on to all fours. "That hurts from that range, that does."

Admiral Rufousrage stood up. "I think we'd better go and see Professor Woollencraft."

Porcwrangler looked up. He was still on his hands and knees and trying to catch his breath. "I'll be there now in a minute."

When they entered his lab, the professor was sitting in a chair, knitting.

"Professor, this is Mr Dafydd Porcwrangler. Porcwrangler, Professor Godwin Woollencraft."

The professor put down his knitting self-consciously and proffered a hand. "The knitting helps clear the mind," he explained.

"Mr Porcwrangler has invented a 'bullet-resistant vest'."

The professor reached for his pistol. "Are you wearing it now?"

Porcwrangler raised his hands, "Yes. No! Yes. I am, but it has already been tested."

The professor looked to the admiral who nodded in confirmation.

"What is it made from?"

"Leather and mercuriumite wire."

"Let me show you something, Mr Wrangler," he marched across to another part of the lab where a metal man stood silently in the corner, its body made from solid mercuriumite. "This is a 'Mechanical Life-form Emulator. It's the prototype – version one. We have ninety-nine of these, only better, marching into battle as we speak. They are following a machine that can wipe out an entire city in one strike. Your vest is a bit… basic compared to what we do here."

Porcwrangler bristled. "It may be basic, but it works."

"The point is, Mr Wrangler, that we could easily design something like this – now that we have the idea."

"It's not as simple as it looks, is it? It took me years to come up with the perfect weave of the wires for maximum effect. *And,* I have the patent on it."

"We could adjust it enough to avoid any problems with patents." The professor shrugged.

"In the time it takes for you to replicate it and adjust it, I could adapt it to work against pulsarnite weapons."

The professor and the admiral gave each other a wary glance.

"Look at the amount of mercuriumite you've used on this metal man! My vests use one hundredth the amount," Porcwrangler continued, "With my vests you could make them for a fraction of the cost, which means you could make more of them."

"He has a point about the cost," the admiral chipped in.

"But availability of mercuriumite isn't what prevents us making more," countered the professor.

Porcwrangler seized on this piece of information. "So, if there's a limit to how many of these things you can make, you still need to protect your regular soldiers," he was on a roll now. "And think of the other ways you can use it! On vehicles for instance."

Rufousrage and Woollencraft exchanged a glance. Woollencraft gave a barely observable nod.

It was the Admiral who spoke. "We're not going to buy your vests Mr Porcwrangler. *But*, if it suits you, we will give you a contract to come and work here. You can show us how to make your vests and we'll give you on the job training for this kind of thing," he gestured to the metal man.

This wasn't what Dafydd Porcwrangler had come for at all. He eyed the metal man up and down. Imagine being able to make one of these. "How do they know what they're supposed to do? Does someone have to control them?"

"We use something we call 'programming'. They think very much like a real human, only it's based on the parameters that *we* program. When they leave the factory, they know their job is to obey orders to defeat the Traditionalists."

Porcwrangler's mind went back to Digby Landowner, leaving him for dead in the pig sty. "So, could you be more specific? Tell them they need to kill a specific person, for instance?"

"As long as they have enough information to identify the target, yes, I don't see why not."

Dafydd Porcwrangler's brain was racing ahead. "I want anything I invent to be branded with my name," he blurted.

The admiral and the professor looked at each other and shrugged. It seemed an unusual request but not problematic.

"I don't see why not – we can certainly call these vests of yours 'wranglers'."

Porcwrangler considered this momentarily. Wranglers had a nice ring to them, but, if he had anything to do with Staff Sergeant Landowners death, he wanted the man to know. "It's *Porc*wrangler."

"Porcwranglers it is then!"

He smiled at the two men and proffered a hand. "Tidy!"

CHAPTER 41
Victoria

It was gone midday, in Traditional time, but the sun had only just risen. The sky was clear, and the air was cold and crisp. It was going to be a beautiful afternoon.

The crew of *The Reliant* were led, in single file, hands tied loosely behind their backs, toward the gallows. It was the first time they had seen each other since the kangaroo court over a week ago.

Five nooses of varying lengths, each with a different number of turns, hung from their own individual broad, oak beams. Just beyond the gallows, a single post with a pile of chains stood alone. A large, excitable crowd had gathered.

Each member of the crew was positioned behind their own, bespoke noose – Aoife at one end, then Gonagain, Bunty, Jao and Bearnárd. Emily Tutu was led to the post and chained to it. There was a hubbub amongst the crowd, until the judge spoke.

"I shall now read the convictions and the sentences.

"Aoife Trustworthy, you have been found guilty

of treason to the cause, sabotage of military operations, and four counts of murder at Stanleyville Airdock. You are sentenced to be hanged until dead.

"Oisín Gonagain, you have been found guilty of impersonating a military sergeant, theft of military property – to wit, a pulsarnite rock – and nine counts of murder at Stanleyville Airdock. You are sentenced to be hanged until dead.

"Bunty Goodtime, you have been found guilty of aiding and abetting a theft, and six counts of murder at Stanleyville Airdock. You are sentenced to be hanged until dead.

"Rajaobelina, you have been found guilty of aiding and abetting a theft, and four counts of murder at Stanleyville Airdock. You are sentenced to be hanged until dead.

"Bearnárd Strongman, you have been found guilty of inciting a riot, and three counts of murder at Isalo Mine. You are sentenced to be hanged until dead.

"Mechanical Lifeform Emulator version two point two, you have been found guilty of attempted massacre at the Hotel de Ville, and existing as an abomination. You are sentenced to elimination by firing squad.

As the sentences were read out, the executioner placed a noose over the head of each person. Bearnárd watched each of his friends, taking one last look.

Aoife looked wretched. Of course, he had never met her as a free woman, but he could tell that she was broken, both physically and mentally. Her skin was sallow and taut, and she couldn't be much more than fifty kilos wet through. She had a vacant expression and her gaze was fixed on nothing in particular.

Oisín was staring resolutely at his shoes. The executioner had to physically lift his head to put the noose around his neck. Bearnárd knew that he was blaming himself for everything. He was willing Osh to raise his eyes and look at him one last time, so he could give him a reassuring smile or a nod. He was a good brother and a good captain – he wanted him to know that. But his eyes never left the floor.

Bunty stood with her feet shoulder-width apart, her back straight and her chin up. She had chosen something to focus on and she barely blinked. She looked proud and strong but, if you looked closely, you could see she was trembling, and her eyes were filling up. As the noose went around her neck, she shed a single tear.

Jao looked positively serene. She was almost beaming. She seemed to be scanning the gathering crowd, as if she was looking for someone she knew. Bearnárd half expected her to give someone a cheery wave. When the executioner slipped the noose over her head, she gave him a polite smile and, as he arranged the knot under her left ear, she actually said, 'thank you'.

Emily's metal face and body language were totally unreadable.

******

When Rajaobelina was born, her grandmother recognised her gift for healing immediately – those with a gift can see it in others. To be born with more than one gift was incredibly rare and, as they knew no-one with the gift of pre-sight, Jao's second gift went unnoticed. She was already living on *The Reliant* when she began to suspect that her dreams and odd feelings were actually the gift of pre-sight, but she didn't know how to hone and develop it, especially in adulthood. As a result, the gift remained uncontrolled and erratic.

As she stood on the gallows with a noose around her neck, she finally understood why she had felt so relaxed about her impending execution. It wasn't because she was in denial – it was because it wasn't going to happen.

She scanned the crowd, searching for something that was going to save them. And then she spotted him. A thin, wiry man with wild eyes, freckles, and frizzy auburn hair – undoubtedly Madakan. She had no idea who he was, or why he would save them, but she knew it was him. He seemed more... vibrant, brighter, more in focus, as if he was more than three-dimensional. It was difficult to describe.

The Madakan's eyes darted everywhere; he seemed to be trying to watch everyone at the same time. He frequently raised his eyes to the heavens, as if seeking divine intervention.

Jao's concentration was broken when the judge spoke again.

"Do any of you have any last words?"

No one spoke.

"Executioner, you may begin."

The executioner nodded. "Sergeant, bring in the firing squad."

A burley sergeant bellowed, "TO THE LEEEEFT – MARCH!" and a squad of ten rifle-bearing privates marched in.

Emily Tutu suddenly became aware that she was to be executed *first*. The ideal opportunity to escape and rescue her friends had never presented itself. It was now or never. She began to strain at the chains. No matter how closely they observed, the firing squad and the bloodthirsty crowd would be unable to perceive the change in her, but, nevertheless, the chains began to creak.

The burly sergeant continued to bellow his orders and the excitement of the crowd grew. The firing squad were about to raise their rifles when the first weak link snapped, and the chains began to whirl away at great velocity. As the unwinding chain grew longer, it skimmed past the faces of the first few soldiers. The fourth member of the squad jerked his head back with lightning reactions, but the fifth caught the chain link full in the face. Blood spattered everywhere and he collapsed to the ground.

The unruly crowd cheered and laughed. They

didn't care *whose* blood was spilled.

The sergeant increased the pace of his orders. "TAKE AAIIMM – FIRE!"

As Emily Tutu freed herself of the last chain, the remaining nine members of the squad, discharged their weapons. Emily magnetised her body with reverse polarity, but the momentum of the bullets was too great – they either ricocheted off her or lodged in her shiny frame. She marched steadily towards the execution squad.

"RAISE WEAPONS – TAKE AAIIMM – FIRE!"

Again, the soldiers fired, and Emily jerked backwards briefly, before continuing stoically towards them.

The crowd began to panic – they screamed and pushed back. People fell and were trampled underfoot.

"AIM, FIRE! FIRE AT WILL."

Emily's tall frame jolted and convulsed, as she was peppered with a barrage of gunfire. She continued forward, but collapsed to her knees. The green lights of her eyes extinguished, and she fell face down with a clatter.

The crowd surged forwards, roaring with delight. If it wasn't for the noise, they would have heard that Emily was still speaking. "Power. failure. Switching. to. stored. power. Resetting."

Jao glared at the Madakan – willing him to make his move. He looked to the heavens once again, but still did nothing.

The executioner nodded to the burly sergeant

and stepped on to Aiofe's gallows. He reached for the wooden lever and pulled. The trapdoor beneath her fell away and Aiofe dropped several feet before the rope halted her fall. Her body jerked and the noose tightened, but the knot failed to break her neck. She swung and convulsed, pedalling her legs, trying to reach the wooden deck.

The crowd cheered and laughed, their mocking aimed more at the executioner, who had miscalculated his victim's weight, than at the woman at the end of the noose.

Still the Madakan did nothing. Jao was starting to think she was mistaken.

The embarrassed executioner ignored his first failure – and moved on to Gonagain's gallows. He reached for the lever again. Suddenly, a white blur launched itself from the crowd and clamped its teeth around his hand. The executioner let out a pained yelp and tried to wrestle his hand free from its grip.

"Go on, Etoile!" Bearnárd shouted.

Someone took a potshot at Etoile, but missed and hit the hapless executioner in the leg instead. He hit the deck clutching his kneecap with one hand, the tenacious mutt still clamped to the other. The crowd roared with delight. This was the best fun they had ever had at an execution.

Emily Tutu had been aware of everything going on around her, despite her inability to move. Her vision had been coming and going intermittently – she could only see the ground she was lying face down on anyway – but she had heard everything. She was running on potential energy stored in the multitude of springs and cells throughout her body. The myriad of cogs within her frame were sliding and rotating methodically, trying to find an alternate route from her pulsarnite heart to her vital modules. With one final click, her power source was reconnected. She began moving her fingers and toes, rediscovering how to control her movements.

The bright sky dimmed, and Execution Square fell into shade, but amid the chaos, the Madakan was one of the few people to even notice. Jao followed his gaze to the sky. The cause of the current gloom was not a *cloud* obscuring the sun, but a dirigible. It was a dirigible unlike any she had seen before. The envelope was huge and flat and triangular, like an enormous slice of pie and, instead of the usual four propellers mounted on the gondola, there were no fewer than six mounted on the hard-shell envelope. Three glass hemispheres protruded from the underside of the envelope, surrounding the integral gondola. In each hemisphere a gunner swivelled to whichever angle they desired.

Jao glanced back towards the Madakan, but he was no longer there. She heard a scream, like a war cry, ring out from Gonagain's gallows. The Madakan mounted the deck and punched the executioner in the neck. Blood spurted out over the crowd as he withdrew his fist, the protruding blade now clearly visible. The cheers from the crowd began to subside, as they got the first inkling that things were starting to go horribly wrong. It was then that the airship overhead opened fire.

The bloodthirsty mob became a throng of terror, as soldiers and onlookers were gunned down. Those who were knocked over in the panic, got trampled underfoot. To make matters worse, Emily Tutu was now slicing through the hordes like an ice breaker cutting through the floe. One arm hung limply by her side but the other thrashed and battered anyone in her path.

The Madakan ran behind each member of the crew, cutting the ropes that bound their hands. They each gave a grateful, albeit confused, nod of gratitude as they slipped off their nooses. Finally, he was at Bearnárd's gallows.

"Thanks, Koko – what's the plan?"

"Run! To *The Reliant*, fast as you can."

Bearnárd followed Koko through the dispersing crowd. Koko was fast and, before long, he was ahead of everyone except Etoile. Emily Tutu was running with an awkward gait and the unconscious Aoife over her shoulder. Bearnárd caught her up as Gonagain was shepherding his crew from the square.

"Emily! Give me Aoife. Your co-ordination is all over the place."

Emily Tutu passed the unconscious spy to Bearnárd and tried to thank him, but just made a noise like fingernails on a blackboard.

"Get moving, Bernie. I'll hold off any trouble here." Gonagain's demeanour had totally changed. He was steely and determined. He was overcompensating for his prior, defeatist manner.

Bearnárd looked back at the throng, who were beginning to regroup. "Hold them off with what?"

Koko shouted from ahead. "You dun't wunt to hang about here. I have guns further up."

The wedge-shaped dirigible had turned and was making another pass, spraying bullets into the mob once more.

"GO! I'm right behind you." Bearnárd broke into a run, the weight of Aoife barely registering. Gonagain took up the rear, glancing behind occasionally.

As Koko and Etoile ran down Victoria Street, they passed an undertaker's shop. An unvarnished, handle-less casket sat on the carpenter's trestles outside. Koko veered over to the coffin and flipped the lid. "Over here! Guns!"

As Jao ran towards the Madakan, he tossed a Peacemaker and an ammo belt to her. She caught the ammo belt cleanly but fumbled the revolver, nearly dropping it before clutching it to her chest. Bunty caught both and had the belt over her shoulder in one swift movement – barely breaking her stride. But Jao had stopped completely. She was craning her neck to see if she could see the captain. Bearnárd appeared first; his distinctive, lumbering sprinting style was unmistakable. Then came Emily Tutu, running like a marionette operated by a drunkard. Finally came Gonagain. He was clutching a walking cane and was only a metre or two in front of the angry mob. Just as he was about to catch Emily Tutu, he turned to face the crowd, swinging the cane wildly. He was holding off the rabble before they engulfed Emily. One final swipe and he began running again.

Jao climbed the trestle and stood in the casket to get a better angle, before firing shots over Gonagain's head. The bullets whistled over the heads of the pursuing hordes. Those at the front stumbled to a halt, only to be knocked over and trampled by those behind. Koko followed Jao's lead and began firing too. Some of his shots went into the crowd, some over their heads and some nowhere near. He was an awful marksman and Jao feared for Gonagain's life.

Gonagain spotted Jao and Koko and made a shooing gesture for them to flee. Jao could see some of the firing squad making their way to the front line. It was definitely time to move. She jumped from the casket and scooped up the remaining guns and ammunition. "Shut the lid!"

Koko slammed the lid shut and Jao left the weapons on top, where the captain and Emily would see them. "Let's get going."

The crew of *The Reliant* were running for all they were worth when the firing squad began to shoot. Bunty stopped to return fire whilst the rest of the crew caught up. She was crouched behind a fruit stall and Gonagain saw a couple of watermelons explode right in front of her. Bunty momentarily disappeared from view and, for a moment, Gonagain thought she had been hit – but she re-emerged firing once again. Bullets ricocheted off Emily Tutu.

One of the marksmen caught Gonagain on the upper arm. He felt the familiar, intense, hot pain and glanced at the shredded tweed on his jacket and the small patch of blood that was growing around it. “Ah feck! Not again!”

The wedge-shaped dirigible had managed to slow to running speed and was now directly overhead. Gunfire was unleashed from all three gunners and the soldiers, and the hordes behind them, were forced back.

When they reached *The Reliant*, the hatch was down, and the engines were running. Gonagain made sure that he was last to board – he wanted to be sure no one was left behind. No sooner had he stepped inside the loading bay, then the tatty dirigible left the ground. It began a slow, erratic ascent – oscillating clockwise then anti-clockwise.

Bearnárd cranked the hatch closed and they all stood momentarily staring at each other.

Gonagain, still clutching his arm, turned to Koko and broke the silence. “Thank you for rescuing us. Who the hell are you?”

Bearnárd threw an arm around the small Madakan. “This, is Koko Stewdiver. One of my fellow escapees from Isalo.”

“Koko *Bladefist* – I'm Koko Bladefist now.”

“And how did you get into *The Reliant*?”

“Jeremiah Lovehats picked the lock – it's wut he does.”

Gonagain looked to Bearnárd for confirmation. Bearnárd shook his head and shrugged.

The airship lurched and swung violently. "Flying an airship is not wut he does. You might wunt to go and take over."

"Skipper… I'm not doing so well here." Bunty was white as a ghost. She had undone her leather waistcoat and her blouse was soaked in blood underneath. She collapsed to the floor.

CHAPTER 42
Victoria

Staff Sergeant Landowner stood at a window in the Commissioners Suite, on the top floor of the east wing of the Hotel de Ville. The suite consisted of private barracks and shared living spaces for visiting officers. There were also tiny offices for their use, and it was from one of these offices that he watched the debacle unfold in Twelve Bells Square.

He wasn't keen on executions at the best of times – there was too much theatre as far as he was concerned – a shot to the back of the head, in front of a hole that the condemned person had dug themselves, was perfectly adequate and not such a waste of time. What he was witnessing was doing nothing to change his mind.

First that dreadful automaton nearly escaped – knocking one of the firing squad unconscious with the end of an unravelling chain in the process – and almost caused a stampede among the crowd.

Then the idiot executioner had got his calculations wrong and left Trustworthy dancing on nothing. Before he had chance to give Gonagain the drop, the scruffy mongrel from *The Reliant* had appeared from nowhere and attacked him.

"This is ridiculous!" Landowner muttered to himself as he marched to the coat hooks to retrieve his pistol from its holster. He returned to the sash window and yanked it upwards, before leaning out of the opening and taking aim at the back of the mutt's head. He squeezed the trigger at exactly the same time as the dog tugged the executioner's hand. The executioner dropped to the floor, clutching his kneecap while the dog carried on pulling at his other hand.

"Ugh! Keep still, you stupid mutt!"

The crowd were finding the whole scene hilarious and the executioner being shot was the icing on the cake. A few were looking around, trying to spot who had done it. Landowner decided to withdraw from the window for a few moments and stepped back, well out of sight.

By the time he had repositioned himself, the hilarity below had turned to panic. The metal monster had resurrected itself, the executioner was lying in a pool of blood and a man, who looked *vaguely* familiar, was releasing the prisoners.

"Right," Landowner said assertively to no one in particular. He put on his tunic and strapped his holster around his waist. "Someone has to sort this out and it looks like it has to be me."

He leant out of the window once more, to make an assessment of the situation, and was just about to head down into the square when the gunfire from overhead began. Bullets rained into the crowd and members of the rabble fell like ninepins. A stray bullet lodged itself in the wooden window frame, an inch or two from Landowner's hand. He jerked his head back in. Perhaps it would be more prudent to just observe. He moved to the window on the other wall – he had chosen the corner office – and watched as the crew of *The Reliant* disappeared between the buildings.

He stood silently, clenching and unclenching his teeth, staring at the open window for several minutes, before *The Reliant* rose up from between the buildings. He took several shots, but he was out of range. He thought he may have hit the envelope but, if he had, the hydrum would have exploded. He remained at the window, watching as the dirigible became a dot in the distance before disappearing completely.

CHAPTER 43
Victoria to Antsirabe

(Minimusday)

The Reliant had escaped from Victoria with the help of covering fire from Charlie Namemaker and the crew of the *Gypsy Tart*. Bearnárd had set a course to Antsirabe. They needed to be somewhere where they could lay low for a little while. None of them could face another stint in Cabinda and, ideally, they would go somewhere time neutral anyway. Skydocks had been suggested, as well as Tana, but there was way too much through-traffic. Eventually Jao had come up with the idea of Antsirabe.

They had dropped Jeramiah Lovehats off on the banks of the Brown Gelada, walking distance from Lubumbashi river dock – Gonagain didn't think it was safe for them to fly back into Lubumbashi itself. He thanked Lovehats and bade him farewell. "You can tell Namemaker that if he thinks we're all square now, he's got another think coming."

"Oh, I nearly forgot. Charlie left you something in the loading bay."

Koko had opted to stay on board, as acting engineer, and had made himself comfortable in the hold. Gonagain had moved into Beagán's cabin, and his own cabin was converted into a temporary hospital. Jao was rushed off her feet looking after Bunty and Aoife, and trying to repair Emily Tutu. Gonagain had refused treatment, insisting that she concentrate her efforts on those that needed it the most.

"You should shut Emily Tutu down and deal with her later," he had said, but Jao insisted that she found tinkering with Emily's innards 'relaxing and therapeutic'.

Gonagain had got Bearnárd to patch him up. He had done a good job, but Gonagain was acutely aware that he wasn't healing like he did when Jao tended his wounds.

******

Jao sat in Gonagain's cabin, watching over her two patients. It was difficult to tell whose condition was most serious. Bunty had a very serious gunshot wound and she had lost a lot of blood. There was no exit wound, and Jao had had to remove the bullet with tweezers. She had stemmed the bleeding by packing the wound with clean fabric and bandaging tightly around her middle – but not before using her healing powers on it. Apparently, a couple of watermelons had taken the brunt of the shot and probably saved her life. Bunty had not regained consciousness since collapsing in the loading bay and she now had a fever. Jao dabbed her lips with water every half a deciday.

Aoife was drifting in and out of consciousness. Jao didn't really know how to treat her or, indeed, what to treat. She was badly bruised around the neck, where the noose had bitten. Her fingers were bruised and scarred, and her fingernails were missing. She was thin as a rake; her skin was sallow and her hair was like straw. For an adult woman, Aoife was tiny. This was accentuated by the weight loss that had occurred while she was held captive in the Hotel de Ville. As Jao tended the wounds on her neck, fingers, and toes, she was unexpectedly overwhelmed by a feeling of warmth and empathy towards her. She looked so diminutive and fragile, yet she fought for her beliefs as hard, if not harder, than any man Jao had ever met.

Jao cleaned the wounds with alcohol swabs and used her powers of healing, one digit at a time. There was little else she could do, except feed her chicken broth whenever she was conscious.

Jao had just sat back and closed her eyes, her mind going to Emily's damage and how to fix it, when she heard Aoife mumbling. She rushed to her side and began spooning broth into her mouth. Aiofe pushed her hand away.

"I'm sorry..." she whispered hoarsely, "... about the captain."

"Don't worry about that, just concentrate on getting better."

"I don't love him. I don't even have a crush on him. I was just jealous... of you and him."

"There *is* no me and him. We're just colleagues, friends at best."

"That's not true though, is it?"

Jao ignored the claim. "Anyway, if you're not interested in him, why were you jealous?" she taunted light-heartedly.

Aoife licked her dry lips and beckoned Jao closer. Jao leaned in, straining to hear what she was going to say.

Aiofe lifted her hand and stroked Jao's face, looking deep into her sapphire eyes. She reached around the back of her neck and, with surprising strength, pulled her closer. "It's *you* I want. I was just trying to come between you and him. If *I* couldn't have you, I didn't want anyone else to." She pulled Jao close and planted a kiss on her lips, softly at first, then with more urgency, pushing her tongue between her lips.

Jao's initial instinct was to pull away but, for some reason, she didn't and just tensed up instead. As Aoife's tongue gently probed and caressed her own, Jao began to relax. Despite her reservations, it felt good. For a brief moment she responded, before pulling away abruptly. "No! This isn't right. Not between two women. It just isn't right." She backed toward the door and fled.

Aoife plonked her head back on to the pillow and closed her eyes. "Bugger," she whispered hoarsely to herself.

Gonagain and Bearnárd were in the mess drinking whiskey when Jao came in. She picked up the coffee pot, feeling it for weight and heat, before emptying the contents and busying herself making a fresh pot. She didn't acknowledge the two men and seemed edgy and flustered.

Etoile glanced up, but soon lost interest and nudged her head back under Gonagain's hand. Gonagain and Bearnárd exchanged a wary glance. "Is everything alright, Jao?" Bearnárd enquired tentatively.

"Yes, why shouldn't it be?" she replied defensively.

"I just thought… you know… with the patients. How are they?"

Jao plonked herself on a chair and stared into her coffee cup, as if the answers were in there. "Oh. Bunty still hasn't regained consciousness. It's not looking great at the moment."

"And Aoife?"

Jao fidgeted. "She's in and out of consciousness."

"Has she been able to say anything?" Gonagain asked.

Jao's edginess returned and she stood up with her coffee. "Nothing coherent. If you need me, I'll be with Emily Tutu." She turned and hurried away.

Gonagain raised an eyebrow at Bearnárd.

“It’s a tough time, Osh. Everyone’s a bit fractious.”

Gonagain shrugged. “Well, I best get back to the bridge. I don’t trust Koko up there on his own. If his piloting is anything like his shooting, we could end up anywhere.”

CHAPTER 44
Victoria to Antsirabe

(Polexday)

Jao awoke uncharacteristically late. She was exhausted from nursing her two crewmates, repairing Emily Tutu, and keeping an eye on the state of the engine under Koko's management. Even so, it had taken her hours to fall asleep. She had tossed and turned for over a deciday thinking about Aoife.

Nobody had ever told Jao that they wanted her before. It was good to feel wanted. She thought about the kiss, and the time that Aoife had brushed her hair at Stanleyville. Eventually, unable to fall asleep, she got up and took out the vanity case. It was beautiful. She studied all the contents, read the pamphlet, and took out the mother of pearl hairbrush and began to brush her own hair. All the things that she had originally found irritating about Aoife, were now the things that made her attractive. And why shouldn't two women be in love? Just because they were both women? Whose business was it anyway? It wouldn't go down well in a place like Antsirabe – it was against all the teachings that Jao had grown up with – but she had stopped believing most of that nonsense a long time ago. Although Jao didn't think she could ever love a woman in 'that way', she was worried that she had offended Aoife by saying it was wrong. She had changed her mind about her completely in the last few weeks, and wanted more than anything to put their past enmities behind them and to become friends.

Jao eventually drifted off to sleep and, despite her feelings, her dreams were peppered with hair brushing and kisses.

The next morning, Jao took more care about her appearance than she normally did when she emerged looking for her morning caffeine fix. But she was also in a hurry – wanting to get to Aoife while she was still clear in her mind about what she was going to say.

On the bridge, Gonagain was grilling Bearnárd and Koko.

"So, when did you *first* notice the steering was so sluggish?"

"Well, we were on course when I first took over from Koko, but a bit low. It was really slow gaining altitude, but I just put that down to Charlie and Jeremiah Lovehats replacing the hydrum with heliagen.

It wasn't until about half a deciday ago that I had to change course to avoid flying over a city."

"Koko, you're absolutely *sure* we didn't hit, or get hit by anything? You didn't hear any strange noises?"

"No. I did wut you said – same direction, same speed, same height. Nuthing happened."

Gonagain and Bearnárd exchanged a suspicious glance. They had definitely lost altitude. Koko was about to protest his innocence when Jao burst in. Her eyes were full of tears that trickled down her cheeks as she tried to speak.

"Jao! What's wrong? Is it Bunty?"

Jao shook her head. "Bunty is the same. It's Aoife. She's gone."

Bearnárd, who was the only one wearing a cap, took it off and held it to his heart.

"I… I thought she was doing okay?" Gonagain stuttered.

"She's not dead; she's just gone."

There was a group sigh of relief, and Koko suppressed a giggle.

"Well, she can't have gone far, Jao – we haven't touched down since Victoria." Gonagain's tone lacked the sympathy that might have been appropriate.

Jao clutched the note in her pocket but decided not to show anyone. It read:

My darling Jao, I'm sorry I upset you last night. I can't stay on board The Reliant now – it's just too awk-

ward. Goodbye. All my love, Aoife.

"We'll do a search of the ship, Jao." Bearnárd said warmly, before looking sternly at Gonagain.

The three men scoured the ship with Jao trailing behind. There was, indeed, no sign of her or any of her things. Eventually they arrived at the loading bay. The engine noise was deafening – the loading bay door was wide open. Koko went dangerously close to the edge, as if he was expecting to find Aoife outside. "Look! There's a bullet hole in the envelope," he shouted over the engine noise.

Bearnárd cranked the hatch closed and the bay was quiet again. "Well, the bullet hole explains the loss of altitude, and the open hatch would explain the clunky steering – it's like having a stuck aerofoil."

Koko puffed his chest out and raised his chin in defiance of the earlier accusations.

"And the missing kite would explain the missing Aoife," Gonagain added. He was staring at the empty space on the shelf that the kite would normally occupy. "Why would she leave like that? Without a word?"

Jao stared guiltily at the floor.

Gonagain's attention was caught by an unfamiliar trunk. A feeling of déjà vu washed over him, until he remembered what Jeremiah Lovehats had said: "Oh, I nearly forgot. Charlie left you something in the loading bay."

Gonagain flipped the catches on the trunk and

opened the lid; the others stood behind him open-mouthed. It was full of money. Loads of it. All in different denominations of ariary. "There must be… fifteen million ariary in there! That's enough for us to lie low for a whole year – maybe two."

There was a moment of silence, broken by a noise from the voice-repeater.

"Hello? Is there anyone there?"

Jao rushed to the voice-repeater. "Bunty! Are you okay?"

"No, I'm not! I'm absolutely ravenous. What does one have to do to get some scran around here?"

EPILOGUE
Victoria

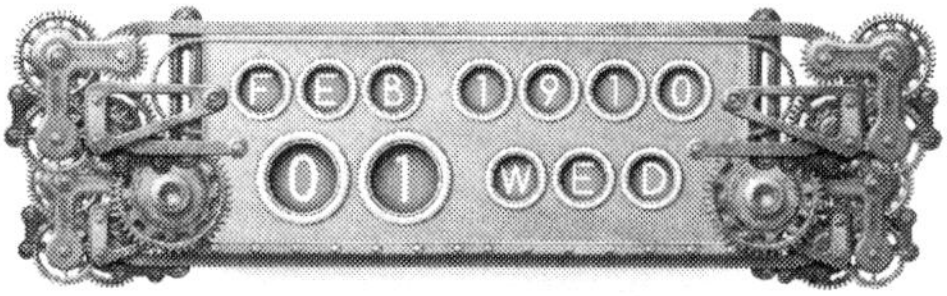

Captain Warehouse stood beside the pulsarnite-powered personnel carrier he had just emerged from. He had followed the First Century of M.L.E.s and *The Smile* through desert, savannah and scrub and they had finally reached their destination. They were in the scrub, about six kilometres outside Victoria, and the city was just visible on the horizon. About fifty metres ahead of him, *The Smile* extended its massive pulsarnite cannon until it towered above them. The pilot of *The Smile* powered up the mighty cannon and a loud deep hum began. Captain Warehouse could feel the ground vibrating beneath his feet.

The colonel in charge of the operation spoke to the captain of *The Smile* over a field voice-repeater. "Perform safety sequence, Captain. Over."

"Wilco. Over."

There was a pregnant pause.

"Safety complete. Ready to fire. Over."

"Fire at will. Over and out."

The human element of the cohort sat in the

scrub, cross-legged, heads down, with their hands over their ears. The automatons stood stoically in rank and file. The massive cannon fired, and *The Smile* rocked slightly, but remained in place. A sonic pulse, the like of which had never been witnessed before, travelled to Victoria in an instant.

Those who were unfortunate enough to be outdoors, on the streets of Victoria, were physically lifted and slammed into the nearest buildings. Many of those indoors fared no better. The newer, more stylish, contemporary buildings were also the weakest. Victoria West Airdock collapsed in seconds, crushing those inside. The trendy boutiques and cafés were obliterated.

Many of the older buildings were more resilient. All of the windows in the Hotel de Ville had shattered and the decorative plaster cracked and crumbled in numerous places. The structure, generally held up well. Only the top floor of the east wing suffered any real damage. Here, sections of the roof collapsed as did the ceilings and parts of the walls.

Staff Sergeant Landowner was pacing up and down in his corner office, chuntering to himself about the ineptitude of the lower ranks and the escape of crew of *The Reliant*. He was facing the window, when it unexpectedly exploded into a million fragments of glass which blasted into his face and torso. He was thrown across the room and slammed into the wall behind him. Blind and bleeding, he managed to get himself on to all fours. He could hear the timber rafters above his head creaking, and pieces of plaster crashed down upon him. Somehow, he managed to crawl under the desk – only his legs were protruding when the room collapsed.

Six kilometres away, the colonel stood and watched the city crumble. He turned to Captain Warehouse. “Okay, Captain, send in the First Century.”

ACKNOWLEDGEMENTS

With special thanks to: Steph Warren @bookshineblog; Dafydd Mihangel, mab y gogledd; Paul Nicholls; Aida Morales; Sara Louise Wheeler; Jade Cumming; Carrie-Anne Heath; Shaun Rogers, for the cover art; and, most of all, to my loving wife Mary-Clair Farrelly without whom this book would not have been possible.

Printed in Great Britain
by Amazon

48803297R10265